Also by Annie Hartnett

RABBIT CAKE

Unlikely Animals

Unlikely Animals

A NOVEL

ANNIE HARTNETT

Ballantine Books

New York

Copyright © 2022 by Annie Hartnett

All rights reserved.

Published in the United States by Ballantine Books, an imprint of Random House, a division of Penguin Random House LLC, New York.

BALLANTINE and the HOUSE colophon are registered trademarks of Penguin Random House LLC.

LIBRARY OF CONGRESS CATALOGING-IN-PUBLICATION DATA
Names: Hartnett, Annie, author.
Title: Unlikely animals / Annie Hartnett.
Description: First edition. | New York: Ballantine Books, [2022]
Identifiers: LCCN 2021026216 (print) | LCCN 2021026217 (ebook) |
ISBN 9780593160220 (hardcover; acid-free paper) |
ISBN 9780593160237 (ebook)
Classification: LCC PS3608.A74936 U55 2022 (print) |
LCC PS3608.A74936 (ebook) | DDC 813/.6—dc23
LC record available at https://lccn.loc.gov/2021026216
LC ebook record available at https://lccn.loc.gov/2021026217

Printed in Canada on acid-free paper

randomhousebooks.com

2 4 6 8 9 7 5 3 1

FIRST EDITION

Map courtesy of Annie Hartnett

Title-page spread images: © iStockphoto.com

Book design by Dana Leigh Blanchette

FOR DREW

FWD: PLEASE READ

CONTENTS

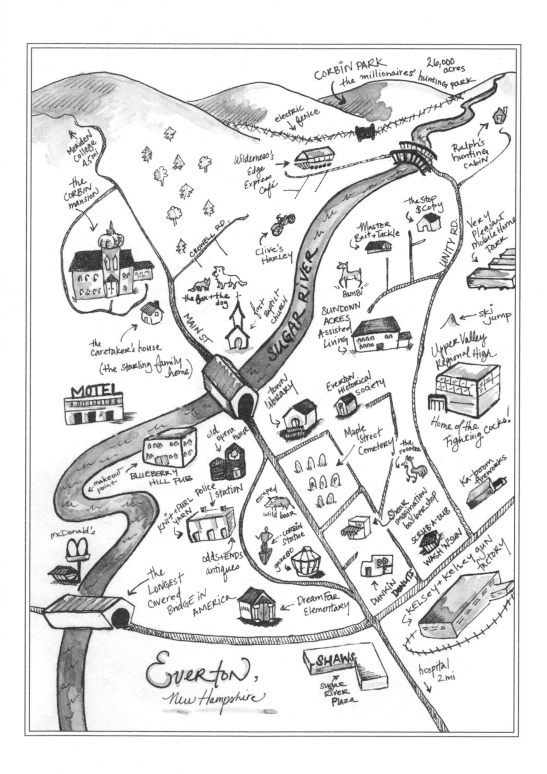

The moose, bison, elk, deer, antelope, boar, goats, rabbits, etc., arrived in town Saturday. The grizzlies have not put in the appearance yet. The fence is to be eight-feet high.

—*THE NEW HAMPSHIRE SPECTATOR*, 1887

Someone's gonna die before this is over.

—OZZY OSBOURNE, 2010

MR. ERNEST HAROLD BAYNES AND HIS TAME FOX.

Photograph by Louise Birt Baynes.

Author's Note

This is a novel. I made it up.

But much of the really neat historical stuff is true.

I have included a more detailed note about my research at the end of the book. Thank you to the local historians who shared the good gossip about Ernest Harold Baynes (b. 1868–d. 1925), the real-life Doctor Doolittle of New Hampshire and alleged total ladies' man. A special thank-you and an apology to Larry, who told me to "keep it positive."

Unlikely Animals

Maple Street Cemetery
Everton, NH
43.3623° N, 72.1662° W

Years later, when people in Everton would tell this story, they would say it was Clive Starling who called the reporter, the way that man loved attention.

But we remember it the way it happened: it was the midwife who slid down the hall to the payphone to get the *Upper Valley New Hampshire News* on the horn. It was a slow news day, so the reporter had zipped right over to the hospital, and he let the midwife go on and on into the tape recorder about a condition called *charismata iamaton,* which translates, from Greek, to "gifts of healing." She insisted that the hands of this newborn baby, tiny hands still coated in the awful gunk of birth, had cured her sciatica. She said most people with natural healing talents are unaware of their gifts, but this baby had the strongest natural talent she'd ever seen.

BABY WITH MIRACLE HEALING POTENTIAL BORN, the next morning's headline read. TOWN OF EVERTON, N.H., REJOICES.

As we recall it, Clive Starling wasn't rejoicing. He was pretty ticked off, actually; the reporter didn't bother to interview him. Not one single question. Not even his goddamn name was printed, mentioned only as a *poetry professor* and *the baby's father.* "Might as well be chopped liver," he said, tossing the newspaper to the side. The reporter clearly didn't know how to do his job; Clive would have been much more forthcoming than his wife. He would have said he'd known this baby was bound to be special.

Clive's wife *was* quoted in the article, her full name was there in black and white, but all Ingrid Starling had to say was that the whole thing was nonsense, to please leave her family alone. Truthfully, Ingrid *did* wonder if there was something different about her baby, but how would she know? She'd never had a baby before. This was her first one. She didn't have anything to say about it yet, especially not to a reporter from the *Upper Valley New Hampshire News.*

Clive and Ingrid took their miraculous baby home, where they learned through a series of experiments that their child's hands weren't *magic*-magic, not exactly, but they sped up the natural healing process. A bad ten-day cold could be knocked down to a three-dayer, a poison-ivy rash could heal in a day, a dog bite could scab up overnight. Clive Starling dubbed it "The Charm," but just because it had a name didn't mean his wife was going to let their daughter use it, not until she was at least eighteen. The people of Everton respected that, for the most part, even if it seemed more than a little selfish, with so many in town suffering from an illness or pain. Still, Evertonians believed a woman should be able to do what she wants with her own kid. The midwife's testimony in the newspaper helped too: *According to most accounts,* she'd explained, *charismata iamaton grows much more powerful after the healer grows into adulthood. It's completely unreliable when the healer is still a child.*

So our town could wait. No one wanted unreliable healing.

As she grew, little redheaded Emma Starling was often asked for high fives around town, just in case any of her lucky health-giving juice rubbed off, but for the most part, everyone treated Emma like a normal kid, albeit one headed for great things. Emma was not only a natural-born healer but *smart* too. When she got to high school, she was top of her class at Upper Valley Regional.

Emma did go through a rebellious period starting around sixteen, when she and her best friend, Crystal Nash, would sit in the McDonald's by the longest covered bridge in America and charge for time spent with a REAL-DEAL TEENAGE HEALER, advertised on Craigslist. But nothing *truly* astonishing ever occurred during those years of adolescent healing, and eventually Emma had to leave our town for college. Fifty-four percent of our students go on to a two- or four-year college, but Emma went farther away than most, to Pomona College in California. Out of our jurisdiction.

Of course, we kept tabs on her through her mother. We listened to Ingrid Starling bragging in the supermarket over the next four years, *Emma this and Emma that,* Ingrid glossing over what was happening with her son, Emma's younger brother, headed to rehab again. We heard when Emma graduated with honors, and we heard when Emma was starting medical school at the prestigious UCLA David Geffen Med. We overheard when Ingrid told her friends at the book club that Emma had agreed to come home for Thanksgiving break. She'd been away for two years, but she was flying back for Turkey Day, to see her dying father, who was suffering from some kind of mysterious brain disease. The man had always been a little whacked in the head, but it had gotten much worse.

"I think it'd do wonders for him if you could come home for the week," Ingrid had said over the phone. And then she'd asked if Emma thought she might be able to do something to help *delay* her father's degeneration, slow it down just a tad, so they could all have more time with him. Ingrid said she'd read on the internet about new research claiming electric shocks could be helpful in preventing the advancement of brain diseases; music and aromatherapy could also help, so yes, they would try all that, but who knows what a dose of the Charm could do? We tittered with excitement at Maple Street. We wanted to see Emma work her magic. We had waited so long.

"I don't know, Mom," Emma said. We could hear Emma breathing through the phone line, and we wished we could hear what she was thinking, but she was all the way out in California. Out of our reach.

"It'll at least give him something else to focus on," her mother said. "Since his retirement . . . well, he's gone a little adrift."

Professor Clive Starling had been forced to retire mid-semester, the end of October, since he had started seeing small animals in the classroom, asking students: "Who let the cats in here?" It was a source of entertainment at Maple Street Cemetery. Both funny and sad, the kind of story we like best.

PART I

The Dog

1

Emma Starling didn't come into Everton the way that took her by Maple Street Cemetery, so she didn't hold her breath when she drove by us, like she used to on the school bus as a kid. She didn't drive by the town square either, so she missed the celebratory sight when the four men and two teenage boys finally caught the wild boar. Emma hadn't seen the way they whooped and slapped one another on the back.

Boars aren't native to New Hampshire, but here in Everton, they often dig out underneath the electric fence to escape the private hunting park that spans the Upper Valley. The park is enormous, 26,000 acres, fenced in about 135 years ago by the nineteenth-century robber baron Austin Corbin as his grand retirement project; he bought up the land from farmers and shipped in animals from all over the world. The Corbin family went bankrupt after the world wars, and today the park is owned by a small club of anonymous millionaires, each member with their own hunting cabin. These millionaires tend to keep to themselves, unless a boar gets out, when park headquarters puts out a call to catch the pig: $1,000 reward.

"Shit," Emma said, her anxiety mounting as she drove. "I can't believe I'm back here."

Even though Emma didn't drive by us in the cemetery, we could hear her muttering to herself; we could see that she had an enormous white dog in the backseat of her red rental car; we were beginning to hear some of her thoughts. We see and hear it all in

Everton, one of the perks of being dead, omniscience within town limits. It's a little frustrating how the living come and go, but we always get the full story eventually.

Emma's story was trickling out of her now. We learned it wasn't a triumphant return for the twenty-two-year-old red-headed medical school student, who was wearing a nice enough gray sweater but had rips in the knees of her jeans that her mother would never approve of. It seemed things had gone all wrong back in California, but right now, she was mostly thinking about what she was driving into. Her father's new doctor said he couldn't be sure exactly what the disease was until an autopsy, which was definitely out of the question as long as Clive remained alive, but it was causing tremors, confusion, and extremely vivid hallucinations.

"Today he says he's seeing a ghost," Emma's mother had complained on the phone. She'd sighed. "Dr. Wheeler says a year, two at the best."

"How can this doctor say it'll be a year when he doesn't know what disease it is?" Emma asked.

"It's not the time to outsmart everyone, Emma. It can be a little tiring. Just come home. I know your brother would like to see you too."

Emma knew there was no way Auggie gave one single flying fart about whether she ever came home or not, but she knew it was time to come home anyway.

"And you need to forgive your father before he dies," her mother had reminded her. "Otherwise, that guilt will eat you from the inside out."

"Okay, Mom," Emma had said, and the phone call was pretty much over after that. Her mom had followed up with an email, had given it the subject line "THINGS TO TALK ABOUT WITH YOUR FATHER," but Emma hadn't bothered to read it. She was angry that her mother had let her dad back in the house after only two months of sleeping under his desk in the Meriden College English Department Building. Emma would have left him there at least a few months more, but her father got away with everything.

The man is dying, she reminded herself as she drove. *Have some sympathy.* The big white dog in the backseat sniffed at the top of the window, wondering if Emma could please crack it a little to let some smells in. We learned then that Emma had picked up the dog only a half hour before. When she turned onto the Route 10 exit toward Everton, the dog had been trotting along, no owner in sight, no collar, matted fur. Emma loved dogs, but she would have stopped the rental car for anyone if it meant she could delay her arrival. She would have stopped for a hitchhiker, a possible serial killer. When Emma pulled the car over, the dog had hopped right in the backseat. He was super-duper glad to see her, nothing close to a killer. She named the dog Moses, after that famous orphan and savior, because Emma felt like she needed a savior right then. Moses put his head between the seats and rested his chin on her bony shoulder. Emma had always been small. She was pale with freckles. A 7 out of 10, according to Jesse Peters (b. 1984–d. 2013), one of our graveyard residents who considered himself an armchair expert on the ladies.

"You're going to live in the palace," Emma told Moses, even if that was not exactly how she felt about her childhood home, but her parents' house was definitely a good place to be a dog. Her mother's last rescue dog had died that summer, cancer, and she had recently said that she had "a dog-shaped hole in her heart," even though her husband was also dying.

Moses went to swipe the side of Emma's cheek with his tongue, and a drool loogie fell from his jowls and stuck to Emma's sweater, which was extremely gross, but Emma's heart warmed. "Good boy," she said. *Friend,* Moses was thinking at that moment. We liked that about dogs, we always had, how clearly they can show a person exactly what they're thinking. We spend most of our time focused on the thoughts of the human beings of our town, but sometimes it's good to be absorbed in the thoughts of a dog.

Emma drove past the sign advertising snowmobile rentals: KIDS UNDER FIVE RIDE FREE! *So many people don't know how redneck New Hampshire really is,* Emma thought, which hurt our feelings a little. We had hoped she would be glad to be back after so much time away. We'd hoped that once she'd seen the traffic of Los Angeles, she could have appreciated our town's charm. Because Everton is really a nice place to live, or it was for us.

Other than the enormous private hunting park, Everton is more or less a normal New Hampshire town. There are pine trees and winding roads and blue-green mountains. Sugar River snakes through the town, dotted with covered bridges, and the water is clean enough to swim and fish in. We're particularly proud of Maple Street Cemetery, which is surrounded by a neat stone wall, with a large iron gate, and is very well maintained by our grounds-keeper, the one-handed Mr. Ridley Willett, an army vet. It's really a town no different from any other, a place where people live and people die.

But maybe, now that Emma Starling was coming back to Everton, things could be different. Just this once, maybe someone would cheat death, edge the Grim Reaper out by a nose. We weren't naïve at Maple Street; we knew about the limits of Emma's abilities from her years of adolescent healing attempts, her days sitting in the sticky red booth at the McDonald's with Crystal Nash, the girls charging forty-five dollars cash for a half hour of real-deal teenage healing. Crystal was the business manager, the entire operation had been her idea. Crystal used to insist that with Emma's power she could be like Jesus. But Emma wasn't exactly Jesus. Emma had trouble getting close to people, and Jesus, well, *that* dude was charismatic. Jesus must have been a helluva guy; not many people can say they came back from the dead. The rest of us stay here when we go.

But Emma didn't have to be Jesus; you don't have to be Jesus to want to save your dad from what's killing him. And at least by now, the time of her return to Everton, Emma was older, more mature. The Charm should have grown stronger, so maybe she could really heal her father, extend his lifeline by a little. We didn't want Clive to live forever, we just wanted a little more time tacked on at the end. Extra time would mean something, for anyone, and especially for a man like Clive, who still had some things to work out with his family.

"Don't hold your breath for a miracle," Charles Tepper (b. 1932– d. 1998) said from his seat on his grave, since he didn't believe Clive's condition was curable. A bunch of us laughed, funny since none of us breathe anyway.

"What about mothers who lift cars off babies?" Mae Belle Henick (b. 1799–d. 1820) argued from her headstone. "Anything could happen, Charles, you know that." Mae Belle had died before the invention of the automobile, but at Maple Street we stay up on current events.

As Emma got closer to her parents' house, more and more of the trees along the road were littered with white flyers staple-gunned to the trunks. Maybe Emma needed her eyes examined, because from the driver's seat, she could only make out the word "missing" at the top. Emma figured it was a missing pet, or a stolen car, or a tractor or snowblower gone missing from a garage. Emma wasn't at all concerned about the flyers, which disappointed us. We thought since she'd stopped for the stray dog on the side of the road, she'd stop to see what those posters were all about, and she would learn what her parents hadn't been telling her.

In the middle of every poster, there was a flattering photo of a young woman. DOB: 04/03/91 HAIR: BLOND (NATURAL BRUNETTE) EYES: BLUE (WEARS MAKEUP, GLASSES SOMETIMES) LAST SEEN: JUNE

2014. NAME: CRYSTAL NASH. Emma's best friend from high school had been missing for several months, longer than most missing people can hope to be found. Emma's dad was the one hanging the posters, and he was pretty much the only one looking for Crystal, because everyone thought there was an easy enough explanation for why young people in Everton go missing. Our town was currently dealing with what the *Upper Valley New Hampshire News* called an *epidemic*. We love our town, we really do, but it had seen a rough stretch of years.

Emma wasn't thinking about Everton's opioid problem as she drove. She was too wrapped up with figuring out how to confess to her parents, the big lie she'd been telling them about medical school. *Wait, what lie about medical school?* The record scratched at Maple Street. We leaned forward on our gravestones, and we learned: *Emma wasn't in med school!* Orientation had started in July, but what her family didn't know was that Emma hadn't shown up to her white-coat ceremony. She simply hadn't gone to orientation. Not even one day of it. It was November now. That ship had sailed.

"I told you that a natural-born healer never needed medical school," Donald Brown (b. 1890–d. 1965) said, because Donald had been a successful enough lawyer without ever stepping foot in a law school, but the rest of us at Maple Street were worried. Something bad had happened out there in California, we could feel it. We weren't sure exactly what had happened yet, but we were likely to find out if we kept listening. "Oh no," we said once we'd heard more, what had happened on the West Coast and how bad it really was. "This changes everything," wailed Donald from his grave.

Soon the Missing posters on Corbin Road were stapled to every last tree. Emma's parents' house was just up this way.

2

Emma had to drive up the curved driveway past the big mansion first. It was built in 1880 by that robber baron Austin Corbin when he came up from New York to retire. He built the animal park pretty far from his mansion, on opposite ends of town. Corbin didn't want the many creatures of the world eating his lawn. The Gilded Age onion-domed mansion remains car-stopping beautiful: a twelve-room yellow house with a green roof and green shutters, white trim, and a wraparound porch. Both the mansion and the caretaker's house behind it are painted the same odd yellow, a bit orange even, like the yellow of Kraft macaroni and cheese.

The caretaker's house, a modestly sized colonial, was the Starlings' family home. Emma could see her dad waiting outside on the porch; his long bright-white hair had always made him recognizable from a distance. Clive Starling still had his full, glorious head of hair at sixty-eight. He kept it long, and braided it sometimes, it was *rock-star hair,* he always said. Clive loved playing with the guys of Blacker Sabbath, his cover band that brought in a regular crowd at the Blueberry Hill Pub on Thursday nights, although the band had been on hiatus lately, hadn't played the past few weeks. Years ago, Emma used to do Clive's makeup for the shows. She'd make him look like a nightmarish clown, and they both used to get such a kick out of that. Her dad was also covered in bad tattoos, a flock of birds on his left arm, his own first name tattooed on his right knuckles, and a skull on his wedding finger, a memento from his first marriage. He had Emma and Auggie's names tattooed over his heart in a terrible script; they were his only kids, which had been Ingrid's big victory, what she had over the previous wives, better than any finger tattoo. Ingrid Starling was competitive, and being a fourth wife came with baggage, even though she and Clive had been married over two decades. She had outlasted them all. One was even dead at this point. Wife number two.

Emma turned off the car, and she sat there while Moses panted and whined in the back. Emma looked at her childhood home from the safety of the car, wanting to keep her distance for just a little longer. She knew her mother would ask her to try to heal her father—and worse, her dad might ask her himself. Up on that familiar porch, she knew the heat lamps would be plugged in, and that her father would have a whiskey in his hand. She knew he would be sitting on a memory-foam pad. She had never been able to heal her father's back pain, not completely, and it had gotten worse these past few years with Emma gone. It's unfair how the body crumbles while the soul still lives in it.

Emma hadn't seen her family for nearly two years. She'd made up excuses, papers to write, MCATs to take, med school interviews to go on, a summer internship. She'd spent last Christmas with Tessie Blatt and her family; Tessie was Emma's college roommate. Normally, Ingrid would have forced her daughter to get her booty back home, but there had been more pressing issues back in Everton. Clive and Ingrid even had to cancel their plans to come out for Emma's graduation, because Auggie was in the middle of a nine-week rehab stay, and it was his second one. Her mother was sorry, of course they were so proud of Emma, but Auggie needed them, and they would watch the ceremony if it was streamed online.

Emma opened the door of the red rental car, and Moses went running for the two men on the porch. Ralph Kelsey was sitting in the other rocker. Both the mansion and caretaker's house belonged to him, the ninety-one-year-old man who owned the gun factory, the biggest employer in town. The Corbin Mansion had gone through a few owners until Ralph Kelsey had bought it for "pennies," in the 1980s. He'd spent millions restoring it.

Emma watched the big white dog bounding forward, and she half wanted to run toward them too. She loved her father; we knew she did. She'd practically worshipped him just a few years ago, but then her dad had gone and had his affair with Sabrina Berkman, visiting political science professor at Meriden College, which was completely boneheaded, since his wife was the campus librarian and bound to find out about it. It was a year and a half ago when Emma's mother called to say there was a divorce in the works. "Dad's always been too friendly with strangers," Emma had said at first, because she didn't believe it. Her dad loved her mother; it was one of the few things Emma knew to be true. He would never ruin their family, would never just move on to the next shiny young thing. Well, Professor Sabrina Berkman wasn't that shiny or young, and the affair lasted only a semester, but that was no solace for Emma. *Who knows what else her dad had lied about?* Emma felt completely betrayed, even though her dad would say you can only cheat on your wife, you can't cheat on your kids. He had barely apologized to Emma. She wasn't even really sure he knew she was angry with him. Really, it would be just like him not to notice, his head always up his own—

"Huzzah!" Clive called from the porch, as Emma approached with her duffel bag. "The prodigal daughter returns!"

"A hero's welcome!" called Ralph Kelsey, and both men lifted their drinks to her. Moses barked in a clear declaration of happiness, not sure what these new people were celebrating, but thrilled to be part of whatever it was. Even Emma smiled, she couldn't help it, and for a second, despite everything, she suddenly felt very glad to be home.

"Here to laugh at the gilded butterflies?" her dad said, not getting up from his rocking chair, and Emma remembered what had kept her in California. Everything had to be a performance. It annoyed her, that her dad was quoting Shakespeare, and especially from *King Lear*. She didn't want to be locked in a prison with her dad. She didn't want to die at the end.

"No, Clive, she's here to bury us," Ralph said, guffawing, reaching over and slapping his friend on the knee. Ralph and the Starlings had long ago become family. "Good doggie," he said to Moses. "Come over here, pal." Ralph made some kissing noises.

The screen door slammed, and Emma's mother appeared, wearing a brown sweater, black jeans, and stiletto boots. Ingrid Starling had always had style. She was looking a little smoother, Emma noticed. Botox. Her mom was fifty-two, sixteen years younger than her dad, but Ingrid Starling liked old things. She was the volunteer president of the Everton Historical Society, as well as the official caretaker of the Corbin Mansion, which was a lot of work on top of her full-time job as Meriden College librarian. "Don't you look like you've been away to war," she said. "Emma, did you sleep *at all* on the plane?"

"Nice to see you, too, Mom." Emma's parents' divorce proceedings had been quickly called off, which had disgusted Emma in a new way. *Where was that woman's self-respect?* Her mom used to be the toughest woman she knew. Moses jumped up to slobber all over Ingrid's sweater.

"And who is this?"

"That's Moses."

"Emma, don't tell me you came home a Bible-thumper?"

Emma shook her head. She hadn't come home anything. She'd come home depressed. "I found the dog wandering Route 10. Maybe not as dramatic as being found in the Nile."

"Oh, you're a sweetie." Ingrid buried her hands in the dog's filthy fur. "It's not your fault you're dirty, of course it's not." Emma's mother didn't always have patience for people, but she had all the patience in the world for dogs. Moses dashed off the porch into the front yard and jumped into thin air, flipped around on the grass.

"He's playing with Harold," her dad said.

"Who?" Emma asked.

"Your father has a new friend," her mother explained.

"He's a friend to all creatures," her dad corrected.

"I mentioned it on the phone," her mother said, reminding Emma with her eyes that they were not using the word "hallucination" or the phrase "visions caused by brain disease." The hallucinations had started out small. First there were rabbits in the kitchen that Ingrid had to pretend to shoo out the door. Then the cats showed up in the Meriden College classroom, causing quite a lot of confusion in Clive's senior poetry seminar, and a week or two after that, the ghost of the long-dead naturalist Ernest Harold Baynes had arrived.

"A welcome distraction," Clive had said, because that was when Meriden was pushing him out. Mr. Baynes was not exactly a stranger to the Starlings; there was a large, framed photograph of him and his pet fox hanging in one of the back rooms of the historical society. Clive had seen the photograph many times, when helping Ingrid organize the place. Ernest Harold Baynes had once been the official naturalist of Corbin Park who let wild animals live in his home. He lived in Everton for over twenty years, where he'd always gone by his middle name. He died in 1925 while still relatively young, his ashes spread in the park he loved.

Dr. Wheeler had warned Ingrid that if her husband was having visions, they were real to him, and so they had to be treated as real, yes, by everyone in the family. He said the worst thing they could do was tell him he was seeing things. Life would get too terrifying. "Don't negate his living experience," Dr. Wheeler warned. They didn't have to pretend they could see the ghost, too, but they couldn't deny that the ghost was there. Ingrid had stolen *The Collected Writings of Ernest Harold Baynes* from the shelves of the historical society; it was her way of dealing with it. She had also scanned an article about Baynes from some ancient newspaper and sent it to the kids.

"Got it," Emma had promised her mother on the phone, but she'd imagined that her dad would only see the ghost late at night, not here in broad daylight.

At Maple Street, we wondered if it was wise that Ingrid had thought to warn Emma about her father's ghost without mentioning his second preoccupation, the hunt for missing person Crystal Nash, hanging hundreds of Missing posters around town. Obsessive behavior is common with the onset of degenerative brain diseases, Dr. Wheeler had explained, but Ingrid didn't want to involve Emma while she was out in California and should be focused on medical school. Ingrid would tell Emma about Crystal's disappearance now that she was home. Once she found the right moment.

On the porch, Emma noticed her father was trembling a little as he lifted his drink. It was the Parkinson's-like tremors, although Dr. Wheeler had said it wasn't Parkinson's. It figured that her father couldn't get some regular disease, a cancer.

"I guess it's true what I've heard, that dogs can see ghosts," old man Ralph Kelsey said, as Moses barked in excitement at the air in front of him.

"I thought that was cats," Auggie said, stepping out of the house to half-hug his sister. Emma's younger brother had recently had his hair buzzed too short by the clipper-happy barber at Shear Imagination, but his skin looked healthy. Seven months sober. Emma hoped it would stick.

"What's new, GG?" he asked, his usual nickname for her. Emma assumed it meant Golden Girl, because that's what the teachers at the high school used to call her, but her brother probably didn't mean it in a nice way. She and Auggie didn't exactly get along. "How's La-La Land?" he asked.

"Sunny," she said, which was the truth, so true it's kind of an idiotic thing to say: that region of California is almost always sunny. But it was a lie, because people associate sunshine with happiness.

"Now I can die happy," Clive said from his seat on the memory-foam pad. "My favorite child is home."

"Clive," Ingrid scolded. "Just how many drinks have you had?" Auggie snorted. But Emma knew it was just like her dad to be so insensitive, and she figured the favorite-child comment was fair, since Auggie was their mother's baby. The one who got all the slack.

"I'm retired, I can drink all day. Did you hear, Emma? Your mother is going to take me out back and shoot me. I'm no use to her now."

"And then she's going to run off with his doctor," Auggie said. Their mother gave him a look. "What? You've got a crush, Mom. It's obvious."

"Just make sure to shoot me first," Clive reminded his wife, then raised his arm to wave goodbye to Ernest Harold Baynes, who had stopped playing with the dog and was headed off down Corbin Road, Harold's restless legs forcing him to get moving again. Up ahead, Clive was sure he saw the silvery specter of a fox emerging from the woods to greet Mr. Baynes. *Who had ever heard of an animal ghost?* Clive thought, tickled by the idea. There were new amusements in this strange final period of his life.

We admit we were jealous of Harold Baynes, to be so clearly seen and heard by someone living, but we hoped Harold could help Clive with his missing-person case, that some good could come from the haunting. A ghost has to do everything in a round-about way to avoid the heavy penalty for meddling in the affairs of the living, but a series of small ghostly nudges could probably work here. We just didn't know quite what to expect from Harold Baynes; not one of us, he wandered the woods alone. We were all glad we weren't cremated. There's too much walking involved, with no final resting place. We get to stay put at Maple Street, even if Ernest Harold Baynes would probably tell you he loves the freedom.

3

AN ENCOUNTER WITH ERNEST HAROLD BAYNES: NATURALIST, WRITER, AND CRUSADER

The New Hampshire Spectator, Vol. XXXVII. August 1904

By George I. Putnam

Photograph by Louise Birt Baynes.

"George, hadn't you better inquire about the way?" says my traveling companion for perhaps the twentieth time that morning. My wife and I are traveling through a quiet county in New Hampshire, and we can finally see a house ahead.

"I'll inquire," I agree, preparing to alight in the dooryard of the red-painted cottage. As luck would have it, we had finally reached the home of Ernest Harold Baynes, and our host welcomes us with the kindly manner that is the key to his success with all the lower animals, man included. Mr. Baynes is a naturalist and a writer who lives on the border of Corbin Park. He is in his early thirties; is of medium height; has maintained a thatch of brown hair; has a noble nose and a most handsome face. He is famous for living with the wild animals he works to protect.

"Where are the critters?" my wife asks, looking disappointed.

"The animals are all around us," comes a cheeky reply from Mr. Baynes. "They are a good deal like children; they never show off well for company."

Indeed, inside the house, we meet a pair of timber wolves named Death and Dauntless. A yellow coyote is curled in an armchair in that corner, and an adolescent deer with a broken leg rests by the fire. Mr. Baynes tells us of raising a baby bear, Jimmie, who has recently moved to a new residence at the New York Zoological Gardens, having traveled from New Hampshire by railcar. "Funny as Jimmie was," he says, "we realized it would be not long before the fun was all on Jimmie's side."

We head out for a walk, leaving the coyote, wolves, and deer behind alone in the house. Once in the field, we smell a familiar smell. Harold Baynes boldly approaches the lady skunk, detaches one of her young, and brings the little black-and-white baby over for our wonder and admiration. We wonder and admire. Nothing unpleasant transpires.

The Sprite joins us on the walk, Mr. Baynes's tame red fox, a pure joyous being. The fox had been off hunting somewhere, Baynes explains, but never wanders far, returns with commendable faithfulness. I simply cannot recover from how charming the red creature is, pouncing on leaves and making regular chirps, almost like the laughter of a child.

I ask Harold Baynes if he would sell me the tame fox, and he names a price of a million dollars. "No more than that," he says, with a good-natured chuckle, "for he isn't really worth it; no less, for moral reasons." I don't have a million dollars; nor would my wife like a fox in the house, not even a tame one; nor do I believe his owner would go through with the sale if I did. "I tell everyone I don't have a favorite pet, that they are all my great friends," he says as we continue our walk. "But between us, that little fox is the creature I love most in all the world."

"What does your wife think about that?" my companion asks, a twinkle in her eye.

Harold Baynes is married to a woman named Louise Baynes, but we do not make her acquaintance. We have heard, also, of Mr. Baynes's charming ways with wealthy women, and the support of the ladies of high society is how he funds much of his work for wildlife, his travels, and speeches about preservation. Perhaps Mr. Baynes was hoping to charm my wife, so he asked his own bride to go to town for the day, but alas, while my wife is easily charmed by handsome men, she is not wealthy.

As we finish a loop around the field, Mr. Baynes invites us for a drink, so we head back to the house. From the veranda of the little cottage on Sunset Ridge, you can see much of Corbin's private hunting park over the fence. The famous Austin Corbin was killed in an accident years ago, so it was his widow Hannah Corbin who gave Mr. Baynes the golden key to Corbin Park and access to its many animals as his study subjects, in the hopes that some good could come of her late husband's final project. None of the many beasts of the park will suffer in Mr. Baynes's presence, as his weapons consist only of camera and notebook.

Even from our distant view on the veranda, it is miraculous how the green-clad land has returned to its virgin state, and the folds of the blue hills inspire restful dreams. When you consider that men have been getting further away from nature for decades, wearing fine clothes and living in cities, it all seems a horrid mistake. It will remain for this generation to see in some measure the folly of this, and to seek a return to the soil. Pioneers like Harold Baynes are needed to forge out—

Ingrid cut *The New Hampshire Spectator* writer off here, didn't scan the next page of the ancient newspaper. The profile went on, but Ingrid knew her kids would get the gist. She did attach another photo, one where she thought Harold Baynes looked a little like Paul Newman in his heyday. According to the gossip mill at the Everton Historical Society, Harold Baynes had once bedded half of the ladies in town, and many more when off traveling, and Ingrid Starling could see his appeal. Of course, Ingrid also felt a little bad for Louise Baynes, with a philandering husband and a house full of wild beasts.

Ernest Harold Baynes and one of his deer friends.
Photograph by Louise Birt Baynes.

4

It was roast chicken for dinner, and Emma had to tell her mom that she was a vegetarian.

"That's so California, GG," Auggie said. "Are you on a cleanse?"

"Well, eat dessert then. The pie," her mom said. "It has apples."

"Just pie is fine," Emma agreed, although the house she'd been living in in L.A. had been a vegan house, no butter or eggs. Twelve people living in a six-room house, more or less a small commune, but rent was cheap, and month to month, while Emma tried to figure out her next step. But her parents didn't know she'd been living in a place like that. They thought she was living in the UCLA David Geffen Medical School dorm apartments.

Auggie farted, his open mouth full of chicken.

"Auggie!" Ingrid said.

"Emma's not a special guest, Mom." Auggie was wearing a black T-shirt, and his chest was built like a bulldozer, always had been, although he'd put on weight since his days as quarterback at Upper Valley High. Auggie wasn't born with healing hands, but he did have nimble fingers: he was something of a prodigy at the piano as a kid, and then later, he was a star on the football field. There had been an athletic scholarship on the horizon, probably to a Big Ten school, but Auggie suffered a bad neck injury his junior year. The doctor prescribed painkillers to get him back on the field. Most people have heard a story like that one, what can happen next. Auggie was soon another Everton teen-ager seriously into drugs.

"Ingrid, leave the boy alone," Ralph said from the head of the table. There were lots of times Ralph Kelsey would act like that, like the patriarch, like the grandfather.

"Yeah," Auggie said. "Leave the boy alone."

Ingrid sighed and returned to her meat. The dog sat at her feet, gazing up adoringly at this wonderful woman who had run out to the store before dinner to buy kibble and a jumbo box of Milk-Bones and who had also given him three pieces of chicken thus far. "No begging," Ingrid said to the dog, and then looked back up at her family. "So, Emma, how's med school going?"

There's the million-dollar question, Emma thought, and she wondered if she should lie again. If she could keep on lying, for-ever and ever, if she could live a secret double life. But no, that was crazy, and probably too hard to pull off, so it was really time to fess up. The time was overdue, even, and Emma figured her mother couldn't kill her, not with Ralph Kelsey there. She took a deep breath, in her nose and out her mouth, and explained to the table that she had never been a student at UCLA David Geffen Medical School. She'd gotten in, but she hadn't gone. The first day came, and she hadn't been able to make herself go. "I've been trying to figure it out," she said.

"What do you mean you didn't go?" her mother asked. "You're telling me you've been hanging out on the beach since your col-lege graduation? Emma, it's November, what have you been doing since *May*?"

Emma poked her fork at a chunk of apple. She wished she could dig a hole in the floor with that fork, hide there for a while. The vegan commune in L.A. had been nowhere near the beach. "I haven't been doing too much, I guess," she mumbled.

Auggie whistled. Her brother looked delighted.

"I never thought you should go to med school," her father said.

"Dad, you always said I would be useful in an emergency room. Who do you think works in an emergency room?"

"Ah," Clive said, nodding, chewing. "You're right, a healer could come in real handy in the emergency room. Someone like you could make a difference."

Someone like you. Her parents and high school teachers had always thought she was so special, just so great, but it turned out not to be true once she left Everton. There were smarter kids at Pomona, and no one really cared that Emma was born with a healing touch that soothed minor aches and pains. "Not much of a party trick," Emma's roommate Tessie Blatt had said, before advising *maybe* Emma shouldn't tell too many people about it.

"How have you been paying for things?" Ingrid asked now, really starting to spiral. "Where were you living? Oh God, were you homeless? That explains those jeans."

"Oh boy," Auggie said. "Here we go."

For the first weeks after graduation, Emma had stayed at Tessie's parents' house. Their mansion actually *was* on the beach in Malibu, but Emma was sluggish, depressed. Med school orientation was weeks away, starting in July. Emma dreaded it. All the competition, more years of feeling like you were just trying to keep your head above water. "Why did you apply if you didn't want to go?" Tessie had asked. Emma wasn't sure, except that she was born a healer, but she didn't want to work out of, like, a tarot card shop by the side of a rural highway, stuck behind a beaded curtain. Med school had seemed like a good idea until it was right about to start.

At the end of the summer, orientation come and gone, Mrs. Blatt said she needed Emma to move out of the pool house, it was due for renovations, but first she had Tessie's father write Emma a prescription for an SSRI.

"I can't believe you really just . . . didn't go to med school," Emma's mother said, letting it sink in. "Unbelievable."

"Unbelievable," Auggie echoed.

"I've been figuring it out, Mom," Emma said, ignoring her brother. "I have a job."

"Oh, thank God. What's the job?"

"I've been, well, a receptionist at a hospice." The 20 mg of Lexapro from Dr. Blatt had been magic in itself, and Emma had perked up. She had moved into the vegan commune, found a job at Guiding Light Hospice, where there was lots of downtime between mounds of paperwork. It might have all been fine.

"I never thought you should go to med school," her father repeated.

"Being a receptionist sounds like a valuable way to spend your time," Ralph Kelsey said. "I'm sure you meet a lot of interesting people."

"Interesting people about to bite the dust." Auggie had never looked more pleased. Emma wished she could wipe the shit-eating grin off his face.

"There are a lot of ways to die," Emma said, poking the apple again.

"Indeed there are," her dad agreed. "Which way do you think is the worst?"

"Clive!"

"I was fired from the hospice, actually," Emma said to her family at the dinner table. "I'm not going back." She sucked air in through her teeth, let it out. "I'm going to stay home for a while. Surprise."

"Oh, Emma," her mom said.

"*Oh, Emma* is right. I fucked it all up."

"Fucked what up?" Ralph Kelsey asked. His eyes were particularly kind.

"My potential," she said.

"Ha," Ralph said. "You've got a long way to go before you know your potential."

"Sounds like she's on a good path to squandering it," her mother said.

Even Auggie looked a little sorry for her then, Emma noticed.

We noticed it, too, and Auggie did feel just a little bad for his sister. A new feeling for him. From where Auggie sat, he felt like his sister had always been Little Miss Perfect, with the good grades, the healing touch, and the no drug problem. "You lied about going to med school," he said, in awe. "You were fired from your first job."

"Yes, Emma, what in the ever-loving Earth did you do to get fired?" Ingrid asked.

"Oh, I'm not sure I want to relive my recent failures." Emma wasn't sure she could do it. This was the worst part. This was the part that she *really* didn't know how to tell her family about.

"Come on, Emma, it'll at least take our minds off it," her mother demanded, and Emma saw that her eyes went to the extra plate that her dad had asked her to set, where he'd spooned out an enormous portion of apple pie for the ghost's dinner.

Emma reddened, but she forged ahead, explaining that out in California, the healing touch had gone wonky. First, it had become unreliable, like the midwife had warned it could: either nothing happened, or the wrong thing happened, and the wrong thing could be something terrible. Tessie had once gotten a gnarly abscess on her foot, one so large it required surgical drainage. At least once she started working at the hospice, Emma figured she could practice on the patients, see if she could get the Charm working again. It didn't matter if a hospice patient sprouted unexplained hair or suffered from complete tooth loss, other side effects she soon discovered. "We're not saving lives here," the head nurse often said at the start of morning meeting.

It was a fine job until Mr. Rawls, dying of pancreatic cancer, accused Emma of touching him. Emma was a receptionist, not really supposed to touch the patients, but this patient, Mr. Rawls, clinging to life, pointed to the place on the CPR practice doll where she had touched him. The CPR practice doll, named Resuscitation Anne, was only the torso, and also supposed to be a female, so Mr. Rawls had to point to a part that wasn't there. "It was a very good touch," Mr. Rawls said, practically panting.

"I did not touch him *there,*" Emma had insisted, but it was too late. Mr. Rawls's roommate claimed he'd seen the whole thing, and they'd been bragging about it to all the nurses, all the other patients. For whatever reason, the medical director, Dr. Megan Farrell, believed these dying men, two men half-crazy from morphine drips, over her employee. "That is the stupidest thing I've ever heard," Emma said, but it was obvious that there was nothing she could say to change Dr. Farrell's mind. And Emma *had* touched Mr. Rawls. She hadn't touched him *there,* but she had touched him, held his hand and tried to heal his cancer. But in Dr. Farrell's office, well, Emma couldn't bring herself to explain to her boss that the reason she'd been touching the dying patients was because she was trying to restore her natural-born gift, a mystical healing power of human touch, so she didn't bother defending herself. Most people outside of Everton would never understand.

At that point in the story, Clive and Ralph Kelsey, the two at the table closest to death, started to holler with laughter. "A *very* good touch," Clive kept repeating, laughing so hard he was crying.

"The healing touch is gone," Emma said to the table, over the laughter, making sure they all understood. "I don't have it anymore."

Her mom said nothing, only closed her eyes. Auggie looked miserable, wasn't laughing along with his dad and Ralph. Emma was sure Auggie wanted her to heal their father, even though her brother, of all people, should know that the Charm wasn't a cure-all. Three years ago, Emma had flown cross-country to try to heal the subluxation in her brother's vertebrae, but a spine is complicated, and the healing would be slow. Auggie's coach had wanted him back on the field. She hadn't been able to do anything to cure his cravings for painkillers either. That was a different kind of disease.

Ingrid opened her eyes and stared hard at Emma. "You're sure it's gone?"

Emma nodded. "It's totally gone now." She held her hands out, palms faceup, signaling emptiness. Emma didn't even get the weird side effects from her healing attempts anymore. When she tried to heal someone, as she'd done with some of her roommates at the vegan commune, nothing happened. "That massage didn't even feel good," her vegan roommates reported.

Ingrid smoothed her hair, a sign she was really upset.

"Sorry I haven't told you," Emma said. "I didn't know how to say it."

"Should we see a specialist?"

"I don't know, Mom, what kind of specialist would you suggest?"

"Okay. You're right. It's fine," Ingrid said, although it clearly wasn't. "You'll find something else to do with your life. You have always had other strengths."

Emma looked over at her dad, who was still chuckling about the very good touch, but he was also now stealing bites off the ghost's untouched plate. Maybe he had not been banking on his daughter healing him, Emma thought, which would be a relief.

"There's always law school," her mom pointed out.

"I'll cut her kneecaps off first," Clive said, snapping to attention. "My daughter is not going to be a lawyer."

"Dad, you're a professor at a fancy-ass college," Auggie said. "Will you stop pretending you're so antiestablishment?"

"*Was* a professor, past tense," Clive said. "And say goodbye to your kneecaps." He pointed his knife at Auggie, and then at Emma, who looked away.

"The point is, Emma, you'll find something," Ingrid said. "I'm not worried."

"Me neither," Clive said, returning his knife to his plate, and reaching for his wife's hand across the table. "I'm just so glad we're a murmuration again." Her dad's fingernails were too long, Emma realized, a little grossed out. She'd find out later that her mother had to cut his nails for him, on account of the tremor. Someone had once told Clive that a gathering of starlings, the birds, is called a murmuration and he'd written it down immediately. He kept a notebook full of slang words and phrases, was always adding to it, from books he read, or things the kids said at the college. He was the one who had named Emma, a name that means "Healer of the Universe" in Teutonic. Emma knew she was lucky that she hadn't ended up named Airmid or Meditrina, two goddesses of healing. She was born years before Emma became the most popular girl's name, after Rachel and Ross's baby on *Friends*. It was a classic name, of course, but if he'd known it would be *that* common, her dad never would have gone for it. Clive Starling had always wanted his family to be standouts in this town.

Over at Maple Street, we were upset about the loss of Emma's abilities—"I'm devastated," Donald Brown (b. 1890–d. 1965) said, because Donald was kind of a drama queen—but we loved Emma Starling, healing hands or no healing hands. Above all, we were glad she was home. We knew she had unfinished business here. Everyone knows how much ghosts care about unfinished business; that old cliché is true.

And we could see that Emma needed some time home in Everton to recuperate from what had happened in California. She needed some time to revive herself. A reboot. A fresh start. There's lots of words for something like that, when someone needs to make a comeback after a major fall. "Resurrection" is another one, although of course that word means something else to us at Maple Street, and a resurrection was really much more than anyone here would ever expect.

5

Emma volunteered to clear the table, wanting everyone to remember she was still the good child. The helpful one. As she loaded the plates into the rack, that was when she spotted the missing person poster. It was displayed up on the fridge, as if it were a good report card or an elementary school art project.

"What kind of weird joke is this?" Emma asked, marching back to the dining-room table with the flyer displaying a photo of her best friend from high school. She was someone Emma didn't talk to anymore, although Emma knew her parents had stayed in touch. Crystal and her dad Bart had once been part of the extended family at the Corbin Mansion and caretaker's house, and Emma's parents still loved Crystal. Felt responsible for her.

"I made those posters," Clive said proudly.

"Oh," Auggie said, leaning back in his seat. "This is going to be good. I can't believe you haven't told her."

"Auggie," Ingrid reprimanded. "We are going to tell her, now that she's here. And I thought you learned to be more sensitive at the Phoenix House." Ingrid could walk the halls of that expensive rehab place in the dark. She had been to so many family group-therapy sessions, stayed in touch with some of the parents, heard what could happen. Because of this, Ingrid was very sure Crystal Nash—who had never gone to rehab, although Ingrid would have certainly offered to pay for it if she'd known what was going on—was dead of an overdose, an unidentified Jane Doe in a morgue somewhere. It didn't take a lot of imagination.

"Mom, cut to the chase," Auggie said.

"Yes," Emma said. "What happened to Crystal?" The last she'd heard about Crystal, she was working as a bartender at the Blueberry Hill Pub. She'd been doing all right.

"No one knows what's happened to her," Clive said.

"What do you mean no one knows?"

"Crystal got on the H-train," Auggie said.

"What kind of train?" Ralph was confused.

"H is for heroin."

"A drug train?" Ralph asked. "Or a metaphorical train?"

"Your father and I didn't know how to tell you," Ingrid said. This is not how Ingrid had wanted to break the news, either. She hadn't noticed the poster on the fridge, or she would have removed it. "No one has seen Crystal for a few months. We know she was using, and it doesn't look good. Your father had her declared a missing person."

"What? Oh my God."

"*I* wanted to tell her," Clive said. "I wanted to tell Emma right away." Clive, unlike his wife, was very hopeful that Crystal Nash was still alive. "Our only problem is that no one knows where she is. But now that Emma's home, she can help me find her." Clive was ready to team up with his daughter, like this was some kind of buddy-cop comedy.

"You told the police?" Emma asked. "What did the police say?"

"Those motherfuckers," Clive said, because he hated the Everton cops, all two of them. He told Emma how they'd searched Crystal's trailer, found it still looked lived in, even if the electric toothbrush was gone from its holder, so yes, maybe Crystal had simply packed a light bag and left, but still, they should find out where she'd gone. "We don't spend too much time looking for grown adults who leave town," Officer Zinger had told Clive. "Not much time on missing drug addicts either." The police had

called off the hunt once they found two lousy bags of white powder in her bedside table.

Emma didn't know anything about Crystal's drug problem,
though it sounded like Officer Zinger had a good point, even if
he'd been kind of a dick about it. Crystal *was* a grown adult, and
if her toothbrush was gone, maybe it had nothing to do with the
drugs. Emma could imagine leaving this town and never looking
back, because that had been her own plan. Crystal simply got out
of Everton, Emma reasoned as she heard more of the story. Who
could blame her? She didn't owe it to the Starlings to tell them
where she was going. She'd moved on. Good for her.

"You should add a reward to that poster," Ralph Kelsey told
Clive. "I'll pay for it." As one of the richest residents of Everton,
Ralph Kelsey knew how money could motivate. Ralph was probably right, because a group of four men and two teenage boys had
just spent all day chasing an escaped wild boar for a thousand
bucks, and those suckers are huge, big enough to wreck your car.
The boar captured in the town square gazebo had battered one of
the Murphy boys in the stomach with a tusk, causing some pretty
serious internal bleeding. Keegan Murphy was currently at home
toughing it out. His dad had given him some of the good stuff, for
the pain.

"I'll consider it," Clive said, about the reward. He didn't want
the poster to be overwhelmed with text.

"Well, Ingrid, I'd like to get out of this hellhole," Ralph announced, which is what he said at the end of every dinner, when
he wanted to be driven back to his Deluxe Apartment at Sundown
Acres Assisted Living. A few years ago, Ralph started to need
more care than Ingrid could give him, so he'd moved across town
to assisted living. The big yellow mansion sat empty, but Ralph
still came to the Starlings' most nights for dinner, and sometimes
he spent the whole day with Clive, yukking it up on the porch.
Ralph had nothing else to do; he'd retired a long time ago. The

gun factory was now run by a youngish CEO, a man in his early forties. Ralph Kelsey kissed both Emma and Auggie on the tops of their heads like he always did when he said good night, ever since they were little, and went out to get into the passenger seat of Ingrid's Subaru Outback, that reliable chariot.

"Emma, come have a drink with me on the porch," her father said, once her mom and Ralph had gone. "There's a lot more to catch up on."

"I'm really tired," Emma said. "The red-eye flight." She wasn't ready to be alone with her dad, she still thought he might ask her to cure him, side effects be damned.

"Tomorrow then," Clive agreed. "I'll update you with the work I've done on Crystal's case. So glad you're home, Emmy. You've been AWOL too long."

"Tomorrow," Emma repeated, realizing she was really home on an open-ended stay. She hadn't booked a return ticket back to California.

"I guess it's just us again tonight, Harold," Clive said, opening the front door to head to the porch, a handle of whiskey in his hand. Auggie was still right there in the kitchen, but Clive didn't ask his son to come out with him, because Auggie didn't drink, even though his main problem had been heroin and Oxys, not whiskey. Auggie got down on the floor to rub the belly of the new dog.

Emma went upstairs to her childhood bedroom, lay down on the quilted twin bed, and thought about what could have happened to her old friend Crystal, not seen for months. She imagined Crystal escaped Everton on her Harley, which is why she had to leave most of her stuff behind. That alone explained why the trailer looked lived in. One of the things Emma's dad and Crystal had in common, their stupid motorcycles. "My crotch-rocket," Clive liked to call his. Sometimes Emma thought her dad would have preferred Crystal as a daughter. Crystal and Clive had the same taste in music, agreed on Black Sabbath, Led Zeppelin, Motörhead, Judas Priest, Iron Maiden, and Deep Purple. They had their big argument about Metallica. Auggie had always said it was weird that their dad was into metal music, that he seemed too old, but Ozzy Osbourne was only a year and a half younger than Clive, born in 1948 and also likely to die sometime soon.

Emma resolved to text Crystal before she fell asleep, but she needed to figure out what to say first. *Sorry we haven't talked in so long, but I'm home now. Everyone here is worried about you, just let us know where you are, send a postcard or something, an email.* Even if Crystal didn't care about Emma anymore, she had to care about Emma's parents, and Ralph Kelsey too. Probably even Auggie.

In the end, Emma texted a watered-down, pathetic version of everything she would have liked to say to her ex–best friend. *Call my parents, OK?* she typed. *My dad is sick.* Emma couldn't bring herself to write *dying*, so she went with *sick* instead. It wasn't fair for Crystal to get Emma's dad all worked up if she'd just left town on her Harley. Emma closed her eyes and smooshed her head into the pillow, even though it was only eight-thirty P.M., and even earlier on the West Coast. At Maple Street, we would love to remember that feeling, what it was like to be so tired and worn-out, the combination of a long trip plus the suffocating effects of a family dinner, chicken and apple pie.

When Bart Nash and his teenage daughter moved to Everton, the Corbin Mansion had already been through a lot of groundskeepers, hired and fired by Ingrid or Ralph. But when Bart Nash came along, he made all their handyman dreams come true. Bart could probably kill any large animal with his bare hands, he was a huge man—six-foot-seven—his head bald as a potato, but Bart was too sweet and fun for any kind of killing. He loved small children, all animals, Jimmy Buffett's music, fruity cocktails, and professional wrestling. When Ingrid learned there was no Mrs. Nash at home, she insisted that Bart's daughter was welcome to come to work with him anytime.

So if Crystal didn't have basketball practice, she started hanging around the Starling house, because there were tons of snacks there and none back at the trailer. Crystal was sixteen, and she had a piss-poor attitude about moving high schools again, especially to a school with a subpar basketball program. She was a really good point guard, even though she didn't look like your typical athlete. She had bleach-blond hair to her shoulders, was eyelinered as heavy as a meerkat. According to Bart, his daughter was going through a witchcraft phase.

"I'm a Wiccan," she'd said, with an eye roll.

Emma had seen Crystal in the halls of Upper Valley High. She was hard to miss, with that hair and that scowl, but Emma was a freshman, Crystal already a sophomore. Crystal showed no interest in Emma, not at first. She would raid the pantry, and then she would curl up on the padded bench in the living room with a book, never one that had been assigned in school, always something from the library that looked like an old spell book. Crystal never did her homework, Emma noticed.

It was Clive who was the first to win Crystal over by giving her a Ouija board and a canister of Morton Salt. He said real witches go through a ton of salt; it's needed in most spells. "And curses," he told her, and winked. He also told Crystal that a spell or a curse usually needs two people to conduct it, if you're going to conjure up any real power, and he gestured toward his daughter in the other room.

Crystal finally approached Emma a few days later. "Someone at school told me you can cure cancer with your hands. They said you won't do it because you suck."

"The people we go to school with are cretins," Emma said, jutting out her chin. Emma hated kids like Samantha Tatro, who did whippets in the bathroom by the gym. Samantha had made Emma's life miserable for years, spreading rumors about how she was giving all the teachers magic hand jobs in exchange for those perfect grades.

"I agree, generally," Crystal said. "But there's usually some truth to every rumor."

"I didn't do anything with Mr. Zammerilli."

"I mean with your hands," Crystal said.

Emma shrugged, and took Crystal upstairs, and let her read the *Upper Valley New Hampshire News* article about the midwife. It was framed in her parents' bedroom, over their bed. Embarrassing, but easier than explaining it herself. "I can't cure cancer," Emma said. "Just minor stuff."

Crystal held out her arm. It was covered in scratches from basketball, Crystal wasn't afraid to fight for the ball. "Show me." Emma held her breath, touched Crystal, and concentrated. The Charm didn't just happen willy-nilly. She'd never healed anyone outside the family, not since the midwife. When she touched Crystal's arm, she concentrated as hard as she could.

Crystal ran to Emma in the hallway the next morning at school and grabbed her shoulders. "You're going to be my best friend." Crystal showed Emma her scratch-free arms. After that, no one said nasty things to Emma in the hallways anymore, because everyone was afraid of Crystal Nash. There was a rumor she'd turned everyone at her last school into toads. That was certainly not true, but Crystal encouraged it, would say "ribbit, ribbit" if Samantha Tatro ever got too close.

Emma and Crystal had sleepovers, stayed up late with the Ouija. They asked the board about whether Crystal would ever be famous, and what for, and the simple *Yes* or *No* on whether the geometry teacher, old Lester Stert, was a pedophile or not. "Lester the molester," Crystal always called him. The Ouija board had said *Yes,* but Emma was sure Crystal had nudged it. They asked it questions about the boys at school, even though the pickings were slim at Upper Valley High, except for Mack Durkee, who Emma said was the complete package, but he was a senior, out of their reach. And they told each other secrets, like what happened to Crystal's mom.

"In another time, I think my mom could have been a saint," Crystal said to Emma. "Locutions," she added. "That's what it's called when God speaks to you."

"Even though she killed herself?" Emma asked. "She should have been a saint?"

"The saints always met violent ends," Crystal said, and shrugged. "I think you could be like that."

"Could be like what? Like your mom?"

"I mean, you could be special," Crystal said.

"I don't want to meet a violent end."

Crystal laughed. "There's only so much I can control, dude."

It was after that that Crystal made *charismata iamaton* her personal research project. She used the interlibrary loan form, which meant you could get books from all over New England, and of course Massachusetts had some really witchy stuff. "It says here it's not a power but an *energy.* You have a natural energy. It's really not that crazy," Crystal explained, looking through yet another library book. "Science shows that touching really does reduce blood pressure, stress, and promote healing. You just have an extra gift. We need to do *something with it.* It's going to waste."

When Ingrid overheard the girls talking about the Charm, she nearly killed them both. "You are forbidden from charging anyone in the school a dime. Especially the boys. No, wait, *especially* the *teachers.* If you want to be a healer, Emma Starling, you let it motivate you to think about what you want to do in the future. A doctor would be a very good choice," she finished. "For someone with your gift of gentle touch."

"Thanks, Ms. Starling," Crystal said.

"For what?"

"Oh, nothing. Just thanks for giving Emma good advice."

The girls had been looking for a name for their healing business, and the Gentle Touch Healing Society was born. Crystal made all the business decisions, such as the decision to meet their clients at the McDonald's, because Crystal knew Ingrid Starling would never be caught dead in a fast-food place. Crystal also made their clients sign a nondisclosure agreement from a template she found on the internet to keep it a secret from Ingrid, and also everyone at school. Crystal said it was important Emma never touch the money, that the clients never saw Emma put her magic hands on those grubby dollar bills. "They have to believe you're the real thing. A big part of *charismata iamaton* is the client's faith in it."

"Is McDonald's the right choice for our offices then?" Emma asked.

"People are comfortable there. Comfort is important too."

During the years of the Gentle Touch Society, Crystal never promised miracles, even if she always put "THE REAL DEAL" at the bottom of their ads. Clive busted them early on, when he walked in for a Big Mac, but he swore he wouldn't tell his wife. He said he thought it was good practice, but what Emma really needed was to get into the ER, reach the people who needed immediate healing, the bleeders, the burn victims. Crystal agreed with Clive, but for now she said she and Emma were stuck with anyone who answered their Craigslist ads.

Emma wasn't sure how strong her Charm really was, but she knew she had helped some people, really helped them, cured some rashes and soothed arthritis, and given at least some comfort to people with more serious health problems. But when Crystal started holding hands with the clients, too, to double up on the profits, Emma was pretty sure that was a scam. Crystal insisted she'd learned to harness her own energy, the natural healing touch we're all born with. She was sure *charismata iamaton* could be a learned skill. "Maybe Jesus wasn't born with it either."

"The whole point is that Jesus was born special," Emma said.

"I mean, who knows what really happened."

And maybe Crystal was right, because none of their clients ever asked for a refund. In fact, some of the clients started preferring Crystal. She had a way of looking at you, as if she were really listening. That would come in handy later, when she became a bartender.

It was three weeks before Emma left for Pomona College orientation when everything fell apart for the Gentle Touch Society. That was when Emma was attacked by a client in the brown-tiled bathroom of the Mickey D's. That was when that horrible man had grabbed Emma's hand and yanked it toward the sweatiest, swampiest part of his khakis. Crystal thought Emma was overreacting, the pepper spray had done its job protecting her. It could have been, you know, *so much worse.* The girls wouldn't go to the bathroom alone anymore. They had the pepper spray, and they could buy a Taser, too, with all the money they had. Problem solved, easy-peasy. But Emma said the problem wasn't solved, she was quitting, it wasn't worth it. She said Crystal had been charging people way too much anyway, people who so obviously had nothing.

Crystal said Emma knew jack-shit about what it's like to grow up without money. Not everyone gets to grow up in a mansion.

"It's Ralph's mansion," Emma said. "We just live in the caretaker's house."

"Have fun in *Los Angeles,*" Crystal said. "Enjoy your ordinary life. I hope someday the babysitter fucks your husband."

"Crystal, come on. You won't be stuck here forever."

"You have no idea what you're talking about," Crystal said, storming off.

When Emma left Everton with her shower caddy and surge protector and tons of new underwear, the friendship was on shaky ground, but Emma didn't think it was over. The nail in the coffin came weeks later, when Crystal's dad died of a sudden heart attack. There would be no funeral in Everton, Bart Nash's body was to be sent to Virginia to be buried alongside his wife. Emma texted Crystal from California: *I'm so sorry about your dad. We'll have a strawberry daiquiri in his honor next time I'm home.*

Crystal responded a day later, said she'd rather eat a can of shit.

"Who put it in a can?" Charles Tepper (b. 1932–d. 1998) had asked from his grave. He loved the insult.

The friendship fell off a cliff after that, like Wile E. Coyote in the Road Runner cartoons. The ground was there, until suddenly it wasn't.

Emma tossed and turned in her childhood twin bed, which suddenly felt more like a coffin. She checked her phone again, but no text in response. She felt abandoned by Crystal, cut off all over again. An old wound torn open on her first night back in town.

6

Now, *we* could have pointed to where the missing woman was, the former Blueberry Hill Pub bartender, the twenty-three-year-old Crystal Nash, but so far no one had asked us. We're not supposed to meddle. We listen, we watch, we hope for the best, but our condition can be pretty limiting. In her worst moments, Mildred Roscoe (b. 1811–d. 1902) says we're nothing but idle gossips.

We know we're not exactly guardian angels at Maple Street, but if we were only given a little more freedom, if there weren't so many rules and restrictions to being dead, we could help out the living. We could make it better for them. Absalom Kelsey (b. 1745–d. 1837), buried toward the top of the hill with an obelisk-shaped headstone, the oldest soul in the graveyard, loves to remind us that the rules are in place for a reason.

The first rule is, of course, No Meddling, and if you meddle too much your spirit can explode. A gone-in-a-flash type thing. A bright light, a puff of smoke, a slight lingering stench.

The second rule explains the Importance of Caring for the People of Everton. If you stop caring about the events of the living, you're in direct violation of the rules of our cemetery, and your soul shrivels up before it disappears, like a browning, withering houseplant. It's less dramatic than an explosion of white light, but the end result is the same. You go Quiet. There are many graves in our yard where there is a stone and no soul lingering above it, someone who has become nothing but a rock.

But we can resist it, the Quieting, as long as we continue to keep tabs on the events of the living. We care for them; we root them on. We try our best not to meddle. Some of the other rules are silly, added over the years, rules like No Lawn Games and No Evil-Doing and No Unnecessary Singing, but we take those first two rules as seriously as we can. We don't know if there's anything after this. Maybe nothing. Maybe this patch of dirt and grass and ice and snow is all there is.

When overdose victim Jesse Peters (b. 1984–d. 2013) first arrived at our iron gate, he was still pretty high as he made his transition between the living and the dead, and he said that that not knowing what happens next and the fear associated with the not-knowing, that uncertainty and anticipation is what makes us human. Jesse Peters hasn't turned out to be much of a philosopher once he was more dead and less high, but we'd be lying if we didn't admit many of us have thought a lot about that ever since, if we're still human or if we're something else.

PART II

The Rabbits

7

⇒·∙·⇐

THE LOYALTY OF FOXES

from *The Collected Writings of Ernest Harold Baynes,* © 1925
This Book Is Property of the Everton Historical Society

"Mrs. Baynes, what is under that there stone?"
Photograph by E.H.B.

Mrs. Baynes and I never had children together, nor did we particularly want them, because we kept such a full and active household of coyotes, timber wolves, skunks, deer, squirrels, a baby bear, and many, many birds. But of all the animals we have ever lived with, it was the fox who was our shared favorite. The Sprite had more personality in the tip of his little blackberry nose than most men have in their entire being.

Mrs. Baynes and I started out with three fox cubs, all taken from a burrow in Corbin Park, sniffed out by a friend's hunting dog. Even at this young age The Sprite was different from his brethren, brighter somehow, smarter, and bent on adventure. Perhaps this was a were-fox, we thought, and in the morning we should awake to find him a human infant curled up in the leaves between two baby foxes. Or perhaps he would change us all into foxes in the night! There was truly something fairylike about the third little fox cub, and so that is why we named him "The Sprite."

Whenever The Sprite saw us, he expressed his delight by wagging his tail, pulling back his ears, and jumping up, much as an affectionate dog would do. In fact, from the time he was a tiny cub, he exhibited great pleasure at being reunited with me or Mrs. Baynes when we had been out of his sight for an hour or two. His expressions of delight were usually accompanied by a vigorous, open-mouthed panting.

His eating habits were a great source of amusement for us. He was particularly omnivorous and ate almost anything we offered him from our own table. One of the few things he would refuse was pineapple, and to that he showed an unmistakable dislike. He never ate all of his food, except for candy (licorice his favorite), but he would hide what was left, somewhere in the house. Once, I saw him mount a chair and place a piece of meat on a shelf. Of the three drinks he was accustomed to, namely, water, milk, and coffee, he had a decided preference for coffee. He would lap up half of Mrs. Baynes' cup most mornings.

His appetite became a problem, however, once he got a taste for chickens. He was very young indeed, no more than a toddler, when he began to take an interest in poultry. I was playing with him in the garden, when through a gap in the fence there flounced a fussy black hen. The fox caught sight of her and his eyes seemed in danger of popping out of his head. If it can be said that a fox "loves" chickens, this was a case of love at first sight, and his love only escalated from that first affair. Poultry hunting soon became The Sprite's favorite sport. He had many interests in life, but that was his chief one.

The fox's other flaw was that he was possessive, and he grew quite visibly in love with Mrs. Baynes as he grew older. He thought she was his mate, and once or twice he snarled at me, his chief competitor. Mrs. Baynes suggested I might trap him a vixen, but I was against trapping another fox, at least for the time being, after the twin tragedies that had befallen The Sprite's poor siblings. I'll spare the details, and of course we were sad about these happenings, the more so because we were to blame. Both tragedies might have been avoided had enough forethought been given and the necessary precautions taken, but until one has had long experiences with young creatures, it is difficult to think of and guard against all the many misfortunes that may possibly overtake them.

Fortunately, neither of these victims happened to be The Sprite, so their loss, much as it distressed us at the time, does not seriously affect the rest of his tale. Isn't that the rule? The hero can't die, at least not until the very end of the story.

8

Clive was the first to rise in the Starling house, except for the odd Sunday when he slept in. It was why he'd always told his wife his drinking wasn't the problem she said it was; he was almost always up at the ass-crack of dawn. Of course, then there was a two-or-three-hour nap in the afternoon. The napping had started many years ago; his teaching schedule allowed for it, but there was even more time for it now, without any job to do. To be asked to retire mid-semester was humiliating, but when Clive started seeing cats in the classroom, President Billings said his hands were tied.

Clive was at least keeping to his schedule, so the day after Emma had arrived back home, he got out of bed at five A.M. and was feeling pretty lonely as he descended the stairs. His beloved daughter seemed like she could barely stand to look at him; her homecoming wasn't the joyful reunion he'd hoped for. When Clive stepped off the landing into the yellow kitchen, he was glad to see Harold Baynes already sitting at the table. Clive needed the company this morning. "Good morning," he said to Harold. "Can I make you some coffee?"

"None for me, thanks." Harold was wearing his gray suit, even at this hour, which made Clive feel underdressed, but we all wear whatever we're buried in, or cremated in. We keep the outlines of our body. The clothes we last wore. We hold on. There were ways that Harold Baynes was just like us, and other ways he was entirely separate. We can hear all the thoughts of the living in town, but none of the cremated, a great barrier between us. We were dying to know Harold's plan here, how he would help Clive without his soul going up in smoke. He drummed his hands on the kitchen table, he seemed to be waiting for something.

Well, aren't we all waiting for something, Clive thought, then pulled the ties on his robe closed before he started the coffee maker. He had never been the kind of man who liked to be naked in front of other men. He was not a locker-room guy, not really into sports. Clive liked poetry, walks on the bird-sanctuary trails, and his 1948 Harley that still ran like a dream, even came with a detachable two-seater sidecar that his kids used to ride in when Ingrid allowed it. Clive knew he'd had a good life, he'd just expected it to go on longer. Clive understood that he was most likely seeing the ghost of Ernest Harold Baynes because he was dying, and Harold was here to shepherd him toward the end and into whatever lay beyond. Clive also wondered if perhaps the ghost needed something from him, some kind of favor. *Wasn't that what ghosts wanted? To put some earthly business to rest?* "Is there anything you need from me?" Clive asked. "Something that could help you . . . rest in peace?"

"I'm fine, thank you," Harold said, the same way he had declined the coffee.

Clive looked miserable. No one needed him.

"Your daughter's return didn't go as you'd hoped?" Harold asked.

"You should have seen the way she looks at me now. Pity and disgust."

"She's still angry about that affair?"

"I suppose so," Clive said. "I don't see why. Her mother has mostly forgiven me. Nearly entirely forgiven me, I would say. And that should be just between me and Ingrid. I don't see why the entire family has to get involved."

Harold tapped the table again. "You know, when I was alive, if I spent too long traveling away from our home, or if I'd accepted a big donation from an attractive socialite, I would bring home another animal. It's very hard to be upset about your own life when you're busy caring for a young and defenseless creature."

Clive considered it, an animal as an apology. "Well, we have the new dog. Moses."

"Your daughter gave that dog to your wife. That was her apology, not yours."

"The dog was an apology?"

"Seemed like it," Harold said.

"I never thought Emma should go to med school," Clive grumbled, although that wasn't exactly true, with all his talk of emergency rooms. Clive thought about it. "Another dog maybe. I could get another dog."

"You could be more creative."

"Ingrid's very allergic to cats," Clive said. "But I'll think about it."

"Okay," Harold said. "You think."

"What in the devil would be the point of a pet for a dying man?" Absalom Kelsey (b. 1745–d. 1837) asked from Maple Street, as the rest of us tried to guess what Harold's strategy was. If the cremated spirit of Ernest Harold Baynes would ever deign to walk by our graveyard, we would simply ask him what his plan was with the haunting opportunity, but he steered clear. There had been some petty fight with Absalom, years ago, and Harold's wife isn't buried with us, so he's not obligated to visit. Still, you'd think he'd want our help with the challenges of a haunting. You'd think he'd swallow his pride and come by.

"What's your plan for today?" Harold asked Clive. "Anything on the schedule?"

"I'll check," Clive said, although he knew there wouldn't be. He hated retirement, with all these open days. He opened his laptop, looked at his calendar: *Band Meeting, coffee shop, 11 a.m.*

Well, that was something. Always good to see the guys, even if they'd lost their regular Thursday-night gig at the Blueberry Hill Pub. A reason to get fully dressed today, he thought.

"I know a nice place to go walking around the coffee shop," Harold said, looking at the calendar. "I could show you, if you'd like." We perked up at Maple Street. A walk might lead somewhere.

But Clive ignored Harold; he was absorbed in the world of the computer now. He went next to his Meriden College email, out of habit. It was the one thing the college hadn't taken from him. There was a parking ban in effect, and students were supposed to see their advisers to register for classes, and one of his former students had emailed him because he needed a letter of recommendation to graduate school. It happened to be one of his least favorite students, and he thought about writing back and saying that he'd write him a recommendation letter straight to hell. What could Meriden College do now anyway? They'd already forced him out. Taken him down a peg. Given his office to some goddamn young person who had been hired to replace him. Not that he hated young people. He wasn't that kind of older man.

He closed the email and went to Google. He typed in: *What is the friendliest rare and unusual pet?* The search engine came back with pages and pages of results. Clive liked that about search engines. They gave you more than you needed.

Clive spent a little time on the Russian website for *Kompaniya po prodazhe lisits,* which translates to "company for the sale of foxes." This Russian company had been working to domesticate the red fox for the past sixty years, an experiment started in the Soviet Union beginning in 1959. The experiment had been meant to understand how domestication worked, but eventually, the Russian scientists started selling the foxes as pets, and the company continues on today, selling and shipping internationally. One such domestic fox could be yours, in four to six weeks, international shipping and "How to Care for Your Fox" instructions included. Eighteen thousand American dollars.

In the end, since Clive kept hesitating over the computer, it was Harold who entered the credit card information, who pressed the Buy Now button. *Click, click, click.* Clive stood back and watched. He was amazed at how well the man who had died in 1925 was able to navigate a computer. Sometimes Clive still had trouble with the damn thing, and he had to ask one of his students or his kids or even his wife how you could get the godforsaken cursor to move again.

We were surprised Harold was allowed to do that, surprised that ordering a wild animal online didn't count as too much meddling, but Harold didn't burst into a bright white light, didn't explode into nothingness. We waited for it to happen, but Harold's cremated soul, the outlines of it, stayed intact. We never know how much meddling will upset the universe.

"Wonderful," Clive said when the credit card information went through. "You see, Harold, you may have trapped your pet fox in the woods, but now we have the internet. Isn't it wonderful?"

"Yes," Harold agreed, but now he looked unsure. "Although I had thought perhaps we could trap you a fox in the woods too."

"Ah," Clive said. "Well, this is certainly easier. Free shipping." Then Clive looked to the door; he heard his wife on the stairs. Harold scrambled to close the laptop, and Harold was long gone by the time Ingrid Starling's big toe hit the bottom landing. Clive had to laugh a little, at the way the ghost so quickly disappeared. Even Harold knew there was something to be afraid of: the wrath of Ingrid Starling, who would never forgive an eighteen-thousand-dollar purchase on anything except a car or a down payment on a house. *Oh boy.* She was not going to see an expensive exotic pet as a thoughtful gift, a stand-in for a real apology. Ingrid was really going to *flip her shit,* Clive realized, as his students would say, it was another one of the slang phrases that Clive Starling loved. He had spent so much time trying to stay young and hip, and here he was, making impulse purchases on the internet like some crazy old man. It was a side effect of certain brain diseases, Dr. Wheeler had mentioned, online gambling, compulsive shopping. Sometimes the disease could mess with a part of the brain that is responsible for impulse restraint and risk management, Dr. Wheeler had explained. Suddenly Clive would remember him saying that.

Clive felt the rising panic. He would need to undo the purchase as soon as possible, but for the moment he would keep his composure. He didn't want his wife to think something was up. Ingrid hadn't even wished him good morning yet; she was busy getting breakfast prepared for her new dog. Clive knew the rules of the morning ritual: he was not allowed to speak to Ingrid until she spoke to him, until after she'd had her coffee, two cups from the pot he brewed for her. She liked quiet in the morning. Clive respected it.

"You're going to have to talk to your daughter," Ingrid said, breaking her own rule, Coffee Before Talky. "Make sure she knows this isn't a vacation."

Clive didn't answer, because he was trying to stay calm, the kitchen filling up with rabbits again. When Clive saw his hallucinations of small animals, we could see them, too, if we focused in on his thoughts. The rabbits were indeed all over the kitchen. Hopping, sniffing, digging, doing general rabbity things, and that was when Clive Starling felt it keenly: he really was losing it. It was terrifying, so much was the same as always, and yet so much had changed, had been rattled around.

9

⤜•⤛

The clock on Emma's phone claimed it was somehow already noon, but she remembered it was nine A.M. West Coast time. We think it's a disgusting habit of the currently living, the need to touch their phones even before their coffee cup, but we understood why Emma immediately grabbed hers, only to find nothing on the tiny screen. No response from Crystal. *I know you hate me and I don't care,* she added to the text thread. *I need to know where you are. My mom thinks you're dead.* Emma put the phone down on the nightstand. Crystal would surely respond to that.

Emma got out of bed and went to the bathroom down the hall to brush her teeth and take her white pill of Lexapro. She heard Auggie in his room, blowing things up, still a videogame addict at twenty. She knew things must have been hard for her family with Auggie's drug problem, harder than she had any real sense of. "I've got a handle on it," her mother used to say when Emma called to ask, and Emma hadn't really believed her, but she'd also tried not to think about it; it was happening so far away. Emma had once told a few friends in college she was an only child, when the topic came up. It was terrible, but her friends would be pissed at their sisters for stealing their clothes, and Emma's brother was stealing her parents' money to buy heroin. Not an easy thing to talk about. It was easier to lie and say: *Nope, no siblings, yes, an only child, ha-ha, yes, I do know what they say about only children.*

Downstairs, Emma was greeted by Moses and his enormous

head, his velvet-soft ears, his fur still wet in places. Her mother must have given him a bath. There was no sign of her parents, so Emma put on her coat and her winter boots, and grabbed an old leash from the junk drawer to take the dog for a walk.

There was a little trail through the woods off Corbin Road, where Emma let Moses off-leash, and he ran into the trees, zigzagging after squirrels. Out there, Emma was bombarded with the missing person posters, stapled on practically every trunk.

"Your dad's cool," Crystal had said back in high school, after Clive had explained the history behind some of his tattoos. A few of them he'd done himself, with a needle and india ink. Crystal had two sleeves of tattoos of her own now. Emma hadn't seen the tattoos in real life, only on Crystal's Instagram. There was a portrait of Joan of Arc, and one of Saint Dymphna, the patron saint of the mentally ill. Saint Dymphna's own father had cut off her head. The tattoos were colorful, beautiful, even if Crystal used to point out that many saints had prayed to be ugly so that no man would marry them.

Moses treed a squirrel and was now trying to climb a big oak without any success. There was a poster there too. "I came home a failure," Emma said to the poster. "You'll be sorry you're missing it."

In the photo, Crystal Nash appeared to tilt her head just a little.

Emma leashed Moses, and she started back to the Corbin Mansion and caretaker's house. Her parents would be back soon, and she would have to face them. Then Emma saw her rental car, glistening like a red ruby slipper in the afternoon sun, parked next to her father's old truck. Her parents must have taken the Subaru wherever it was they'd gone. Emma would have to return the rental car that night to Big Willie's Towing, but she still had it for a few more hours. She hadn't even had her own car in Southern California, where everyone says it's impossible to live without

one. The rental-car keys were in her coat pocket. She could still
escape, drive far away from here and never ever come back.

We understood that it overwhelmed her, what she had come
home to. It should be natural to go home to be with a dying parent, the cycle-of-life sort of thing, but it's harder than anyone pre-
pares you for. And she knew her dad was not the type to go quietly.
She had heard about the retirement party in the English Department lounge, how her dad had smashed the sheet cake onto the
floor, frosted with the phrase *Parting is such sweet sorrow.*

She opened the car door and Moses jumped right in. He'd been
in that car before. It had taken him someplace nice. To a warm
house, a family who was forthcoming with the Milk-Bones. He
saw no reason to believe the car wouldn't take him someplace
good again.

On their way down Main Street, Emma and Moses drove by the
little steepled church, and Emma thought how the church looked
like something out of a storybook; there were things Emma could
appreciate about a small town. The marquee out front read:
DON'T LEAVE YOUR SOUL OUT IN THE COLD. We liked that one, even
though the weather doesn't bother us. Emma approached the
town square, its white gazebo. We'd heard that Maple Street
would be getting a new member; Keegan Murphy didn't survive
the night after what had happened with the boar.

From behind her windshield, Emma could see Ralph Kelsey
and his friends from Sundown Acres Assisted Living protesting
on the town green. They called themselves the Enraged Old Bags,
and they protested every afternoon. The Sundown Acres van
dropped them off. The five members all protested something different, since the group could never agree on their politics. Ralph
always said the cause didn't matter; it was simply good to be pas-
sionate about something. Eunice Vandervoss held a sign that read

THIS OLD BAG IS FOR GUN CONTROL, so Ralph hated her. And for years Bubba Reid had been holding up the same sign: BUBBA REID DEMANDS RIGHT TO DRIVE. Bubba's license had been revoked a decade ago.

The copper statue of Austin Corbin in the town square looked down over the protest signs, looking amused and a little evil, as he always did. And Corbin *had* been evil, an anti-Semite and a total douche, but no one in Everton had suggested taking down his statue yet. Someone had even put a knit hat on the statue's bald head to keep it warm as the weather turned colder. We admit, we are a little jealous of the statue, the people of Everton so often touching him and talking to him as they do and saying his name every time they talk about *Corbin Park,* or the *Corbin Mansion,* or *take a left on Corbin Road.* Of course, Austin Corbin isn't around to hear it, since he's not buried at Maple Street, although he did die in Everton in 1896. His wife had him sent to be buried in New York, and Austin went to his final resting place in the same carriage that killed him. He'd spooked his horses when he opened an umbrella, and he was thrown from the carriage into a wall that would crack his head like a chestnut. He lived for six more hours as he repeated one word over and over again: *Bang, bang, bang, bang, bang.* His wife did not know if he was instructing her to shoot him or to shoot the horses, so Hannah Corbin did neither. She also didn't call for the doctor; there seemed no point.

In her red rental car, we realized Emma was driving to the McDonald's by the Covered Bridge, and we felt sad for her. She really did miss her friend. She kept waiting for a text to come in from Crystal, saying she was fine, still alive, but that Emma could go fuck off and die.

Moses whined from the backseat, signaling his need to pee.

"Didn't you just go?" Emma asked, but she agreed to stop. She was about to drive past Dream Far Elementary, a red building with white pillars, and she pulled into the school parking lot. There was a big field behind the school, and she took the dog out on his leash. Moses lifted his leg in relief. And then he looked around. *Another great place,* Moses thought. *Smells amazing.* There was a swamp near the school that gave off the strong scent of sulfur.

Recess should have been over at Dream Far this late in the afternoon, one-thirty already, but there was a group of kids out in the middle of the field, all crouched on the ground, looking at something. *Oh-boy-oh-boy-oh-boy,* Moses thought, before he lurched, and the leash broke in two pieces; it was a leash made for a much smaller dog. Moses took off, running straight for the kids like they were a flock of geese, like he was waiting for them to scatter and fly away. Emma knew he wasn't dangerous, but he might be scary, so she called after him to stop, to come back, "Moses, Moses, Mo, Mo, Mo, come!"

The dog kept running, maybe he didn't know his damn name yet. Of course he didn't, he'd only been named yesterday. The kids saw the big dog and most of them greeted him with open arms, and then Moses grabbed it, whatever it was on the ground that the kids were looking at, and he tried to get the kids to play chase.

It took Emma a second to see what Moses had. A plastic bag, which Emma worried he could choke on, so she grabbed it as quickly as she could. But she knew as soon as it was in her hands what it really was by the distinct texture, not a plastic bag at all, but a condom. She screamed, and flung it on the ground. "Where is your teacher?" she asked. "That isn't a plaything."

"We weren't playing with it," one of the girls said, her hands on her hips. She was wearing all pink, down to her shoes, and her hair was in braids. She looked to be around ten. "And our teacher is dead."

"She's not dead," a boy said. "She is so definitely not dead."

"I'm telling you, she's dead," the girl said. This girl was Leanne Hatfield, a fearless kid who would walk through Maple Street Cemetery even after dark, but Emma didn't know that yet. Emma imagined this girl didn't have an easy time making friends, thought of herself at about that age. Her dad had always told her she was special, smarter than most, and Emma wondered if this girl in all pink was under the delusion that she was special too.

"Aren't we feeling sorry for ourselves," Mildred Roscoe (b. 1811–d. 1902) said from her grave.

"Give her some time," the ever-hopeful Mae Belle Henick (b. 1799–d. 1820) advised.

"Patience," Bill Casey (b. 1955–d. 2004) agreed, a man whose headstone claimed he'd been a very good father.

Moses went for the condom again, pouncing like a cat on a mouse. It was an expression of pure delight, the kind so common to see in dogs, so rarely seen in people.

Emma left the kids and the condom, told the kids again not to touch it, then she and Moses hightailed it out of there. She started down the street when she realized how wrong it was to leave the kids with the thing she'd told them not to touch. She didn't know too much about kids, but one of them would surely touch it. Emma turned the car around and parked in front of the school, left Moses in the car, went into the front office. There was a woman wearing cat-eye glasses at the desk; Emma told her what she'd seen on the playground.

"That must have been the fifth-grade class. They're supposed to be planting seeds. We don't have a substitute teacher for the second half of the day . . ."

"What?" Emma asked. "That's awful. Is that legal?"

"We're looking for someone more long-term. A good teacher is hard to find, you know." According to the nameplate on her desk, the secretary's name was Doris. Doris leaned forward. "You know what happened to their teacher, don't you?"

"They killed her?"

"Oh, no, nothing like that," Doris said. "Sid Wish was her husband."

Emma said nothing. She didn't want to be in that office anymore. She had done the right thing, reporting the condom.

"Oh, honey, you haven't heard?" Doris asked, and she looked so happy. Emma realized it was the second time she'd seen that much joyful delight in one day, and what's more, in one hour. There was joy everywhere in Everton. Doris promised she wasn't going to leave out any of "the juicy details." The opioid problem had been getting worse and worse in Everton, and Doris said it had changed the town *completely.* "The worst calls the police used to get were for abandoned vehicles. Some guy beating up his wife. Now it's all drug dealers and overdoses. Trash."

"I see." Emma agreed with Doris, in some ways, that this small town didn't have a whole lot to offer, but then again, there was her brother. He was *awful,* but he wasn't trash.

"This year is the worst we've seen the problem," Doris went on. "But I totally understand why they never suspected him. He owns the car dealership! I bought my Mazda from him!"

Emma remembered the dealership: Sid's Car Korner. He spelled Corner with a *K,* but Car with a *C.* Her dad would always point it out, what a kick that was. He also loved the sign at the Fish & Tackle Shop: COME BE A MASTER BAITER! and he would probably love that Sid of Sid's Car Korner was a drug dealer on the side. Her father often said that a poet loves anything that better illuminates the daily horror of being alive.

"And what are you going to do about the condom?" Emma asked.

"I'll send out the janitor. Arthur will get to it," Doris said, waving it off, before leaning forward with more gossip. "And you know what happened to Claire Wish?"

"She's dead?"

"Oh no, no. She's not dead. Claire Wish just had a bit of a breakdown, after the cops busted her husband. Of course she did, wouldn't you? That's why she had to leave our school, at least for a while. Principal Jefferies wasn't going to fire her, that would be silly, not for something her husband did, but we're also quite relieved. It's such a mess!" She leaned forward and lowered her voice. "I heard she's in a locked ward."

"That's terrible."

Doris nodded, smiling, and her voice returned to a normal volume. "And it's too bad, because those kids really loved Ms. Wish. I've never seen a group of children love a teacher so much. You know, if you're looking for a job, the long-term substitute pay is really very good, and there's no experience needed. A young person like you could be a real hit with the kids. Do you have a job?"

"I don't—"

"Great. I'll schedule you next Monday at seven A.M. for an interview. Principal Jefferies will want to meet you. He never checks his emails. He prefers face-to-face."

Emma didn't know what to say. She'd never imagined herself as a substitute teacher in her hometown. She heard the dog barking. "I have to go. Moses is waiting."

"And may God bless you, too, dear. I'll see you on Monday. Seven A.M. The kids will just love you. So young and pretty."

Emma had only come into the office to address what she'd found on the playground. She wasn't looking for a job. Even if, actually, she *did* need a job. She needed money, she had college loans, credit card debt. She didn't want to ask her mom to bail her out. "I'll think about it," she told Doris. "Please don't forget about the condom."

"Oh, yes," Doris said, and she pressed the button for the loud-speaker, which meant the entire school would now know about the condom, not just the janitor who would need to clean it up.

When Emma got back to the red car in the lot outside Dream Far Elementary, Moses wasn't in the backseat, or the front seat. She'd left the window open, and the dog must have jumped out. Her chest tightened in panic. Then she heard more barking. She turned around, and Moses was across the street, barking like a maniac at a squirrel up a tree. She ran over to the dog and grabbed his collar. There were missing person posters on these trees too. The posters were everywhere. By the time she pulled the dog back to the car, Emma didn't want to go to the McDonald's anymore. This was all too much too soon. She needed a cup of good coffee. A quiet place to sit.

10

→·←

Emma headed to the north part of town, toward the Wilderness's Edge Express coffee shop, a repurposed old-fashioned train car on the side of a wooded road. Her father loved Wilderness's Edge Express. It was where he had liked to do his grading, and where he brought his poetry students to write their odes to New Hampshire. It was peaceful there, and close to the entrance of Corbin Park. Her dad loved to tell his out-of-state freshmen about the park, how enormous it was, about the eccentric millionaire who had built it and had animals shipped in from all over the world, and who-knows-what was in there now. The Meriden College students who hailed from the manicured suburbs of New York and Connecticut and New Jersey were always impressed. They all found New Hampshire to be much wilder than they'd expected.

Emma parked in the little dirt lot, and she left Moses in the car, the windows only slightly cracked so he couldn't jump out again. The dog wouldn't boil to death in a hot car; it was November in New Hampshire. Emma walked up the steps of the train car and was immediately greeted by a community bulletin board inside the door, littered with posters. Babysitters wanting to babysit. Firewood hoping to be sold. Crystal Nash waiting to be found.

"Would you look who's back in town," Crystal Nash said from her missing person poster. "Never thought we'd see her again, did we, Sparky?" There was another poster tacked up nearby, for a lost dog. *Responds to Sparky,* the writing underneath the photo said. *Please do not chase.*

Emma had never had bad effects from her Lexapro before; it wasn't even supposed to be habit-forming. Hallucinations weren't one of the listed side effects; Emma had been mostly worried about possible weight gain. She reached out to touch the words underneath the poster: HAVE YOU SEEN THIS PERSON? That feeling gathered in her throat, the one you get before you're about to cry, but she swallowed it down. Emma had never had a friend like Crystal, not before or since. Her roommate Tessie Blatt didn't even come close. Tessie was fun, and really very generous, but she was also obsessed with her boyfriend, the one who was always cheating on her.

"Where did you go?" Emma asked the poster. "Where did you fucking go?"

The poster said nothing in response, only stared blankly.

"Who are you talking to?"

Emma looked up, and it was the girl who worked at the coffee shop; she was the only other person there. It was midafternoon, Emma remembered, so that wasn't unusual. A coffee shop has a morning crowd. "Oh, I was on the phone. My mother."

The girl grunted. "My mom sucks too." The girl was wearing a brown visor and had a tattoo of Hello Kitty on her arm. She couldn't have been more than seventeen, but that Hello Kitty would be around a long time. The name tag on her shirt said *Angell,* spelled with two *l*'s, and her hair was dyed blue. Emma ordered a latte and a raspberry-orange scone, and hoped she wouldn't have to make small talk.

"Hey, aren't you Clive Starling's daughter?" Angell asked. Emma didn't think she knew this girl, but they must have met before, it was such a small town, and of course it made sense that she knew her father. He was a regular.

Emma nodded.

"He talks about you. He was in here just a few hours ago," Angell said, pointing to the booth in the corner of the empty shop, where a coffee cup was broken on the floor in the train's aisle and a muffin was crushed, it looked like it had been stomped on by Clive's big motorcycle boot. "He had a big fight with his friends this morning," Angell explained. "I haven't had time to clean up." Angell Kimball played a game with herself while she worked, and the game was to see how little work she could do. She spent nearly her entire shift staring out the back window behind the register. The window looked out into the woods. It calmed Angell down, all those trees.

Emma didn't know if she was supposed to pick up the broken coffee cup, pay for it, or something else. She had no clue what this Angell expected of her. She did know her dad often met his bandmates at Wilderness's Edge Express. Dennis Hollingdrake, the band's drummer, was her dad's best friend, other than Ralph Kelsey, and a pretty big hothead. "I'm sorry for the damage," she finally said to Angell, and offered to pay for the coffee cup and the smashed muffin. "He's been going through a hard time."

But Angell said she already knew all about it, she'd overheard the argument. "It's no big deal," she said. "But if you could give me, like, seven or eight bucks, I think that would cover it. Then, like, the owner won't be mad."

Emma forked over the rest of the change from the twenty she'd used to pay for the coffee and scone. Now she watched Angell pocket the money, and Emma wondered if it should have gone in the register, but well, what did it matter? What did any of it matter?

Emma was almost done with her latte and scone when she heard a voice she recognized. She looked up and saw Mack Durkee, her high school crush, perfect SAT score, total dreamboat, a look-alike of Jim Halpert from *The Office,* standing at the coffee counter. He was holding a baby goat in his arms. She thought it was another hallucination, was ready to go cold turkey on the Lexa-pro. Mack was the last person Emma would have expected to see still stuck in Everton. Maybe he was just back for Thanksgiving.

"Emma Starling," Mack said. "I heard you were home."

"You did?" Emma could not remember when she'd ever talked to Mack Durkee. He had been a senior when she was a freshman, but now Emma stood up to hug him as if they were old pals. *Be cool,* she said to herself. He'd gone away to New York for college, she remembered. "How are you?" she asked. "Still in New York?"

He shook his head. "Came back here after college. Only the big-time smarties move out to California."

Well, this certainly lifted Emma out of her doldrums. She couldn't believe Mack Durkee knew so much about her life. She liked that he called her a smarty. She liked that he knew she knew she was too good to stay in this town forever. "And who is this?" Emma asked, pointing to the baby goat in Mack's arms.

"I'm Mack Durkee, remember?" he said with a sly little grin.

"I meant the goat," Emma said, and laughed. *Emma was flirt-ing!* She was euphoric. *Look at her!* On top of the world.

The goat struggled a little, baa-ed. "How rude of me, to not introduce you," Mack said. "This is Doris Durkee, and she's a baby pygmy goat."

"This is the second Doris I've met today."

"Must be fate."

"A coincidence," Emma agreed. What Emma didn't know was that this goat had been named for Doris Jones the Dream Far secretary by the high school students, because Doris Jones always called the cops on any cars she saw parked at Make-Out Point. In return, the teenagers egged her house and named this goat after her.

"And why is Doris in the coffee shop?" Emma asked.

Mack Durkee, with his goofy smile and his floppy brown hair and generally lovable face, said he was now a biology teacher at

Upper Valley High School. Emma thought of the job interview she'd just been offered, and wondered if everyone with a college degree was offered a job in the Everton schools. But she didn't see how that explained the goat.

"Part of my job is to teach sex ed," Mack explained. "That's where Doris comes in. We started a 'No Pregnancy Until Graduation Pact,' although now we're calling it 'Kids, Not Kids.' That was the girls' idea. I think it's pretty clever. I thought the sophomores could take care of a goat, to prove to them how hard it is to take care of a baby."

"All the kids have their own goat?"

"Oh man, no, I think it would get pretty chaotic if we let every student have a goat. We can only handle Doris, and honestly, she's turned into something of a distraction in class. And the students aren't allowed to take her home at night, so I guess I'm the only one who's really learning how hard it is to take care of a baby. Isn't that right, Doris?" He patted her rump.

"What happens to Doris when she isn't a baby anymore?" she asked. "Is there a sad ending to this story?"

Mack opened his mouth to answer, but he pointed out the window, taking a hand off Doris, leaving her front end unsupported. "Oh my God," Mack Durkee said as he pointed. "Your father."

There, in the middle of Unity Road, was Clive Starling. He was walking along the yellow line of the road, strewing missing person posters on the ground behind him as he went. He was wearing a red ski parka, and no pants, no underwear. It wasn't a busy road, but the cars went fast around there. "Your father," Mack Durkee said again, proving to Emma it wasn't another hallucination, and then he put the baby goat down on the floor of the coffee shop and she teetered on her unsteady legs. Mack ran out toward the road. Emma rushed out after him, after she'd stood there shocked for a second, and Angell, still behind the counter, yelled after them: "Your dog! Your dog! You forgot your dog!"

And even as Emma's brain was mostly full of thinking about her father, and how scary and embarrassing this moment of her life had turned, there was also a part of Emma that still felt euphoric, that wanted to stop and laugh at her father's bare butt, at how he looked like Winnie-the-Pooh in the red top, no pants, and also at this girl who had pocketed her money, who couldn't tell the difference between a goat and a dog.

Together, Mack and Emma shepherded Clive Starling into the front seat of the car, where Moses was waiting in the backseat. Clive wasn't talking at all. He was in some kind of trance. Didn't even react when the dog licked his face. Mack said he'd follow Emma in his Jeep once he retrieved Doris the baby goat. "You can't leave a human baby on the floor of a coffee shop," Emma said, trying to make a joke, a joke in this big mess, because Mack had just touched her dad's penis accidentally as he'd buckled his seatbelt. Emma would have left her father unbuckled, but maybe Mack thought Clive Starling needed restraining, so he wouldn't wander off again.

"A goat isn't a human baby," Mack said. "They can walk almost immediately after birth. It's not a perfect experiment, I admit."

"I'm sure you're a wonderful teacher," Emma said. It looked like she had hurt Mack's feelings, and she hadn't meant to. She'd meant to be funny.

"I had to come home to care for my mom," he said, gesturing to half-naked Clive Starling in the front seat, as if he represented all aging parents.

"I'm sorry," she said. "Is she—"

"She's hanging in there, stage-three breast cancer, but in fact, actually, I was hoping to run into you while you're home. Your mom told me you were coming home, and I was hoping you might . . ."

Emma could see why Mack Durkee cared about her, why he knew who she was. He wanted her to heal his mother. Of course. *Of effing course*. She shook her head. "I'm sorry," she said.

"I figured," he said, and straightened himself up. "Go on ahead, I'll follow you."

"You don't need to," Emma said. "Thanks for your help." She got in the car with her dad. She turned the key. As she drove, she noticed Mack's Jeep was behind her, following anyway. Some guys won't take no for an answer, Emma thought, but she couldn't help but smile a little in the rearview.

11

—➤·◄—

The Corbin Mansion and caretaker's house were about three miles from Wilderness's Edge Express coffee shop, and on the ride back, Emma's dad started rambling. He had the time alone with his long-lost daughter, and instead of telling her anything that mattered, how much he loved her or how sorry he was for some of the bad shit he'd done, he was telling her some story about how when Ernest Harold Baynes was a college student, he'd walked seven miles in one of the worst blizzards on record, and it was then that he became a true naturalist.

Emma drove past her dad's red motorcycle with its double sidecar abandoned on the side of the road, which explained how her dad had gotten all the way over to Unity Road, three miles from the house. Someone would have to come back and get the bike later, and her dad would have to be banned from his motorcycle for a while, possibly forever.

"Let's go inside, Dad." Emma tried to coax him out of the car when they got to the house. Her dad really flipped out then, yelled "No, no, no!" so many times that Auggie came out as Mack pulled up in the Jeep.

"Doin' the No-Pants Dance, huh, Dad?" Auggie said.

"Where's Mom?" Emma asked.

"At the store," Auggie said. "Tomorrow's Thanksgiving," he said, as if Emma didn't know that. "But I can handle it. Come on, Dad."

Clive went fairly willingly with Auggie, and Mack grabbed Clive's other arm to steady him. They went into the house like that, and Emma followed behind them on the stairs, trying not to look at her dad's bare bottom. Moses was circling, too, the dog all worked up. Auggie got some clothes from the dresser. He put their father's underwear on, and then his pants, coaching him to step through each leg hole.

"This is humiliating," their father said with sudden clarity.

"Nothing to be embarrassed of. Just the imperfect human body having a hard time," Auggie said, with a kindness Emma didn't know her brother possessed. "Mack, you can go," Auggie said. "It might help us more if you go."

"Auggie, don't be rude," Emma said, horrified.

But Mack said of course he would leave, and wished them luck. Emma watched him go. He hadn't gotten ugly since high school, that was for sure.

"Oh," Clive said, remembering something. "Emma, by the way, your mother wanted me to tell you that she's not running a Bed and Breakfast."

"What does that mean?" Emma asked.

"You're going to have to help out. No sleeping until noon."

"I just saved you from getting hit by a car. And Auggie—"

"Please don't shoot the messenger," her father interrupted, putting his head down on the pillow and closing his eyes. He was ready for his afternoon nap, in his jeans and ski parka. He never missed his afternoon nap.

"Well," Auggie said, after their parents' bedroom door was closed. "That Mack Durkee's kind of an ass, huh? I don't know why Mom thinks he's so great."

"He didn't have to help us."

"Oh right, I forgot. He was GG's big unrequited love."

"How did you even know that?"

"I lived in this house." Auggie gestured to the hallway where they stood. "Did a lot of eavesdropping. You loved him and Crystal loved the math teacher."

Crystal had actually thought the math teacher was a pervert who should be arrested, but Emma didn't correct him, he would think she only wanted to argue. Her brother had wallowed in a puddle of anger and resentment since his eleventh-grade spinal subluxation in the third quarter of the game, and all that wallowing had left him pretty nasty. Auggie went back into his room, probably back to his videogames. *Not my problem,* Emma decided. She didn't want to deal with Auggie. She didn't care. She'd come home for her father, not her brother. She was headed for the real, final loss of her dad. Yes, her dad exhausted and frustrated and embarrassed her, and she hadn't forgiven him for having an affair, but she also couldn't imagine the world without him. Her father had always taken up so much space. All the oxygen in the room.

Emma went to her dad's office. She wanted to feel close to who he used to be, or who she'd thought he was. His office was the room on the second floor with a cherry-wood desk and matching bookshelves. She sat down at his desk, a chair she'd sat in so many times. There was a bulletin board propped up, a corkboard full of clues and pictures of Crystal. This was her father's shabby detective work. The work of a madman, or a man suffering from a serious brain disease. There were pictures printed out from Crystal's Instagram, which hadn't been updated since she'd gone missing, and scribblings of Crystal's last known whereabouts. There were cut-out newspaper articles of unrelated kidnapping cases, and a list of all the cults in New England, which appeared to have been printed out from a Wikipedia page. Nothing that amounted to real evidence or a clue.

On the desk was *The Collected Writings of Ernest Harold Baynes,* the book her mother had stolen from the Everton Historical Society. She read the first few pages, which recounted the story her dad had been telling in the car: as a college student, Baynes had walked seven miles in a blizzard to go see Louise Birt O'Connell, his future wife. *It might have been foolish,* Harold wrote, *but I cannot regret that walk in the blizzard, for it proved the depths of my love for Louise, and at the same time it brought me face to face with the relentless powers of nature. It was instrumental to my life as a naturalist, in that it greatly deepened my sympathy with the wild creatures whose daily portion it is to face the possibility of death and tragedy at every corner.*

"My daily portion," her dad had murmured over and over on the ride home, from the comfortable-enough microfiber seat of the red rental car.

The book also said the Baynes cottage in Everton had been on Unity Road, on Sunset Ridge, near where Emma had found her father. In his confusion, her dad was lost in time. He had probably thought if he knocked on the door of the little red house, Ernest Harold Baynes would answer with a squirrel on his shoulder, and welcome Clive Starling in to sit by the fire with all the critters of the world from Corbin Park. It made sense to Emma that her dad was drawn to the park at the end of his life. He had always loved the park history. The lore it invited. He said it was one of the special things about living in Everton.

Emma remembered the elaborate bedtime stories her dad used to tell, stories that almost always ended with one of her mean classmates left to the jaws of the crocodiles of Corbin Park. If Emma's mother was in earshot, she would say that there had never been crocodiles in the park, even if Rudyard Kipling had said there were. Kipling had lived in the area for a few years with his American wife in the late 1800s, around the time the park opened, and he said the park was full of "lions an' tigers an' bears an' buffalo an' crocodiles an' such all." Ingrid insisted a crocodile would never survive a New England winter.

"There's definitely crocs in Corbin Park," Clive would say. His wife could naysay all she wanted, but the best thing about the private hunting park, built in 1887 and fenced in ever since, is that no one knew what went on in there. Not even Ralph Kelsey, local millionaire and gun-factory owner, had gotten an invitation to visit. He always joked it kept getting lost in the mail.

"They hunt children," Clive would say in another bedtime story, this one to both Emma and Auggie. "They make the most beautiful taxidermy out of little kids." Then her dad would start the tickling. The tickling was the part Auggie liked best, but Emma always wanted her dad to get back to the story. To tell them what else happened in the park, if any of the children ever escaped.

"Who cares how the jaguar feels?" Ingrid would say from the doorway, quoting the classic story "The Most Dangerous Game," to make her husband laugh. There had been so many happy times like that in their marriage, when Clive and Ingrid would team up against their kids.

12

We know Corbin Park is a big mystery to most people in our town, but *we* could have told anyone what was beyond those Jurassic Park–style wooden gates, if anyone ever stopped by Maple Street to ask. From the outside, the fence isn't much to look at, just chain-link and electric wires, but inside the park, we could tell you how dense those woods are. The trees have been allowed to grow and grow, like nature intends for trees to do. The park is enormous, 26,000 acres, which is 19,696 football fields; that's three-fifths the size of Washington, DC. There is one road that loops around the entire park, one loop that connects all twenty-five cabins, each complete with a huge parcel of land. Corbin Park would be the largest national park in New Hampshire, if it were public land. Many of the residents come in and out of the park by helicopter, and most of the cabins are second homes, hunting retreats for the weekend. But there are a few hardcore residents, full-timers.

Eighty-six-year-old Mavis Spooner, for example, hadn't left the park in nearly ten years. The older she got, the more time Mavis wanted to spend in the woods. She loved the proximity to wildlife, although sometimes the wildlife of Corbin Park got a little too close, even for Mavis. Earlier that day, for example, the day of Clive's walk through the imagined blizzard, Mavis Spooner had overslept, and when she awoke she could hear Jack on the porch. Jack was not, had never been, a patient bear, but this was the first time he'd come up on the porch. Mavis got out of bed, her bedroom was to the left of the kitchen, and she shuffled across the rug. She looked out her sliding-glass door to the porch to where Jack was pacing.

"Don't be huffy," she called. "I'll be right out." Jack stopped pacing, turned, licked the glass. It would need windexing later, Mavis thought, but she also knew she was unlikely to do it. Mavis had given up on most of the housecleaning, her husband had been gone so long. It was just Mavis and the bears, most of the time, and the raccoons in the garage, the deer and elk on the lawn, except for on Saturdays, when the little girl would show up for her lesson. Decades before, Mavis Spooner had been on the faculty at Boston Conservatory. She still taught voice lessons in her home, but only to children; she made their parents wait in the car. Adults made Mavis nervous. Mavis only had one student these days, a little girl named Leanne Hatfield, because Everton was short on young vocal talent, and park headquarters put up such a stink about residents giving out too many day passes. She'd had to make several phone calls for Leanne Hatfield and her grandfather to finally get a sticker for their windshield.

Mavis used a walker, and it took her a while to get Jack and Jill's breakfast together. That morning, breakfast was dog food and a pint of yogurt and a dozen hard-boiled eggs. "He'll be sorry he got so upset," Mavis said, balancing Jack's bowl on her walker. She'd have to come back inside for Jill's. She knew Jill was waiting for her breakfast at the edge of the woods, down off the porch where good bears belonged.

Outside, Jack went right to it, eggs first, his favorite. Mavis had named the bear for Jack, her husband, dead nine years of lung cancer. It felt good to say his name. And she named the other bear Jill, because they were a pair, and she couldn't exactly name the other bear after herself. It was against the law to intentionally feed bears in New Hampshire, but no one ever bothered Mavis Spooner in Corbin Park. She didn't receive calls of complaint, no certified letters in the mail. "The single sole good thing about really rich people," her Jack used to say, "is that they respect your privacy."

Sometimes we wondered who we'd get first, Mavis Spooner or Ralph Kelsey or Clive Starling. They were all to be buried at Maple Street, even the reclusive Mavis, because Jack was put to rest in town and she was going to be laid next to him. Jack Spooner (b. 1926–d. 2005) had been a social guy; even though he did appreciate his privacy, he liked a good party too. His wife, Mavis, had only *gone weird,* as he called it, after he'd kicked the bucket. "All that time alone," he would regularly complain. "It hasn't been good for her."

It very rarely is, we agreed, very rarely good for the living to be alone too long. It can even make the dead strange. Harold Baynes helping a man sick with brain disease order a fox as a pet off the internet, for example. Idiotic, frankly. We're lucky to have each other here at Maple Street for company and conversation.

One thing we've learned from one another, chattering away as we do, is that a good story doesn't always follow an arrow, sometimes it meanders a little instead, so we hope you'll excuse this tangent about Mavis and her bears. It might seem unrelated, but sometimes a minor character doesn't become important until later, so don't forget about Mavis Spooner. The lives of the living often get tangled up in unexpected ways, especially in a town as small as ours, even when an eight-foot electrified fence splits it up.

13

On Thanksgiving morning, Emma found the turkey sitting naked on the counter, the potatoes not yet peeled. She'd set an alarm so she wouldn't be accused of being on vacation in her own home, but her mother must have gone out for a run to blow off some steam before the holiday. Her dad was at the kitchen table, clicking away at something on his laptop, and Emma watched him from the doorway. His silver-white hair was in a single braid. He was wearing a blue plaid flannel, the sleeves rolled so you could see the flock of tattooed birds. He didn't look so near death, even if he looked old. Well, she admitted, the hallucinations weren't a good sign. What had happened yesterday in the middle of Unity Road really wasn't a good sign. There was a book next to her dad on the table, the English to Russian dictionary.

"Good morning," she said, and he looked up. "Catching up on your Russian?"

"*Da*. Did you sleep well?"

"Not great," Emma lied. "Hard not to sleep in my own bed." Truthfully, the bed upstairs was the only bed she'd really ever felt was her *own* bed. All the other beds in her life had been temporary. It was just a passive-aggressive way to remind her father that she had grown up and moved out.

But her dad didn't seem to notice. "Hey, I could use your help with something," he asked. "If you can keep a secret from your mother."

"I can't," Emma said, because honestly, *What the hell?*

"It's just something I need your help with on the computer. A mistake I made."

"I'm taking the dog for a walk," Emma said, pouring her coffee into a travel mug. "Ask Auggie."

"Fine. I'll figure it out myself." Clive went back to clicking madly at the laptop. "Now, what was I doing," he muttered, which Emma didn't think was unusual, it was obvious her dad had memory problems, and he'd been frustrated with the computer long before that. Emma didn't know that her dad had been trying to undo yesterday's ridiculous purchase, but during the course of their conversation, he had forgotten why he needed the English to Russian dictionary. So instead, Clive went to his Facebook page, clicked on some of his old colleagues. An econ professor he hated.

By noon, the turkey was in the oven, and Dr. Wheeler arrived to examine Clive at the house. Dr. Wheeler had shown up in a Prius as white as his lab coat, like some kind of TV doctor. He was tan with Ken-doll blond hair. He had a slight scruff. He looked to be in his mid-forties, and Emma was a little bit disarmed by his beauty. Emma had never heard of a doctor who still made house calls, not these days, especially not on a major holiday, but her mother had called the doctor in a panic after her husband was found on the road without his pants. Dr. Wheeler said he'd come for an exam as soon as he could, and that meant noon on Thanksgiving Day.

"What disease does Clive have exactly?" Ralph Kelsey asked the doctor, once Clive was out of earshot, gone upstairs for his afternoon nap. "I haven't been told." Everyone was in the living room. Ingrid had put out some appetizers on the coffee table, stuffed mushrooms and a wheel of brie.

"Well, it's not exactly clear. We know it's causing cognitive and motor problems," Dr. Wheeler explained. "Hallucinations of small animals or children are common in people who have certain types of dementia."

"Children?" Ingrid said. "That would be awful."

"How would that be worse?" Emma asked. She thought of the fifth graders on the playground. They were no worse than small animals.

"Well, Ingrid," Dr. Wheeler said, concluding his notes. "He's going to need a legal guardian. Things have escalated to the point where a guardianship is our best option." He explained that in his experience, these neurodegenerative diseases follow a similar pattern: Clive would likely have good days and bad days, but there would be a noticeable loss of physical and mental function as time went on. A guardianship would mean Clive would have to be declared incompetent in front of a judge, so that his wife could start making all his choices for him, financial and health-wise. And so that he couldn't get arrested for indecent exposure, if something similar happened again.

"He's not going to like losing all his rights to his wife," Ralph Kelsey warned.

"He's going to have to deal with it, Ralph." Ingrid was annoyed that Ralph needed to add his two cents.

But it was true that Clive didn't take it well, once he was up from his nap. "Well, doesn't this get more humiliating by the day," he said.

"I'm sorry, Clive. We don't have a choice."

"Can Emma do it then? Can Emma be my guardian? There's something horribly degrading about my wife being my guardian. Especially since it looks like she's got her hands full with the good doctor here."

Ingrid turned bright red. Emma realized her father was having a good day, and he could see, clearly as anyone, that something unprofessional was going on. More than once, Dr. Wheeler had touched Ingrid on the shoulder. A year ago, Emma would have said maybe her dad deserved it, that what's good for the goose is good for the gander and all that, but now her father was dying. It was too late for any kind of revenge. Her mom could have all the boyfriends she wanted once her husband was dead.

"What do you say, Emma?" Clive asked. "You'll guard your dear old dad?"

"I think it's a great idea," Ralph said. "Emma would be my pick too."

Ingrid smoothed her hair, tried to regain her composure. "Well, Emma, you're home, you might as well be useful. And it would give you two some nice time together."

"I don't know how long I'll be home." Emma had no immediate plans to leave, but she didn't have plans to *stay* either. She was only home to figure it out.

"Please?" her father asked.

Everyone was looking at Emma, waiting for her answer.

"*I'll* do it," Auggie said. He was sitting on the couch next to Emma, eating yet another bowl of Corn Pops, his favorite sugary cereal. No one said anything about the cereal, even if they were about to have Thanksgiving dinner, because sugar can help keep drug cravings at bay. Emma knew her brother was not on the guardian consideration list. No one puts someone recently out of rehab in charge of someone else's health care, especially after the fiasco with all those checks Auggie had cashed. But Emma also felt ashamed that her brother would so quickly offer to be guardian, when she was a total coward about it. "Well, maybe . . . if I could be the guardian for a little while, until I figure out what I'm going to do next. And then Mom can take over?"

"It means more paperwork to change a guardianship," Dr. Wheeler said, still looking a little flustered from Clive's accusation. "But yes, that would be fine."

"So, I'll do it," Emma agreed, unsure of what she'd agreed to exactly.

"GG saves the day," Auggie said, sarcastically.

"It is a big responsibility for you, Emma," her mother said.

"I'm happy to do it," Emma said, not happy at all. She didn't want to get stuck in this town forever to guard her father as he died, however long that took. The old man might live another decade, even two, no matter what the doctor said.

"I'll get the paperwork started," Dr. Wheeler said.

"We'll have more time together then, Emma, your mother is right," Clive said, clearly very happy. "And we can really get to work on our missing persons case."

"One thing at a time, Dad."

"It would be helpful if someone finished setting the table," Ingrid said, standing up to go check on the turkey.

"Emma's all over it." Auggie settled deeper into the couch.

It was always easier to do their mother's stupid chore than to argue about why Auggie should do it this time. Emma went into the dining room, the table already set with a white lace tablecloth and goofy turkey-shaped candles Ingrid had bought at the Dollar Store. As Emma circled the table with the silverware, she noticed the sixth table setting. Emma knew her mother had invited Crystal to every single Thanksgiving ever since Bart Nash died, but Crystal always declined.

Back when Crystal and her dad came to Thanksgiving at the Corbin House, the dinner was in the great dining room of the mansion, a room with a carved wooden ceiling and elegant candelabras on the table, not shitty turkey candles from the Dollar Store. Back then, Emma loved Crystal with an intensity of a teenage best friendship, stronger even than a romance, and just as obsessive. Emma hadn't minded being Crystal's sidekick, not when Crystal knew so much more about everything. She was so much more worldly and self-assured. Crystal had lived with her dad all over the country, had already lost her virginity to an older guy she'd met in Asheville who smoked clove cigarettes and who still wrote her letters sometimes. Emma was more excited than Crystal every time a letter arrived, but Crystal was too tough for romance, and she let Emma keep the letters. To be fair, Crystal had never made Emma *feel* like a sidekick, not really, Emma felt instead like Crystal and their friendship protected her from harm, like as long as they had each other things would be okay. But it hadn't. A best friendship protects you until it breaks.

"Who is this extra table setting for?" Emma yelled back into the living room.

"What?"

"There's six chairs here."

"That's Harold's seat," Clive called back.

"Dr. Wheeler, would you like to stay for dinner?" Ingrid asked, playing coy. "I know your ex-wife has the kids, and we have extra space. Plenty of food."

"I'd love to stay," Dr. Wheeler agreed.

"Oh my God, this family," Emma muttered, rolling her eyes to the ceiling. She picked up one of the Pilgrim turkey candles and looked him in his googly eyes. "Are you a little liar too?" she asked him. She didn't believe for one second that the lonely, divorced doctor was staying for Thanksgiving dinner just because he happened to stop by for a holiday medical call.

"The more the merrier," Ralph Kelsey said from the living room. Ralph Kelsey loved absolutely everybody.

"You're going to have to set another place for Harold then," Clive called. "He said he's coming hungry."

"Dad—" Emma started, but her mother interrupted.

"Just do it, Emma, please," Ingrid said.

An hour later, they were all seated at the table, the Pilgrim turkeys lit, and everyone had to say what they were thankful for. Emma thought about Mack Durkee and his floppy hair, but of course she didn't say that. But she *was* thankful that someone like Mack was stuck in Everton. He had come home to care for his sick mother, he'd gotten the job at the high school, and yet—he seemed happy. Well adjusted. Someone who didn't need an alarm to get out of bed in the morning.

If Emma was the kind of person to believe in signs, well, those two Dorises, the secretary and Mack's goat, had to be a sign. A coincidence like that had to mean something. If she was going to be her dad's guardian, she should take the job at Dream Far Elementary, too, so she wouldn't be stuck with her father for his every single dying minute, like two birds in a cage. A substitute teaching job wouldn't be hard, hadn't Doris the secretary said something like that? It could even be fun. She liked kids. *Didn't she like kids?* Of course she did, she thought, she wasn't a monster.

"Heaven help her," said Mary Garvin (b. 1945–d. 2001), a former schoolteacher in our graveyard.

"What if I get a job?" Emma asked Dr. Wheeler across the table. "Can I still be the guardian if I had a job?"

"Oh, a job would be fine," Dr. Wheeler said. "Most guardians also work regular jobs, of course they do. The important thing is to monitor your father, and report it when he gets worse."

"Worse?" Clive said.

"What kind of job did you have in mind?" her mother asked.

"Substitute teacher at the elementary school," Emma said, feeling suddenly more important. More together. She didn't even have the job yet, but Doris had made it pretty clear that the job was hers if she wanted it. Emma told the table that the teacher was out for her husband's drug-dealing trial, and the school was in dire straits. She tried to make herself look like the hero.

"Oh," her mother said. "I think that sounds like a fabulous way to spend a year before you get serious and go to law school."

"I'm not going to law school. But thanks, Mom. Nice to have your support."

We cheered at Maple Street, even Mildred Roscoe (b. 1811–d. 1902). We didn't know if the guardianship was enough to keep Emma in Everton, but a paying job might. We were sure Emma could get her mojo back if she just stayed here in town. Clive Starling, lover of words, could have told us that "mojo" used to mean "witchcraft" in the 1920s, probably of Creole origin, and Sara Ford (b. 1986–d. 2012) explained from her grave it was yet another slang term for heroin, but we only meant Emma could get back to her old self if she stayed home. If she got to know those kids, she might feel like she was someone special again.

"The teacher's husband is Sid Wish?" Ingrid asked. "I hope they fry him."

"They don't fry people for drug dealing, Mom," Auggie said.

"I heard he sold to teenagers when he was teaching driver's ed," Ralph Kelsey said. "That's pretty despicable." Sid's Car Korner also offered driving lessons.

"Yeah," Auggie said. "Let's kill him." He was having fun with this. "I saw his wife in the newspaper. She looks like a Victoria's Secret model."

"Did you ever buy drugs from him?" Ralph asked Auggie, and the table went quiet. They weren't supposed to ask that kind of question. It made everyone feel bad. Auggie mumbled something, but no one could understand it.

"Has someone dealt with the rabbits?" Clive asked, breaking the silence, looking from the dining room into the kitchen. "You know I'm up to my ears in rabbits every time I go in there."

"Have you tried calling the exterminator?" Auggie asked.

"Oh no, I don't want to kill the rabbits," Clive said to his son. "I just want them to know that rabbits belong outdoors. Harold kept wild animals in his house, but I'm not sure I'm up to it. Too much upkeep. Rabbits can make such a mess."

"Clive," Dr. Wheeler said. "Try to take some deep breaths."

"It'll be good for you," Ingrid said, ignoring her husband and

Dr. Wheeler and turning back to Emma. "Taking care of these kids in need should help you find yourself."

"What makes those kids *in need*, Mom?" Auggie asked.

"They lost their teacher. You don't realize how important a teacher is at that age. A good elementary school teacher is your second mother and your first crush."

"Okay, Mom," Emma said. "That's a little more pressure than I need." But she remembered her third-grade teacher, her favorite one. How Ms. Skornicki had protected her from the bullies in the classroom who made fun of the town story about her hands. She remembered once Ms. Skornicki had made T. J. Horton stare at the wall for an hour because he said Emma had a magic butt and he'd seen sparks flying out of it.

"I'm sure they all had a crush on *this* teacher. I know I would." Auggie had pulled up a photo of Claire Wish on his phone. She did look like someone who moonlighted in lingerie catalogues. Like a thirtysomething Cameron Diaz with a boob job.

"I hope they fry him," Ingrid said again. "I heard he was laundering money through the community theater. You know he was the director of the community theater?"

Ralph nodded. "I saw *Les Mis* last year."

"Mom, Sid Wish isn't some mastermind," Auggie said. "I don't know why everyone thinks he is. He's lower-rung, a cog in the machine. You know how much heroin they found at the car dealership?"

"I don't, August, how much?"

"I've probably had more stashed in my room at some point."

At that, Ingrid reached over and grabbed the empty plate set for Harold Baynes, and she threw it at the wall, where it broke into a dozen pieces. It was her wedding china, but she didn't care. Her marriage wasn't doing her any favors lately.

"Auggie," Ralph said. "You've upset your mother."

"To state the obvious," Emma said, her eyes wide.

"I'm sorry, Mom," Auggie said.

Dr. Wheeler stared into his lap, wishing he hadn't agreed to stay for a family holiday dinner.

"And what about the rabbits?" Clive asked. "Can something be done?"

Ingrid pushed back from the table and grabbed the broom, unclear if it was for the broken plate or to shoo out the rabbits in the kitchen.

Ralph hated awkward silences, so he launched into a story about Ben Laurasseta, a recent resident of Sundown Acres Assisted Living. The week before, Ben was having sex with Katherine Bagley in the Sundown Acres hot tub when he had a heart attack. "Died instantly. The sad part is, then he drowned Katherine," Ralph explained. "By accident, of course. He was already dead. I don't know why they have a hot tub in an old-folks home. The thing is a death trap."

"Really burst her bubble," Clive said, and started to laugh. Auggie and Emma started laughing, too, and even Dr. Wheeler cracked a smile.

"Not funny, Clive," Ingrid said, sitting back down. She was calm now, the plate swept up, the imaginary rabbits shooed.

"We all have to go sometime," Ralph said, shrugging. Death didn't bother Ralph. He wouldn't be upset if he didn't wake up tomorrow, with the excellent life he'd had.

"May our lives end with a bang," Clive said, lifting his glass.

"When's the duel?" Ralph asked, and Clive laughed and pounded the table. Underneath, the poor dog flinched.

14

If he was being honest, Clive wasn't all jokes about the end of his life, as much as he liked to laugh with Ralph Kelsey, or listen to old stories from Harold Baynes. He was up late that night with his whiskey and the embers in the fireplace in the living room, wondering if this was really it for him. His last Thanksgiving. *Had there even been green bean casserole?* He didn't remember a casserole. But if Clive had to go soon, he hoped it didn't take too long. He didn't want his family to remember him as a dying man. He didn't want to be a burden, didn't want to be an eyesore. Adult diapers and all that. He'd seen how his wife looked at the young doctor, and he wanted his wife to remember how good-looking he'd once been. Not classically handsome, maybe, but Clive Starling felt he'd had sex appeal, with his long silver hair and tattoos and a leather jacket. And Clive knew he was loving, really loving, when he remembered to be. Sure, he could get distracted. Ingrid said he was a starling through and through, birds known for loving shiny objects.

"A coward and a liar," his wife had said about him. Which wife had said that? Helene or Ingrid? Clive even couldn't remember now. He'd spent so much time trying to forget, and now his brain was doing it for him. Helene had been his second wife, and their marriage hadn't ended well. It started when Helene found a love poem to Diane Festershaw, her friend from two houses down. His subsequent marriage to Diane was his most unhappy one, out of the four.

But with Ingrid, Clive finally met the love of his life, settled down and had a family, and he'd only had one affair in twenty-five years. Those stats were pretty good, considering how his other marriages had gone. Clive Starling was capable of change.

But no one's perfect; Clive had slipped up.

"A slipup doesn't last an *entire semester*," his wife had said, which is how long the affair had gone on. Nearly as long as Sabrina Berkman was visiting faculty. "I suppose your son picked a good time to steal my engagement ring to pawn," Ingrid had also said, because that was when things with Auggie really weren't going well. Clive tried to tell her how neglected he'd felt, since she'd been spending all her time focused on their son, but that really didn't help his case. "You selfish bastard," she'd said instead.

When Ingrid kicked Clive out, he had gone to live in his office at Meriden College, sleeping under the desk. He'd spent all his time at the pub, when he wasn't teaching. It was never too lonely and too quiet there, televisions blaring from every corner. Crystal Nash was there to talk to, behind the bar most nights. Crystal had become a real friend to him. She would have told him if she were planning to leave town.

Clive was waiting to hear an update from his PI sometime soon, any news or leads on where Crystal might have gone. Maybe he should check in with Roy Briggs again, but Clive vaguely remembered he'd vowed to call the private investigator only during business hours. It was well after midnight in Everton.

The ghost of Ernest Harold Baynes appeared in the other armchair by the fire, showing up suddenly as he sometimes did. Clive asked if Harold knew anything about the current whereabouts of Crystal Nash, but Harold only shook his head. It would be too easy, if ghosts could simply dole out answers to the mysteries of the living just because they were asked directly. The universe would never allow it.

"I figured you wouldn't know," Clive said, poking the fire. "No one seems to know."

"Indeed," Harold said, a cloud of clear annoyance crossing his face. Ghosts hate to be lumped in with everyone else. "So, Mr. Starling, I heard about what happened the other day on Unity Road."

"What about it?"

"Well, I suppose, how humiliating, to be out and about without your trousers."

Clive felt ashamed for a minute, but then he remembered what his son had said. "That was only the imperfect human body having a hard time," he told Harold Baynes. That line was actually something his wife had said first, to Auggie, as a way of comforting him, one of the times Auggie was trying to get off heroin. He was having bad diarrhea, a common side effect of the detoxing process. Auggie had shit his bed, Ingrid had cleaned it up, and that was exactly the kind of reassuring thing you say to someone you love when they are being an awful burden but you're trying to convince them that you don't mind. Not at all. No big deal. *For you?* Anything.

PART III

The Deer

15

~>-*-<~

JIMMIE THE BEAR OVERDOES IT

from *The Collected Writings of Ernest Harold Baynes,* © 1925

This Book Is Property of the Everton Historical Society

At first, Jimmie was too little to cause much trouble.

Photograph by Louise Birt Baynes.

Jimmie, because of the young age he'd been orphaned, would never again be a wild bear, but Mrs. Baynes and I did what we could to give him every happiness. He was treated to bowl after bowl of banana pudding, and he clawed more than one piece of fine furniture to splinters. It made no difference what he destroyed,

Mrs. Baynes always defended her cub. She also knew the way to his little heart was straight to his tummy. When he was hungry, he would begin to grumble, deeper and louder, until at last came an uncontrolled outpouring of ursine profanity, and Mrs. Baynes would scramble to bring him crackers and a pail of milk.

One day, Mrs. Baynes and I came back from a drive, and when we pulled up to the house, Jimmie didn't come to meet us as usual. A window opening onto the roof had been left open. We entered the house and found that the pantry door had been left open too. It was a door we usually shut up from all the animals, even the well-behaved ones, for obvious reasons. What a sight met our eyes when we reached the doorway! The floor was strewn with paper bags and boxes left by the grocer that afternoon, all of them burst wide open and with their contents sifted through. I never saw such a mess in my life. In one corner of the room a molasses jar had been overturned, and the syrup lay in golden pools and shining smears, and in the middle of it wallowed Jimmie, the author of all this deviltry—sticky, utterly unpresentable, and supremely happy. For about five seconds I felt angry, but I glanced at Mrs. Baynes and saw that she was trying very hard not to laugh.

"Yes, it's awfully funny, isn't it?" I remarked. At the sound of my voice Jimmie looked up, with a jam label glued to one cheek.

I can't remember which of us laughed harder, me or Mrs. Baynes, and the argument we'd had in the carriage was forgotten, I hoped for good. Mrs. Baynes is not typically a jealous woman, she knows we are uniquely suited to be together, but any word spent too long on another woman makes her prickle, and somehow I had provoked her suspicions while we were out in the carriage. Jimmie saved me from a longer tongue lashing.

The young bear wobbled up on his two hind legs to come meet us, and we noticed something we'd seen once before when the bear had eaten too much molasses. All that sugar made him act quite *silly*—I dare say it had made him drunk! He attempted a somersault that would have done discredit to an intoxicated clown, and then he seemed to wait for applause.

"Bless his little heart," Mrs. Baynes said. "He was only hungry."

Jimmie tottered over to her, and looked up at Mrs. Baynes with a smirk, his eyes half closed in ecstasy. He threw both paws over Louise's shoulders. His paws were growing bigger and bigger, I had noticed, no longer a bear cub but an adolescent bear. Jimmie gave her the gaze of a loving drunkard, a look that begs a woman for affection or forgiveness or some of both things. It was a look I imagined I could get myself, when I'd been out on the speaking circuit too long, and had returned home with mud-caked boots.

16

>-·-◄

The next Monday, at an absolutely ungodly hour of the morning, Emma drove her dad's beloved 1985 powder-blue Ford F150 to Dream Far Elementary for the interview. Clive was no longer allowed to drive, per the rules of the guardianship, his truck keys taken away along with the ones to his motorcycle, so Emma had her own set of wheels.

Principal Jefferies, a tall man in a brown suit and a green bowtie, was extremely glad to see her. "Wasn't sure you'd come," he said. "Doris said she was 50/50 on whether you would show, but she said you were perfect for the job otherwise. Looked responsible."

"Oh," Emma said. "That's nice to hear."

Principal Jefferies told her they would hit the ground running. They would put her right in the classroom with the kids, but she'd get the boot if the background check came back with any red flags. "We didn't used to background-check," Principal Jefferies said. "It's expensive. But I'm sure you've heard about our past problems. You'll get fingerprints done at the police station after school, and a drug test, if you don't mind."

"No problem at all," Emma said. She wasn't sure if the Lexapro would show up on a drug test, but she would google it. "If you don't mind me asking, what have you told the kids about their teacher? One of them seemed to think she's dead." The Wish trial was starting up next week, the newspaper had said that morning.

"Yes, they're very interested," Principal Jefferies admitted. "The kids don't quite understand the situation, I think. Not because they're not capable—they're probably old enough to grasp it all—but because everyone around them tells a different story. Sometimes lying to children is easier than explaining the truth. Teaching Lesson Number One."

"What's Lesson Number Two?"

"Oops, there's the bell. Better get you down the hall."

"I'm Ms. Starling and I'm going to be your substitute teacher," Emma said to the class after Principal Jefferies had left her to sink or swim. "Long-term," she added, because that's what her contract had said. *Long-term substitute teacher.* The class said they already knew all about her; Doris had announced it on the loudspeaker. Doris abused the loudspeaker.

There were eight of them, four boys and four girls, but Emma felt there might as well have been forty. They made so much noise. She tried to steady herself, get her bearings; this was all happening a little fast. That one girl was still in all pink, and that one tall boy was still wearing a Viking helmet, and he said, yes, he always wore it, no he wouldn't take it off. Principal Jefferies had handed out the sticky name tags before he'd retreated to his office.

"Are you a cowgirl?" someone asked.

Emma had worn her turquoise cowboy boots. They were her lucky charm. She was also wearing a J.Crew blazer, which felt more like a costume than the cowboy boots did. She was wearing a Blacker Sabbath T-shirt under the blazer, some of the band merch her dad had ordered once. "I'm not a cowgirl anymore," she said, because she did not want to admit she'd never ridden a horse. "I'm your teacher, at least for the time being."

One of the boys, whose name tag said Adam D., said his mother worked at the Meriden College Library with Ingrid Starling. "What happened to med school?" Adam D. asked. "My mom said you were supposed to go to med school."

"I decided I didn't want to go," Emma said. She had not been prepared for this question.

"Did something bad happen?" Tobey L., the shrimpy boy in the green glasses asked.

"Yeah," another kid said. "How bad was it?"

Emma did not want to tell the kids how bad it was. She asked if anyone knew the capital of North Dakota. She couldn't remember the capital herself, couldn't remember any city in the state other than Fargo. *Was Fargo the answer?* She didn't think so. But she decided you didn't need to know the answer to ask the question. Maybe *that* was Teaching Lesson Number Two.

"It's Bismarck," one kid muttered.

"State capitals are covered in fourth grade," another kid piped up. Her name tag read Nicole P., and she was wearing purple glasses and had jet-black hair.

"We want to get to know you," said one of the girls, wearing her name tag upside down, but Emma was pretty sure it said Olivia.

"The subs always tell us whatever we ask," the one named Michael B. said. Michael B.'s head was shaved into a mohawk, but it was uneven, not a good haircut. "Mr. Vale told us about his goiter surgery. He brought it in to show us, in a jar. Best sub ever."

"That was so gross," Nicole P. said. "I hated him."

Emma wanted her students to like her. Emma did not know that Teaching Lesson Number Three is: Who Cares if Your Students Like You; You Are Not Their Friend. There were several former teachers in our midst at Maple Street, and they had a few shared opinions about the profession. That was one. "Well, what do you want to know?" she asked.

"Tell us anything," Tobey L. said.

"I want to know why you're not going to med school," Adam D. said. "I want to be a doctor."

"I want to be a Viking," said the boy in the Viking helmet, whose name tag said Ulf, but the attendance book said his name was Daniel.

And so, here was her first real rookie mistake: Emma caved, and she told the story she was all of a sudden dying to tell. She said she was born with a natural healing ability, and explained a little about her hands. She went ahead and told her students about what had happened in California, how the touch had stopped working, how she'd been trying to get it back. She tried to tell the PG-version of what had happened at Gentle Touch Hospice.

"You're a witch doctor?" Adam D. asked.

"My grandmother sees a psychic twice a week," Nicole P. said.

"I don't believe in nonsense," the girl dressed in all pink said. She had written her full name on the tag in impossibly neat lettering: Leanne Hatfield. "Are you lying?" Leanne asked.

All the kids looked at Emma with slitted eyes. *Fifth graders hate liars,* she noted. "It's the truth," Emma said.

"Prove it," Leanne Hatfield said. "Heal something."

"I can't heal anything. I just told you, the healing touch is gone."

"We'll help you get it back," Tobey L. said. "Class project!" he yelled.

"I'm not sure I want it back," Emma admitted. It felt good to tell the truth, even to a bunch of kids. That she was actually kind of relieved she didn't have it anymore, that it wasn't her responsibility to heal her dad, even when that had always been more healing than she'd ever been able to do. She was relieved that she didn't have to go to med school to fill some kind of destiny. Maybe she was free of the pressure to be special at all, she could just be something like a substitute teacher and that would be fine. But then Emma realized she'd revealed a little too much to these kids. She didn't want anyone in town asking her about the hospice in California, about the patient she'd touched and why she'd been fired for it. "Please don't tell your parents this story," she said.

"We won't tell our parents," Olivia said. "We love secrets."

The rest of the class was quiet. They'd just met Ms. Starling. They didn't owe it to her to keep secrets.

"I live with my grandfather," Leanne Hatfield said. "But I probably won't tell him either."

"Thank you," Emma said. "It means a lot." She remembered what her mom always said about training the rescue dogs, that it never helped to show your fear, so she was trying to stay calm.

"Fifth graders aren't exactly dogs," Mary Garvin (b. 1945– d. 2001) said from Maple Street, unable to keep her opinions about children to herself.

At that point, all the other kids chimed in with who they lived with, after Leanne started it. Michael B. had his mom, his older brother, away in juvie at the moment, and his little sister. Nicole P.'s parents owned the Scrub-a-Dub Wash-and-Sun, the combo laundromat and tanning salon. Olivia's parents owned Shear Imagination, the one hair salon in town, which specialized in buzz cuts of different lengths. Tobey L. lived with his mom and dad and six siblings, and his dad worked at the gun factory. Daniel said his parents were still on the other side of the ocean; he had been kidnapped during a Viking raid and raised on the ship, and Leanne Hatfield rolled her eyes and said that was absolutely not true, don't be so stupid.

"What about you?" they asked their new substitute teacher. "Who do you live with?"

Emma didn't feel like much of a grown-up when she told them she lived with her parents, her brother, and a big white dog.

"I know who your dad is," Adam D. said. "He's the crazy man who puts up the posters. My mom says it's littering."

It stung a little, for Emma to hear her dad described as crazy, even if it certainly wasn't the first time. He'd always been more eccentric than other dads, not the kind of dad who putters around the house fixing things. Instead, he was riding his motorcycle, practicing with his metal band, drinking too much, and reciting poetry when no one was asking for poetry. "He's trying to do a good thing," she explained. "It's not littering if it's for a good cause." And she thought about adding, *he's looking for my friend*, but she didn't, because Crystal Nash wasn't her friend. Not anymore.

"Okay," the students said, not caring enough to argue with their substitute teacher about what constitutes littering, because it was lunchtime, and kids love lunchtime.

During recess, Emma at least had a twenty-five-minute break while the fifth graders went to the playground with the gym teacher, who was also the recess monitor. Emma used the time to look through the stack of student files that Principal Jefferies had given her. The manila folders contained the students' grades and personal information, vaccination records. Tobey L. had seven siblings, not six. Michael B.'s father was dead, an overdose. Dan in the Viking helmet had not been raised on a ship. He was in foster care, three homes in two years, so Emma decided she would let him wear the helmet as long as he wanted to, and maybe she would even call him Ulf, although a note in the file warned her against it, because Ulf means wolf in Viking and Daniel was historically a biter.

"There's something in common with dogs," Bill Casey (b. 1955–d. 2004) pointed out from his plot at Maple Street.

"Oh, be quiet," Mary Garvin (b. 1945–d. 2001) said. Bill Casey could drive Mary Garvin up the wall.

Emma was most surprised by Leanne Hatfield's file. The girl

lived with her grandfather, like she'd said, because her parents had died in a murder-suicide. It said it, simply like that, no news clippings or elaborations or psych evals, as if it were a detail the same as any other. Leanne Hatfield had also gotten the chicken-pox vaccine, which we had forgotten was a disease that could now be protected against. Those of us who had died of polio or had gone deaf from the mumps marveled at that kind of thing, modern luxuries.

While Emma was reeling from the news of a murder-suicide, she noticed the note, tucked into each one of her students' permanent files: *Death of a classmate.* And recently, sometime over the summer. Dead parents were one thing, and so was foster care, and a former teacher who'd had a mental breakdown after her husband was arrested for drug trafficking, but it hit her harder that these children knew someone their own age who had died, so much loss already in their short little lives.

Emma looked at the framed photo that had been left on the desk of the extremely blond and beautiful Claire Wish, her arm around her husband. Sid Wish had slicked-back hair; he looked like the kind of man who golfed on weekends. Claire Wish had Barbie-perfect teeth and breasts. She looked like the kind of woman who was a second mother and a first love, all at the same time, and yet she'd abandoned her students only a few weeks into the school year to go have her breakdown over what her husband had done.

That was when Emma felt the choking realization that substitute teaching was just another thing she could fail at. Another person who could mess up these kids.

"I hope you can at least teach us something," Tobey L. said at the end of the day as the kids were all putting their backpacks on. "The subs never teach us anything."

"One let us watch *Dances with Wolves*," Nicole P. pointed out.

"We saw Kevin Costner's bare butt," Olivia said. "But the sub said it was probably a butt double. An actor who played his butt."

"I can teach you something," Emma promised. "Something more than that." She had seen *Dances with Wolves,* but it had been a long time ago, and Emma was surprised that the fifth-grade class knew who Kevin Costner was—*was Kevin Costner still famous? Still alive?* In truth, Emma didn't know if she could in fact teach these kids anything. She'd been overwhelmed by what it said in the binder Principal Jefferies had given her, one she'd only had time to glance at that said "Things Fifth Graders Need to Know" on its cover. The binder contained everything that the state, or maybe it was the federal government, mandated that the kids learn that year. It was a lot. Children need to learn so much.

"Smell you later, Ms. Starling," Michael B. said, going out the door. The other kids laughed, and Ulf howled. Not howled with laughter but howled like a wolf. Like a wild animal. Emma wondered then what had happened to Mr. Vale and his goiter, why he'd quit when he probably had medical bills to pay.

"What did you expect?" Mary Garvin (b. 1945–d. 2001) asked from her grave, when Emma sat down exhausted at her desk. "Did you think the children would instantly *love you?*" Doris the school secretary had promised they would, because Emma was pretty and young, but the students loved the prettier and still-youngish Claire Wish. They missed her positivity, her blond hair, her corny bulletin-board decorations, the stories she used to tell about her cat, Lady Marmalade. They didn't have room in their fist-sized hearts for someone new, certainly not yet.

17

A brief correction here: *almost* all the fifth graders loved Ms. Wish. One of them did not. One of them decidedly did not. Leanne Hatfield did not love Claire Wish, and she did not miss her either.

No, Leanne did not miss the Word-of-the-Day, she did not miss the smiley faces on the top of her homework, she did not miss Claire Wish's world map of "Where We Have Been and Where We Hope to Go." The map was still in the classroom, but no one updated it anymore. It was your standard classroom-issue map of the world, and it was stuck with red pins for places kids in the class had visited and blue pins for places they hoped to see in their lifetime. Michael B. had gone absolutely crazy with blue pins, adding upward of four a week, even though Leanne Hatfield was pretty sure that Michael B. would not see much of the world except for prison. Leanne had watched a documentary called *What Famous Serial Killers Were Like as Kids,* and she thought Michael B. fit the profile. Ms. Wish had written what she'd called a "Letter of Concern" home to Leanne's grandfather after Leanne mentioned the documentary, but her grandfather was only upset with Ms. Wish. "Don't you know what happened to her parents?" her grandfather asked when he called the school. "Of course the kid is curious about what makes a killer."

Leanne's parents, Travis Pammett and Rebecca Hatfield (b. 1979–d. 2004), had been dead since Leanne was a baby. Only Rebecca was buried with us at Maple Street; Travis had been cremated by the state of New Hampshire; no one claimed his body. Leanne's grandfather had his granddaughter's last name changed from Pammett to Hatfield as quickly as he could. Rebecca Hatfield still cried over the cremated Travis Pammett, and he wandered by us sometimes, but he never stopped by her grave, never apologized.

"The man killed you," Mildred Roscoe (b. 1811–d. 1902) reminded Rebecca Hatfield regularly.

"He didn't mean to," Rebecca Hatfield said, although Travis definitely did.

But for Leanne Hatfield, there had been an even worse loss than the loss of her parents, if losses were to be rated: her best and only friend, Isabella Eaklin, the only girl she thought was worth being friends with at Dream Far. Isabella had missed out on most of the fourth grade, sick with what the doctors said appeared to be a rare form of leukemia. Izzy had finally left the hospital over the summer, when it was time to go home to die. There was nothing more the doctors could do.

"It's a lot of tragedy for one kid," David Hatfield would tell his friends, his neighbors, anyone who came over to the house. He used it to explain why Leanne Hatfield was the way she was. A brilliant kid, but bossy. Sometimes a little mean. We loved Leanne anyway, at Maple Street. She walked on the gravel path through our cemetery every day, even if it was after dark, always stopping at Isabella Eaklin's grave, and sometimes also her mother's. She liked to leave trinkets on Izzy's headstone, little plastic poison dart frogs she bought at the Dollar Store. "Looks like the frickin' rain forest over there," Sara Ford (b. 1986–d. 2012) complained. We were all envious of the frogs. Colorful little guys. Izzy loved frogs; they were some kind of Eaklin family emblem.

But without Isabella, Leanne didn't love anything quite as much as she used to, not even her Saturday singing lessons, and Leanne certainly did not love her classmates. Izzy used to tell

Leanne to "be nice, be nice," but what was the point in being nice now? It was with meanness when she told them over and over again that Ms. Wish was dead, because even if they didn't believe it, it upset them. Their precious teacher.

Ms. Wish was never coming back to teach, Leanne Hatfield knew that, even if the other kids didn't. The other kids kept telling one another: "she'll be back, she'll be back," as if no one in her class had ever lost someone before. As if they had all forgotten about Izzy. How thin her wrists got at the end. How everyone had raced to bring the best and biggest Get Well Soon balloon and teddy bear to the hospital, even though, before Izzy got sick, no one else was her friend. It was Izzy and Leanne, in their own little world, singing songs, acting out skits, or pretending to shoot the boys with their pointer-finger guns from behind the cover of the birch trees at the edge of the playground. Leanne never really cared about shooting anyone, but Izzy liked guns, because her father did: he was the CEO of the gun factory. Her dad loved her a lot, Izzy always said. He used to leave work early to pick her up from school on Wednesdays.

No one picked Izzy up anymore, not Wednesdays or any other day of the week. And that was why Leanne Hatfield felt so sure that Ms. Wish wasn't coming back. No one ever does. Not once they leave. Leanne Hatfield was a know-it-all, and she knew that leaving was always for good.

"She was as nervous as a whore in church," Leanne Hatfield reported back to her grandfather that afternoon when he asked about the new long-term sub he'd gotten an email about from the school secretary. He didn't scold his granddaughter for her language, she'd learned the expression from him.

"I hope you can give her a chance, kiddo," he said instead.

18

"So, tell me about teaching," Clive said to Emma that evening as they sat by the fire with the dog. "What's on the syllabus?"

The fifth grade doesn't have a syllabus, but according to the Common Core binder, the kids had to learn about both world wars before the end of the year. The key terms that all fifth graders are supposed to learn are: *depression, superpower, democracy, human rights, suffrage, genocide.*

"Heavy stuff," her dad agreed. "Do you want my advice?"

"Can't hurt."

"You should feed them all to the crocodiles."

"Dad." Emma rolled her eyes, but she was also kind of happy he remembered that, the stories he used to tell her. She should be more patient with him, she thought. So what if everything was a performance? There was only a little bit of the performance left. Maybe she should forgive him and try to enjoy the show.

"If you really want my advice," he said. "Really, don't try to do *too good* of a job. Students can smell desperation, and they don't like it. If you just try to do a C-average job at teaching, you'll end up better off. A better teacher."

"Huh. An interesting theory, Professor."

Her dad sighed. "It's such a shame Meriden wouldn't let me finish out the semester."

"A real shame," Emma agreed, even though she definitely agreed that forced retirement had been the right decision by the school. She'd seen the video of her father's final day in the classroom. It had been uploaded on YouTube by one of his students in his senior poetry seminar, where the breakdown had occurred. Auggie had sent her the link.

Her dad was standing on a desk in the beginning of the video, which is why the student must have taken his phone out to record. Clive was still amazingly agile, for a dying man. "Who brought the cats in here," he yells from above. "Bethany Tinkham, I'm going to have to dock your grade."

"What? Why?" the girl named Bethany asks. The camera goes to the girl's face, and she looks both horrified and amused.

"Absolutely no cats in the classroom. Who the hell told you that you could bring cats to school?"

"You did," Bethany says then, and a look of real confusion crosses Professor Starling's face, and he climbs down off the desk, and starts to cry. He gets down on his knees in front of this girl Bethany, and hugs her around the waist. She looks so uncomfortable when he does that, her professor clutching her while he sobbed. It was sad stuff, hard to watch. It had over four thousand views. Emma wondered if her dad had seen it. If he knew it was out there, humiliating him on the internet.

"She could be anywhere, you know," he said now, by the fire. He was talking about his detective work again, the case of missing person Crystal Nash. He said it as if he were marveling at it, as if Crystal had performed the best magic trick. Emma listened as he ran through his wacky theories, the cults she might have joined, or maybe it was a kidnapping.

"Alien abduction?" Emma asked.

"Now you're thinking," Clive said. "We're casting the widest possible net. And of course, we should never forget about murder. That's not my hunch here, but we have to cover all the bases."

"Maybe she simply left, Dad," Emma said. She did not want to have to worry about Crystal being murdered.

Her dad went upstairs and came back with the corkboard from

his office, all his detective work so far, what cults were based in New England, a chart of how other missing person cases had been solved. "It's all about getting the word out, and then hoping you get lucky," he said. "Look at this case. A delivery man opens the wrong door, but hears someone in the basement calling for help. Or here, someone watches the exact right TV program and sees the missing kid in the library the next day. And here, a dog digs up a human bone. Even that's lucky, to find a bone."

Moses lifted his head, hearing several words he knew.

Clive also mentioned hiring a private investigator, and Emma said that was probably taking it too far, especially since her parents' finances were a mess after Auggie's rehab stays, plus her father had a bit of a spending habit. Emma didn't know her dad already had a PI on retainer, a man named Roy Briggs, someone he'd found online with good recommendations and cheapish rates.

But Emma agreed with one thing: Crystal could be anywhere, just when she had come back to Everton. To be a substitute teacher. To watch her father die.

19

"We have a surprise for you, Ms. Starling," Tobey L. said first thing in the morning after the bell.

"What kind of surprise?" Emma asked, nervous.

"More like a test," said Leanne Hatfield. She was holding a shoebox.

"An experiment," said Zoe F. in her teeny-tiny voice, and everyone agreed that was the word they were looking for. Because Ms. Wish had taught her students in the first month of the school year about the scientific method, the need to conduct an experiment when you've got a working theory.

Inside the box was a sparrow, brown feathers, a bit white in the chest, and very, very dead. The bird was a perfect specimen, not dead for any obvious reason, no car tracks or cat claws, just dead, but in perfect shape otherwise. As if the bird had fallen from the sky. Michael B. had found it on the playground, and they wanted their new substitute teacher to heal it.

"Touch it," the students commanded. "Touch it."

Emma was still rattled by what she'd read in the student folders the day before, the losses these kids had suffered, and so she stammered that she had always heard, hadn't the students been told, not to touch dead wildlife? That it carries diseases? Mites? Never touch something dead or sick without gloves, hadn't they heard that many times?

"Touch it," they chanted, and Leanne Hatfield was the loudest, her lungs the lungs of a future Broadway star.

"Touch it, touch it, touch it," they went on. Their classmate had died, and some of them had dead parents, too, how could she ever say no to these kids? She wasn't a monster. So Emma Starling, new to teaching, who didn't know yet that you shouldn't always do what your students tell you to do, well, she made another rookie mistake. She touched it. She held the limp little thing in her hands. The feathers were soft, and its body so delicate. She could almost feel its heartbeat. She held her breath. The kids were as silent as a group of fifth graders could ever be. Emma couldn't help it, even though she'd certainly never resurrected anyone or anything, she hoped *something* would happen. That she would find a way to impress these kids. She thought of touching Crystal's arm for the first time, healing those scratches from basketball, when Emma had really wanted nothing more than to make Crystal her friend.

After a few minutes, when nothing happened to the bird, nothing at all, no flutter of the wings or flicker of the little yellow-rimmed eyelids, the kids all sighed loudly, dramatically. "Told you," Leanne Hatfield said to the rest of the class. It was only Michael B. who wasn't giving up, said he'd keep the shoebox in his cubby overnight. He would check again in the morning. Maybe the healing took some time to work.

"Let's open our earth science books now," Emma said, because she thought that was a good segue to start learning something. The children groaned. Ulf took out a rubber band and shot it at her. It hit Emma smack in the cheek, narrowly missed her eye.

After school, Emma had to lie down in the dark of the arts-and-crafts closet for ten minutes, exhausted and battle-worn, and she still had to head to the police station for her drug test and fingerprints. Principal Jefferies had reminded her in the teacher's lounge. She'd lied and said she'd forgotten the day before, but really she'd hoped it wouldn't be necessary. She didn't want the entire town to know she was on Lexapro, but then she had googled it, and anti-depressants shouldn't show up on a routine drug test. There were things to be thankful for.

The police station was in the town center, straight across from Maple Street Cemetery. It used to be a candy store, wedged be-tween Odds and Ends Antiques and the Knit & Purl Yarn Store. Officer Zinger was behind the desk. Officer Zinger and Officer Gene had a good cop/bad cop thing going on, and Zinger was the bad cop. He was thin, with a flattop haircut.

As Officer Zinger inked her fingers, Emma asked him if there were any updates in the Crystal Nash case.

"Listen, like I told your father," Officer Zinger said, pulling out a urine-sample cup. "It's just not worth it."

Emma's hackles went up. "Not worth it?"

"I don't mean any offense, princess." He snorted. "What do I know. Maybe she joined the circus. Or a lesbian cult. But there was dope in her trailer. Not exactly a mystery."

Emma did not like being called princess. She did not like any-thing Officer Zinger said. He wasn't doing his job, wasn't protect-ing and serving. She went into the bathroom with the sample cup and when she came out, she handed it directly to Officer Zinger, even though he'd said to leave it on the tray behind the toilet. He was so surprised that he took it.

"Still warm," she said, and left.

We cackled with delight at Maple Street. "That's almost as good as a can of shit," Charles Tepper (b. 1932–d. 1998) said.

"Teaching will toughen you up," Mary Garvin (b. 1945–d. 2001) said with pride. "Let's just hope she doesn't quit."

As Emma left the police station, she ran smack into Lottie Evans, who owned the Knit & Purl. Lottie Evans was wearing an all hand-knitted outfit, her lipstick not exactly done in the lines. Lottie had been one of the most faithful clients of the Gentle

Touch Society, years ago, coming into the McDonald's for arthritis treatments. As they chatted, Emma had to break it to Lottie that she couldn't heal anymore, that she'd lost her abilities. No, she wasn't going to medical school either. "Too bad," Lottie said. "I'm sure your mother is upset."

"She's coping," Emma said.

"And poor Crystal. She was such a nice girl. Never as good as you, though." Lottie said her arthritis had gotten so bad she couldn't even knit anymore. "But now I take these." Lottie pulled out a vial of pills from her purse and rattled them. "Magic beans," she said.

"I'm happy you've found something that helps," Emma said. "Be careful with those."

Lottie kept talking, updating Emma on what her grandkids were up to, how some of them were doing quite well and some of them were really in the shitter.

"Glad to hear it," Emma said before she was finally able to pull herself away from Lottie. Emma ducked into the safety of the old powder blue truck as quick as she could, before she ran into someone else she knew. This town was crawling with people she knew.

Back at the house, Emma's dad was on the porch with his drink and his heat lamp, plus a heavy wool blanket. Moses was lying at his feet, where the dog could almost always be found these days. Moses had heard the Starlings say several times that Clive was not supposed to be left alone, and yet they all kept leaving him unattended, going out of the house, doing whatever it is people do without their dogs. Moses was not a fancy, trained service dog, but he was a Great Pyrenees mix, a breed whose job was guarding livestock, known to be a trustworthy dog with the defenseless creatures of the world. He was very happy to guard Clive.

Emma collapsed in the rocking chair next to her father.

"Where've you been, Emmy?" Clive asked, offering her a Bud from the cooler. His memory wasn't having the best day, plus he was a few beers deep.

"Teaching." Emma took the drink. "And then I had to go to the police station to get fingerprints."

He chuckled. "Always knew you'd take after me."

"Dad?" Emma asked, ignoring that comment, not sure if it was about teaching or the fingerprints, but never mind, there were more important questions. "Do you know who Crystal hung around with?" she asked.

"Oh, you two were always together. Shared the same brain, practically."

"I mean, recently."

"Well, let's see, me, and Dennis, Philip, and Kurt. And Old Ivan of course."

Those were the names of the men of Blacker Sabbath, and also Ivan Goodman, constant barfly. "Dad, I mean her friends, not her customers. People her own age?"

"Hmm," Clive said. "No one I knew, I suppose. I mean, I suppose she had her co-workers. But mostly I know she was saving money. She wanted to get out of Everton."

"So maybe she left. If she said she was going to leave, maybe she left."

"She would have said goodbye," he said, shaking his head. "I gave her five hundred bucks toward the cause. It would have been rude not to tell me."

"Did Mom let you do that?"

"Oh no, no, don't you go getting me in trouble. But I think your mom gave her money too. Crystal was like another daughter to us, but you know that. You two will be friends again, eventually. She always asked about you, wanted to know how you were doing."

"She asked about me?" Emma wasn't expecting that. She had assumed Crystal pretended she didn't exist when talking to Emma's parents.

"I always told her there wasn't much I had to tell. All the way out in California, who knows what you were up to. Might as well have been Timbuktu."

Emma didn't respond, didn't say it was a direct flight from Boston, because she was lost in the possibility that Crystal might have been missing her, too, all these years. People talk a lot about first loves, or the love of your life, but people don't say as much about the friend of your life. Emma still loved Crystal, the friend of her life. And Emma knew she had to find out where she really was, what had happened to her. If things had gotten bad with the drugs, maybe she was still alive but needed help. Emma certainly couldn't leave Crystal's fate up to the two Everton police officers; her dad was right, they were bozos. She couldn't leave it up to her dad either. She had seen the corkboard.

20

Emma knew from watching crime dramas that a detective usually starts with canvassing the town, going to all the places the missing person was last seen. She decided to start at the Blueberry Hill Pub after school on Friday, after surviving her first week of teaching. Snow was just starting to fall. The Blueberry Hill Pub was in a redbrick building, with an outdoor deck that overlooked the Sugar River. The first floor was a family restaurant, where they did a good brunch on weekends. The bar was on the second floor, and the music stage was up there, too, where Blacker Sabbath had their regular gig on Thursday nights, until they'd gone on hiatus. The walls on the second floor were decorated with sports paraphernalia from all the New England teams. Big Hank O'Sullivan, who owned the place, was a professional sports freak.

"Did your dad send you?" Hank asked, running the bar top over with a rag. He was wearing a Celtics jersey, had Tom Brady tattooed on his bicep. His skin was the color of Silly Putty.

Emma shook her head. "I'm just trying to find out what happened to Crystal. My dad doesn't know I'm here."

"Not much to tell, I'm afraid," Hank said, pouring Emma a beer on the house. "She was a good bartender, but she got sloppy at the end. She kept missing shifts. I told her I would need to fire her soon if she didn't shape up."

"Did she shape up?"

"Nah, not really. Crystal did what she wanted. She told me she didn't plan to be bartending for much longer anyway. She was destined for something much greater than working at this restaurant. This shitty-ass restaurant, is what she actually called it, but I let it slide."

"Did she say what she was going to do? Where she was going to go?"

Big Hank shrugged. "She said she was going to make her mother proud. What we all want, I guess."

That really wasn't what Emma wanted to hear, that Crystal was becoming like her mother. Emma knew schizophrenia often strikes first in one's early twenties, which was when Crystal's mom had heard those locutions from God that told her to kill herself.

Big Hank leaned forward over the bar. "Speaking of mothers, I've got a nasty rash. Is your mom letting you heal people with those magic hands yet? Us lowly villagers?"

Emma grimaced, and realized she needed it out in the open that her healing touch was gone, so she didn't have to keep having similar conversations. If she told Big Hank, the entire town would know by noon tomorrow; that was the way gossip worked at the bar. "I can't heal anymore," she explained. "I lost the ability. It's all gone. I don't know what happened, but one day it just didn't work anymore. It's super strange."

"Huh. Just like some guys can't throw anymore."

"What?"

"You can't do what you used to do for no good reason, happens all the time to athletes. They're born with a talent, but they lose it. Always a tragedy. Some of these guys were at the top of their game."

"Oh," Emma said. "Okay. Well, you'll have to see a doctor about the rash. Sorry I can't help."

"That's all right," Hank said. "Maybe I'll try another oatmeal bath."

Yuck, Emma thought, but she tried not to make another disgusted face. "Do you know if Crystal had a boyfriend?" she asked next. That was the other big rule she'd learned from detective dramas: if a woman goes missing, it's always the boyfriend.

Big Hank shrugged. "Not that I know of." But then he called for Brayden, who was in the back running the dishwasher. Brayden came out with his flat face; his nose had been broken in hockey several times.

"Crystal, a boyfriend? Nah," Brayden said, after Hank asked. "She was only into women. But no girlfriend either. She complained about poisoned well water in the dating pool, whatever that means."

Emma reddened. She was embarrassed; it had been a long time since she and Crystal had actually been friends, had talked about boys, girls, whatever. Emma felt like a fraud looking for her, but she also didn't see this guy Brayden doing much. "Were you friends?" Emma asked him.

"I mean, just at work, but we liked to shoot the shit. Super sad what happened to her. You shouldn't mess with the white horse."

"You think it was an overdose."

"Definitely. They'll find her in the woods, one of these days. That's where they found my cousin, a long time later too. I think there's some instinct to head to the woods to die. That shit's primeval."

"Thanks, Brayden," Big Hank said, trying to get rid of him now.

"If you want the truth, I blame Kade."

"Who's Kade?" Emma asked.

"He was a line cook here," Hank said. "I had to fire him."

"Do you know where I can find him?"

"He wrapped his car around a pole last spring."

At Maple Street, Kade Stockman Wright (b. 1984–d. 2014) flinched at the memory.

"Kade liked to party after work," Brayden said. "He *always* had drugs. I know Crystal used to hang out with him."

"I did always have drugs," Kade agreed from his grave. "That's fair."

"I didn't know any of this," Big Hank assured Emma.

"Drugs are always part of the restaurant scene. You just gotta be smart about it." Brayden tapped his temple.

"Thanks, Brayden," Hank said. "You're dismissed."

Brayden gave a thumbs-up. "I hope that was helpful," he said to Emma, and she thanked him. It *was* helpful, to have some sense of how or why Crystal had started using. It was probably a simple case of small-town boredom, if she had guys like Brayden and Big Hank for company, and this guy Kade didn't sound much better. That set Kade off, bitching about people speaking ill of the dead as Emma finished the last of her drink.

"How's your dad doing, by the way?" Big Hank asked. "He really didn't send you over here to sweet-talk his way back onto the stage?"

"What do you mean?"

It turned out that her dad's cover band Blacker Sabbath wasn't really on hiatus, like he'd been claiming. Dennis Hollingdrake and the others had kicked Clive out of the band, and they'd continued to perform without him. They were playing as a ZZ Top cover band now, calling themselves ZZ Rock Bottom.

"Wow," Emma said. "That's awful."

"I feel terrible about it. I really do. But last time your dad performed—that was a real disaster for my business, and I know Dennis had no choice, it was your dad or the band. But hey, make sure your dad knows that his friends just don't have the magic without him. The Thursday-night crowd isn't impressed."

"Why not have him back? I'm sure he'd come."

Big Hank shook his head, no way. "The health department

came after that stunt he pulled." From the Blueberry Hill Pub stage, Clive had yelled into the microphone that he was seeing rats everywhere, *didn't everyone see, rats all over the goddamn restaurant!* It was another hallucination, another symptom of the brain disease, but of course the good patrons of the bar and restaurant didn't know that, and neither did the health department. The pub had to be closed for a deep cleaning, and Clive Starling was banned from his favorite watering hole, the place he always called his port in the storm.

Emma felt bad for her dad, how lonely he must be without his band or his job or his bar. When she got home, it was getting dark, and she found him sitting outside in the snow underneath the birdfeeder, holding a lump of black sunflower seeds in his palms. Her dad had started feeding the birds; that was his new hobby. He told Emma that the ghost of Ernest Harold Baynes had promised him that the chickadees would eat straight from his hands eventually, if he remained patient enough. Chickadees are always the friendliest of birds.

21

$\rightarrow\!\cdot\!\leftarrow$

"I wish you wouldn't do this," her mother said on Saturday morning when Emma told her dad to get ready for a day of detective work, and he'd gone scooting upstairs to get ready. "I wish you wouldn't indulge him. The police are looking for her. Let the police do their job."

"Mom, come on, the cops aren't doing anything. Officer Zinger told me they think she joined the circus or a cult."

"I hope she did join a cult."

"Maybe she did, we'll find out."

Ingrid had let her husband make his posters and his corkboard because there was no stopping that behavior, but Ingrid had no hope Crystal Nash would ever be found, considering the drugs she was on. Ingrid knew too much from the Phoenix House. She had seen how this could go. She had friends from group family therapy who had lost their children. "This is just not what I wanted you to come home for," she told Emma.

"Tell me, Mom, what did I come home for?"

"To spend some time with your father. To get back on your feet."

"We *are* spending time together. That's just what we're doing. And my feet are fine. I have a job. I'm working on it."

"Fine. Do whatever you want, Emma, but I don't want to be involved. I can't take it. My heart cannot take it." Ingrid closed her eyes then, and breathed in through her nose, as if she were in pain. "I just want you to know, this isn't a game."

Emma was annoyed her mom was acting so tortured, when no one had asked her to do anything. Her dad came down then, ready to go, so at least Emma didn't have to continue the conversation. She could walk away.

Emma and her dad drove to the Shaw's Supermarket in Sugar River Plaza. That was a sure way to talk to a lot of people. In the supermarket aisles, Clive handed anyone who would take one a missing person poster. They asked everyone they saw if they'd seen Crystal Nash at any point over the last few months, or if they'd heard anything.

"It's not like anyone hurt her," the checkout boy said.

"How do you know, Julian?" Clive said, pointing his finger in the boy's pimply face.

"I'm not supposed to let you harass our shoppers anymore, Mr. Starling."

Julian finally called the manager, and Emma learned her dad had been badgering people in the supermarket for months. Emma pushed him out the sliding doors.

T. J. Horton was tailgating in the parking lot, selling hot dogs out of the bed of his truck; he had a small charcoal grill going. Emma had never had a use for T. J. Horton, he had a Confederate flag sticker on his rear windshield, but she figured she still had to ask him about Crystal. "Oh yeah, she was buying up Oxy the last time I saw her," he said. "I had to tell her I wasn't selling anymore. I've gone straight. Just pork products and fireworks now. You need any fireworks, Mr. Starling?"

"Yes," he said. "And a hot dog."

But Emma said no, she wouldn't let her dad buy anything from T. J., not even a hot dog. She was in charge of how he spent his money.

"Fine," Clive said, pouting. "I thought this was supposed to be fun."

"Come on," Emma said, pressing him toward their truck, and she saw what her mother meant, about this being a game.

They drove next to the Very Pleasant Valley Mobile Home Park, where they found Crystal's trailer locked up with a great big chain. Emma knocked on the door of the neighboring trailer, and a woman answered, wearing a sweater with a sequin snowman on it. "Hi, Mrs. Maas," Emma said. "Do you know why Crystal's trailer is chained up?"

"Oh that," she said. "Yes, the landlord is such a tough cookie about money. He wants to be sure he gets his rent if she comes back for her things."

The owner of the trailer park, Graham Leeches, was not known to be a charitable man; he was always evicting people in midwinter. Graham didn't live in the trailer park but across town in a four-bedroom house with his wife and two kids. He worked full-time at the gun factory, a higher-up with an office, Percy Eaklin's right-hand man.

"We're closing in on an answer!" her father called out to Mrs. Maas and the rest of Crystal's neighbors as they left the Very Pleasant park. "We'll let you all know!"

The gun factory was closed on weekends, so Emma had to wait until Monday to reach Graham Leeches to see if he knew anything about the whereabouts of his former tenant Crystal Nash. She called while her students were out at recess, and the receptionist politely asked what this was regarding, but quickly turned unfriendly. She said not to call again about Crystal Nash, this was harassment, all these phone calls. "I know Clive Starling is behind this," she said. "Officer Zinger was very clear with him that he wasn't allowed to call here again. I don't know what he's paying you, but don't call here again, got it?"

Emma felt like a scolded little kid, and she apologized before she hung up. Her dad had worn out everyone on this investigation long before she had gotten home. She wasn't sure what else she could really do at this point, months after Crystal had gone missing. If only her mother had been honest with her from the beginning. Well, then again—Emma was lying back then, about being in her first weeks of med school. No one had been perfect.

At the end of the day, the fifth graders presented their first big homework assignment, a project called "The Future of the World," and they were each supposed to describe what they thought life would look like in a hundred years. Michael B. went last, and he poured a bucket of ice water over Ulf's head to show what would happen when the polar ice caps melted. He had ten other buckets lined up to show how much water it would be, and he planned to keep pouring them, which Emma actually thought was pretty clever, but she had to stop him before he drowned his classmate. She was only trying to be a mediocre substitute teacher, but there were still certain rules.

22

It was late that night, and getting later, Monday turning into Tuesday, but Emma tossed and turned, just couldn't get to sleep. Eventually, she climbed out of bed, crept downstairs, and headed straight to the liquor cabinet. Moses arrived on the scene to check if they were being robbed, but Emma reassured him with an ear rub. It was good to not be completely alone. Together they went to the porch. Emma thought fresh air might help clear her head. The moon was full, and she looked across the lawn to the hulk of Ralph's mansion, that big yellow house. All those empty rooms. Emma saw the *Upper Valley News* headline: MISSING WOMAN HIDES OUT IN MANSION FOR MONTHS, RIGHT UNDER STUPID FAMILY'S NOSE.

She marched across the yard in her winter boots. Moses followed her without enthusiasm; he was a dog who needed his twelve to fourteen hours of sleep. She went right up to the heavy front door of the Corbin Mansion, punched in the code on the keypad—"1880," the year Austin Corbin came back to Everton to retire and build his grand animal park.

In the great hall, all the lights switched on as if by magic, as if the big house had been waiting for Emma. Her mom must have installed motion sensors. That was new, even if everything else looked as it always had. When Ralph Kelsey moved into the mansion back in the '80s, he had hired a New York City designer to restore the original grandeur, after the previous owner had let it

fall to shambles. Ingrid kept it up now, hired repairmen when repairmen were needed, now that Bart Nash wasn't around to take
care of everything for her. Ingrid hadn't been able to bring herself
to hire another full-time groundskeeper.

Emma climbed the stairs to the bedrooms and went room by
room, searching the place. There was a queen-size four-poster
bed in each room, except for Ralph Kelsey's master room, which
had a king. But no one was living in the mansion now. The sheets
were unruffled, tightly made by Ingrid Starling herself; she had
rules about hospital corners. Crystal wasn't hiding out.

Emma went back downstairs to the great hall, where Moses
was waiting for her. He cocked his head. "I know, I know," Emma
said. "Don't you start. I know it was a crazy idea. I still had to
check."

Emma picked up the bottle of Jack Daniel's from where she'd
left it next to the umbrella stand in the front hall, then went into
the hunting-trophy room. Ralph had collected the taxidermy over
the years, hadn't actually killed most of the animals himself.
There was a taxidermy zebra shipped over from Africa; there
were deer, antelope, and mountain goat heads on the wall. Moses
growled at the sight of all those dead animals before he realized
none of them were growling back.

In the center of the room, there was an enormous mahogany
desk, which had become Ingrid's office, a quiet place for her to
think away from her family. Ingrid had forever been planning to
write a book about Everton's history. So far she had only a long,
rambling chapter on Austin Corbin and his hunting park, his two
sons both named Austin Corbin Jr., the mistress who hung herself, the failed artist son-in-law who shot himself in a room full of
blank canvases, which Corbin said only left behind more paint-
ings that wouldn't sell. Legendary bastard Austin Corbin had not
even been kind to his own family, but it would be quite the book
if Ingrid ever finished it.

Emma sat at the desk in the high-backed leather chair, and Moses collapsed in a furry heap next to her, with that satisfying sound of a big dog lying down. She poured a drink. She felt like a kid pretending to be someone grown-up and important, a game she'd played by herself so many times in this mansion as a little kid, before Crystal had moved to town, when Emma played most of her games alone.

She sifted through the stacks of paper on the desk, grant applications, proposals. Her mom was trying to get Ralph to turn the house into a museum, now that it was no longer a private residence. She pulled open the top desk drawer, where she found paper clips, pens, a tray of staples, a protein bar, a tightly rolled joint, and a letter folded into three sections. Emma opened it. It hurt to see Crystal's handwriting. So familiar and yet so strange. *Dear Mrs. Bird,* it started. Crystal had always called the Starling parents "Mr. and Mrs. Bird."

Dear Mrs. Bird—

Mr. Bird is at the bar every night, and he asked me to put a good word in, so here's my good word. My dad would tell me to stay out of it, but my dad's not here, and having you both as surrogate parents has meant a lot to me. Mr. Bird can be a real moron, but he loves you. I hope you can forgive him. I know you had a good reason for kicking him out, and I won't blame you if you divorce him. But if you want my opinion, and I know you didn't ask for it, the affair was his way of dealing with Auggie's drug problem. I think he's afraid he's going to lose his son, and sometimes that kind of fear makes people do reckless, hurtful things. Now he's going to lose you, too, through no one's fault but his own. But I do know he's really sorry. It's all he talks about.

Love, Crystal

Emma was annoyed. *Give me a break,* she thought, reading the letter. Was this why her mom had forgiven her dad, and let him back in the house and called off the divorce—because Crystal had asked her to? That seemed ridiculous. And it really wasn't any of Crystal's business, the affair or Auggie or anything else.

It was pretty meddlesome, we agreed.

Emma threw back the rest of the whiskey and stood up. She walked around the office, stroking some of the stuffed animals. She touched the bristled face of the wild boar. The look on the boar's face was one of openmouthed horror.

It was then that she heard footsteps.

Emma was drunk enough not to be scared. She fell back into the big office chair and watched the doorway of the trophy room, waiting for the ghost of Crystal Nash to appear from underneath the mahogany stairs. Maybe that would be a relief. Just to know for sure where her friend was, what had happened to her. There would be closure then.

23

It was not the ghost of Crystal Nash but only Mack Durkee in the doorway, holding up a flashlight like he was ready to hit someone with it. Moses hadn't barked once, just lifted his big head and wagged his tail. "Oh," Mack said. "It's you."

"What are you doing here?" Emma asked, because she had certainly not expected Mack Durkee to walk in. She was in her favorite pajamas, printed with flamingos wearing Santa hats, a Christmas gift from a few years back. She pulled her winter coat closed. Mack was wearing a white T-shirt and jeans, a blue flannel over the T-shirt. He was even wearing a belt.

"You set off the alarm," he said.

"What alarm?"

"The motion sensors." Mack waved his hand in the air. "Your mother never told you? She hired me as the night watchman, I get a text when they go off. The last time it was a bat, and it took me forever to get the bastard out. But otherwise, it's not a hard job."

Emma wondered why her mom didn't hire Auggie to be night watchman. He needed a job. He was right across the lawn. He could have caught Emma before she'd ransacked all the bedrooms, before she'd found the joint in the desk drawer, her old best friend's handwriting. "Well," Emma said. "It's just me."

"Breaking and entering in your jammies."

"Yup," she said. And even in her embarrassing outfit, Emma found she was relieved to see Mack, and not just because he wasn't a ghost. She didn't want to think about her dad cheating on her mom because he was worried his son was going to die. It was easier to think about Mack Durkee's hunky oval face and floppy hair. She held up the bottle of Jack Daniel's, the maple-syrup-colored liquid sloshing. "You drink?"

"Definitely," he said, pulling up a chair. Emma poured some whiskey into a coffee cup her mother had left on the desk. It looked reasonably clean.

"What are you doing here in the middle of the night?" Mack asked.

Emma blushed, embarrassed. Even the dog had thought she was being ridiculous, searching the bedrooms for Crystal Nash.

"I'm only asking because I need it for the logs. As night watchman, you understand." He winked.

Now, we're not psychics at Maple Street, but we knew where this was headed, two good-looking young people, so alive still, both lonely, both dealing with ailing parents. The kissing was bound to start soon.

Emma swallowed her pride and explained that she was trying to find Crystal Nash, in case she was hiding out in the mansion. Sounded crazy, she knew. "And I didn't know my mom had hired a security guard," she said.

"And now you can tell your mother he's doing an excellent job."

"I am definitely not telling my mom about this." Emma laughed. "She would have my head for touching her stuff."

"Snooping on your own mother, huh? I hear you and your dad are local detectives?"

"Where'd you hear that?"

"Not many secrets in Everton. Plus your dad knocked on my mom's door."

"We're looking for her, yeah. Got anything for me, Durkee?"

He shook his head. "It's definitely too bad, whatever happened to her. I know it's hard to lose a friend."

"I'm just trying to find *something*. I need something before I give up on her."

"Well," Mack said, and rubbed the back of his neck. "I saw her at the pub all the time, but we never really talked. I think she thought I was corny. The only thing I know that might help you . . . I heard she'd been buying from Sid Wish."

"That's something. Who told you that?"

It was Mack's turn to blush. "One of my students."

"Your high school students?"

"From the mouths of babes."

"Well, that's more than T. J. Horton gave me."

"Ew, don't let that guy give you anything."

Emma laughed.

"And I heard you took Claire Wish's job," Mack said. "I play basketball at the rec with Jefferies. He was excited about you."

"Yup. No more California for me. Not so smart after all."

"No, that's great," Mack said. "That's really great. Those poor kids can really use someone like you."

"Someone young and aimless?"

"I'm serious. It's making a big difference to have someone who cares show up day after day, instead of a revolving door of people who work other jobs. It might change the entire direction of their lives."

Emma already knew there was a possibility she could fuck these kids up forever. It wasn't comforting to hear Mack confirm it. "Any teaching advice?" she asked. "My dad told me not to try too hard."

Mack laughed. "Don't try too hard. That's good. I would say—listen to the kids. They'll trust you if you listen to them. Respect what they think."

"Well, that sounds easy," she said, sarcastically. She wanted the kids to like her; did they need to trust and respect her too? "And how's your goat project going?"

"Not well," he admitted. The students left the goat in the hallways, tied to the handles of their lockers, or set Doris to graze on the baseball field. Mack sounded dismayed. "It's just no way to treat a baby."

"But it's a fine way to treat a goat."

"I suppose next year we'll just give out more condoms." He sighed and drank more of his whiskey from the coffee cup. It said I'M THE BOSS on the side. Emma had bought it for her mom for Mother's Day, years ago.

"Condoms might be more effective," Emma agreed. "But I'm sure they'll never forget their biology class. I certainly wouldn't, with you as a teacher." She reddened. She was drunker than she thought.

"Shucks," Mack said, and gave Emma his cute, crooked smile.

"Get to the good stuff," Charles Tepper (b. 1932–d. 1998) urged, and for once, we agreed with Charles, that horny toad. Yes, it took another two hours of drinking and talking and flirting, but we got our payoff in the end. Mack and Emma made a new use for the bearskin rug before dawn, and the poor rug was so old that two of the bear's teeth fell out from the action. As they got dressed, Mack pocketed the fangs, but Emma didn't notice. "Cool souvenirs, man," Patrick D. Braeburn (b. 1948–d. 1972) said. Patrick was still stuck in the free-love era. He hadn't made it out of Vietnam.

Midmorning at school, Emma was so hungover, she had to throw up in the girls' bathroom, couldn't even make it to the faculty bathroom down the hall.

"You're sick?" Leanne Hatfield asked. Emma Starling hadn't noticed the pink sneakers the next stall over. "You should go home," Leanne said, putting a cup of water underneath the stall door. "You could be infectious. My voice needs to be healthy. Rehearsals for the musical should start soon. We just need to find a new director."

"It's not contagious." Emma took a sip of water from the Dixie cup and sloshed, spitting it into the toilet bowl. She emerged from the stall, found Leanne standing by the sink. "I'm feeling much better," Emma tried to reassure her.

"You don't look better, Ms. Starling. You should go home. We'll be fine on our own."

"You're not fine on your own. You're little kids."

"Okay," Leanne said, and nodded. She respected that. Leanne wanted people to treat her like a kid, and sometimes it seemed like they forgot to, since she didn't speak or act like one. But when they went back to the classroom, Leanne announced that Ms. Starling was sick. The rest of the class freaked out, telling Emma to go to the nurse.

"I'm not sick," Emma told the class again, but she also didn't want to come clean about being hungover, because the fifth graders would think that was worse. Her students all agreed she looked pale, wouldn't give it up, so finally Emma said they could raid the arts and crafts closet, and do any kind of art project they wanted for the rest of the day. They'd leave her alone then. She opened the closet door and let them have at it.

When the bell finally rang, Olivia, Zoe F., and Adam D. all handed her a Get Well Soon card on their way out the door, which hadn't been the assignment. There had been no assignment. Emma was overwhelmed with happiness. She was winning them over; some of them thought she was a good teacher, worthy of a Get Well Soon card. She was getting her shit together, she thought for a second, until she remembered she had thrown up at school earlier that day. Her hangover was mostly gone. There was a thick dusting of glitter on the industrial carpet, like the floor of a strip club.

Emma leaned back in her teacher's chair and pulled out her

phone. There was a text from Mack. A gif of two cartoon bears hugging. Her high school self would be so, so happy. But Emma wasn't sixteen anymore, and she didn't want to get stuck in this dead-end town just because she'd fallen for a hunky high school biology teacher who did goofy small-town things like raising a goat with his students to teach them the dangers of teen pregnancy.

Now that she was feeling more clearheaded, the fog of the hangover lifting, she thought about what Mack had said about Sid Wish, how he was Crystal's supplier as well as selling to the teenagers in driver's ed. Emma looked at the framed photo of Claire and Sid Wish on her desk again, wondering what Claire knew, if she really could have been so oblivious, if Sid ever bought her expensive presents or had unexplained cash.

Claire Wish's phone number was written on the top of the telephone tree in Emma's teacher's desk. Before she chickened out, Emma dialed. She was immediately greeted by a very cheery hello, but it was a recording, the call had gone straight to voicemail. Maybe Claire Wish really was in a mental hospital, a locked ward, like Doris had said. Or maybe Claire Wish just wasn't taking phone calls from strangers. Even if Emma could reach her, Claire Wish probably wouldn't answer questions about someone like Crystal Nash, a known drug user, heroin found when the police searched her trailer. Claire Wish wouldn't say anything that might incriminate her husband, not when his trial was due to start soon, if she had any loyalty to him left.

24

❧

Clive woke from his afternoon nap to find the ghost of Ernest Harold Baynes sitting at the edge of his bed. This was unusual, Clive thought, the ghost had never showed up in the bedroom before. *Death must be coming soon.* What a lonely thought. Clive bravely dragged himself out of bed anyway, and noticed he'd been napping in his undershirt and undies. It was two P.M., but he threw on his bathrobe and slippers. He saw no reason to get dressed, with nowhere to be, no classes to teach. Clive and Harold went downstairs, with Moses on their heels, and they found the house was empty. Yet again, Moses was the only Starling family member standing guard.

In the bright kitchen of the Corbin caretaker's house, Clive poured out an afternoon snack: three bowls of cereal, one for him, one for Harold, and one for the fox, in case the ghost of Harold's pet fox finally decided to show up, the ghostly vision Clive had seen only once, standing at the edge of the woods that day, the day Emma had finally come home. Clive knew the fox was the creature that Harold loved the most in all the world, but he never came around with Harold. Clive was a little miffed by it. Still, Clive was glad his friend had some company, since Harold had said his wife, Louise, wasn't with him in the woods. She went to travel the world after his death, Harold had explained, she'd outlived him by many years. She'd been a successful photographer in Europe and had ended up buried in Nova Scotia; she'd always wanted to be nearer to the ocean. It made Clive awfully happy he still had his own wife, to hear Harold talk about Louise.

Clive went to put his cereal bowl in the sink, and he looked out the kitchen window onto the front lawn. There in the midday sunshine was a deer, standing in the snow. "I'm sure she'd like a snack too," Harold said. Clive agreed, and so he went out with a box of cereal. More Corn Pops from the Starlings' endless supply. When Clive extended the yellow puffs to the deer, he felt like he could read her mind. He felt that he knew everything about her. How glad she was to see him.

Now, *most* deer would have run from Clive Starling. He was wearing a bathrobe and an undershirt and what Clive's students would call tighty-whitey underwear. But this particular deer was remarkably bold, and had been fed by children before, had discovered the joys of the packaged foods available on the playground at recess time. The children at Dream Far Elementary had fed this deer Fruit Roll-Ups and peanut butter sandwiches, carrot sticks and Ritz crackers, and even, once or twice, a slice of ham. The children had the good sense not to feed the deer any chocolate items, since they knew that chocolate can kill a dog, so it could likely kill a deer too.

So, this particular deer, whom Clive Starling quickly named Bambi, as though he were a man with no imagination and not a professional poet, ate Corn Pops straight from Clive's palm. "That tickles, Bambi," Clive said. The deer had whiskers underneath her jaw. Clive Starling reached into the cereal box again. Boy, did he feel like a friend to all animals at that moment. He was inhabiting the spirit of the noble Harold Baynes. *If there was only so much life left in this skin*, Clive thought, *I am glad I have had this experience*. And he looked the deer over lovingly.

It was only then, he reported to everyone later, that he noticed that the deer was speckled with some kind of pearlescent paint. This deer, his Bambi, had been shot, but only by a paintball gun.

Clive had heard about this, why someone would do this. The high school kids were into night hunting, or flashlight hunting, which is illegal, because a deer will freeze when you shine a light at it, and that unfair advantage makes it poaching, not hunting. The high schoolers had started shooting deer up with glow-in-the-dark paint, in the hopes that they wouldn't have to use flashlights to find the deer at night.

"Let's get you cleaned up," Clive said to Bambi. "I'll get a wet towel." And then Clive realized, this was the ultimate test: Ernest Harold Baynes had not only fed wild animals, he had lived with them. Invited them into his home.

Clive Starling did not stop to think of any of the consequences. What his wife might say. Clive Starling didn't think of Ingrid at all as he lured the deer into the house, one Corn Pop after the next Corn Pop. He walked backwards, and soon they were up the four porch stairs—Bambi took the stairs one by one, like she'd been walking stairs her whole life—and soon they were in the house. Poor Moses ran upstairs to hide. Clive and the deer were in the front hall, then they were in the kitchen. Bambi was standing in the kitchen! Bambi's back was as tall as the countertops. It struck Clive only then how large this animal was, and how hooved.

"What the fuck do I do now, Harold," Clive said to the ghost, but the ghost was not around. Ernest Harold Baynes was no longer at the kitchen table, and even Moses was nowhere to be seen. And then Clive remembered that he had to wash the paint off the deer. He poured the remaining cereal into a bowl and left Bambi munching away as he went upstairs to get a towel and some paint-removing supplies.

In the bathroom cabinet upstairs, Clive found the thing he was looking for: nail polish remover with acetone. He knew that this was the best thing to remove paint quickly, his wife had taught him that much. He splashed acetone on the towel and went downstairs toward the deer, the open bottle in one hand, the towel in the other. He wanted to clean her up quickly, while he still had cereal left to feed her.

It might have all worked out fine, but Bambi had lived long enough to associate certain smells with fear and otherwise bad feelings. What Clive Starling did not know, because he was not a gun man, had never been a gun man, was that acetone is often used in a homemade mixture to clean your gun. Many hunters in New Hampshire used a homemade mixture, and Bambi knew the smell of acetone. Clive could tell, as soon as he was face-to-face with her again, what she was thinking, and that he'd made a major mistake.

In the sunny yellow kitchen of the caretaker's house of the Corbin Mansion, Bambi went berserk.

25

When Emma pulled up to the house, the Everton Volunteer Fire Department was out front, all remarking about how much damage a grown deer could do in such a short time. Her father was wrapped in an aluminum blanket, the kind they give to marathon runners, and Moses was sitting at his side, trembling.

"What the hell happened?" Emma asked, and her dad explained the whole story, or as much as he could. "Oh my God," Emma said, in wonder and disbelief. Then she felt a lump in her throat. She was his guardian. She was supposed to prevent disasters like this one.

Ingrid drove up, the fire department had called her and asked her to come home. She stormed up to her husband, and Clive quivered from the Parkinson's-like symptoms as he explained what had happened, how the ghost had told him to do it.

"You expect . . ." Ingrid said, already furious and she hadn't even seen the inside of the house yet, how much had been ruined, how many of the cabinets had been kicked in, windows broken. The deer climbed the stairs in the house, which only made things worse. Just like cows, deer can walk upstairs just fine, but cannot go back down. The firemen had poor Bambi cornered in Clive's office, and were waiting for someone to come with the tranquilizer gun, and that someone was taking their sweet time. Clive had forbidden the men from shooting and killing her, not on his property. Emma talked to one of the firefighters about it.

"We don't want to kill the deer either," the firefighter said.

"And we're all hunters. But it's shooting fish in a barrel, and all that. It's not right."

As they waited, Bambi had gone through two more boxes of cereal. "She's stress eating," Clive claimed, as though he could possibly know what the deer was thinking.

The man with the tranquilizer gun finally arrived, and it was someone Emma recognized. It was Peter Foots, Auggie's old best friend, the one who hadn't come around in a long time, since Auggie got on drugs and Peter had stayed off them. He was wearing a Sullivan County Animal Control T-shirt, a black tee with a white logo. It said STAFF on the back. Emma felt the unfairness of it, Peter Foots had always been so much dumber than Auggie; why did he turn out okay? On staff somewhere. Maybe now that Auggie was clean, he could get a job like that one. Peter looked happy.

"Sorry it took me so long to get here," Peter Foots told the Starlings after Bambi had been shot with the tranquilizer. Four of the volunteer firemen had put Bambi gently in a truck and she would be laid out in the woods where she'd wake up several hours later, a little groggy but likely no worse for wear. "I couldn't find the tranquilizers," Peter Foots said, "people steal them from Animal Control."

"I'm sorry for the trouble," Clive said. "I'm embarrassed. I'm really embarrassed."

"You should be sorry," Ingrid snapped.

"Mom," Emma said. "He's sick."

"We're all sick," Ingrid said, although that wasn't really true.

The Starlings went into the house to look at the damage, and Peter Foots tagged along. It seemed like every single cabinet in the kitchen had been kicked through, even the ones that looked too tall for a deer to reach. Windows were broken, dishes were smashed. Upstairs, the deer had broken the bed in the master bedroom. There were white feathers everywhere from several busted pillows.

Emma thought her mother was going to cry, but then it was her father who really broke down. The deer had pulled a bookcase down in his office. It was the room the firemen had finally trapped her in while they waited for Peter Foots to arrive with the tranquilizer. Bambi had released a stream of urine all over the pile of books. No one had seen it happen, but it was obvious from the smell. At least Emma had borrowed the first edition Ernest Harold Baynes book. It was in her desk at school; she'd taken it to read while the kids were out at recess. When they had a minute alone, Emma would tell her father that something so special to him had been saved. The bulletin board of clues from Crystal's case was untouched, too, hanging on the wall, Clive Starling's half-baked detective work still intact.

Her dad lay down on the floor near his urine-soaked books, stomach flat, moaning.

"Oh, so you're upset when your things are ruined," her mother said.

"Jimmie used to destroy the house too," Emma said, thinking of something that might be a comfort.

"Who's Jimmie?" Auggie asked.

"He was Ernest Harold Baynes's pet bear."

"Do not mention that man," Ingrid said. "Please leave him out of this."

"Who?" Peter asked, and Auggie took him aside to explain. Peter looked over at Clive very sadly, very tenderly. Peter had known Clive Starling back when he had seemed like the coolest dad any little boy could ever have. The guy with the rock-star hair and the motorcycle. Who made them watch old Dracula movies at sleepovers, instead of "whatever crap" they really wanted to see.

Clive wiped his face, pulled his silver-white hair back into a ponytail. He was still shaking from the tremor. He looked up at Peter, and asked, "Why do people steal the tranquilizers?"

"What?" Ingrid asked.

"He said people steal tranquilizers from animal control."

"It's cheaper to mix heroin in with something else," Peter explained. "Animal tranquilizers are one of the most popular mix-ins. And it's free if you steal it."

"That's the great thing about stealing." Clive smiled as he said it.

"Hey," Peter said. "How's the search for Crystal going? I've been praying for her."

"Praying doesn't do much good. You keep your eyes peeled, son."

Peter Foots nodded. "You know," he said, "she was my first kiss."

Emma remembered. Crystal and Peter had both been sleeping over, and Crystal went downstairs to the kitchen and she came back and said she'd made Peter Foots a man. When Emma asked what that meant, Crystal was seventeen and Peter only fourteen, there were practically laws against that, Crystal said relax, I just kissed him, but it was a kiss he would never forget. It looked like that was true, the way Peter Foots was biting his lip now at the memory.

"Oh my God," Ingrid said, remembering something, her voice suddenly panicked. "How am I going to tell Ralph? It's his house. We don't own the house. It's his house."

"We'll go tell him together." Emma wanted to help her mother. To step up as guardian. To take responsibility for some of this, the mess her ward had caused.

"GG to the rescue again." Auggie rolled his eyes toward his skull, and Emma regretted hoping Auggie could pull his life together. In fact, she didn't care if anything good ever happened to him.

26

By the time Emma and her mother got in the car to head to Sundown Acres Assisted Living, Ingrid was in hysterics. She was terrified to tell Ralph that his house had been wrecked. She didn't want to disappoint him, she said. It was a side of her mother that Emma had never seen before. She was usually cool and composed, even if sometimes she'd snap, throw plates at the wall. But she never showed weakness like this. Never showed fear.

"Mom, Ralph will understand," Emma attempted to reassure her. "It was an accident, and he has the mansion, and the apartment in Sundown Acres. He even has that little hunting cabin he never goes to. It's not like he needs the caretaker's house."

"I hope he hasn't heard about what happened yet. Can you drive a little faster? We should be the ones to tell him."

"We're almost there," Emma told her. "Mom, calm down. See if you can calm down." Sundown Acres Assisted Living was only three miles from the Corbin mansion, but it was possible that Ralph *had* already heard about what had happened. In such a small town, and with something as big as a deer in a house, that news would travel fast. And knowing the Sundown Acres gossip grapevine, Ralph was sure to hear it the wrong way. The gossip at Sundown Acres Assisted Living was like a game of telephone: many of the residents couldn't hear very well, but they all loved to gossip, so they would pass the half-heard news on and on and by the time the last person heard it, it barely resembled the original information.

When Emma and her mother pulled up outside the entrance to Sundown Acres, there was an ambulance out in front, a common sight at any assisted-living home.

"Oh dear," Ingrid said. Emma knew her mother wasn't trying to be funny about Bambi, it was her honest reaction to the ambulance. The red flashing lights were turned off, and no one was rushing around, which meant that the person they'd been called to save was now someone already dead.

When Emma and Ingrid walked into Sundown Acres, everything was still chaos, since Ralph Kelsey had been dead for just over an hour. Officer Gene was there taking notes—he was the nicer cop, short and shaped like a guinea pig. The police investigation was under way, but Officer Gene said he could tell the Starlings most of the story. Ingrid was listed as Ralph's emergency contact. She was his legal caretaker, which Emma had never known before.

About two hours before, Angus Dagit had been the first resident at Sundown Acres to hear that there was a deer in the Corbin Mansion, or "that huge yellow house on Corbin Road," as Angus's son had told him over the phone. Angus Dagit's son was forty-four-year-old Angus Dagit Jr., and he was known as Gus-Gus to just about everyone—one of those silly childhood nicknames that had stuck. Gus-Gus was in the volunteer fire department, and he called his father to explain why he wasn't coming by Sundown Acres until later.

"He called from the fire truck and told me about the deer," Angus Dagit had explained to Officer Gene.

Gus-Gus Dagit had to come give a statement, too, and he said he'd told his dad that he couldn't come golfing today, that his help was needed, but that he'd be by to visit before dinner. "I said I'd call when I was in the lobby and we'd have a few fingers of Mak-

er's Mark together. It's my dad's birthday today," Gus-Gus explained. "I didn't want him to think I'd forgotten, so I called him
on the way to the fire. I mean, to the deer."

Angus Dagit was one of the residents who didn't hear very
well, but who suffered from such terribly good confidence that he
thought he heard just fine. Emma remembered him from years
before, from volunteering at Sundown. He was the kind who
pinched butts.

What Angus Dagit had heard his son say on the phone was
half-correct: he heard that there was a deer in the Corbin Mansion, trapped upstairs, and it was really the caretaker's house, not
the mansion, but that's close enough. Angus also heard his son
say that they needed his help to shoot it. Gus-Gus said he would
be by soon to pick him up, he was on the way in the fire truck, and
he'd call when he was in the lobby. Angus was sure his son had
said they needed *a couple of trigger marksmen,* which Angus
Dagit had been, at one point. He'd been a sniper in World War II.

"Here was a chance to be a hero again," Angus Dagit told Officer Gene. "Do you know how bored I've been here?" A chance to
be a hero, alongside his son, Gus-Gus. He wasn't sure why one
deer needed two marksmen, but Angus Dagit knew something
about the Corbin Mansion. He'd heard about it enough from his
friend Ralph Kelsey, who owned the place and would never shut
up about the history of it. "I never knew why he didn't keep living
there and hire full-time help," Angus Dagit was quoted as saying
in the police notes. "He could certainly afford it, and his daughter
and her family lived right next door."

When her mother read that quote, Emma saw that it just about
killed her. Because they both knew that Angus Dagit was one of
Ralph Kelsey's best friends at Sundown Acres, but Angus was
confused. Ralph didn't have a daughter. Ralph didn't have any
family left; his wife had died so many years ago, but Ralph did

have the Starlings who lived next door. He had Ingrid and Clive and Emma and Auggie, and they had him. Emma realized that Officer Gene probably thought they *were* Ralph's family, that her mom wasn't just his healthcare proxy, which is why they were getting the entire story of his death. Well, they were family, just not tied together by blood.

"I know this is a lot," Officer Gene said at that point, stroking his round face with a look of serious concern. "Would you like me to stop for now?"

"No, no," Ingrid said, wiping away some tears. "Go on."

More excited than he had been in decades, Angus Dagit went downstairs to tell Ralph Kelsey the news. That there was a deer stuck in Ralph's house, and Angus said isn't that strange, and that he hoped the doe wouldn't cause much damage. Angus bragged to his friend that he was being called in as an expert marksman, and he assured Ralph that he didn't have much to worry about. "The deer will be dead in no time, as soon as my son comes to pick me up in the fire truck."

"And what was . . . his reaction?" Ingrid asked. "What did Ralph say about the deer?"

"According to Angus, Ralph laughed his ass off," Officer Gene said. "He laughed so hard he said he was going to wet his pants."

Emma could see her mom's face relax. Ralph wasn't mad at her, in his last moments.

Angus Dagit had gone back upstairs, furious and humiliated by Ralph's laughter. And he took out his gun. And he sat down on the edge of his La-Z-Boy chair to wait for his son to call. He took out his cleaning solution, the stuff that smelled something like acetone nail polish remover, and he began to clean his gun.

"And then, I don't know how it happened, but it went off in my hands and then . . ." Angus Dagit explained. In parentheses the police report read: *(At this point, Mr. Dagit begins to cry, and could not finish his sentence).*

The gunshot went right through the floor, and right into the identical apartment below, and straight toward the identical brown La-Z-Boy chair that came with the Deluxe Retirement Package, but first the bullet went through the chest of Mr. Ralph Kelsey. He'd had to lie down for a minute, tired out from that last good laugh.

PART IV

The Fox

27

ANOTHER HOME FOR DEATH

from *The Collected Writings of Ernest Harold Baynes,* © 1925

The author with Dauntless.

Photograph by Louise Birt Baynes.

I left the New York Zoological Park with a pair of grey wolf cubs in a box, covered with wire netting, ready for their journey to New Hampshire. I was going home by way of Boston and my train left New York at eleven in the evening. Presently the little captives began to scratch on their side of the box.

"Hello," said a nearby good-natured fellow passenger. "What have you got there?"

"Hush," I answered, putting my finger to my lips. I did not want to get thrown from the train. "Tomato plants."

"Ah, I thought so by the sound," he replied. "Well, for my sake, I hope they won't grow through the side of the box before morning."

When I arrived in New Hampshire, Mrs. Baynes joked we should name them Tomato and Basil, but in the end we named them Death and Dauntless, because of their dark colors and fearless natures. I never saw animals with such ravenous appetites and for the first time I fully appreciated the meaning of the saying "as hungry as a wolf."

As Death and Dauntless grew rapidly, the pair became unmanageable. I hated to wake my wife from a fine sleep to get her outside to chase escaped wolves, but I was forced to do it more than once. One night, we found the wolves in a neighbor's hog sty. Dauntless was chasing five or six pigs round and round at a pace much faster than they would have travelled for their health, while Death sat on his haunches and expectantly licked his chops. The wolves were about to win the game, when Mrs. Baynes and I stepped in to intervene. The wolves ran from us, sailed over the farther wall. They first ran through a flock of ducks, which scattered to the four winds of the night. The wolves were seeking an entrance to the henyard when the farmer and his sons joined the hunt.

From one part of the farm to another we went, until at last an idea occurred to me. After giving my companions brief instructions, I went into the barn and sent up my best imitation of the long-drawn howl of a timber wolf. Presently, the wolves came to investigate what other wolf had arrived, and Death and Dauntless were captured once more. Before I went to sleep that night, I had come to the conclusion that one full-grown wolf might be better than two, so I decided to keep Dauntless, and find another home for Death.

Dauntless was very lonesome without his brother and for months afterwards he howled at night, long and mournfully. The howl of a timber wolf comes from deep down—it is a half-human cry.

"A sorrowful sound indeed," Mrs. Baynes remarked regularly. She had not agreed with splitting up the pair, as troublesome as they were. Mrs. Baynes is so forgiving and tender-hearted, I believe she would have gotten up twice a month in zero-degree weather to chase the wolves around every hog sty on every farm in the county. It is a trait I always found admirable in my wife, as impractical as it could be at times.

28

※ ·-·※

"I'm so sorry to tell you," Ingrid said on the phone to everyone she'd been calling to invite to the funeral, to be held that coming Saturday, "Ralph was killed earlier this week." She kept saying it like that: *was killed,* instead of *died* or *passed away.*

"He was ninety-one," Emma tried to remind her mother. "And it was over so quick." She thought those things should be a comfort. They'd all had several good long cries about it, because they all loved Ralph, but *most* of the Starlings knew Ralph would have loved the way he died. A better story than the lovers who died in the Sunset Acres hot tub.

"Out with a bang," Auggie said, sniffing.

"It was a good death," Clive agreed, wiping his eyes with his sleeve, and Ingrid told them all to shut the hell up or she'd kill them too.

After the wrath of the deer, the caretaker's house was most certainly uninhabitable, and Ingrid was busy setting up the mansion for the wake and funeral, so the Starlings all moved temporarily into the Rodeway Inn, a clean and simple motel with red doors. Clive and Ingrid were in separate rooms; Ingrid said she couldn't stand to look at him, much less sleep in the same room. But she also only rented three rooms, she insisted she wasn't made of money, which meant Auggie and Emma were sharing a room. Truthfully, Ingrid wanted someone to keep an eye on Auggie. She was pretty sure there were drugs being done in some of the rooms at the inn. She didn't want him to be tempted.

Emma wasn't thrilled to be sharing a room with her brother, but she assumed they'd all move into the mansion after the memorial service. All those empty bedrooms, beds already made with perfect hospital corners. Everyone would have a little more space. She and Auggie could surely put up with breathing the same motel-room air for a few days.

But the night before the funeral, Auggie rolled over in his bed and faced his sister in the next double. "You really think it's good for Dad?" he asked. "To run around playing detective? Show everyone just how crazy he's gone?" Their dad had printed a fresh stack of posters at the Stop & Copy and he said he was planning to hand them out at Ralph's funeral, until Ingrid had gotten wind of it, and they'd all gone in the dumpster.

"Dr. Wheeler said it was fine," Emma said, defending herself, even though Dr. Wheeler hadn't exactly said that. He just said obsessive behavior was to be expected with their dad's condition. "And I just want to know if Crystal's okay. I don't see how that's a bad thing."

"You know, I was on the exact same shit as Crystal, GG. You never called."

"What? I called."

Auggie shook his head.

"You know I called. Mom told me what was going on, how you were." Emma had called her mom every Sunday, always hoping her mom wouldn't pick up. She'd always called, even when she was at her lowest point in Tessie Blatt's parents' pool house, wondering how easy it would be to drown yourself in an infinity pool. That phone call was her great performance every week, ten minutes of pretending she was totally fine.

"You know you can call the Phoenix House? Send letters, postcards, flowers? Stuffed animals?"

"The rehab center?"

"No. Disneyland."

"Jesus, Auggie. I had my own shit going on."

"Losing your magical charm, I know, what a tragedy."

"What the hell is your problem, Auggie? Seriously. Can you really hate me that much?"

"Probably."

Emma was about to cry, but she was trying hard not to. She didn't want to give her brother the satisfaction. "And what did you want me to do, Auggie? Come home every time you went back to rehab?"

"Nice, Emma. Very supportive."

"I don't get what you're so mad about. I'm just trying to help Dad find my old best friend."

Auggie snorted. "You should have at least called."

"Auggie," Emma snapped, full-on pissed now. "If I could get into my time travel machine, I would go back and call the Phoenix House. I would send a huge care package. I'm sorry about that, I really am."

"You should have called *her*," Auggie said.

"What? Who?"

"When Crystal's dad died. She was waiting for you to say you were on the first plane home, and you texted instead, something stupid about a strawberry daiquiri? She showed it to Mom. Crystal said you'd had some big dumb fight, but it shouldn't matter, because her father had *died suddenly*."

Emma's stomach sank. "Oh my God."

"Yup. Not the best way to treat your friend."

"But there wasn't a funeral."

"Who gives a fuck about a funeral? Don't you remember when Bart got into topiary and made you that shrub shaped like a big-ass hand? Or all the times he came to my football games? I don't think he missed one. Or blasting Jimmy Buffett from his stereo while he worked, just to drive Crystal crazy. Bart Nash was part of our family, and *you texted*."

"Oh my God," Emma said, again.

"Yup. *That's* why she hates you. Not because you quit your dumb society. Not because you went to college. Because you didn't come home when she needed you."

Emma was surprised Auggie had known about the Gentle Touch Society, but apparently her brother had paid a lot more attention than she'd ever given him credit for. And Emma could see how awful she had been. Auggie didn't need to hammer it home. She should have called. She should have gotten a ride to the airport right away. She should have asked her parents to bring her home. Her best friend's dad had died.

"Sorry, GG. You really didn't know, huh? I was never sure whether you didn't know or just didn't care."

"Why do you call me that?" she asked. She had a sudden feeling it didn't mean golden girl.

"You don't know?"

"No. I don't."

"Giant Grouper. Always thought you were too good for everyone here. Big fish in the small pond."

"I never thought I was too good for anyone."

"Oh, *come on,* Emma. Look around."

Emma's eyes filled up, and she turned away from her brother into her pillows. Auggie had been harsh, but she deserved it. She deserved every bit of it. Why hadn't her parents spoken up? Why hadn't Auggie said something before, if he'd always had all the answers? *Someone* should have said something. *Of all the other times her mom had tried to control her life!*

But Emma knew it was her fault. No one's fault but her own. You spend years thinking that you're the golden girl, and you find out that you're a giant grouper. A big ugly fish.

29

That Saturday at eleven A.M., Ralph Kelsey's funeral service was led by the director of assisted living at Sundown Acres, Tanya Harris. She had a soothing voice and made everyone feel like maybe Ralph was still with them, lurking somewhere above. Ingrid had said no Jesus stuff, because it was well known that Ralph Kelsey was an atheist, but Tanya Harris slipped a little in anyway.

Emma was going out of her way to be nice to her brother, saving him a seat and offering him a bottle of water as a peace offering. He took it and smiled a little at her, even if it was without teeth. They knew Ralph Kelsey would want them to get along.

The members of Blacker Sabbath were in attendance, or "had dared to show their ugly mugs," as Clive Starling muttered when he saw them. Dennis Hollingdrake wore a ratty brown suit and had shoulder-length hair, but Dennis was bald on top so he always wore a baseball hat, even at a funeral. "Why not bury the hatchet before you die," Harold nudged Clive. Clive said he'd do no such thing. He was mad at Dennis, so mad, but it sure would be nice if he could remember why.

Ingrid knew she wasn't up to the task of giving the eulogy; she didn't want to cry in front of everyone, so she'd asked the current CEO of the gun factory, Percy Eaklin, to do it instead. Percy had a '70s porn-star mustache, and he got up to the podium and made a quick speech about Ralph's legacy at the gun company, and all the jobs he'd provided for so many years to the town of Everton. "I'm going to have a Ralph Kelsey statue erected outside the factory," Percy Eaklin promised, and he paused for applause. When no one applauded, he said he envisioned it to be a working fountain, too, with the flow of water spouting from Ralph's rifle.

"What a weird gift," Ingrid said, accidentally into her microphone.

Percy had really missed the mark with his eulogy, but people were impressed by Percy Eaklin no matter what he did. His young daughter, Isabella, had died only a few months ago, after a long illness, and he still ran the gun factory, still organized charity events. He was still an active member of the community, when a lot of people were sure they would just lay down and quit breathing if their ten-year-old daughter died. His wife, Geraldine, had stopped coming out in public, which people could understand, she was in mourning. The Eaklins had sold their big old house in the center of town—too many happy memories, everyone figured—and had gone to live at their second home, the hunting cabin, which Percy used to use to get away from his family. You know you're really rich when you own two houses in the same town—something Ralph Kelsey and Percy Eaklin had in common.

After Percy's speech, there was a procession to Maple Street Cemetery, and Ralph Kelsey's body was put into the ground, his final resting place. The ground was frozen this time of year, and often bodies in New England will be kept on ice until spring thaw, but Ingrid had paid extra to have our groundskeeper, Ridley Willett, jackhammer through the frozen ground to dig the grave. She didn't want her precious Ralph to be kept in any kind of limbo. Ridley was a little peeved that Ingrid didn't seem to appreciate how hard it is to use a jackhammer with only one arm, but he'd gotten the job done.

Once Ralph was buried, Ingrid stayed by his grave for a long time. She left her pocket revolver behind, in the spot where his tombstone would go when it got back from the engraver. Ralph

had given the revolver to her, but Ingrid had no use for guns anymore. We squealed when Ingrid put it down. We'd never had a
gun left in the cemetery. Flowers, sure, and sometimes food, which
was a horrible idea, since we couldn't eat it, and sometimes the
squirrels would die from toxicity. Candles were everywhere, as
well as laminated pictures of Jesus or Mary or various saints.
Once, we'd gotten a Monopoly game, since Jesse Peters (b. 1984–
d. 2013) had loved to play as a kid and again, later, in rehab. We
loved any objects left in the graveyard, really, even the food, because they felt like offerings to the dead. Acknowledgment we
might still be around, watching the living, protecting them. More
people used to believe in that kind of thing. Leanne Hatfield is the
only person in the entire town who regularly leaves anything in
the graveyard, all those plastic frogs stacked on her friend Izzy's
headstone.

When Ralph Kelsey (b. 1923–d. 2014) arrived at Maple Street,
he would not stop laughing, which isn't unusual, people often
showing up still doing the last thing they were doing when they
were alive. It takes them a few days to settle down. It's awkward
when people die in the middle of coitus, and they show up to
Maple Street thrusting, like Ben Laurasseta (b.1929–d. 2014) had
done recently after the heart attack in the hot tub. The thrusting
of the spirit does no good, even though we do our best to hold on
to our human shapes. The pleasure of life is gone.

During the reception back at the mansion, all Ralph's friends in
Everton mingled, feeling a little more social and celebratory than
they had when the coffin was in sight. They were now cracking
jokes and smiling, pouring drinks, marveling at the mansion
where Ralph had once lived and wondering who would get all his
money now. The process of moving on was under way.

Ralph was the last of a long line of Kelseys, so most of his millions were going into the Ralph Kelsey Historical Trust, which
Ingrid would oversee, using funds to preserve Everton's history.
Ingrid could start a Corbin House museum if she wanted to, but
the Starlings weren't suddenly rich. Ralph had left them each only
a very modest sum. He did leave Ingrid the deed to the caretaker's
house, so the Starlings finally owned their own home, damaged as
it was. The mansion still belonged to the trust; it would be Ingrid's job to make sure it was preserved.

Emma wanted to do the rounds and ask about Crystal Nash,
talk to anyone she hadn't already asked, but somehow she got
stuck in one corner of the trophy room, talking to Patty Gutterfield about how her healing touch didn't work anymore, and no,
she wasn't sure why, and yes, it was too bad that Patty's shingles
had come back again. Finally, Mack Durkee sauntered in, holding
a beer in one hand and a plate of egg salad sandwiches and cookies in the other, looking every bit like her knight in shining armor.
Patty Gutterfield walked away, leaving the young people to talk.

"Hey," he said. "I'm sorry about Ralph."

"Thanks. I know he really liked you."

"I was hoping to ask for his blessing," Mack said, putting his
plate and his beer down on the table next to the stuffed boar, and
got down on one knee. Emma's eyes bulged. "Emma Starling, will
you . . . go to dinner with me?"

Emma laughed. "Now?"

"We're at a funeral right now, Emma." Mack stood up and
brushed off his pants. "Please be respectful."

Emma was gleeful, and Ralph would have been happy that
these crazy kids were flirting at his funeral. Ralph had always
been up for a love story. "Where would we go?" Emma asked, as
if there weren't three perfectly good restaurants in Everton.

"Anywhere you like." Mack raised his brown bottle of Budweiser to his lips, and Emma watched him do it, but that's when she heard screaming. It was her mother railing at her father, the noise coming from outside.

"Oh, she did crack under the pressure after all," Mack said.

Emma was surprised at how well Mack knew her mother. She rushed out to mediate, to keep her mother from humiliating herself in front of the entire town, and spotted a man climbing into a UPS truck to make his getaway. Ingrid picked up a rock and hurled it at the truck. It bounced off the side, probably making a dent. Ingrid's hair had come out of its bun, her black silk blouse untucked from her dress pants, her lipstick smudged. Not so stylish now.

"Ingrid, this is not what I had planned," Clive said.

"What the hell was your plan then? To ruin every single part of my life before you die? To bankrupt us?"

"You're getting some of Ralph's money. We all are."

"You monster. You unbelievable gremlin of a man."

"What's going on?" Emma asked. A crowd had gathered on the porch.

"From Russia, with love," Ingrid said, pointing to the beige dog crate in the driveway. Inside the crate, a little Pomeranian was chewing at the bars.

Nope, not a Pomeranian. A fox.

"Your father spent twenty thousand dollars on a pet fox."

"Eighteen thousand," Clive corrected. He remembered now. He remembered some of it now. That morning with Harold at the computer. *Click, click, click, Buy Now.* How he'd tried to undo it a few days later, but trying to write an email in Russian had gotten confusing, and his daughter had refused to help him.

"How could you make even Ralph's funeral all about you?" Ingrid asked. "You selfish man. Just another episode of *The Clive Show.*"

"I'm dying too," Clive said, and Ingrid let out what sounded like a growl from a nonhuman creature, which made the fox go nuts at the crate's bars.

"I still don't understand," Emma said. "How did Dad buy a fox?"

Ingrid handed Emma the pamphlet from Kompaniya po Prodazhe Lisits, the company for the sale of foxes. And a receipt with her father's name on it. *Eighteen thousand dollars.* It was dated before she was declared guardian, Emma noticed, which was something of a relief. It hadn't been her failure. All of her father's credit cards were safely tucked in her wallet.

"You're going to have to get him out of my house," Ingrid said. "I cannot be around that man anymore." Ingrid Starling did not see the fox as one last fun present from her dying husband. She saw it as a big mistake, a symptom of a ravaging brain disease, and the absolute last straw in what had been a tough couple of years.

"Mom, come on. That's not fair."

"I need you to take him away from me."

"He's sick."

"I can't do it anymore. Waiting around for someone to die. It's your brother all over again." Ingrid had been so worried her son, her little boy, her baby, was going to die of an overdose, and her husband had done almost nothing to help, had gone around gadding with Professor Sabrina Berkman. "I'm moving in with Gary," she said. "Emma, you take care of him. I'm done."

"Mom," Auggie said, from the crowd on the porch. Some people had gone back inside, uncomfortable. The fox threw itself against the bars. Dr. Wheeler was standing outside the front door of the mansion, a few feet from Auggie. Emma did not know his first name, but it must be Gary.

"You're punishing Dad now?" Emma asked. "Kind of a shitty time, Mom. It's too late."

"Oh, you've been punishing your father for years. He was

dying then too. We're all dying. I'm dying this minute. And I'm going to go stay with Gary for a while. I'm taking a break."

"Mom," Emma pleaded. "Don't run from this." Emma didn't want to get stuck being guardian forever. This was all only temporary. This was really her mother's job.

"It's too much, Emma. I can only take so much."

"I can live in the mansion?" Auggie asked. "While you're off with the good doctor?"

"Absolutely not," Ingrid said. "I won't have you leaving your dirty dishes everywhere. Your filthy clothes. No one is staying in the mansion. It's a place of historical significance."

"And what am I going to do?" Auggie asked. "Where am I going to live?"

"August, you're an adult. Figure it out." This surprised us, that Ingrid would throw her baby bird from the nest.

"You can come with us," Emma said to her brother, although she didn't know where they were going to live either, but she wanted to show she was doing her best, she was trying to help her family, she was not such an ugly fish. And she knew their mom would come to her senses soon. It was only temporary. Emma had her father's credit cards in her wallet; they'd be fine. They could keep renting the rooms at the Rodeway Inn; the motel allowed pets. "And we're taking the dog," Emma said, because she knew that would hurt her mother.

"Take everyone," Ingrid said. "Take the dog, take the fox, take the deer, take the whole forest."

"She's lost it," Eunice Vandervoss said from the porch, and several people murmured in agreement.

"Show's over," Ingrid said, turning to the crowd. "Funeral's over. Time to leave. Be gone. Skedaddle." Dr. Wheeler started helping her shoo people out the door and off the porch, off the lawn, into their cars.

"He sure is obedient," Auggie said about Dr. Gary Wheeler.

"You can all stay in Ralph's hunting cabin," Ingrid said, after most people had left. She tossed Emma the keys. "It'll be good for you both, having some time alone with your father."

"Screw you, Mom," Auggie said. "Screw you and your dumb doctor boyfriend."

Emma agreed with her brother for once, but she was also glad for the gift of the hunting cabin, a better idea than the Rodeway Inn. It was only five miles north, at the edge of Everton, and it was free. The conversation turned businesslike then; Ingrid said the kids could take both the Subaru and the truck, because the truck wasn't always reliable, as old as it was. She said Dr. Gary Wheeler could drive her to work; the hospital was near the college.

Clive was ignoring the logistics of who was living where, and he let the fox out of its crate. "A male fox," he reported from the paperwork. "He'll need a strong Russian name." Clive didn't care that his wife was mad at him, Ingrid had thrown plenty of fits before. She'd never left him for another man, but Clive didn't completely understand what was going on. What he did understand was that he and Ernest Harold Baynes had mail-ordered a fox. And the fox had arrived, and he was glorious.

"Isn't he something?" Harold asked.

"He's really something," Clive agreed. The fox cooed.

After her mother drove off in Gary Wheeler's Prius, Emma walked over to where her father lay on the ground, wearing his red parka over his good funeral suit. The fox rolled over and offered his white belly; Emma reached down to pet him; he was as soft as a kitten. She knew what her roommates in L.A. would say about this, how it was cruel, or inhumane, disgustingly selfish and entitled, and a big part of Emma felt that way, too, that wild animals are meant to be left wild. The other part of her felt a pure childish delight at the idea of a fox as a pet, who smiled and chuckled and wagged his big brush tail at her touch.

30

At Maple Street, when Ralph Kelsey (b. 1923–d. 2014) finally stopped laughing, the remnants of his final earthly moments fading, he took to kissing his wife, Marilyn Boyd Kelsey (b. 1923–d. 1997), with nearly as much passion as the couple had as teenagers, although we could tell that Marilyn was faking it. She had liked it better when Ralph was still alive, because it had tied her closer to her own life. While they kissed, Absalom Kelsey (b. 1745–d. 1837) began to read his distant descendant the long list of Graveyard Rules, starting with the first rule, No Meddling in the Affairs of the Living, and the gravity of its consequence: if you meddle too much, your spirit can explode. "The second rule," Absalom continued, "details the Importance of Caring for the People of Everton . . ."

Ralph Kelsey took a break from kissing Marilyn to interrupt Absalom. "But where do you go when your spirit explodes? There's something after this?"

"No one knows."

"So, it might be a much better place?"

We were all a little insulted. Marilyn Boyd Kelsey especially.

"There might be eternal nothingness after this," Old Abe clarified. He gestured around him to the gaps in the hill, where gravestones had been returned to mere rocks. No soul perched above.

"Meddling might still be worth it, if it could help out your family," Ralph Kelsey said, musing. He had long been prepared for nothingness after death. He wasn't afraid of it.

"It's harder than you think, to meddle," Sara Ford (b. 1986–d. 2012) said, pointing out something we rarely like to admit. How little danger there is of meddling, when it's so difficult to get anyone to listen to us. At the moment, Harold Baynes was the only one with a real chance of meddling, the only one in a haunting position, the only one with the attention of the living. We'd hoped to finally talk to Harold when he came to Ralph's interment at Maple Street, give him some advice, but he'd stayed behind at the mansion, waiting for the after-funeral party to start. We loathe the cremated sometimes, how freewheeling they can be. A terribly cheap imitation of the living.

31

Ingrid had banished her family to the far reaches of our town, to Ralph Kelsey's old hunting cabin. It was not on the same property as the Corbin Mansion, and there was nothing moneyed about it. It was at the very north edge of Everton, just within our sight, and down a long dirt road into the woods. The kitchen in the cabin had a sticky white tile floor, an electric stove, a few copper pans hanging above, a table to sit at that was covered in a plastic tarp to protect from dust and bugs. When she looked, Emma found nothing in the cabinets, except for a can of roach killer. The living room was wall-to-wall with an awful mustard yellow carpet, a small couch that faced a fireplace, and a boxy television. There were bunk beds in the bedroom—two beds, with four bunks—and then a little bathroom, with only a toilet and a shower. The only sink was in the kitchen. The windows were small, so it was pretty dark in there, even in the daytime, and felt darker because of the wood paneling. Emma did not want to live there for long.

"Paradise," Clive said. "Isn't it?"

"I guess," Auggie said. "That TV looks pretty ancient."

"Harold agrees that it's paradise," Clive said, and then he bent and released the fox from his crate into the cabin as the 120-pound dog cowered in the corner. The fox weighed fifteen pounds, according to the manual from the company for the sale of foxes, which Emma had flipped through. U.S. Customs had let the fox in, so Emma guessed that the whole exchange was legal enough.

Emma had read somewhere once that people often hide drugs in shipments of exotic animals; no one wants to open a crate full of rattlesnakes to search for cocaine.

"What should we name him?" Auggie asked.

"I've already named him," Clive said. "It's Rasputin."

"How about Tails? Or Big Red?"

"Nope. Has to be Rasputin."

"Why does his name *have* to be Rasputin? Most people have never read *War and Peace*."

"Rasputin didn't write *War and Peace*," Clive said, looking disappointed at his son. "He was a Russian monk who had magic healing powers, and he was a sexual deviant."

"Oh."

"And he rose from the dead. Amazing guy."

The fox cooed and clicked. "How long do foxes live?" Auggie asked.

"Fourteen years in captivity," Emma said. "Twoish years in the wild. It said in the manual."

"Long time," Clive said.

"Ouch." Rasputin was nipping at Auggie's fingers.

No species can become completely domesticated in the span of sixty years, the pamphlet of instructions from Russia said. *Your fox will still have days of wild animal. Do not expect a fox to be as tame and predictable as a dog.*

Moses growled whenever Rasputin got too close to his corner of the cabin. Emma wished that she had named the big white dog something else, any other name—Rover or Koda or Thor, or maybe after some other Biblical figure, one not quite so well known for his powers of prophetic sight.

That night, Emma lay in her top bunk, giving Auggie and her dad the two bottom bunks. She was sweaty with anxiety, or maybe just from the heat. Even though it was seventeen degrees outside, it was a hot little sauna in the bunkroom, the place too small for three grown-ups and one large dog, everyone breathing in there at once, plus the radiator heat seemed impossible to regulate. Emma envied the fox, his own quiet crate out in the living room.

In the morning, the fox jumped up on the table and peed in Emma's coffee cup, but otherwise, the first twelve hours in the cabin went fine. The fox had dry cat food for breakfast, what the manual had said to feed him. Clive scolded Emma for getting the cheap Meow Mix at the Shaw's; he said he'd have to go to the pet store to get the good stuff.

"*I* wanted to go to the pet shop," Auggie said, because he had gone grocery shopping with Emma the day before. "I wanted to get the fox some toys."

"I'm going to make sure Auggie's in charge of my feeding tube," Clive said. "Emma will get the cheapest brand of mush."

Which really wasn't funny, Emma thought, since she *was in fact* in charge of her dad's feeding tube, should he ever need one. Still, she gave her dad and Auggie some cash for the expensive cat chow, and they came back from the pet store with about a dozen neon-colored feather toys, much to the fox's immense delight.

Da, da, da, Rasputin thought, when presented with the toys. He was excited by the training the Americans were putting him through. It was immediately obvious to the fox they would be training him to hunt and kill small birds, a skill which comes naturally to a fox. Much easier than what the Russian scientists had wanted, teaching him how to cuddle, how not to bite.

32

On Monday morning, on her new route to work from Ralph's cabin to Dream Far Elementary, Emma had to drive past Upper Valley High. She scanned for Mack's Jeep in the faculty lot, but it wasn't there yet. So Emma had a real crush. She planned to text Mack later, accept his invitation to dinner. A dinner date would be an excellent excuse to get out of the cabin for a night; Auggie could watch their father.

At school, Emma learned it was Olivia's birthday, and birthdays are a big deal to fifth graders. Olivia had brought in cupcakes for the entire class, yellow frosted ones that looked like roses, because she said that yellow roses mean friendship. Michael B. was allergic to all sorts of things, even cupcakes that were a symbol of friendship, but he said he kept a bag of quarters in his cubby for occasions like this. Ms. Wish used to let him buy something from the vending machine in the teacher's lounge so that he wouldn't be left out.

"Ms. Wish thought of everything, didn't she?" Emma said, the resentment coming through a bit too much. The kids didn't notice, except for Leanne Hatfield, who rolled her eyes. Leanne rolled her eyes every time Ms. Wish was mentioned.

Michael B. went to his cubby to get his quarters, and that's when Emma saw it: the shoebox. It was right there, still in his cubby, all these days later. "Is the dead bird still in that box?" Emma asked, trying not to panic. "Can you please bring it over to me? Michael. Bring it to me. Right. Now." She could not let an animal continue to decay in their classroom. That would be a failure. Not a C-average teaching job, but a *real failure.*

"No, she's gone," Michael B. said. "She escaped." He picked up the shoebox and showed Emma a ragged bird-sized hole in the cardboard. There was one single downy feather left in the box.

"Oh," Emma said. *What the fuck,* she thought.

"You're magical," Olivia said.

"I don't think a sparrow could chew through cardboard like that," Emma said. *It must have been mice,* she thought to herself, but she didn't want to say that to the kids, some of them were afraid of mice. But it had to be mice. They chewed through the box and then dragged the sparrow carcass back to their little hidey-hole in the wall. Mice will eat anything, won't they? Or maybe a rat?

"We saw the sparrow on a tree out on the playground," Michael B. claimed. "It came back to life."

"Yup, we did," Olivia said, and all the rest of the kids nodded. Even Leanne Hatfield nodded, a girl who had probably never bothered to leave cookies for Santa.

"How did you know it was the same sparrow?" Emma asked. "Sparrows all look the same."

"It was definitely her," Zoe F. said, and then everyone else agreed. It was definitely that same sparrow. "We tied a piece of red string to her leg," Zoe F. explained. "We told you it was an experiment."

"We didn't want to tell you," Tobey L. said.

"Why?" Emma asked.

"Because. You'd quit. Leanne said you'd quit."

Emma looked around the classroom, eight faces, eight open mouths with baby teeth still to lose, sixteen wide eyes. She was so touched. They cared if she stayed. She had barely taught them anything at all, and they still wanted her to stay. "Why would you think I'd quit?" she asked.

"It's a matter of time," Leanne Hatfield said.

"My mom said she would quit motherhood if she could," Michael B. said.

"If you're a healer again, you'll go to med school," Adam D. said.

"I'm going to stay," Emma told the children. "I don't want to go to med school."

"Oh," the kids said.

"You'll stay all the way until June?" Ulf asked.

"Yes," Emma said, because what else was she going to do.

"June is a long time from now," Olivia pointed out. "It's December. It's my birthday."

"We know it's your birthday," Leanne Hatfield muttered.

"You'll stay until after the trial," Nicole P. said, and it was a statement, not a question. And then several of the students started to cry. Tobey L. held up an article from that morning's newspaper. He had clipped it out. Tobey L. wanted to be a journalist, even though the profession barely existed anymore. The headline read: WISH TRIAL PUSHED BACK AGAIN.

"You read the newspaper?" Emma asked.

"Don't insult us," Leanne Hatfield said.

"Ms. Wish *is* coming back, right?" Ulf asked.

"I don't know, I'm sorry. She might, but I can't promise."

"We just want to know when our teacher is coming back," Olivia said, tears in her eyes. "We love her."

Emma thought about what Mack had said the late night in the mansion. *Make sure to let the children know you respect them,* he said. *Respect and trust.* Principal Jefferies had warned her against telling the truth to the kids, but she trusted Mack more than she trusted dumb Principal Jefferies. "Would it help if I let you talk about the trial?" she asked the kids.

They all nodded eagerly and formed a semicircle on the carpet. The fifth graders loved to sit in semicircles on the carpet; it was hard to keep them at their desks. Tobey L. handed her the article, asked her to explain some of it. There were problems with jury selection, and that might take a while. The fifth graders were anxious for it to get going; they wanted justice for Ms. Wish, and Emma wasn't sure if that meant putting her husband away or setting him free. Olivia wanted to know if Mr. Wish would get hanged if he was guilty, and if Ms. Wish would have to watch.

"Of course not, idiot, he'll just go to jail," Leanne Hatfield said, and Emma made Leanne apologize to poor Olivia.

"Why do people take heroin if it's poison?" the children asked next. "How many people has Mr. Wish killed? Will Ms. Wish ever come back to teach? If I see Ms. Wish in the supermarket, should I hug her? Or should I leave her alone like my mom says?"

Emma did the best she could with these questions. She knew from the school files that Michael B.'s dad had died from an overdose, so she had to be careful what she said, not to put her foot in it. She told them about her friend Crystal and her brother, Auggie. She said it wasn't *always* a sad ending, but that the kids should never take up the habit. She said maybe she could have her brother Auggie come in sometime and talk to them. "A survivor and an inspiration," she called him, even if that didn't sum up Auggie at all. He had let that stupid football injury derail his life. She knew the addiction wasn't his fault, but then again, she blamed him for it anyway. She felt bad about that, so she forced herself to say something nice: "He used to be really good at the piano. His teacher always said he could be a conductor on Broadway, if the NFL didn't work out." Maybe that was *too nice,* Emma thought. She knew her brother was back at the cabin, trying to get the PlayStation hooked up to the ancient TV.

"Do you think your brother would want to direct the winter musical at the community theater?" Leanne Hatfield asked, perking up. "We really need a director if the show is going to go on, and it would be *great* if he could play the piano."

Emma remembered that Sid Wish had been the previous director of the community theater. "Maybe," Emma said, even though she felt she knew pretty well that Auggie's pianist days were behind him. "What's the show?"

"*Titanic the Musical!*" Leanne said. "It's a huge cast, so we need everyone to sign up. A lot of bodies. Everyone gets a part. It doesn't matter if you suck at singing." She looked straight at a few of her classmates, so that they got the message that they did, in fact, suck at singing. "Can I have his number?" Leanne asked, pulling out her phone. Not all the kids had phones, but Leanne Hatfield did.

It might have been crazy, but Emma wrote her brother's number on the whiteboard.

"Thank you, Ms. Starling. I'll call him today."

"Don't tell him I gave it to you," Emma said, backtracking. "He might not say yes if he knows it's my idea. Tell him you heard from someone in town how good he is at piano. Say an old lady recommended him." Eunice Vandervoss, one of the Enraged Old Bags, had been Auggie's first piano teacher. Some of the fifth graders nodded; they understood sibling rivalry. Then they asked what happened with Crystal Nash, the other drug user. Emma said that was a story for another time.

"She's missing," Adam D. said. "Haven't you seen her name on those posters?"

"Your friend is the kidnapped woman?" Olivia asked.

"She wasn't kidnapped," Emma said. "She's just missing."

"A serial killer got her," Leanne Hatfield said. "That's what my grandfather thinks."

"There are barely any serial killers left," Tobey L. said, and Leanne gave Tobey a dirty look. "What?" he said. "They would be in the news." Tobey L.'s mom had recently gotten him a *New York Times* subscription for his birthday, because Tobey L. said he wanted the paper delivered to the doorstep every day, "just like in olden times." The *Upper Valley News* only came once a week, on Wednesdays, and the rest of the week the articles were only published online.

"I think Tobey L. is partially right," Emma said. "DNA evidence makes it much harder to be a serial killer than it used to be." *You should not be having this conversation with your students,* a little voice in her head said, but she ignored it. She had just gone over the different classes of drugs.

"There's definitely still serial killers," Leanne said. "My grandfather says there definitely still are." Leanne Hatfield's grandfather remembered the 1980s, when Everton was visited by the River Valley Killer. The man had murdered at least three women, and their bodies were found in a wooded area off Unity Road. "My grandfather says serial killers nowadays just kill people no one checks up on. People who are invisible."

"Invisible people? You mean ghosts?" Olivia asked.

"No, stupid. Like women of the night."

"What's a woman of the night?" Ulf asked.

"Is that like Batman?" Tobey L. wanted to know.

"All right, all right, Leanne, that's enough," Emma said, recognizing that things had definitely gone too far.

But Leanne Hatfield wasn't done. She was trying to prove a point, and Leanne Hatfield liked to be right. She liked being right better than anything else in the world. "That's what my grandfather says, every single time he sees the posters everywhere. He says that woman was on drugs that made her invisible, so no one cared when some guy picked her up off the side of the road and murdered her."

"There's a drug that makes you invisible?" Tobey L. asked. He liked superheroes almost as much as he liked *The New York Times.*

Tears filled Emma's eyes. It was sudden. Like she'd been hit on the back of the head. It took her by surprise, to hear that no one cared about Crystal. She cared about Crystal. She had never stopped. She had made a mistake not calling home, not coming home when Bart died, but Emma had always cared about her friend.

"Look what you did," Michael B. said. "You made our teacher cry. Who's a psycho now?" Leanne Hatfield was always accusing Michael B. of being a psycho.

Ulf and Michael B. both started chanting, *"Psycho, psycho, psycho,"* at Leanne, which Emma should have put an immediate stop to, but she also had to stop crying first.

Emma had to step out in the hall, where she couldn't hear the chanting, so she could pretend it wasn't happening. If Principal Jefferies stopped by, she could play dumb. Emma knew that Leanne Hatfield was right, sort of. Even if what happened to Crystal likely wasn't *serial-killer bad,* whatever had really happened probably wasn't good. There also wasn't anything Emma could do about it right now. She took some deep breaths before she went back into the classroom and scolded the boys for name-calling and bullying. She wasn't a completely terrible teacher. She just needed one single sole minute to collect herself.

33

On her drive back to the cabin, Emma considered it: she most likely hadn't healed the dead sparrow, but—what if she had? What if the Charm was back, and better than ever? By the time she pulled up to the cabin, she had steeled herself to try it. She didn't care if it made all her father's beautiful moon-white hair fall out, or even his teeth disroot. She couldn't be afraid of what might happen. Not if it might save him.

Her brother and her father were inside playing videogames, Auggie had gotten the PlayStation hooked up, was teaching their dad to play *Call of Duty*. Emma stood in front of their screen, and Auggie protested until he saw what she was doing. She put both her hands on her father's face. She concentrated on the transfer of energy. Her dad didn't move, didn't talk for once. She waited for the buzz in her ears, the heat in her hands. She waited to feel something happen in her father, the illness to retreat.

When she let go, her palms were wet with his tears. "Thank you, Emma," he said, and then he stood up and said he was going to go for a walk.

"I'm sorry, Dad," Emma said. They both knew it hadn't worked.

"Don't be. I just need some fresh air." The dog and the fox both followed him out the door, and Emma collapsed into the couch, feeling drained and defeated.

"Worth a shot," Auggie said.

"Yeah."

They were silent for a minute. "Hey, guess what," Auggie said.

"What?" Emma snapped. She was exhausted. She didn't need Auggie to pile on.

But it was good news: Leanne Hatfield had already called and offered Auggie the job as community theater director, and Auggie was going to do it. Emma pretended to be surprised, although her surprise was genuine that he wanted the job. "Actually," Auggie continued, excited. "I got two phone calls today, both offering me jobs."

"What? Who called?"

"Percy Eaklin is throwing an anti-drug youth banquet, and he wants to pay me a bunch of cash to give the keynote. I guess someone at the gun factory told him I was an inspirational speaker? I thought it was a joke, but I guess not."

"Oh," Emma said, and then a little smile spread on her face. It didn't take her long to figure out how it had all happened: Tobey L.'s dad worked at the gun factory, and Tobey must have told his dad about the school day, how his teacher's brother was a recovering heroin addict and an inspiration. Mr. Lee must have known his boss was looking for a keynote speaker for the big benefit, and so he passed Auggie's info along to Percy Eaklin, looking for some brownie points with his boss. Tobey had Auggie's phone number handy to give to his dad, because Leanne Hatfield had asked for it, Emma had written it on the whiteboard, and Tobey Lee, future journalist, kept perfect notes.

34

According to Clive's watch, it was eight A.M., later than he usually slept. His back was killing him; bunk beds are never good to people with chronic back pain. There was Ernest Harold Baynes, sitting at the end of his bunk, but Clive recognized little else about his surroundings. Clive and his kids had been in the cabin for almost a full week, but every morning, this was all new to him. It was new to him again that morning.

As he got up, he pieced it together: he was at Ralph Kelsey's hunting cabin; he'd been there with Ralph a few times before. He learned that his kids were in the cabin with him; their belongings were everywhere, and yes, look, Auggie was still asleep in that bunk, and their dog had come, too, this sweet white dog at his feet. *Moses,* his collar said. But there was no sign of his wife. He was not heartbroken about her absence, because he could not remember that Ingrid was off having an affair with Gary Wheeler. There were useful things about these periods of forgetting. Clive *could* remember most things eventually, if you jogged his memory, gave him a little extra information, the right information, but his kids weren't mentioning where their mother was, so Clive didn't remember.

Clive put his bathrobe on over his pajamas and headed out of the bunkroom to Ralph's small kitchen. He made a full pot of coffee as usual because he didn't know how to make a half pot. He couldn't remember if Auggie drank coffee, and he couldn't ask; Auggie was still asleep. Clive remembered Emma was a coffee-drinker, but he could also remember she wasn't in the bunk room because she was off teaching; she had to get up so early to teach at the elementary level. If she needed coffee, she would have to drink the rocket fuel in the teacher's lounge.

And Clive didn't know this, but across town, at that very moment, his wife was drinking a lukewarm, watery coffee from Dr. Wheeler's Keurig machine. Ingrid missed Clive most in the mornings. Their morning rituals. He would have the coffee made, she would read the newspaper, and he would wait patiently until she was ready to chat with him. Then the floodgates would open. Clive always had so much to say, and sometimes he would read her the Poem of the Day that came to his email, and he would go on and on about whether it was an excellent poem or a very bad one. But Clive could be a good listener too. Ingrid would complain about the kids. She'd admitted once that their shortcomings were maybe her fault, putting so much pressure on them, but Clive assured her she'd been the best mom possible, given the circumstances. Given who she'd procreated with, he said, she'd done a bang-up job. Those conversations, those rituals, were the kinds of things that make up a life. The things Ingrid was missing now.

But Clive didn't remember where his wife had gone, so he didn't pick up the phone while she was feeling lonely over her morning coffee. "Is today the day?" he asked Harold after his fourth cup. The pot seemed endless.

"What day?" Harold replied.

"The day I die."

"I don't think so," Harold said. "Unless you take some drastic measures."

"Right." Clive nodded.

Harold reminded Clive that there was a fox in the living room, locked in his crate, and a domesticated fox is an animal that needs a lot of human interaction and attention, or it will start destroying things. "So, we'll play with the fox then," Clive agreed, and he shuffled into the living room, the dog behind him, an enormous white shadow. There was a name tag on the crate that said *Rasputin*. The name tag was from Principal Jefferies's office, Emma had slapped it there so her dad would stop musing about what to name the animal, which he'd done for several days in a row, only to always settle on Rasputin.

"Where did you come from?" Clive asked the fox as it purred in his lap. "I found you in the woods?"

"Yes," Ernest Harold Baynes confirmed. "We trapped him together." Even Harold lied to Clive sometimes. It was easier than explaining everything from the beginning.

Rasputin rolled over for a belly scratch. The fox made all kinds of noises, purrs and coos and clicks, and Clive felt very, very lucky to have caught this fox. He wondered if Ingrid would set the fox free when he died, or if she would keep him. *Oh right*, he remembered, his wife was mad at him. *What for?* He wondered.

"Perhaps you should apologize to your wife," Harold said. "She didn't like the fox as much as I thought she would."

"I trapped the fox as a present for Ingrid?"

"Yes." Harold sighed. "We thought she would like a fox."

"Hmm. I would have thought she would have preferred a dog."

"She already had a dog."

"Never stopped her before," Clive said. Ingrid had once brought home three dogs from the Humane Society. "Well, I like this fox, very, very much," Clive admitted, as the fox purred and clicked. "Rasputin, you said his name was? It's a perfect name."

"Indeed." Harold was noticeably bored, having this conversation about the fox's name yet again. He walked over and flipped on the TV. Thanks to Ralph's premium cable package, the hunting cabin had about a million channels, even if the television set was an older one.

"We trapped him in Corbin Park?" Clive asked.

Harold's face lit up, and he snapped his attention away from the television screen. "Yes," he said. "Yes."

"You know, it's so strange, but I don't remember trapping him."

"That's not that strange."

"What's it like inside the park? I've always wanted to see inside. A secret forest. It has to be a special place."

"I could show you," Harold said. "If you want."

"Corbin Park?" Clive asked, and Harold nodded. Clive would have liked to see Corbin Park, but he was also a recently retired poetry professor, and he understood that a secret forest was an obvious metaphor for death, something his college students could have come up with. When Clive was ready to die, Harold would take him to Corbin Park, and there Clive would finally meet the ghost of The Sprite, Harold's pet fox that Clive had only seen once at the edge of the woods. The Sprite was the Grim Reaper in this metaphor. "I'm not ready yet," Clive decided. "Maybe once the snow melts."

"Okay," Harold agreed, deflating into the brown tweed couch. A show called *Celebrity Psychic Medium* came on, a program where the host communicated with the dead loved ones of celebrities.

"What's this trash?" Clive asked, and he sat down to watch.

The celebrity psychic medium, an anemic-looking blond man, was helping solve a crime that had never been solved. In this episode, a pop star's long-missing uncle and former manager was found buried in the foundation of her pool. "Wow, did you see that?" Clive asked Harold. "That was nearly the perfect murder."

And that was what led Clive straight to the computer. It was what made him look up the string of words: "Psychic Medium Upper Valley New Hampshire Real." Clive clicked on the first link that came up, and the website said the woman was no longer local, but she took clients from all over the world over the phone. Clive went to fetch a credit card, only to find his wallet almost empty, save ten dollars in cash. His daughter had his credit cards, he had forgotten that was the dynamic now. Parent had become child. Clive would have to remember to ask Emma for a credit card. Sessions started at $199.99 for forty minutes, the website said, and Clive knew it would be money well spent. Because he was sure that this woman he found online, Barbara Anne Lavoy, four and a half stars on RateMyPsychic.com, could help him find Crystal Nash, missing person, twenty-three, nearsighted, five-foot-seven, not a natural blonde, gone for nearly six months. Through all his forgetting, Clive Starling had not forgotten about her.

35

"No, no, no, Dad, no, you may not spend your money on a telephone psychic," Emma said on Friday, the last day of teaching before her much-needed winter break began. The fox had gotten everyone up early with a series of horrible screeching noises, and Clive asked about the credit card at the breakfast table. "No, Dad. I want to find Crystal, too, but you just spent twenty thousand dollars on a pet fox."

"Eighteen," Clive corrected her. For some reason, he could always remember the exact amount. "I need to speak to a psychic. She's reputable, I'll show you the reviews. We need to find Crystal. We need to know what happened to her."

"Crystal's dead," Auggie said, his eyes bleary.

"You don't know that," Emma and Clive said at the same time. Auggie hated times like that. When his sister and his dad were so closely aligned.

"You don't have to be so horrible, Auggie," Emma said. "You really don't."

"Sorry, GG, I didn't mean to be horrible. I just think it's the realistic conclusion. I'm glad you've looked for her, but maybe it's time to call it quits."

"We'll quit when *I'm* dead," Clive said.

Auggie tapped his wrist. "Should be any minute now."

Clive laughed, and slapped the table.

"I'm going to work," Emma said.

"Me too." Auggie had started work at the theater. The rehearsals were at night, but Auggie also had to build the entire *Titanic* set. Their dad would be spending his days alone, with only the fox and the dog. Emma figured he couldn't get in too much trouble, she would have the truck, Auggie had the Subaru, and his motorcycle was back at the Corbin caretaker's house, safe in the garage. He could watch all the TV he wanted, he had the fox and dog for company, and she'd bought him a new bird feeder and hung it up outside the cabin. He could feed the birds.

As she drove off to Dream Far Elementary, we hoped Emma would come around on the psychic, especially this particular one. Licensed medium Barbara Anne Lavoy used to live right here in Everton, and once, years ago, when an old woman escaped from Sundown Acres, all Barbara Anne Lavoy had to do was see the photo and smell the missing woman's dirty blouse, and she immediately knew that Nana Hubert was near water, and that the old woman couldn't see. Volunteers found poor Nana on the bank of Sugar River, her eye poked out by a tree branch, but otherwise unharmed. After the story made the national news, Barbara Anne Lavoy packed up and left town for Phoenix, where she claimed the pay for psychics is much better. Even though she'd left town, we thought she could help here, if Emma would only pony up the Visa.

It was the last day before winter break, and Principal Jefferies had the gall to tell Emma that there would be a new boy in her class that day. The children were multiplying, growing in power, just when she'd learned all their names and could rattle them off at a quick pace. Some of the children were more memorable than others, and she didn't know why only some of them always wrote their last initials on their homework worksheets, but she knew all the children. She didn't need another, but he was in her classroom anyway. The new boy had yellow-white hair and very light blue eyes. He had come from Florida, but he looked like he'd never seen the sun in his life. Principal Jefferies had already slapped a name tag on his chest, and asked if the boy could stand in front of the room and introduce himself. Emma wasn't sure it was so kind to put the new kid on the spot.

"My name is Rat," the kid said.

"His name is Jonathan Nelson, not Rat," Principal Jefferies jumped in. "Aren't kids a hoot?" he said to Emma before waving and heading out the door.

Emma told the new boy she was going to keep calling him Jonathan, John if that was better, but the kids could call him whatever they wanted. She had made the same rule for Daniel, so it was only fair. She only called him Ulf in her head.

"I like to be called Rat," the boy repeated, and Emma said she would think about it. Jonathan Rat was wearing a gray sweatshirt. He had gremlin-like ears.

Leanne Hatfield wanted to know if he would consider joining the cast of *Titanic the Musical!* She had persuaded almost the entire class to join, with Zoe F. the only holdout. Community theater was supposed to be for all members of the Everton community, but the usual players had quit after Sid Wish got arrested, so the cast had become anyone Leanne Hatfield could recruit on the playground, and a few kids from the middle school who had been orphans in last year's *Les Mis*. Jonathan Rat Nelson said he would only join the show if he could be a pirate.

"Sure," Leanne agreed. "You can be a pirate." This was way out of character for Leanne, Emma noted, but she didn't think too much of it until the beginning of silent reading hour, when Leanne offered the new boy access to her private collection of World War I books, the war they were studying in their history unit. "I usually bring extra reading material," Leanne explained. "There are so many things they forget to teach us."

Emma tried not to be offended. There *were* things she forgot to teach.

Jonathan Rat lay on his stomach on the carpet and flipped through all of Leanne's books, books she'd never let any other kid touch before. Leanne spent the entire reading hour staring at the new boy. Emma chuckled to herself. Leanne had it bad. Emma reached into her desk and texted Mack. *He's just a fun distraction,* she repeated to herself every time she texted him. *It's not serious.* They were going on their first real date that day after school, meeting at the Blueberry Hill Pub.

"Mr. Wish's trial *finally* starts in January, after the break," Tobey L. reminded Emma after lunch. "You said we could watch it on TV. You promised."

Emma did not remember promising this, she did not even know that the Wish trial was going to be televised, so how could she have promised? But then again, there had been that day after what had happened with Mack, after she'd drunk god-knows-how-much of that bottle of Jack Daniel's, she might have promised just about anything then, as long as the kids agreed to work quietly. "I promised?" Emma asked, waiting for Leanne to pipe up and say that she had never promised any such thing, and the rest of the kids were pulling her leg, that they were being manipulative little poops. But Leanne said nothing, too busy staring at Jonathan Rat Nelson, whose nose was buried in another World War I book, the one about fighter planes. Emma didn't see a way out. "Okay," she said. "If I promised." She didn't have the strength to fight them, not on this, and not with only forty-five minutes on the clock before vacation. She would need to put an order in for the school's television, so Janitor Arthur could put the TV in her classroom for the Monday after break. She would have to re-member to stop by the janitor's closet on her way out, to put her name and the equipment she needed on the clipboard. Arthur was about eight hundred years old, but Principal Jefferies had already warned Emma never to offer to help Arthur do his job. "He's a proud man," Principal Jefferies had said. "Just write in all caps on the clipboard, so he can read it."

36

Mack and Emma had agreed on an afternoon date at the Blueberry Hill Pub, three P.M., right after school. A dinner date would no longer work, Emma had to be home at dusk for her dad; Auggie would be out at rehearsal and couldn't watch him. Worst case, this also gave Emma an excuse to bail early if the date wasn't going well.

The Blueberry Hill Pub was decorated for Christmas, with red lights and wreaths and garlands, so it actually looked pretty cozy and romantic. When Emma walked up the stairs to the bar area, Mack Durkee was already in a corner booth, wearing a scarf, an accessory not many men can pull off. He was reading a book. There was something tucked into the pages, she noticed as she approached, and he didn't close the book fast enough, so she saw what it was. "Is this"—she grabbed the list out of his hand—"a list of conversation topics?"

Mack blushed. "My mother's idea."

"This is terrific," Emma said, reading. "*What is your greatest fear?*"

"Being boiled alive," Mack said, pouring a glass from the pitcher he'd ordered. It had been that kind of teaching day for Mack too; the day before vacation always is. "What's yours?"

"Being trapped in a cabin with my dad and my brother and a tame fox from Russia for the rest of eternity."

"What about the dog?"

"I *like* the dog."

"Ha," Mack said. "Okay, next question."

"Three dinner guests living or dead?"

"I'd want someone who could tell a really crazy story that no one else knows," Mack said. "Like D. B. Cooper."

"Who's that?"

"He hijacked a plane in the '70s and extorted, like, two hundred k in ransom, and then he parachuted out of the plane. No one knows what happened to him."

"And who else?"

"Amelia Earhart. Keeping with an aviation theme. And my dad, I guess," Mack said, opening up a little more to Emma. He shrugged. No one in town knew who Mack Durkee's dad was, Mack included. *We* knew, of course, it was Jett Bass, who owned Odds and Ends Antiques. He'd agreed to be a sperm donor for Mack's mother, no strings attached. Jett still quietly loved Mack's mother, and Mack, too, from the respectful distance she'd requested. "What about you?" Mack asked. "Three dinner guests?"

"Hmm," Emma said. She thought about Crystal and Bart and Ralph. The dinners at the mansion they used to have. The gilded age of high school. Not that Emma was the kind of person who'd peaked in high school. "Well, let's see. I think you're right, what you want most is to hear a good story. Okay, I've got one: Cher, Diana Ross, and Gene Simmons. I read they were in a love triangle in the '70s. I'd like to hear more."

"The guy from KISS?"

"Yeah."

"Whoa. Kudos, Gene."

"I know."

The Blueberry Hill waitress arrived at their table, wearing a white T-shirt and a green apron, and holding a blooming onion. "On the house. From Big Hank." She pulled out a napkin from her apron, where Big Hank had written: *Hope your love blossoms.*

"Jesus. Everyone's a cupid," Emma said, and rolled her eyes. She looked to the bar for Big Hank, but Brayden was the one tending bar, and not working very hard, because the only patron was Percy Eaklin, drinking alone except for his mustache. Emma felt pained for him, and she whispered to Mack that Percy's daughter was supposed to be in her class, if she were still alive. She asked Mack if he thought she should go talk to him. She could say she was sorry and tell him his daughter's classmates really missed her. But maybe he just wanted to be left alone?

"I don't know," Mack said. "If you want to be left alone, you stay in your house."

"What if your house is full of people?" Emma asked, thinking of the tinderbox she would be going back to. But then again, Emma thought it was likely Percy's problem with his house was that it was empty, save for his depressed wife, Geraldine, whom no one in Everton had seen since her daughter's funeral.

Before Emma could muster up the strength to go have an awkward conversation with Percy, to thank him for making Auggie his keynote speaker for the anti-drug youth banquet, Percy stood up and paid his bill, then tipped his baseball hat to Brayden behind the bar. Percy was wearing a baseball hat, even though he was also wearing a suit, which looked out of place in Everton, everyone else in flannels and jeans. Well, Percy was a CEO, Emma figured. This town didn't have many CEOs. "Next time," she told Mack. "Next time I'll tell him how much the kids miss his daughter."

"Next time," Mack agreed. "Now, tell me more about . . ." He looked down at the questions his mother had written for him. "What you'd take to a desert island?"

After their date, despite a double case of onion breath, Mack and Emma did some serious making out on the bench seat of Emma's dad's Ford F-150. The truck wasn't exactly comfortable, but they couldn't go back to his mom's place, and they couldn't go back to Ralph's cabin, and they probably shouldn't break into the mansion again, and Mack's Jeep was currently occupied by the goat working through a bale of after-school alfalfa hay, enjoying her life as a symbol of fertility and youthful mistakes.

"What now?" Mildred Roscoe (b. 1811–d. 1902) asked, cranky as usual. "Emma's going to get pregnant and rot in this town?"

"Mildred, for Pete's sake," Michelle Blake (b. 1914–d. 1942) scolded. "Let the young people have a little fun."

"Attaboy," said Charles Tepper (b. 1932–d. 1998), which is what he always said when anyone got frisky in the backseat, or in this case, the cab of a truck.

When Emma got back to the little cabin, she was luminous from all that kissing. It was after dark, but her dad was outside in the yard, squatting in the snow. He was holding out birdseed, trying to get the chickadees to eat from his hand while the fox and the dog watched. The chickadees by the cabin were even less friendly than the ones at the Corbin caretaker's house, which might have had to do with the little red fox waiting for them below, licking his chops.

The dog howled when he saw Emma, and Emma realized her dad was wearing only his parka and had lost his pants again. *Try to act normal,* Emma repeated to herself, which had been Dr. Wheeler's advice whenever their father acted strange. Emma hated Dr. Wheeler, for whatever was happening with him and her mom, but she didn't think his advice was all bad. "Let's go inside, Dad."

"I'm feeding the birds."

"I can see that, but let's go inside and get warm. We'll feed the birds tomorrow."

"You'll help?"

"Sure."

"Wonderful," he said. "That's wonderful."

"Come on, Dad. Let's get inside and warm up."

Years ago, when one of their dogs was dying of cancer, Emma's favorite dog they'd ever had, a border collie mix named Dexter, they'd taken Dexter to a vet who had said not to act sad around the dog as his health failed. That the dog would absorb that human sadness, as dogs are prone to do, and that would make everything worse. So that's how Emma was trying to think about it: her dad was a dog with cancer. He couldn't fully fathom what was happening to him as his mind slipped away, but he could absorb her pity, her sadness. She would have to hide it from him. Pretend everything was fine.

37

> — • ◄

It was Emma's sacred Christmas break, but her dad asked if they could spend the day hanging missing person posters. He hadn't been covering much ground on his own, he complained, no longer allowed to drive. "And you know how people tear them down," he said. The Everton Beautification Committee, led by Patty Gutterfield of the Enraged Old Bags, had hired a group of teenagers to tear down the posters. The committee was paying two dollars over minimum wage.

Emma agreed to take her dad; they would go as soon as she finished her coffee. Auggie emerged from the bunkroom rubbing his face, wearing a black T-shirt and the blue gym shorts he always slept in. He opened the cabinet for the Corn Pops. He complained that Emma had bought the generic brand again. "Puffed Sugar Corn Cereal" in a bag, not the brand-name yellow box. "It is exactly the same," Emma snapped at her brother, and then she remembered why he wanted the sugary cereal in the first place. Her mother had texted her three times about it. Their mother hadn't entirely disappeared. She was in their texts, their emails. She was calling Auggie all the time. It was only their father who hadn't spoken to their mom, who didn't seem to know where she was, and his kids didn't want to confuse or upset him, so they were tiptoeing around the issue. Lying when they had to.

"Merry Christmas," Auggie said as he sat down with the cereal.

"What's that?"

"It's Christmas, Dad."

Emma sighed. This could get ugly.

"I don't think so," Clive said, looking around the cabin for evidence of the holiday. "Your mother would never miss Christmas."

"Okay." Auggie shrugged. "It's *not* Christmas."

"It's not Christmas," Clive repeated firmly, gruffly. "It's not."

"I agree," Auggie said. "It's not."

"Come on, Dad," Emma said, putting her coffee cup down. "Let's go hang some posters."

So that day, they hung posters. And that night, they had frozen pizza and watched whatever showed up on TV. As they watched the second half of *Die Hard,* Auggie worked on his keynote speech for Percy Eaklin's charity banquet, coming up on New Year's Day. He wouldn't let Emma help him write it or even edit it. *Well, it was his own rope if he wanted to hang himself,* Emma decided.

All night, they didn't talk about Ingrid, their wife and mother, who always went all out for Christmas. She would go absolutely balls to the wall with ornaments and evergreens. Ingrid would have objected to the crassness of that phrase, and Clive would have explained that *balls to the wall* originated from the air force in the '60s, and it means pushing the ball-topped joystick all the way down, sending the plane into a dive.

"Nothing to do with the male anatomy," Clive would have told her, if she were there.

Emma had hoped to spend the week not thinking at all about the fifth graders, but the community theater couldn't afford to skip a week of rehearsals for Christmas and New Year's; the show went up in the beginning of February, so of course Emma got dragged into Auggie's drama with the kids. "Can you talk to Leanne for me?" he asked after one rehearsal went particularly badly.

"Probably not," Emma said. "What did she do?"

Leanne had gotten into a fight with Bruce, the middle schooler who was supposed to play the captain of the *Titanic*. Bruce was the only one with a voice big enough to carry the role of captain, but Leanne took issue with how many times his voice was cracking lately, and she also wanted to know if he had a plan for clearing up his acne. Bruce said he was quitting unless Leanne apologized. Leanne would not apologize.

"It's a community theater, right?" Emma asked. "I mean, it's not just a kids' theater. Can an adult play the captain?"

"Anyone can join, yes," Auggie said. "But you can't really sing."

Emma looked over at their father, who was caught up in an intense game of *Call of Duty*. Her dad, who had never shot a gun in his life, now loved this shooter videogame, said it was no wonder no one reads poetry anymore when there are videogames to play. "What about Dad? He can sing."

Auggie considered it. "At least Leanne couldn't bully him."

"What's the show?" their dad asked. Clive thought most musicals were so corny. *RENT* and *Wicked* and *Cats,* all horrible, *Les Misérables* and *Pippin* were worse. But he was delighted when Auggie said it was *Titanic the Musical!* Clive thought that was really funny, to turn such a tragedy into a singing and dancing routine. "What's the part?" he asked, very interested now.

"We need a captain for the ship. Someone with a big singing voice. The rest of the cast is all little kids with kid-sized voices; no one can do it."

"No one else can do it?" Clive smiled big, but then his face dropped, remembering something. "I would say yes, Aug, I absolutely would, but if you haven't noticed, I'm dying."

"It'll give you something to live for." Emma nudged her father. She desperately wanted the musical to be a success. She was a little afraid of what Leanne would do if the play failed, who she would take it out on.

"You only have to live until February eighth," Auggie said. "That's when the show goes up."

"Oh, I think I can live until February. I had thought the play was this spring. Yes, I'll do it. I'll be the star."

This spring. A lump rose in Emma's throat, but she swallowed it down. And then she got distracted anyway, because her dad and Auggie started to campaign to take the fox with them to rehearsal that night. Emma did not think that was a good idea. "It'll be too stressful for Rasputin," she argued. "And I'm sure animals aren't allowed in the Old Opera House."

"No one is ever there but us," Auggie reassured her about the beautiful old building that housed the community theater. "And Rasputin really likes people."

"He never hides," Clive agreed.

In the end, Emma agreed that they could bring Rasputin, but she would come along, too, so that the fox would only have to stay for twenty minutes or so, and wouldn't be a distraction. She had to bring the dog too; Moses barreled out the door when they tried to go without him.

The kids *ohhed and ahhed* over the fox, of course they did, but they were also fascinated to meet their teacher's father. "This is your dad?" Adam D. asked Emma. "Who puts up the posters?"

"Yup. That's him."

"My mom says you're littering our town."

"It's important to get the word out," Clive said.

"So, do you think that missing woman is dead?" Leanne asked, her hands always on her hips.

"To be honest?" Clive shook his head. "I don't know."

The fifth graders liked honesty, but Emma was upset to hear

her father say that. He had been the one who usually stayed hopeful. Dogged in his search.

"Why do you keep looking for her?" Olivia asked. "If she's in heaven?"

"Everyone deserves to be looked for if no one knows where they are," Clive said simply, and the children nodded. That was a satisfactory reason for kids who knew the rules of Hide-and-Seek. Then they returned their attention to the fox, and it was all going fine until the fox bit Ulf, who was probably playing too rough. Emma packed Rasputin up in the crate, put Moses on his leash, and had to drag the dog away from her father. She paused at the exit of the auditorium as she listened to Leanne Hatfield sing a lament for her drowned husband, one of the finale numbers of the show. The beauty of Leanne's voice was overwhelming.

Emma loaded the animals into the truck, and then she climbed in and felt a straining feeling in her chest as if her heart were really trying to break itself in two. *By the spring.* Her dad might be dead by spring. *Anticipatory grief,* it's called, when you're sad about something that hasn't happened yet. *Oh man,* we thought at Maple Street, how we missed the excruciating pain of being alive.

While his daughter's heart was breaking in the parking lot of the Old Opera House, Clive was standing on the polished stage, already wearing the captain's hat from the costume trunk, wishing Ingrid was there to see it. He would like to take the hat home so he could chase his wife around the kitchen, singing that song about the girl whose eyes could steal a sailor from the sea, and she would yell, *Stop, stop, Clive stop!* And swat at him. His wife was sure to be home soon, from whatever trip she was on. *Where had she gone again?* France maybe. She'd always wanted to go to France. *And why hadn't he gone with her?* Paris was for lovers.

"You're dying," Ernest Harold Baynes said, ever helpful. The ghost had a glow to him, thanks to the stage lights. The year before, Sid Wish had done a big fundraiser for the new lighting system, and it was so state-of-the-art that Auggie didn't know how to use all the features. Auggie mostly just turned the overheads on and off, but there was still time to learn the bells and whistles before the show. Six weeks until opening.

PART V

The Rooster
(And the Frog)

38

➤ ◄

Photograph by Louise Birt Baynes.

Toward the end of the following spring, marking one year since the bear arrived in our home, we knew that Jimmie was getting too large. Good-natured as he was, he was growing very strong, and quite too demonstrative for some of the people he made it his business to meet. If he saw a man coming up the road, the man was in for a wrestling match whether he was in training or not.

A very nice young man walked all the way from Lebanon one day to try to sell us a copy of *To Heaven Through Nature,* a slim book about how being in the natural world brings us closer to God. Jimmie met him a quarter of a mile down the road, and by the time I reached the salesman, calling vigorously for help, and yelled, "Down! Down! Down!" to Jimmie, the poor chap looked like he'd walked through a field of barbed wire, torn up and bloody as he was. As the Bible-pounder was leaving, Mrs. Baynes's eyes twinkled as she called to him: "When you get out a new edition of your book, don't forget a chapter on bears!"

But the true climax for Jimmie was reached when Mrs. Baynes was coming home from a walk, and Jimmie seized her, took the knot of her hair in his mouth, and threw her onto the snow. It was all in fun from his point of view, but not from hers, and certainly not from mine. As much as I loved our bear, I loved my wife much, much more.

I had already heard from the director at New York Zoological Society that they'd like to buy Jimmie, and I could not accept the offer because I'd made it a point to never sell an animal that had been a member of my household, as I believe that animals are not our belongings. When I thought again of how Jimmie had pushed my wife's face into the snow, I decided it would be fine to *present* him to the zoo.

It was not two months later when I went to New York and naturally the first person I called on was Jimmie. The director of the zoo gave me a warm welcome and took me to the bear enclosure so I could see my friend. From a distance, I could see Jimmie lying in a corner of the den, his head on his left paw and fast asleep.

"Jimmie!" I called. "Jimmie! Come, Jimmie!"

Jimmie's head came up from his arm, and he scrambled to his

feet. He came trotting along the inside of the pen, and he stood on his hind legs and I gave him my hand through the bars. He grasped it in both forepaws. The onlookers gasped; I suppose because they thought my hand was about to be eaten.

Jimmie gave way to that queer, continuous, bubbling sob he often made when greatly stirred. "Ubble-uble-uble-uble-ubble," he blubbered, and he kept it up until I thought I would cry myself.

It was clear what the bear was saying, and everyone at the zoo heard it. Jimmie was saying: *Hello, I love you, I missed you, I'm glad to see you, take me home.*

>-·<-->-·-<

39

The Inaugural Heroes Against Heroin Spaghetti Banquet was to be held on New Year's Day in the rec center, the first town event of the new year. It was forty-five dollars a ticket, not exactly cheap, and people weren't really sure what kind of event it was— *Was it supposed to be fancy or casual? How do you dress for a spaghetti dinner? Would there be food to eat besides spaghetti?* Percy Eaklin, the organizer, had not provided enough information on the invitation. It was clear he was trying to do something good for the community, but everyone needed more information. Some people showed up and felt really overdressed. Some people were in jeans, sweatshirts. Clive wore his leather jacket. Auggie's old suit didn't fit him well anymore—he'd put on weight—so he'd gone to the Salvation Army over in Claremont and he'd found a three-piece gray suit. It was perfect, he thought. He looked dapper as hell. Emma wore a short black velvet dress, black tights, her turquoise cowboy boots, and dangly gold earrings. Mack was going to be there, so Emma was bringing her A-game.

The football team came wearing their jerseys, even though football season was long over. Little Glenny Anderson was wearing the bottom half of his mascot costume, the head of the rooster under his arm. Glenny was too small to be on the football team— there was a weight limit for safety reasons—but he was still one of the Everton Fighting Cocks.

At the Enraged Old Bags table, Eunice Vandervoss was in her purple dress with her red hat. Eunice hadn't been sure about com-

ing to an event sponsored by the gun factory; she thought the
NRA were some of the worst fink bastards out there, but Auggie
Starling had sent her an invitation thanking her for all she'd done
for him; he never would have gotten his new job without her. Who
knows what the boy meant by that, but she did believe in helping
the town's youth stay off heroin. Also, Eunice really loved a party.
Who knew how many parties Eunice or any of the Enraged Old
Bags had left?

There was an open bar set up in one corner of the basketball court and Clive headed straight to it. The round banquet
tables dotted the court, covered in white tablecloths. There was
a podium and a microphone under the basketball hoop. And in
another corner of the gym, there was a sign for donations, surrounded by boxes and trash bags. The invitation had said to bring
clothes for the homeless shelter up in Claremont, with a note that
clothes were especially needed for teen moms. Percy Eaklin was
really trying to do a good thing here, even if he had forgotten to
tell people what they should wear to this event.

Auggie found his seat at the Reserved table, which was right in
front of the podium. Auggie was nervous, Emma could tell. She
watched him from afar as she waited for a drink. He was leaning
over his backpack, like he might throw up into it. He was talking
to his backpack, actually. *Maybe practicing his speech?* She hoped
he didn't mess it up. She wished he'd at least let her read it, but
he'd refused.

After Emma had secured a drink, some kind of peachy spe-
cialty cocktail, she took a lap around the gym. She came to the
Memorial table, where photos of young people who had overdosed in recent years were displayed. People had been asked to
bring framed photos of lost loved ones. "Look, it's me!" said Sara
Ford (b. 1986–d. 2012) from her grave. "Why does my mother always use that picture?" "There's me," said Jacqueline Castle
(b. 1995–d. 2014), a newer overdose victim, still finding her foot-

ing in our graveyard. And then we flinched when Emma saw it. Middle of the table. She felt punched. It was the same photo of Crystal from the missing person poster. *Who had put that there?* Crystal wasn't dead, not officially. She didn't need a memorial table.

"Hey," someone behind her said, and Emma turned to see Mack, wearing a black T-shirt with a bow tie and cummerbund drawn on in white cartoon outline. *Nice suit,* she would have joked, if she wasn't so upset by what she'd just seen.

"I need to find out who put this picture up," she said. "I need to find out who the hell they think they are."

"I'm sure they were just trying to be nice," Mack said, trying to comfort her.

"It's not fucking nice," Emma snapped. She reached out and put the frame facedown. *Why was she so angry?* She had thought it herself, that Crystal must be dead. It just hurt to see it in such certain terms.

The table of high schoolers were pointing at Mack and Emma, making kissing noises. The one wearing the bottom half of a chicken suit was clucking. He was holding the mascot's head underneath one wing and making some sort of lewd gesture with his other wing.

Emma looked around and saw Percy Eaklin standing at the podium, adjusting the microphone. He would know who had brought the picture.

"We should sit down," Mack said. "Percy's about to start."

"I'll be right back," Emma said, and she marched right up to Percy. "Why is there a photo of Crystal Nash on the memorial table? I haven't seen a body."

Percy's mouth fell open a little, he looked surprised to see Emma Starling so worked up. Most people knew Emma as generally composed, on the quieter side, a little icy like her mother. "I

put it up," Percy admitted. "I didn't mean to upset you. I was trying to honor her memory."

"What do you know about her?" Emma asked, her eyes nar-
rowing. "How do you know her?"

"Everyone knows her," Percy said, his arms crossed. "And everyone knows she was struggling with addiction. I thought it was
appropriate to make sure she was remembered today."

Emma's anger began to cool, and she felt embarrassed instead.
That was not how she'd wanted to talk to Percy Eaklin. She had
wanted to say something sensitive about the daughter he'd lost,
who should have been in her class, if the girl had lived. "I'm sorry,"
she said. "I guess you're right."

"No problem," he said, uncrossing his arms. "I know it's
hard."

Emma thanked him and headed to her seat at the Reserved
table, where Auggie looked pale, like he really might vomit into
his open backpack. Percy Eaklin was up at the podium, and he
said he was so glad everyone was here, grateful they had all come
together to raise awareness about their town's youth drug problem.

Spaghetti was served, and Emma noticed her dad's seat was
empty, he hadn't sat down yet. She looked around to find him, to
make him eat some spaghetti, but she didn't see him anywhere.
Her brother was getting up to speak, and Emma didn't want to
miss it. She had promised she would record it for her mom. Emma
and Auggie had decided their mom was not allowed to come to
the event; it would only confuse their dad.

"Break a leg," Mack told Auggie, and Auggie gave a weak
thumbs-up.

At the podium, Auggie cleared his throat into the microphone,
and he thanked everyone for coming, wished them a happy New
Year. He said he was going to tell the story of his addiction, in

case it helped someone who was there that night, someone struggling now or anyone who might struggle in the future. He said the easiest way to deal with heroin is not to start using it, but it's not that simple for a lot of reasons.

Auggie explained the way it began for him, the football injury, the pills, but he knew it could begin tons of ways, especially since it was so easy to get and then so hard to stop doing. Even with his parents so involved with his life, even with all the resources the Starlings had, they'd been fighting an uphill battle. "I didn't want to go back to rehab a second time," Auggie explained. "I got in a fistfight with my dad, and I took off. I went to live with friends, slept on couches, slept wherever. I didn't really care what happened to me." Eventually, Auggie said, he hit rock bottom. "Rock bottom looks different for everyone. For me, it looked like standing on the bridge above Sugar River and deciding whether or not to jump."

The crowd gasped. Emma's heart fell. She hadn't known how dark it had gotten. But of course it had gotten dark.

"I did jump, actually, but I didn't die," Auggie said. "Obviously." He waved his hands to show he was very much alive. "I hit the water and I felt afraid. I wanted to live. That was the first time in a long time I actually wanted to live. I walked back to my parents' house, two or three miles, soaking wet and missing a shoe. My mom wasn't home, but my dad was. He told me he loved me, and he drove me straight to rehab."

Everyone looked around for Clive Starling, to see his proud, beaming face, but no one could find him.

"I can't believe he's missing this," Bill Casey (b. 1955–d. 2004) said from Maple Street. "This is the part where he looks like a good dad."

In the corner of the gym, Percy Eaklin was rattling the rooster's cage. Every few years, the 4-H Club at Upper Valley High, the same one that had given Mack Durkee his goat, raised a rooster from an egg, and this live rooster was brought in a big carrier cage to all football games and all pep rallies and all-school events. Sometimes the rooster was even let out onto the football field if the game was a real blowout. This rooster's name was Ulysses, and it was his first public event, after the previous rooster had been retired, gone to the big bird farm in the sky. Percy Eaklin wanted to release Ulysses at the end of the keynote; he thought it would be a nice symbol of Upper Valley High pride and a moment of levity in what was sure to be a downer of a speech. People were always so happy when the football coach let the rooster out onto the field.

"The rehab center doesn't let non-patients stay over," Auggie continued, ignoring whatever it was Percy Eaklin was doing. "But my dad parked his truck in the lot so I could see it from my window, and he stayed parked there for five days while I detoxed. The old man slept in his truck, so I could know he was there for me. On the fifth day, my mom came to get him, and she was really mad; he hadn't told her where he was. He hadn't remembered to leave a note or take his cell phone." Auggie chuckled at the memory.

The crowd didn't know whether to laugh with Auggie. Many people remembered how Ingrid had panicked when she couldn't find her husband or her son for nearly a full week. Auggie wasn't allowed to have his phone in rehab. Ingrid had to call Sabrina Berkman to ask if her husband was there with her, the woman he'd had the affair with. It was humiliating. Ingrid finally tried the front desk at the Phoenix House, where Auggie had been once before, and they told her Auggie was indeed there, and so was Clive, wearing out his welcome camping in the parking lot.

Emma couldn't believe she didn't know this story. Nothing about the fistfight, the suicide attempt, or that her dad had been the one to drive Auggie to rehab the second time. She'd only heard her mother say, time and time again, that her dad had refused to go to any of the family therapy sessions at the Phoenix House because he said he didn't need therapy, goddammit. Emma had heard nothing about her dad sleeping in his truck.

"My dad isn't a perfect father," Auggie admitted onstage. "Most of you know him, and you know that's true. But that old truck in the rehab parking lot, blasting Black Sabbath all day— a band I actually loathe—it got me through the worst five days of my life. My wish for the parents of Everton is to try to love your kids like that, when they need you most," Auggie said. "Flick your headlights for them, all night long, every hour. Let them know you're always there in whatever way makes sense to you."

We wondered if we should flicker the lights of the rec center then, ghosts sometimes like to have a little fun with electricity, and we're out here in the metaphorical parking lot all night long, loving the people of Everton from a distance. But we missed our opportunity with the lights, because Ulysses the rooster was strutting across the stage. "Hello, Mr. Rooster," Auggie said from the podium. "Can I help you?"

Everyone laughed. Percy was right, the crowd was delighted by the big bird onstage, lifted right back up after Auggie's speech.

"Cock-a-doodle-doo!" someone on the football team called.

Ulysses wasn't used to the war calls of the football team yet, this being his first public event, and swiveled his head at the sound of that noise, and that's when he saw another rooster, across the room. Ulysses had not been bred to fight, he had been bred to attend football games, but all roosters have the fight in them. It can't be taken out. Ulysses was ready to peck the other rooster's eyes out. The other rooster was bigger, but he looked slow. Ulysses was ready to go to war.

Now, roosters don't fly very often, but they aren't ground birds. They *can* fly short distances, twenty to forty feet, so Ulysses took to the air. Ulysses was ready to do some damage to Glenny Anderson's beautiful, youthful face. Glenny was still not wearing the head of the rooster costume, only the body. He didn't see Ulysses coming at him, his attention was elsewhere, with one of the cheerleaders. Someone yelled "duck," but Glenny Anderson didn't duck, because people were always yelling the names of birds at him, calling him "Big Bird" or "Daffy Duck" or "Hey, KFC." Glenny was used to that, the names didn't bother him, he was a member of the football team. But now Ulysses the rooster was going to scratch Glenny's eyes out. Ulysses was going in, talons first, wings flap-flap-flapping.

In the cozy burrow of Auggie's backpack, Rasputin the fox was curled up asleep, but he got a sudden whiff of the bird in flight, and his eyes snapped awake, because, as everyone knows: *foxes love chickens*. Auggie had brought the fox for emotional support, and to show him off to a few of his old friends, but hadn't planned to make a big show. But now, Rasputin sprang from the backpack and jumped up on the table, where he immediately understood what all the training had been about these past two weeks, those little neon feather toys. Rasputin now had to kill this rooster before it killed that boy. This was all some sort of elaborate American game. The Russians had warned him about the Americans, how stupid and weird they can be. But no problem, Rasputin would slaughter this rooster and it would make his American friends happy. Rasputin jumped, and he was so very quick, and the rooster's neck was soon in his jaws. The people screamed. The white tablecloth and the fake lilies were soaked in blood, splattered on the white football jerseys, on the feathers of the mascot suit. Who knew there would be so much blood in a single rooster?

"My goodness," said Eunice Vandervoss. "And after that beautiful speech."

"It's the end of innocence," someone else said.

Auggie hadn't moved so fast since his days on the football field to get to the fox, weaving through tables and people, ending by scooping up his blood-soaked fox. "I'm sorry," he said. "I'm sorry!" But no one was angry. People were clapping. It was a standing ovation.

"Great speech," called out one of the football players.

"Don't do drugs!" called another.

Everyone in the rec center agreed, talking at one another over all the applause: Auggie Starling had given quite the keynote. Heartfelt and inspirational and entertaining, a heck of a way to begin a new year. He just might have the chops to replace Sid Wish as community theater director. Auggie beamed, and took a bow, as the fox in his arms struggled to be released.

40

Of course, Clive Starling missed the entire dang thing. Emma and Mack finally found him in the hallway of the rec center, sitting on a cardboard box and finishing up a phone call. No one in the rec center had realized their wallets were missing yet, but Clive had played pickpocket in the line for the open bar. He finally had more than enough credit cards to call Barbara Anne Lavoy, telephone psychic.

"You did what?" Emma said, when her dad explained who he'd been talking to, why he'd needed to skip Auggie's speech. The people of Everton were beginning to trickle out, wishing each other a happy New Year. Auggie was still hanging back by the podium, mobbed by admirers and people who wanted to pet the fox.

"I called the psychic," Clive explained to Emma and Mack. "She agreed the college should not have fired me. She said it sounded like I was a really good teacher. She said she was glad you were following in my footsteps; she said the children would be the answer."

"Was this therapy or a psychic session?" Emma asked. "Whose credit card did you use?" There were eight wallets on the floor in front of Clive.

"Oh, one of them."

Mack had to turn away, he was laughing so hard, then he stooped to gather the wallets. "I'll go give these back," Mack said, and went off to locate their owners. No one would be mad at Mack Durkee, would not accuse him of stealing their wallets. Such a wholesome young man. Many people would probably give him a twenty-dollar reward for being kind enough to return a lost wallet.

"Well, Dad, did the psychic tell you where Crystal is?" Emma asked.

Her father only sighed. "It turns out, *most* of her psychic services can be easily done over the phone, but not a missing person. Barbara Anne said she would need to smell an item of clothing in order to learn what happened. It's just impossible to do from a distance. I can understand that. I tried to hold up a piece of clothing to the phone, but of course a person can't smell through a phone."

That was when Emma noticed what was written on the cardboard box her dad was sitting on. On its side, in Sharpie, in all caps, the box said: CRYSTAL NASH TRAILER. "Dad, where did you get that box?"

"Lucky, huh? I saw Graham Leeches come in and put it with the clothing donations, and I thought it might have some clues inside. But it's just clothing."

Graham Leeches. The owner of the trailer park. Percy Eaklin's right-hand man. Emma had never been able to reach him on the phone in his office at the gun factory, not that she'd tried that hard. Maybe Graham Leeches knew something. He had to know something. Emma grabbed Officer Gene, who had been out in the parking lot directing traffic, and she told him they might finally have a real lead on the Crystal Nash case. She showed him the box of Crystal's clothes that her father had been sitting on. She didn't mention the psychic or the stolen wallets.

"I'll check it out," Officer Gene promised.

"We'll come with you," Clive said, and Emma agreed, they would.

It was another stroke of luck that Graham Leeches was still in the rec center, helping Percy Eaklin put away the folding chairs and banquet tables. Graham's dress shirt was untucked, and he was sweating up a storm. Officer Gene asked Graham if he could explain the box of Crystal's clothes. Why he was giving her things away.

"All her stuff belongs to me after ninety days if she doesn't pay her rent," Graham Leeches said, wiping his brow. "Percy said the shelter really needed clothing for teenage moms, and that I should donate Crystal's stuff. I thought it was a nice idea."

"It's really appreciated," Percy said, stacking more chairs.

"Doesn't mean I know jack about what happened to her," Graham said, holding up his hands in a gesture of innocence.

"All right, no more crying wolf," Officer Gene said, pointing to Clive, then pointing to Emma, with his ruddy red finger. "And hey, nice speech, Auggie. Proud of you."

"Thanks, Officer." Auggie had rejoined his family in time to watch them accuse Graham Leeches of murder or kidnapping or both.

"I'll take those." Percy Eaklin said, scooping up the box of clothes. "I'm meeting the director of the homeless shelter in fifteen." Emma almost objected, but what was she going to do with a box of Crystal's clothes? It was pathetic. It was time to let her go. No more missing person posters, no more half-baked detective work. Crystal Nash, her old best friend, was gone. She had tried to find her, but it had been too late.

"There's blood on your hands," Clive said, but he was talking to Auggie. "Why is there blood on your hands? Was there a fight?" Rasputin was stashed in Auggie's backpack, the rooster blood drying on his fur. The fox would need a bath when they got home, and foxes absolutely loathe baths, hate them worse than cats do. "Was it a pillow fight?" Clive asked as they all headed toward the door of the rec center that opened to the parking lot. "What's with all the feathers? What did I miss?"

———

"I think Dad's going to get in real trouble if we keep leaving him alone," Auggie said to Emma, late that night. "I think we need to listen to what Dr. Wheeler advised. He needs to be supervised at all times." That's what the mentally incompetent paperwork had said, in red ink: *Needs Constant Supervision.*

"It's not practical," Emma said. "Dr. Wheeler also said it's not practical."

"Listen: I think you should take him to school with you. He clearly misses being in the classroom. He can be your teacher's helper."

"Aren't you home most of the day? Can't you watch him?"

"No, I am not home most of the day. I'm building the *Titanic* set, and it would be dangerous to have Dad at the theater when I'm building. He'd nail-gun his hand or something. Mack said that schools are looking for parent volunteers all the time. He said Principal Jefferies would totally go for it."

"Mack means parent volunteers of the children, not parents of the teachers."

"You know, Mack's not so bad," Auggie said. "It's fine with me if you date him."

"I'm glad you've come around on him. Big of you."

"His mom does the costumes at the theater, and he helps her out. You know she has cancer? And he's pretty good with a drill, helps me build when he has the time."

"I thought you said no one was helping."

"Do you know how hard it is to build a good stage replica of the *Titanic*? It's simply not a one-man job. But Emma, seriously, please take Dad with you tomorrow, just show up with him. Mack says Jefferies is an idiot, and he'll let you get away with anything. And the kids already know Dad; they love Captain Clive."

Emma sighed. Mack was right. She could probably get away

with it. "I'll try it," she agreed. "We'll see what Jefferies says. But otherwise . . . I guess we could hire someone, a nurse or something."

"You said you'd take care of him. You promised."

"Jesus, Auggie."

"Just telling it like it is."

The idea was pretty insane, Emma knew, but it wasn't like Principal Jefferies would fire her. Not for bringing her dad to school, just a few times, until they figured something else out. It was temporary.

41

Of course Clive loved the idea of being teacher's assistant, it was only Moses who objected. When Clive went to leave the cabin with his daughter, the dog howled as if being tortured, begging to be taken along too. Auggie would have to spend his morning dealing with the distress of the dog, the poor animal's separation anxiety. Emma thought that was a pretty good punishment for this horrible, dumb-as-hell idea, taking her father to work with her.

"I don't see why you can't have a teacher's assistant," Principal Jefferies said when they got to school. "If I don't have to pay him. I think it's great, you know, father and daughter spending time together, doing something good for the school community." He gave Clive Starling a name tag that said Teacher's Assistant, and Clive looked down at it proudly.

"Hi, Captain Clive," the kids said in a chorus when they saw him, not really surprised to see the captain there in school. They were much more interested in Janitor Arthur, who had just wheeled a television set to the front of the room.

"Shit," Emma muttered under her breath, remembering it was the start of the Wish trial. Her father would find out that she was planning to spend the entire day watching Court TV with fifth graders. He was the one who told her to do a C-average job at teaching, but this was probably pushing it. Emma had already known it was a bad idea, but since her classroom was at the very end of the hall, and Principal Jefferies almost never dropped in, she had also planned to get away with it. But now her father would be there to witness it. There was no backing down now or the kids would riot.

"We're watching TV?" her father asked. Emma lied and said the students had earned it, that they had won a countywide spelling bee, and this was their prize.

"Wow," Clive said to the kids. "Congratulations."

No one corrected Emma Starling about the spelling bee, didn't scold her for lying, not even Leanne Hatfield. They weren't paying attention to her. While they waited for Arthur to get the TV going, they were picking each other up. It was their new thing; it had started right before the break began. They loved being picked up, they loved picking each other up. It was either the first spurts of hormones or it was a deep desire to remain a baby, Emma wasn't sure which. Whenever they asked if they could try to pick her up, Emma always said no, even though there was also part of her that wanted to see them try.

"It's working, Ms. Starling," Arthur finally said, and Emma took the remote and flipped to Court TV. There was Sid Wish, in a nice suit, purple tie, black hair slicked back, looking like a cleaned-up car salesman indeed; a little too smooth, a little arrogant, the kind of guy who would say something insulting to the waitress.

"We're watching the Wish trial?" her father asked. "Why is this on TV?"

"It's not hard to get on Court TV," Leanne Hatfield said. "They play trials 24/7. All you have to do is write in; there's a form on their website. That's what my grandfather said. It's nothing impressive."

"I'm impressed," Clive said, and Leanne rolled her eyes.

The camera panned around and there was Claire Wish, in the front row, shoulder-length blond hair and a white silk top, looking impossibly radiant, someone whose skin had been scrubbed by the wings of angels. The camera hung on her for longer than necessary as *Defendant's wife, elementary school teacher* appeared at the bottom of the screen.

"Wow," Jonathan Rat said. "That used to be our teacher? She looks like a supermodel."

Emma Starling and Leanne Hatfield felt a similar feeling at the same time: a hot flash of anger. Leanne had that new crush on Jonathan Rat, so that partly explained it, and she also hated Sid Wish for screwing up his job at the community theater. They had lost so much rehearsal time; they might now end up with a real slipshod production. For Emma, Claire Wish had become her nemesis, *the world's most perfect teacher,* and then Sid Wish appeared again, and she felt rageful about the pills and powders Crystal and her brother had gotten hooked on. Sid Wish was someone pretty easy to blame.

The defense lawyer's opening statements were pretty ridiculous, Emma thought. He claimed Sid Wish could not be a major heroin dealer, could not be mixing elephant tranquilizers or anything else into the heroin, something that made the drug cheaper but so much deadlier, not when he was married to that beautiful, simply lovely, Claire Wish, and not when he had been the director of the community theater. "How many drug dealers do you know that are into Broadway musicals?" he asked the jury. The jurors' faces were blurred out on television for privacy reasons, but they appeared to nod their blurry heads, seeming to agree that the lawyer made an excellent point.

"I just want revenge," Emma complained to Auggie one night later that week as the trial continued on and it looked like Sid Wish really might be acquitted. Auggie was boiling water for macaroni, had volunteered to make dinner for everyone.

"Revenge for what?" he asked.

"For dealing."

"A lot of people do."

"Well, not selling just to anyone. To you and Crystal."

"Wow, GG, I didn't know you cared so much."

"Of course I care," Emma said. *Why did her brother always make her feel like that?*

"Well, I don't think I ever bought from him anyway. And what you really should want is revenge on the people at the top. The kingpins. People with a lot more money than Sid has; maybe someone like Percy Eaklin."

Emma snorted. "Percy Eaklin is *not* a kingpin."

"Okay, no, but someone with that kind of money. That kind of power. You know where I think the kingpins are?"

"Massachusetts?" she asked.

"Corbin Park."

"Huh," Emma said. It was entirely possible, she agreed. From Ralph's cabin, they saw the helicopters flying in and out of the park all the time. The millionaires coming and going, no one asking questions. No cops to pull them over.

"Still," Auggie said, pouring the box of shelled pasta into the bubbling water on the stove. "We should definitely send Sid Wish to the electric chair, just to be safe."

"Shut up, Auggie."

"Off with his head. Lethal injection. Bring out the firing squad."

"Shut up, Auggie. Just shut up."

"Tie a millstone to his neck and drown him. Burn him at the stake. Let Emma Starling cast the first stone."

"I'll stone *you* to death."

Auggie grinned. "Thanks for caring, sis," he said. "I mean it."

Emma looked up and saw that he did. Mean it, that is. She smiled back at him. Her stupid brother.

"Hey," he said. "I know you got me the director job. Those

students of yours aren't exactly vaults. And actually, you have no idea what it means, to get a second chance. So really, thanks, Em."

Emma sniffed, trying not to cry, but for a good reason this time. A happy one. She was about to say more to Auggie, how glad she was that he was alive, and how sorry she hadn't been home when he jumped off a bridge, that she hadn't been able to heal him when he needed it, the drugs or the spinal subluxation, but their father called out from the bunkroom that he was pretty sure a chipmunk had gotten into the cabin. This was a possibility, but it also could have been another hallucination. Auggie and Emma searched frantically around the cabin for a chipmunk anyway, because they didn't want it getting into the food, or chewing the electric wiring. The fox and dog ran around the house, too, both animals thought it was an excellent game. Rasputin and Moses had gotten used to each other, living in such close quarters, and they shared the common love of the long-haired man who was so generous with the treats. So generous, in fact, it was almost as if he'd forgotten he'd just given you one just a few minutes before. *Here was another and another and another.*

42

A week into the Sid Wish trial, Emma and her dad arrived in the fifth-grade classroom to find it held a somber tone, no one picking anyone else up, no one stealing dry-erase markers from Emma's desk to write on the board, no one turning on Court TV. The trial was dragging on, and the kids didn't seem to care anymore. Emma thought they were upset because Ms. Wish hadn't come back to teach yet, and she really didn't want to hear anything more about Claire Wish and how great she was, so she wasn't going to say anything about their obvious melancholy. It was Jonathan Rat who finally asked what was up. Or, "Who died?" is what he actually asked.

"Isabella E.," the rest of the class chorused.

"And today is her birthday," Leanne explained. "She was my best friend."

"Oh, you poor kid," Clive said, seated near Leanne in one of the empty desks. He looked enormous in the small chair.

Leanne nodded, glad for her special grief to be recognized. But Leanne was also thrilled by how sad the entire class was acting that day. Leanne had been worried everyone else had forgotten Izzy; it seemed that way, most of the time. But no, they had all remembered; Olivia had even worn black. Leanne wished she'd thought of that, but she was decked out in her signature pink. Jonathan Rat wasn't that sad, but no one could blame him. He'd lived in Florida last year, and before that it was North Carolina, and before that Arizona. His parents had promised him they'd stay in New Hampshire for a while.

Emma was alarmed by the reminder that her students had lost a classmate, and so recently. She was supposed to be a source of love and stability here, and there was her dying father, wedged into his tiny desk. There was nothing stable about him. *What the hell had she done,* bringing him here? What if Captain Clive went for his daily afternoon nap in the arts and crafts closet and didn't wake up? She wasn't supposed to mess up these kids even more, didn't want to be yet another person who hurt them. But she didn't know how to undo it, her father as their assistant teacher. She couldn't ask him to leave. He was so happy in the classroom. "What would cheer you all up on this very sad day?" she asked the kids instead, in her most nurturing tone of teacher voice.

The students put their heads on their desks, they said they didn't need cheering up, they needed to be sad. Emma had to admit that was a good answer. "What if Captain Clive tells you more about his friend Harold?" Emma suggested. That was the kind of wacky thing that the kids really liked, and she might as well make use of her father. She had told him he wasn't allowed to talk about Harold before, but the ghost kept coming up, and the kids were curious.

"Yes," Michael B. said.

"Yes," the rest of the kids agreed.

Clive's eyes went bright like the fox's did when the baggie of liver treats appeared. "Really?" he asked.

"Really," she said.

Her dad stood up in front of the classroom to tell the class about Ernest Harold Baynes and his wife, and the animals they shared their home with: timber wolves, foxes, skunk, deer, one bear, countless birds, especially chickadees. And two bison. The only tame bison in the world. "There used to be lots of bison in Corbin Park," Clive said. "At a time when bison were almost extinct. Some of them were sent to Yellowstone to help replenish the wild population. That was Harold's idea."

"His wife let him live with a bear?" Tobey L. asked. "My mom won't even let me have an iguana."

"His wife edited his books and got them published," Clive said. "She took almost all the photographs. And it seems like the fox and the bear both liked her the best, or at least as much."

"Sounds like she's the really cool one," Leanne Hatfield mumbled.

"You know what, Leanne," Clive said. "You might be right; I don't think his wife gets the credit she deserves." We knew Louise Baynes would have liked to hear that, but she was too far away from Everton at this point. Buried up in Canada. And Leanne smiled; she liked to be told she was right.

That was when the cupcakes arrived at the door. Emma had slipped out during the lecture to call Gertie's Bakery, and Gertie had brought the cupcakes over herself when she heard the situation. Gertrude Whipple remembered Isabella Eaklin. How could anyone forget that sad story? The cupcakes were the yellow-frosted ones that looked like roses, that symbol of friendship.

"She's still your friend," Emma reassured the kids, who didn't know if it was right to eat the cupcakes. "She's gone, but she's still your friend, and your friend would want you to be happy. And she would want you to celebrate in her honor." The room was quiet for a minute, but then Leanne agreed, and after that everyone else agreed too. Leanne was the best friend. She got to call the shots.

Of course, Emma was thinking about Crystal during her little speech, and she hoped Crystal was happy, maybe on some ranch in Wyoming, where the buffalo roamed, the bison population brought back from the brink of extinction. But it probably was childish to believe that. Sometimes young people do end up dead for horrible reasons. That much was clear that day in the fifth-grade classroom of Dream Far Elementary.

While the kids and her father were eating their cupcakes, and after Michael B. had been sent down to the teacher's lounge to buy something he wasn't allergic to from the vending machine, Emma went into the closet to gather some art supplies for the next unit of the day. She'd decided she was going to have them all make Birthday/Goodbye cards for their friend Isabella E., a physical symbol of both remembering and letting go. She felt like she was being a good teacher, giving these kids some lessons on closure, what she'd never gotten from Crystal's disappearance, since no one knew what had happened, where she'd gone. There had at least been a funeral for Isabella; Emma had looked up the obituary online.

"Loss isn't a competition," Ralph Kelsey (b. 1923–d. 2014) reminded her from his grave.

From the closet, Emma grabbed the usual construction paper and glitter, and then she noticed the white plastic bucket labeled "Balloons" in Ms. Claire Wish's perfect penmanship on one of the top shelves. A birthday party needed balloons, Emma thought, even if the party was for a dead person. She stood on a chair to get the bucket down.

We'd all stopped celebrating birthdays long ago at Maple Street, even though everyone's birthday is written right there on our tombstones. Our birthdays were one of the earthly things we forgot about, the way we all forget what cake tastes like, or what exactly it feels like to be hugged. We'd love to be hugged again, but we can't quite re-create the sensation in our minds. A hug must be so comforting, we think, and warm.

Emma took the bucket from the top shelf, climbed off the chair, and brought it back to her desk, putting it next to the construction paper and the glitter. She opened up the white plastic top, and in the bucket there were colorful balloons, a ton of them. Emma had seen it packaged that way before, in some of the evidence photographs shown at the Wish trial.

Balloons full of heroin.

43

When Emma got over her shock, after sitting there at her desk for several minutes, she wondered if she should wait until the end of the day to do something about the bucket. She did not want to get her father involved; she wasn't sure he would be any help. He was distracted anyway, going on and on about Harold Baynes to the kids who were still paying attention.

Emma decided the right thing to do was to put the burden on Principal Jefferies. This was over her pay grade as a long-term substitute teacher of the fifth grade. This was a Class-A substance that came with a huge amount of jail time. She stepped into the hallway and called the office from her cellphone.

"Speak up," Doris said.

"Can you send Principal Jefferies to my classroom?" It was way too hard to explain over the phone; she didn't want the kids to overhear.

While she was waiting for the principal to get there, Emma knew she wanted the kids to be as distracted as possible. The TV was in the classroom, but the trial wouldn't be enough to distract her students; they were bored of it by now, and she didn't want Jefferies to know they'd been watching the trial either. She hooked her laptop up to the TV and went to Netflix and searched for something to watch. She went to the Netflix Classics section, and there it was: the perfect movie, one of her dad's old favorites. It was black and white, so it passed for educational. Her dad had always said it was the best Jimmy Stewart movie, to hell with *It's a Wonderful Life*.

The kids were already absorbed in the movie when their principal finally got there, and they barely noticed him. Principal Jefferies didn't recognize what the balloons were, so Emma had to explain in a hushed whisper.

"Jiminy," Principal Jefferies said, at full volume. "Claire Wish. Worst teacher of the year."

All the kids looked up then, their eyes glaring.

"I'm kidding," he said. "I miss her, too, of course, of course I do, that was only a joke. And what's this movie?" he asked.

"It's a really old movie called *Harvey*," Adam D. said.

"About a drunk guy with an imaginary rabbit for a friend," Ulf explained. The kids moved their stares back to the TV. "Ms. Starling wants us to understand what's wrong with her dad."

"That's not why . . ." Emma said, but then she realized, yes, maybe it was. Her dad had always loved the scene where the friendly and charming alcoholic Jimmy Stewart introduces people at the bar to his imaginary friend, a seven-foot-tall rabbit named Harvey. Her dad loved to quote a favorite line: "Nobody ever brings anything small into a bar." Everyone in the bar was glad to meet a huge imaginary rabbit, because it made their own problems shrink. No matter how big a problem was, at least it wasn't a seven-foot-tall invisible rabbit. But her dad wasn't saying anything about the movie or the rabbit now. He was asleep in his chair, head slouched, time for his daily afternoon nap.

Principal Jefferies told Emma he'd go down to his office and call the police, and he'd let her know what to do next, but don't let the kids know what's going on, sit tight for now. Principal Jefferies left the bucket of balloons, didn't remove it from the classroom. He said he didn't want to tamper with evidence.

Emma sat on the floor, far away from the balloons, near where

her father's chair was, and watched the movie with the kids.
Emma had never realized it before, but the movie was about grief.
It's about the loss of the main character's mother, how the pain of
her absence follows him around, like a seven-foot-tall rabbit. And
the best part of the movie is toward the end, when his sister says
she can see the rabbit too. When Jimmy Stewart is not all alone in
the world with his grief.

Her father snorted loudly in his small metal chair, but not
loudly enough to wake himself up.

Or actually, Emma thought, maybe Harvey really is an enormous invisible rabbit. Maybe it's not a metaphor at all. Sometimes magic might just be magic.

44

Once Principal Jefferies got his shit together down there in his office, the entire school was dismissed early, so the drug-sniffing dogs could come in and search the school. It would turn out that Claire Wish, and, most likely, her husband, had hidden a whole lot more heroin in the ceiling of the fifth-grade classroom, stuffed behind the removable cheap white panels. When they got there, the drug-sniffing dogs simply sat in the center of the classroom and barked toward the lights until the police looked in the ceiling. These were cops sent over from Concord, the nearest bigger city, because the Everton police force, made up of two cops and several volunteers, wasn't equipped with drug-sniffing dogs, no room in the budget. Officer Gene stayed in the hallway, sweating and pacing. His daughter went to this school; she was never in that classroom, she was a second grader, but what was happening was still crazy enough for any parent to get worked up about.

Emma stayed behind to watch what happened, how it all unfolded, and also because the police told her she'd have to answer a lot of questions, to clear her of possible involvement. Her father stuck around, too, since Auggie wasn't answering his phone. Emma really wanted Auggie to come pick their dad up, to take him off her hands for this. She even tried her mother, but her mom didn't pick up either. She considered calling Mack, but she wasn't ready to ask him any boyfriend-type favors yet.

"This is so exciting," her dad said. "I've never been part of a drug bust before."

"Yeah, Dad," Emma said. "Super exciting."

Emma was being sarcastic, but as the cops and their dogs patrolled the other classrooms, looking for more hidden drugs, she did take a few photos with her phone. She did feel a sick sense of satisfaction in revealing Claire Wish was not such a good teacher after all, but that good feeling lasted only so long, because when the cops had finally asked Emma all their questions and told her she could go, it was pretty frustrating trying to corral her father, who was trying to talk with every single police officer from Concord about Crystal's case. Emma was *really* pissed when they got home and Auggie was sitting in front of the TV. "Where the hell were you?" she asked.

Auggie laughed—he really laughed—when he heard about the balloons of heroin. "Sorry, GG, I got another job," he said, once he'd calmed down from the laughter. He'd been hired as a crew member at the LumberBarn and Yard, where he'd been buying wood for the *Titanic* set. He would work there during the day and do the community theater at night, with a few hours off in-between.

Emma snapped at him that he still needed to answer his phone, because what if it was an emergency, and you know what, *it* had *been an emergency*. But still, she had to admit, it was good news for Auggie, about the job.

After the Possession-with-Intent-to-Distribute charges, the kids didn't love Ms. Wish anymore, because fifth graders are, as a whole, extremely anti-drugs. They hadn't blamed Claire Wish for her husband's problems before, but now there was no escaping it: Ms. Wish was caught up in it too. There was no point in not sharing the events with them, Emma realized, no hiding something that big. "Tell us more," they said, when Emma opened it up for discussion. Her dad embellished a few details, but Emma let him brag, even if the cops had certainly never asked Clive Starling, retired poetry professor, for help solving the case.

Mostly, the kids wanted to hear about these hero dogs, the ones from Concord, the dogs who could smell the heroin in the ceiling—a big, bad drug, a poisonous drug, a real killer that had been sitting above their heads for who knows how long and none of the people walking in and out of the classroom had ever suspected it. There had even been a parent-teacher conference in September, one-on-ones with Ms. Wish, and not even their parents had picked up on it. *Was no adult able to protect them?* the students wondered, growing more and more freaked out.

"Did it get in our lungs?" Olivia asked. "Did we breathe it in?"

"Are we addicted?" Zoe F. asked.

"Good question," Clive said, and Emma shook her head at her father. She sent him out in the hall with Michael B., who had been through so much of this already when his father overdosed. Emma instructed her dad to take the boy for a walk and talk to him about anything, anything at all, except for heroin, and except for Crystal Nash.

"You are not addicted," Emma promised the rest of her students. "I swear on my life, you are not addicted. I promise. You're all healthy as horses."

"If Ms. Starling says we're okay, we're okay," they said to each other.

"She's a healer," Olivia reminded everyone. "She brought a bird back to life."

Emma sighed. It was time for the truth. "I didn't heal that bird," she said. "You are all old enough now to know I didn't heal the bird. I think it was eaten by mice."

"Oh," they said, letting this news sink in.

"You must have seen another bird on the playground. You're sure it had a red string on its leg?"

"Zoe, did it really have a red string?" Tobey L. asked. Everyone

looked at Zoe F., who had been the only one who had actually
seen the bird, everyone else just lied and said they did. Zoe F.
shrugged. She didn't really remember.

"That's okay, Ms. Starling," Adam D. said. "It's okay if you
didn't heal the bird."

"We still love you," Nicole P. said. "You protected us from
drugs."

"She's a protector, not a healer," Olivia said.

"*What* happened?" Jonathan Rat asked, and someone filled
him in on what had happened to the sparrow in the shoebox before he'd joined the class, which Ms. Starling *apparently* hadn't
really healed, but it was still a pretty fun class activity. It had
brought them together. It made them see Ms. Starling was different from the rest of the substitutes. She was going to try to teach
them something, and not just boring facts. The real stuff. Life and
death.

Captain Clive and Michael B. came back in from the hallway,
holding each other by the hand. Fifth graders are generally considered too old for handholding, but no one made fun of Michael
B. Everyone was sorry for him about his dad, and besides, no one
wanted to get pounded on after school.

During the last unit of the day, Leanne Hatfield approached Emma's desk while the rest of the class was struggling through a science project. Ms. Starling had tried to give Isabella a nice birthday
party, even though Izzy was dead, and that had meant a lot to
Leanne. "Ms. Starling?"

"Yes, Leanne?"

"I'm sorry for what I said a long time ago. I'm sorry for what I
said about your friend getting killed by a serial killer."

Emma was a little taken aback. Leanne never apologized, but
here she was, apologizing. Leanne sat down in a chair by the desk

and quietly told Emma what had *really* happened to her best friend Isabella Eaklin. "It wasn't even cancer," she said. "The doctors were wrong." Izzy had been in the hospital for a year, sick from what the doctors had thought at first was leukemia, but then it turned out to be something else, a misdiagnosis, a disease with no cure. The doctors said they had done all they could do; Isabella should go home and rest. Izzy couldn't have visitors at home, her parents said, germs, so Leanne hadn't seen her again after that. The funeral was in August. "I really miss her," Leanne said to her teacher.

"I'm so sorry, Leanne. That is really, really unfair."

"She would have told me to be nicer to you." Leanne reached into her pocket and came out with a frog, a little plastic poison dart frog, a lime-green one with black spots. She put it on the desk right next to the framed photograph of Claire and Sid Wish.

"What's his name?" Emma asked, picking up the frog, feeling like she was finally connecting to the kid.

"It's a symbol of your grief," Leanne said, not at all amused by the babyish question.

"You should name him Terry," Olivia said, coming up to find out why her science experiment wasn't working.

Emma asked Leanne to go help Olivia with her experiment, and then she stared at the frog on her desk. It stared back at her with its plastic black eyes. Crystal Nash hadn't even been Emma's friend when she'd gone missing, yet she was someone Emma felt she'd desperately miss all her life. No one ever stops loving their high school best friend, no matter how we lose them. Some of us at Maple Street had lost our childhood best friends to world wars, to polio, to childbirth, to other violent ends, or just to plain old boring time and separation, but we'd all taken a piece of that love to the grave. That first love. It had shaped us all.

It had been a strange form of grief for Emma since she'd come home, losing someone whose friendship she had already lost.

There wasn't a name for it, the death of a best friend who wasn't your friend anymore. Someone you had failed to always be there for, like you'd sworn you would, sworn best friends forever and ever, two halves of the same heart, unable to survive without the other. Someone who you hadn't been able to help, in the end. There was no name for that mixture of grief and guilt and shame. But here was a name. It was Terry.

45

"You're doing an important thing," Emma's dad said later that week as they were riding home. "You're giving these kids someone to count on. It's no small thing for children. I know that's what your mother would say."

"Thanks, Dad." Emma clutched the wheel as she drove. It was uncomfortable whenever her dad brought up her mom. For some reason, he had decided his wife had gone on a trip to France, so Auggie kept showing him pictures of the Eiffel Tower.

It did mean a lot to Emma, that her dad thought she was a good teacher. She had just gotten her check from Ralph Kelsey's last will and testament; he had left her enough money to pay off her credit card debt and some of her student loan, too, so the need for a paycheck wasn't so pressing. But when Emma thought maybe Claire Wish was going to take back her classroom after the trial, something had become clear to Emma: she *wanted* the job. It's easy to figure out how you feel about something when you think you're about to lose it.

"You know, Dad," Emma said, looking ahead at the road, wondering if she really wanted to have this conversation with her father, but if she didn't say it now, then when? "It really messed me up when you cheated on Mom."

"Oh, Emma."

"I just needed to say that."

"Well, I made a mistake. And I never wanted to do anything to hurt you or your brother, and especially not your mother, but you should know my parents died when I was very young."

"Glad to know I'll have that excuse."

"What do you mean?"

"You're dying. I'm still young."

"How old are you?"

"Twenty-two. Almost twenty-three."

"A little young to be a teacher, don't you think? I wonder if you should go have a little fun before you get such a serious job."

"Okay, Dad. Useful."

Clive sighed. "If you want to know the truth, Sabrina was a distraction."

"From Auggie's drug problem?

"Yes, I suppose. That too. But I started up with her when I realized I was dying. I knew long before those idiot doctors did, well before I let on to your mother that anything was wrong. Really, I knew as soon as I saw the first cat in our house. A symbol of death, cats, and your mother so allergic. I don't know how that cat got in."

"Dad, the realization that you're going to die is not an excuse for an affair."

"Oh, my dear daughter. You'll find dying is an excuse for everything." He reached over in the truck and patted her on the knee. "But really, what you're doing for those children is just terrific, and I'm so proud of you. You're not too messed up at all. You're just as messed up as you should be."

At Maple Street, we knew those four words—"I'm proud of you"—outrank "I love you" in terms of how much we need to hear them, especially from our parents. Emma teared up. "I wish I hadn't lost it," she said. "I really wish I hadn't lost it."

"Lost what? What'd you lose?"

"The Charm."

"Emma, don't you be sorry about that." Clive shook his head.

"Why do you think I called it the Charm? It was just that, charming. Somewhat helpful, but never a miracle drug. You were never going to save the world with it."

"Okay." Emma remembered that her dad *did* pressure her to try to get into emergency rooms to heal bleeders and burn victims, but this was her father. He had never been totally consistent. Something in her released. Her dad truly had never expected her to heal him. She hadn't failed him. She lifted one hand off the wheel of the truck to wipe her eyes. "Dad?"

"Yes?"

"I wish you didn't have to die."

"Me too, Emmy. Me too."

Emma glanced away from the road to look at her dad, his silver hair in a braid, wearing his old red winter parka. He was looking away from her, out the window into woods, but she could tell he was crying. He was holding a stack of missing person posters on his lap. He still always had a pile with him, and he kept putting them up in the teacher's lounge, even though Principal Jefferies had specifically asked him not to; the bulletin board was really for elementary school news only.

Emma would miss him so much.

46

➤·◄

Over the coming weeks, Emma still worried sometimes that she'd failed the fifth graders by bringing in her dying father, like a really awful adult version of show-and-tell, but then Ulf bit Leanne Hatfield, and Leanne clocked him right in the eye, and Adam D. went ahead and peed right then, and Emma had to admit her dad was helpful. He offered to take Adam D. down to the nurse for a change of clothes, and then he and Ulf would have a chitchat, *man-to-wolf.*

And Michael B. was her dad's new little buddy. Michael B. had told Captain Clive that he wanted to grow up to be a biologist, not a serial killer, no matter what Leanne Hatfield said. Clive had treated that goal seriously, and had given Michael B. a list of endangered and threatened wildlife in the Upper Valley area, everyday ways to help populations bounce back. Emma had noticed that Michael had stopped pulling the smoke alarm in the hall.

But not *everyone* loved Clive, or not without reservation. At rehearsal, Leanne Hatfield said she wanted to recast the captain of the *Titanic* again. "We need someone younger," she said. "It's supposed to be tragic when he dies, and no one will care if the captain is a crazy old man."

"Who's the director, Leanne?" Auggie asked. "The show goes up in two weeks. We're not replacing anyone."

"If you kick out the captain, I quit," Michael B. said. Adam D., Ulf, and Olivia chimed in that they would quit too.

"No one is quitting," Auggie said.

"I'm definitely not quitting," Captain Clive said.

Emma was sitting in the front row, with Moses the dog, because he still howled whenever their father left the house, even if Emma was home with him. Auggie had suggested that Emma start bringing the dog to school with her, too, but she said that was out of the question. They could leave the fox in his crate, no problem, Rasputin would curl up, use his tail as a pillow. Who knew the dog would be the harder pet to have?

"But Dad, you are not allowed to talk to Harold when you're onstage," Auggie said to their father. "It does make you look crazy; Leanne is right on that one. Do you hear me? You have to stick to the script only."

"Well, it'd be easier if he'd stop talking to me," their dad said, crossing his arms.

"Yes," Auggie agreed. "It would. But either way, you have to show some self-control." And then Auggie went over to the piano and he started up the opening number yet again.

Emma felt so glad she wasn't in charge for once, that it was up to Auggie to manage it. *If Dad can survive the school year,* she begged as she watched her father goofing around with the kids onstage. He and Michael B. had a secret handshake, and Ulf let him wear the Viking helmet sometimes. *Just get us through the school year,* she prayed. Who was she bargaining with? She had always said she was an atheist, or at least an agnostic, whenever the topic came up, but secretly she thought it would be nice to believe in God sometimes, really go whole hog on the Jesus thing. It would be so great if you really felt like there was someone out there who listened to your bargains, your pleas, your promises to yourself. Like someone somewhere was keeping a lookout.

We're here, we told her, as we often did.

47

One afternoon, when Clive and Emma got back to the cabin after school, there was a man sitting in a white van out front. "Must be our private investigator," Clive said when he saw the van.

"We don't have a private investigator."

"We do. I'm sure he's here because the credit card was declined again. Or maybe he's solved the case."

"Did you just hire him?"

"Oh, no, months and months ago," Clive explained. "Before you came home." He unbuckled his seatbelt and jumped out of the truck into the icy driveway. Emma turned off the truck engine, took a deep breath. This was it. This was the way it ended, with a private investigator she hadn't known about. Her dad, still full of surprises.

"Nice to meet you, Emma," the man said, extending his hand. He was a tall man with blue eyes that nearly bulged out of his head, like a goldfish. "I'm the private investigator who had been working on your friend's case. My name's Roy Briggs."

"What did you find?" Emma asked, not shaking his hand. "Is she dead?"

"Emma," her father scolded. "Don't be rude."

"Let's go inside. Cold out here, and this might take a while to explain."

"Cold as a witch's tit out here," Clive agreed.

Emma scrunched her nose, she hated that saying, but she wanted to get inside too. It was freezing, and the sun was going down already at only four in the afternoon. Whatever the investigator knew, it wasn't good. He would have told them immediately if it was good. She wasn't sure she wanted to hear what he had to say at all. She thought she was about ready to let Crystal go. If she had a time machine, things could have been different, but she didn't, and so they weren't. End of story.

Auggie was still at work at the lumberyard, so once in the cabin, Emma had to let the fox out of his crate. Rasputin and Moses took turns greeting them, tails wagging, the fox chirping, the dog howling and barking. Emma found that Moses had ripped open a bag of flour on the couch, another way the dog was dealing with his separation anxiety: challenging himself to make messes that were increasingly difficult to vacuum up.

"I saw a while back that you bought a fox," Roy Briggs said. "At first, I thought it couldn't be real, but I found out that it was something you can do, if you're crazy. Now my wife wants one."

"What do you mean you saw a while back?" Emma asked.

"Oh, I track all your family's credit card statements. In a case like this, everyone's a suspect."

"Oh. That's cool, that's just great."

"He has excellent references," her father said. "I hired the best."

"Has he found anything?" Emma asked. She felt icky about this whole thing, knowing that she had been watched all this time. Well, that amused us at Maple Street.

"It's a strange case," Roy Briggs said once they had all sat down at the kitchen table with a beer each. Emma needed a drink for this. "There's really very little evidence," Roy went on. "I wanted to give you all the information I found on her because I do have to throw in the towel here. That's why I wanted to come in person, after you called me on the phone again. No more phone calls after this, understand?"

This was, Emma realized, apparently not the first time that

Roy Briggs had quit this case. Her father probably either kept forgetting that Roy had quit, or he wasn't willing to accept it.

"There's no real leads, but I have found a few things," Roy Briggs said. "And maybe they'll help you as you keep working on the case, but any further investigating must be done on your own, is that clear?"

Clive nodded, looking sheepish.

Emma sighed. If a licensed private investigator couldn't find anything, then Crystal really had to be dead. It didn't really matter where her body was. *We* could have told Emma that it *always* matters where the body is. Emma Starling didn't understand the importance of a proper burial. Those left unburied can never fully rest. It's worse than being cremated; much, much worse. We don't even like to think about it.

Roy pulled an enormous manila folder out from his briefcase and plopped it on the table. "This is all my work on the case. I must warn you your friend was engaging in some awfully risky behavior in the year before she disappeared, from what I've found. Drugs, strange men, accepting money for sex."

"Sex?" Clive asked.

Emma opened up the folder and flipped through. He knew Crystal's blood type, her medical history; her old high school report cards were all there. And there were printed screenshots, grainy photos from what appeared to be a surveillance camera, time-stamped. It was stills from security footage of the trailer park. People going in and out of Crystal's trailer.

"Mr. Leeches keeps cameras everywhere in his park," Roy Briggs said, explaining how he'd gotten the photos. "He said he was trying to avoid this type of at-home business in his park."

Emma kept flipping through the photos. It wasn't exactly the idea of prostitution that surprised her, but it was the shapes of the people in the pictures. Their faces weren't any easier to see than the faces of the jurors blurred on Court TV, but you could make out the basic outlines of the bodies.

"You learn not to be surprised at who will pay for sex," Roy Briggs said. "When you've been in the business as long as I have."

The pictures were grainy, but Emma recognized one of the people by the way the lady was slumped forward a bit and wearing such a long scarf. Lottie Evans, who owned the Knit & Purl. Lottie, who had told Emma she missed going to the healing sessions but found the painkillers to be more effective. She didn't say *when* she'd started taking painkillers instead of going to the healing sessions, just that she'd made the switch. *Crystal had started her own Gentle Touch Healing Society.* Well, a one-woman show, which isn't really a society. It made perfect sense. The money had always been good. Crystal could work out of the comfort and safety of her own home, as long as she could get it past Graham Leeches. "She was accepting money for *touching,*" Emma said.

"I just told you that," Roy said.

Emma shook her head and told the PI about the Gentle Touch Healing Society, as if it were any of Roy Briggs's business.

"That's very interesting," Roy said, although he clearly didn't care. "Hey, I got to take a piss. Where's the little boys'?"

Clive pointed to the door between the kitchen and the bunkroom, and Emma kept flipping through the papers. One of these clients might have hurt or killed Crystal, or at least know what had happened to her. But the problem was, the surveillance photos weren't any good. Most of these people were impossible to identify from just these pictures. Lottie Evans certainly had not killed Crystal, not with a crochet hook.

"Sorry that took me so long," Roy said when he came out of the bathroom. "Got a bad case of Peyronie's disease. Maybe the Gentle Touch Healing Society can heal it," he said, snorting a laugh.

Emma ignored the comment; she didn't know what Peyronie's disease was, nor did she want to, it was likely gross. "Can you tell me who these people are in the photos?" she asked instead.

"I would if I could," Roy said, shaking his head. "Tried to figure it out; that might have cracked the case, if we're looking at a homicide, but you really can't tell one person from another."

"Thank you so much, Mr. Briggs," Clive said. "I think you've done a great job."

"Has he?" Emma asked.

"I have to get on the road, but I hope you find her. I'm sorry I can't be more of a help. And Clive, I'm sorry about your situation, but sometimes I wish my wife would leave me too." He chortled.

"What's that?" Clive asked.

"My mother's in France," Emma said. "She'll be back after her vacation."

"Oh, that's right, that's right," Roy Briggs said. "The Eiffel Tower. Well, it was nice to meet you, Emma, and nice to see you again, Clive. No more phone calls. I'm blocking your number. Case closed on my end, all right?"

After Roy Briggs left in his creepy white van, Emma continued to leaf through the security photographs, trying to recognize people by their outlines. Some of the photos were dated last June, the month Crystal had gone missing. She had still been seeing Gentle Touch Society clients, up to the end, even as her drug problem seemed to be getting worse, from everything Emma had learned from people around town. One of the grainy photos was a man in a suit, that was easy enough to make out. Most people don't wear suits in Everton, unless to a funeral or a spaghetti banquet.

Percy Eaklin. He always wore a suit, even at the Blueberry Hill Pub, even to work at the gun factory, even on weekends. Maybe Percy had asked Crystal to go see his sick daughter in the hospital, a last-ditch effort. Emma wondered how much Crystal had charged him, knowing how rich he was. Maybe she'd really gouged the price and it was enough for a plane ticket to Mexico. Maybe she was on the beach somewhere and Crystal's phone didn't work internationally. Maybe that would be the story Emma would choose to tell herself. It was as good a story as any other, and one that didn't end with the more logical conclusion: Crystal was dead. She had been working a side job because she needed more money because heroin is an expensive habit. And eventually, she had overdosed. That's how the story often ends. Emma knew that.

Emma put the folder away in one of the kitchen cabinets. It was clear her dad needed a break from it if he'd been harassing the detective, so she hid it above the fridge, where she was sure he wouldn't go rooting around; there was no food in that cabinet, just her antidepressants and a can of cockroach killer.

While his daughter opened and shut the kitchen cabinet, the one above the fridge where he knew she liked to hide things, Clive sat and absorbed everything the PI had said. Not much new information about Crystal Nash, but there was something else Roy Briggs had said as he was leaving, and Clive paired that comment with the conversation he and Emma had recently, how she was still upset about his affair with Sabrina Berkman. A lightbulb went on above Clive's head. Clive could remember things, if given a little information, if his memory was jogged. Clive remembered his wife wasn't in France. She wasn't cutting loose on wine and brie. No, Ingrid had left him, had driven off in a Prius, not much of a car. Clive Starling was dying, but his fourth and final wife had left him first. For his own doctor. That white-coated son of a bitch.

48

>-·-<

Clive spent the next two days in bed. There was no one home at the cabin to watch him because Auggie was at the lumberyard or working on the *Titanic* set, the show going up so soon, and Emma had to teach, and her dad was supposed to come with her, but you can't make a dying man do anything. Especially not a depressed one. Emma said he could stay home as long as he promised not to leave his bed.

"No problem," he said. "Leave me here to die."

But on the third day, after both his kids left for work, Clive rose again. The first thing he would do, he thought, would be to show Ingrid that he'd gotten closer to their kids in her absence. His wife loved their kids more than she loved anything else in the world, and she would come back to him if she saw he'd put in more effort. Hadn't made it all about him. He was paying more attention to Auggie. He was helping Emma get back on track. He'd promised Ingrid he'd be a good father, back when she first learned she was pregnant with Emma, and maybe sometimes he'd let her down. But Ingrid would be proud of how the kids were doing at the moment, Emma in the classroom and Auggie with the musical. Even if Emma wasn't living up to her potential. Even if Auggie was kind of letting that Leanne Hatfield girl run the show.

Since Clive had missed the past two nights of rehearsals to lie in bed, Auggie was starting to freak out about who was going to play the captain, asking Emma if Mack Durkee could carry a tune. But no, Clive wasn't going to let his son down, not this time, not ever again. The show was going up next week. Everything would be fine. He would not talk to Harold Baynes during the performance, no matter what the ghost said during the one hour and forty-three minutes of the show. Clive would make sure Auggie's opening night was a big success, and that Ingrid was there to see it.

Across town, Ingrid was standing in Gary Wheeler's hyperclean kitchen, outfitted with all new appliances, when she got the text from her estranged husband. She was proud of him for texting; he'd resisted using the phone for so long. *One night only!!!* the text read, inviting her to see *Titanic the Musical!* the very next week. *Please come,* he typed. *And Mr. Wheeler is not a very good doctor if you ask me. Still dying over here.*

It made Ingrid laugh, and she hadn't laughed in a while. The relationship with Gary had not been the breath of fresh air she thought it would be. *I'll be there,* she typed back. And then she felt giddy. A little naughty, even, like she was breaking the rules while Gary was still sleeping upstairs. It was the way she had felt about Clive in those early days, when she was the new librarian at Meriden, and Clive would come by the library all the time to pick her brain about any new books worth reading when he was still married to his third wife.

All Ingrid's friends had said men like Clive don't change, to be wary because eventually Clive would find a fifth wife. It was only a matter of time. But Ingrid would only laugh and say, "Good, he'll be someone else's problem." Ingrid knew Clive would never leave her. He was devoted, like one of her clingiest rescue dogs. Really, he was such a needy man.

But children had needs of their own, and when Auggie's addiction and recovery became Ingrid's full-time job, on top of her job at the college, on top of being president of the historical society, on top of being the sole caretaker for Ralph Kelsey's mansion and grounds, which was so much harder without Bart Nash around to do all the groundskeeping . . . well, Clive's needs had to take a backseat for a while. Or rather, his needs had to get out of the car completely. They had to be curbed. Not forever, but for the moment.

And then. The affair.

"You were neglecting me," Clive had whined.

Ingrid hadn't been able to forgive him, as much as she'd tried, even though she'd let him back in the house. *How could she forgive him?* Her heart was broken. He hadn't been there when she needed him. When *their son* needed him. Refusing to go to family therapy at the rehab center during either one of Auggie's stays, that alone was unforgivable. And now Clive was dying, and Ingrid couldn't bear it. She was so angry, so hurt, and yet she loved him still.

But it was just then that Dr. Gary Wheeler came down the stairs, and he was so handsome, and so young and healthy, and neither of them had hurt the other one yet. *It's not exactly a no-brainer,* Ingrid thought, and then she realized that was a phrase her husband would have gotten a real kick out of, given the situation, what he was dying from.

Ingrid wanted to at least do something nice for her husband, so she texted her kids, said she'd gotten word that the Corbin caretaker's house was move-in ready after the wrath of the deer. She thought Clive and the kids might like to go home, that it would be more comfortable there than the cabin. She imagined things were getting cramped.

Thanks, Mom, Emma texted back. *That will definitely help.*

Clive was overjoyed when he heard that news. He was sure Ingrid would be joining them back at the Corbin House soon, and they would finally be a real murmuration again. And even if Ingrid didn't return to him, even if she was gone forever, Clive wanted to go home anyway. Those goddamn bunk beds would kill him soon, if the brain disease didn't get him first.

PART VI

The Bears

49

> ⇢ ·•· ⇠

ANOTHER END TO JIMMIE'S STORY
from *The Collected Writings of Ernest Harold Baynes,* © 1925
This Book Is Property of the Everton Historical Society

At the Risk of Upsetting My Canoe I Helped Him Aboard

Photograph by Louise Birt Baynes.

I did not take Jimmie home with me, that day in the spring when
he blubbered as he held my arm through the bars. It was heart-
less, Mrs. Baynes said, that I should go to see him. It would be

better, she thought, if I never went to visit him, if I let him think me gone, or dead. If I let the poor bear focus on catching peanuts and popcorn thrown through the bars by the young boys in defiance of the NO THROWING FOOD AT THE BEARS sign.

I did not always listen to Mrs. Baynes ("Never," she says over my shoulder as she reads what I have written. "You should write you *never* listen to Mrs. Baynes"), so I traveled down to New York again to see Jimmie in the zoo. It was only a few months after my first visit. As I approached the bear enclosure, I could see Jimmie, who had grown into quite a specimen of a bear. "Jimmie," I called. "Jimmie, old friend, hello!"

The bear stood up on his hind legs and looked at me with a puzzled expression which seemed to say: *It seems to me that I have met you somewhere before, but I'll be hanged if I can remember where.*

➤·◄·➤·◄

50

February had come to Everton, the coldest month of the year, and the *Titanic* was due to set sail in two nights. Three-quarters of the Starlings had come home to roost. The Corbin caretaker's house looked great with all the floors redone and fresh coats of paint where the floral wallpaper had been, and everyone had been sleeping well in their own beds. That morning, snow had been dumped overnight, and there had been brief hope for a snow day, but the superintendent had decided on only a two-hour delay. Emma, at least, had time to make herself toast and eggs while the plows cleared the roads. Clive put more sugar into his oatmeal. The fox had a little bowl of oatmeal all his own, too, and was lapping it up from his perch on the table. Moses kept eyeing him, the dog wondering why he so rarely got people food, why the fox so often did.

"You're not coming to school with me today," Emma explained to her father as he ate. "Mom texted. She wants to come over and talk to you." Emma's mom had the day off because the college had called a snow day, which was totally unfair when the public grade schools were open.

"What does she want to talk about?" Clive asked, thrilled by the idea of time alone with his wife.

"Beats me."

"Dad, remember, tonight is our final dress rehearsal," Auggie said, grabbing a Pop-Tart. "I'll swing by to get you after work, if you could be in costume when I get here."

"Aye-aye, sir." Clive saluted.

"Have fun with Mom," Emma said. "She should be here any minute. She said she was on the way."

"Have either of you seen Harold? He keeps disappearing on me."

"Have a good day, Dad," Auggie said. "I'm sure he'll turn up."

Five minutes later, Ingrid arrived in Gary Wheeler's Prius; he'd let her borrow the car for the day. She walked into her own house, and there her own husband was at the kitchen table. He was reading the newspaper and having his coffee. There was a dog at his feet. The fox was curled in the fruit bowl.

That was what Ingrid was here to talk about. She did not approve of the fox as a pet. Ingrid had made some phone calls, and she had to give the San Diego Zoo an answer by the end of the week. They were willing to take Rasputin, they said, even though they were over capacity in the Foxes/Badgers/Weasels department, but it sounded like this was a fox that they could use in educational programming.

"Good morning," Clive said, looking up from the paper. "You're finally awake." He stood up to kiss her, but she dodged him. Clive didn't think that was strange. She hadn't had her coffee yet.

"There's something I need to talk to you about, Clive," she said.

"Me too," he said. "About how sorry I am. I hope you know how much I love you. The affair meant nothing, it meant less than nothing. I was only trying to fund my wildlife research."

"Your research?" Ingrid asked, because Clive was mixing up his story with Harold's. "Wait, Clive, please, let me talk first," she said, because she needed to get this out or she wouldn't have the strength. She knew her husband would throw a fit, that this wasn't going to be easy. She tried to help Clive understand about the opening at the San Diego Zoo, *the opportunity of it,* how hard it had been to reach anyone, how many phone calls she'd had to make. Ingrid said she thought it was the best thing for the fox, given that they could not send him back to Russia. The zoo would do its best to re-create the conditions of a healthy wild habitat. They would stimulate the fox in all the ways a wild animal should be stimulated. They would know what to feed him. Maybe Rasputin could even have a mate.

Clive looked horrified, and also really confused, but hadn't started yelling yet, when Ingrid's phone rang in her purse. "Just one minute," she told Clive, because the call was coming from the college. It was the janitor; the pipes had frozen at the library. He was going to thaw them out, but he wanted Ingrid to come in and move her most important documents before he warmed up the pipes with the space heaters and the blow-dryer. "In case the pipes burst," he explained. "I don't want you to lose anything important to you." The janitor knew how professors and librarians can get about paper. He had made mistakes before.

"I'll be right there," Ingrid said to the janitor. "I'll be back in an hour," she said to her husband, since President Billings had warned her that Clive really was not welcome on campus, not after he'd hugged that student without her explicit permission, that day with the cats in the classroom. Ingrid did not want to lose her job because of her husband. "Watch him," she said to the dog as she went out the door. Moses, of course, was already watching Clive. He always was. It was his duty, the thing he was absolutely best at.

51

With the rest of his family gone, and Harold nowhere to be seen, Clive started to wonder what he was supposed to do that day. Surely there had to be something. He went to his computer and checked his Meriden College email. The college had declared a snow day, he saw, which meant he didn't have to teach today. That was good because he couldn't remember what classes he was teaching this semester.

He looked at his calendar, and there was a recurring event, the Blacker Sabbath meeting. The band met at the coffee shop twice a week. He looked at his watch. He should be heading out if he was going to make it to the coffee shop on time to meet his friends. But no, wait, he didn't go to Wilderness's Edge Express anymore. His friends had kicked him out of the band, in his eleventh hour, before his death. Judases, all of them.

"Maybe you should still go," Harold said, appearing suddenly in the kitchen. "Go see your old friends. Go to the coffee shop."

"No, thanks." Clive sat for a minute more. Looked at the empty bowl in front of him, wondered what happened to his oatmeal. He looked at the big white dog at his feet, the fox on the armchair in the corner. Clive really should do something with the day. He had so little time left. So few days in front of him. Even when he forgot everything else, he never forgot that his time was running out. "I suppose I can head to the printing shop," he said. "And make some flyers for Crystal. Yes, I'll do that."

"Maybe swing by the coffee shop after," Harold suggested one more time. "Might be nice to see your friends."

"I'll think about it," Clive said, getting up to put his empty bowl in the sink.

"And I agree that it was hurtful, what your wife said about San Diego."

"Oh, she knows how I feel about California," Clive grumbled. He didn't remember exactly what Ingrid had said about San Diego, but he hated the entire state after Emma had chosen to go so far away to college. He was relieved she'd finally come home.

Harold was still talking: "Louise and I weren't always on the same page with our animals. We did always give our fox room to roam, though. The Sprite could come and go into the woods as he pleased. Those woods are a wonderful place for any fox. Much better than a cage."

Clive ignored Harold, the ghost was talking about his own marriage again, and Clive knew he had someplace to be. He went upstairs to get his motorcycle keys from his wife's underwear drawer, where he knew she'd hidden them months ago.

Moses, sensing that Clive planned to leave the house, started his anxious howls, his frantic pacing and panting, as Clive put on his boots and his red parka over his plaid pajamas. Clive remembered to leave a note for his wife on the kitchen table so that she wouldn't be angry with him. He had forgotten about Gary Wheeler; he only knew that his wife had been angry with him lately. They had just been sitting at the kitchen table having some kind of argument, he knew, but he couldn't remember about what. Better to play it safe, communicate a little better, like Ingrid always asked. He scribbled a note: *Gone out to work on the case.* He could have texted Ingrid, of course, but Clive forgot about his cell phone. It was in his office, plugged into the wall.

Clive started out the door, but because the dog was really putting up a stink, howling like he was being hit with a tire iron, Clive decided he'd bring Moses with him. And yes, the fox could come too. He let them out into the yard and then he loaded them into the double-seated sidecar of the motorcycle. Harold tried to protest, tried to tell Clive it wasn't a good idea, but both animals jumped in no problem, as if they had been trained to ride in the sidecars of antique motorcycles all their lives. Clive got a purple bicycle helmet for the dog from the garage, but there was nothing small enough to fit the fox. *It's New Hampshire anyway,* Clive remembered, there's no helmet law here. Clive decided he wouldn't wear his helmet, either, because *Live Free or Die.*

It is very dangerous to ride a motorcycle after a snowstorm, and without a helmet, almost no one would do it, except for someone suffering from a serious brain disease. We hoped Clive wouldn't crash; it was not a day we wanted to see innocent animals die. We had gotten rather attached to the fox and the dog. Harold was really very upset about the whole thing, begging Clive not to take the animals in the sidecar, but Clive ignored him, leaving the ghost behind in the driveway. We could see that Harold hadn't thought some of his suggestions through, pushing Clive to leave the house. Of course Clive was going to take the motorcycle, his daughter had his truck.

Clive turned the Harley onto Corbin Road, started up Main Street, and took the turn north up toward the Stop & Copy. He put his sunglasses on, snow from the drifts kept blowing in his face. The animals looked miserable, weren't enjoying the wind in their faces at all; this was nothing like a car ride. But somehow, Clive made it to the Stop & Copy safely, and we hoped he could make it back home. We figured the printing shop would be closed, and he'd have to turn right around. But we remembered then that Mr. and Mrs. Misto lived above the printing shop, so the Stop & Copy was never closed as long as the Mistos were home. Mrs. Beverly Misto came down in her robe when Clive rang the bell.

"What a nice surprise," Beverly Misto said, since she was always happy to see Clive. Between Clive's days at the elementary school and his nights rehearsing for the musical, he hadn't been coming around for a while, and he had been a reliable source of income for the printing shop, something of a rarity in Everton. The Stop & Copy even kept his credit card on file, so it wouldn't even matter that Clive's wallet was an empty fold of leather, all his cards with his daughter, his legal guardian.

"I'd like to change the poster a little," Clive said. "Why didn't we ever add a reward?"

"I told him to," Ralph Kelsey (b. 1923–d. 2014) said from Maple Street. "I said I'd pay for it."

"A reward is a good idea," Mrs. Misto agreed. She was not in the business of talking Clive out of making more copies. And a redesign would cost extra. "How much for the reward?"

"A million dollars," Clive said. "No more, because she isn't really worth it; no less, for moral reasons." Clive had no idea where he'd gotten the saying, but he loved how it sounded.

Mrs. Misto nodded, thought about how much worse Clive Starling seemed than when she'd seen him last. More disheveled, and wearing his pajamas underneath his winter coat. She hadn't even seen the motorcycle parked in her driveway with the fox and the dog sitting in the sidecar, one of them whining anxiously, the other sitting patiently, both waiting for their master to return. If Clive could have seen the two animals from the Stop & Copy window, he might remember that it was a tame fox that was worth exactly a million dollars, according to Harold Baynes, not a missing person.

On his way home with his package of two hundred fresh missing person posters, which now advertised a million-dollar reward, Clive made up his mind to drive to Wilderness's Edge Express.

His bandmates didn't own the place. He would like to see Dennis Hollingdrake's face when he walked in, and he remembered how good the coffee was there, and their scones. And besides, a local café like that one might have a community bulletin board, a good place to hang up a missing person poster. Clive didn't remember he had already hung up posters there before, in fact, many, many, many times.

When Clive pulled up in front of Wilderness's Edge Express, he saw Harold Baynes outside the shop, leaning against the green dumpster. "What are you doing here?" Clive asked Harold, looking around, wondering how the ghost had gotten to the coffee shop, when he'd just left him back at the house. Clive had to yell because the motorcycle's engine was still running.

"I wanted to meet your friends," Harold said. "The band."

"Are they inside?" Clive asked.

"No," Harold said, a bald-faced lie. Clive's bandmates were, indeed, inside the café. A little snow wouldn't keep them off the roads; they all drove trucks. If Clive had looked around, he would have seen Phil's Silverado, Dennis's Ford Ranger, Kurt's F-150. But Clive wasn't thinking clearly.

"Oh," he said. His face fell. "I thought they were going to meet me here. Dennis said we would meet here at eleven." Clive got off his bike to talk to Harold, the ghost who felt like his only friend in the world at that moment. He left the bike's engine running. "All traitors, but Dennis is the worst. I started that band, you know."

Dennis Hollingdrake had been the one to throw the coffee cup, that day the men fought at Wilderness's Edge Express coffee shop. Dennis had wanted Clive to apologize to Big Hank for the stunt he'd pulled at the pub, so Clive would play with them again, get the band back together. Clive wouldn't do it. Clive was too proud; he had seen all those rats from the Blueberry Hill Pub stage that night, the ones running all over the place. It wasn't his fault the health department had to be called. Big Hank should run a tighter ship.

"I bet there's a way to get your friends back for kicking you out of the band. Show them you don't need them. What about this Dennis? What would make him extremely, extremely jealous?" Harold gestured over his shoulder to the woods behind the dumpster, where you could see a large portion of the Corbin Park fence peeking through the trees. Clive had seen that portion of the fence many times before. There were all those TRESPASSERS WILL BE SHOT signs.

"I could start my own band," Clive said. "I'll start my own band."

"Is there something else Dennis loves?" Harold asked, growing visibly frustrated. "Something Dennis loves besides music?" Dennis Hollingdrake was a hunting fanatic, and more than anything, he wanted to hunt in Corbin Park. Dennis's obsession was why the band had started meeting at the coffee shop in the first place, because even though it was out of the way of absolutely everything, it was close to the front gate of the park. Dennis simply liked to be close to the park, even if he couldn't go inside. "What else does Dennis like?" Harold Baynes said, trying to push Clive as far as he could without breaking the invisible boundary of meddling. We knew Harold might explode any minute. You never know how much meddling will upset the universe.

"I don't know, they're all traitors," Clive said. "All of them traitors. They're not worth my time, Harold, they're not worth our time." Clive went to hug Harold, his dear friend, but stumbled flat onto his face. "*Et tu, Harold?*" he muttered as he pulled himself out of the snowbank, humiliated. He dusted the snow off his pajamas and decided he'd get back on the motorcycle and go home to his wife, someone he could always count on. He noticed the two animals in his sidecar, animals he'd forgotten about. *Why had he brought the animals with him?* he wondered. That was such a strange choice. Then, as he looked into their clever furry faces, Clive remembered something his wife had said, sometime recently . . . *When was that?* Anyway, his wife, his darling wife, had said she was going to call the San Diego Zoo, which is the best zoo in the world, she claimed. She called it the Harvard of zoos. Ingrid Starling said if they sent him to the zoo, Rasputin could have every happiness of a wild fox.

That awful witch, Clive Starling thought. *Over my dead body will that fox go to a zoo.*

But Clive also knew he *was* dying, and really sometime soon. *You know what,* Clive thought, the fox wouldn't like a zoo, he felt sure of it, but he might like Corbin Park, which was somewhere right around here, the fence right nearby. There was all that freedom to roam. Sure, there were hunters in the park, but really very few, for land that size. Rasputin's odds would be good in the park, and his namesake had been shot three times *and* poisoned, and survived. Clive would set the fox free in the park. Not the dog, he didn't think. You shouldn't set a dog free, even Clive Starling knew that, and Ingrid would take good care of the dog. "Can you show me how to get into Corbin Park?" he asked Harold. "Didn't you say you could take me to the park?"

"I thought you'd never ask," Harold said, his face bright with excitement. "There's something I'd like to show you in there."

"You'll show me your pet fox? I'd love to finally meet him," Clive said. "He never seems to want to meet me."

"The fox?" Harold asked, looking at Rasputin still in the sidecar.

"The Sprite?" Clive asked. "I saw him once, walking with you. The day Emma came home. Doesn't he keep you company on all your walks?"

"Oh right, right," Harold said. "Yes, The Sprite might be ready to meet you now." Harold was lying to Clive again, easier than explaining the truth. At Maple Street, we knew there was no ghost of the fox, no little red grim reaper waiting for Clive in the woods. In fact, Harold hadn't seen The Sprite in over a hundred years; not since 1911, when the fox had been ten years old. It's another one of the mysteries of the universe, what happens to animals when they die. We like to think all the animals are waiting for us, somewhere off this earthly plane, once we let go of the rule of Caring for the People of Everton. We can imagine a place beyond Maple Street, but we can't risk letting go. Not yet. The people of Everton need us here, watching them. Cheering them on. They need to have that occasional eerie sense that someone, somewhere, is keeping a lookout.

We watched as Harold Baynes started toward the woods behind the coffee shop. It wasn't too far to the dirt road that led to the Corbin Park service gate, but Clive and Harold would have to walk through the woods a ways. A half mile or so, along the fence; that would be the most direct route. The service gate was well hidden. It was designed to be, since it was left unlocked most of the time, with so many deliveries coming in. At the edge of the woods, Harold turned around and waited for his friend.

First, Clive took the helmet off the dog, who looked very relieved not to wear that thing anymore. Rasputin jumped out of the sidecar too. Then Clive, because he wasn't thinking clearly, put the purple bike helmet on his own head, and clipped it on. He left the motorcycle's engine running, forgot to turn the key, but he remembered to take his box of fresh photocopies and the staple-gun he always kept in the storage compartment of the bike. He could staple the signs to some of the trees along the way. He could even put up some flyers in the park; there were bound to be lots of trees in there.

52

That snowy late morning at Dream Far, the fifth graders were miserable; they had thought for sure a snow day would be called. They were also pretty mad that Captain Clive hadn't come into school. Why should he get the day off when he was too old to go sledding anyway? Emma reminded them that her father was an unpaid classroom volunteer, but the kids said they weren't paid to be there either. Emma tried to cheer the kids up, revealing she'd brought a bag of marshmallows and a tin of hot cocoa, and all they would need was hot water. She wasn't a rookie teacher anymore.

"And you'll read to us?" Olivia asked.

Emma agreed she would; she loved reading to the class. Sometimes the fifth graders would try to convince Emma that they weren't babies, but when they all sat down for reading time, one or two kids put their thumbs in their mouths, and all of their faces softened, their lips relaxed into o's. Emma would think then about how innocent they all were, even Michael B., who had written "Principal Jefferies Sucks Butts" on the whiteboard just last week.

Emma read to them from a book of Greek myths, but she couldn't read on forever; her throat would get so dry. They moved to the history unit, the horrors of war. Emma had been letting the kids conduct mock trials for the war criminals they studied, having already learned so much about the legal system from the Sid Wish trial.

In a crazy turn of events, Sid Wish had somehow still gotten acquitted, even with the heroin found in the ceiling. His lawyer had been able to pin the entire drug-dealing operation on Claire Wish, his wife, the mastermind, the femme fatale, now in jail awaiting her own trial. Emma had acknowledged to the kids it was pretty unfair that their former teacher was taking all the blame, and even if they didn't love Ms. Wish anymore, they were sorry for her. So far, in the fifth-grade classroom mock trials, none of the war criminals had been acquitted for their crimes. They all died in some horrible form of fifth-grade justice.

"Sorry to interrupt . . . this," Principal Jefferies said from the doorway, because Adam D. was standing on a desk and pretending that he was about to have his head chopped off by a guillotine. "Adam Delaney, please get down from there," Principal Jefferies said. He looked over to the whiteboard, where "Principal Jefferies Sucks Butts" was still written, because Michael B. had used permanent marker, not dry-erase. Emma Starling had put it on Janitor Arthur's TO-DO clipboard list, in all caps, but he hadn't gotten around to it yet. Emma surprised herself and realized she didn't care that Principal Jefferies was seeing her classroom in such chaos. She was doing her best. The kids were learning something, even if she was allowing them to use a papier-mâché guillotine.

"Ms. Starling," Principal Jefferies said. "It's the police on the phone. It's about your father."

"The captain was arrested?" the kids asked.

"Not exactly," Principal Jefferies said. "Ms. Starling, perhaps best to talk in the hallway?"

Emma's stomach dropped. She had taken her eye off the ball. She had left it up to her mother, who was supposed to be at the house in five minutes when she'd left for school. *What could have happened in five lousy minutes?* She told the students she'd be back, and she flipped on the TV, which was still in the classroom.

Emma didn't care what channel it was. She went out into the hall, following Principal Jefferies. She felt like she might vomit.

"Dennis Hollingdrake found your father's motorcycle outside the Wilderness's Edge coffee shop, and the engine was still running," Principal Jefferies explained in the hall. "And Angell Kimball said she saw him wander off into the woods with his two dogs, about an hour before that. Officer Gene hasn't been able to reach your mother, and he's concerned, given the weather and his . . . condition."

Emma wanted to sit down. The coffee shop girl who couldn't tell the difference between a goat and a dog, also couldn't tell the difference between a fox and a dog, but who could really blame her for that? No one expected to see a man wandering around with a fox.

"What happened to Captain Clive?" Leanne Hatfield asked, standing in the doorway. The kids had muted the soap opera.

"They're getting a search party together right now," Principal Jefferies said. "Ms. Starling, you need to get to the police station. I'll come after school."

"Good luck, Ms. Starling, good luck, we love you!" the kids called after her.

When Emma got to the police station, Auggie and her mom were already there; someone had gotten ahold of them. Her mother explained about the frozen pipes. She said she'd swung back by the house after the police called, to look for Clive, just in case, but he wasn't there, and neither were the animals. "Of course he left his phone at home, but there was a note on the table. It said he'd gone out to look for Crystal."

"He really hasn't let that poor girl go," Officer Gene said.

"No," Ingrid agreed. "He never has."

"Why didn't you take Dad to the library?" Auggie asked.

"He's not allowed on campus. A situation with a student."

"What?" Emma said. Ingrid started to explain, but Emma and Auggie already knew about the cat video. They just didn't know it had been enough to get him banned from campus.

Auggie groaned. "Mom, you could have taken him to campus and left him in the car."

But there was no use in arguing really; it was too late now. Twenty people had gathered in the police station parking lot, word was traveling fast. There was a lot of snow on the ground, and most people knew about Clive Starling's condition. He could be in danger before nightfall. If he were stranded overnight, he would certainly freeze to death.

"I got here as soon as I could," Mack said, huffing and puffing, having run over from the high school after Auggie had texted him. Mack was in a cast, making running more difficult. He had broken his arm in a pickup game with Principal Jefferies.

"Thanks for coming," Emma said meekly. She was comforted by the sight of Mack.

Officer Gene addressed the crowd: "Angell Kimball said Clive went into the woods behind Wilderness's Edge Express. He was likely walking toward the Corbin Park fence, and we have confirmation from Corbin Park headquarters that it's *possible* he could get into the park along that part of the fence; there is a service gate that was left unlocked today." Officer Gene said that the president of Corbin Park had agreed to open the park to outside visitors, just this once, in case Clive Starling had found his way in through that service gate. The search party was divided into two groups, one to walk the road and fence near the coffee shop, and a caravan to be sent into the park to explore the area on the other side of the service gate entrance. Mack said he would take Emma, since she didn't look like she could drive. They would be part of the caravan going into Corbin Park.

"Okay," Emma said, still unable to form much of a sentence.

She did not know where her mother or Auggie had been sent, she couldn't remember, she was doing as she was told. She wanted to go home and wait for her father there, hide under the covers until it was all over. But that wasn't the way you found someone who was lost. You had to get the whole town out looking for them. That was probably why no one would ever know what happened to Crystal. Not enough people had bothered to look for her. Then again, Emma's dad had made sure the entire town of Everton saw Crystal's face every day, usually multiple times a day, on the trees and bulletin boards in town. Even if Crystal Nash was never found, she wasn't forgotten in Everton. She wasn't invisible. She was everywhere.

It was about twenty minutes later when Mack Durkee's Jeep approached the front gate of Corbin Park. The large wooden gate swung open slowly. A man in a dorky green uniform gave them a map, and gave them some pointers as to where it made sense to start the search. Inside the park, the forest on either side of the dirt road looked denser than any forest Emma had ever seen. It had been untouched for more than one hundred and thirty years—a pure natural world left only for the millionaires. Each tree looked taller, thicker, and healthier than the ones outside the fence. The air felt cleaner and the snow was pure white, not the yellowed slush of the outside. A deer came out of the woods and watched them drive past.

On the map, Emma counted twenty-five cabins total, spread out over 26,000 acres. Emma wondered how many animals the park held, what kinds. Emma looked back at the trees. God, so many trees. On the map, all the cabins were named after animals: Elk House, Boar House, Hummingbird House, Antelope House, Bison House, and so on.

The Corbin Park gatekeeper said Emma and Mack should

park and get out on foot near the sign that said THE HUMMINGBIRD HOUSE and start their search there. Even if they could narrow his location down to this section of the park, the stretch near Unity Road where her dad might have entered, it was still a real needle-in-a-haystack situation.

"We'll find him, Emma," Mack said, sensing she was giving up before they even really started looking. They got out of the Jeep to walk toward the woods. The road in Corbin Park was well maintained, for a dirt road at least, as of course the roads would be with only the extreme-rich allowed inside. The snow was plowed, it wasn't slippery, and there was salt spread out. Emma saw what must be the Hummingbird House up ahead, a brownish-red log cabin, smoke coming from the chimney. Emma hoped her dad had gone straight to that cozy-looking cabin for a hot chocolate. How easy that would be.

But she also knew it was more likely that her father was still wandering in the snow, probably on the other side of the fence, not in the park, but lost in the woods either way.

"Look," Mack said. "Bears."

There were two bears ahead, in the front yard of the small log cabin. Black bears with brown snouts. Emma gasped. She had seen bears before; having grown up in New Hampshire, anyone would. She'd seen bears in dumpsters, bears tearing down the bird feeder, bears lumbering across the road. But these were Corbin Park bears. These were special bears. Extra-wild bears.

Well, they couldn't be that wild, because there was a woman dressed in a long white parka standing between the two black bears. She was feeding the two bears something from a red bucket that hung from her walker. Her white coat was trimmed at the hood with brown fur, and her silver walker glinted in the sun. The bears were eating from her hand. We told you Mavis Spooner would make it back into our story eventually.

And maybe Emma had read too much of *The Collected Works*

of Ernest Harold Baynes over these past few months, or spent too much time with Rasputin, so she trusted wild animals in a way that she shouldn't have, but she wasn't afraid of these bears. Instead, she wanted to know if this old woman or these bears had seen her father. "Hello!" Emma called out. The bears looked up, startled, and then turned away and galumphed off into the woods.

"Shouldn't the bears be hibernating in February?" Mack asked, thinking like a biology teacher. But Mavis Spooner's bears had no reason to hibernate, not when Mavis served dog food by the bowlful, as well as eggs, peanut butter, and tuna fish. Bears don't hibernate if they're well fed.

"Private property!" Mavis Spooner called, taking a hand off her walker to wave these strangers away. "This is private property!" The park had sent out an email to all the park residents, explaining that there would be a search for a missing person going on in the park today, but Mavis Spooner had not made it to her computer yet.

"We're looking for . . ." Emma started.

"If you're looking for the Eaklins, they live in the Frog House," Mavis Spooner said to this young woman and her boyfriend, or her pimp, whoever he was. Percy Eaklin was evidently starting some kind of harem over there at the Frog House. A few weeks before, when Mavis was driving past Frog House on her way to pick up her groceries at headquarters, she'd seen Percy and another woman standing close to the road, someone who was definitely not his wife, Geraldine. A blonde, and much younger. *Bastard,* Mavis had thought, but she'd kept driving. Not her business.

But now more young people were arriving, and on her property, so it *was* her business. "Tell Percy Eaklin to keep his sex party on his own property!" Mavis yelled. "I'm not interested!"

Emma didn't have time to clarify that she was looking for her father, Clive Starling, and that he would be lost and confused, because it was then that they all heard a howl. Emma would recognize that specific howl anywhere. *Moses! Without a doubt!* The dog would be with her father.

53

Emma and Mack ran toward the woods, trying to follow the sound of the distressed dog. It was slow going, trying to run through deep snow, but Moses kept up his howls. Soon, there was a fence in front of them, eight feet of chain-link, and on the other side, Emma saw the big white dog, that perfect beast, and Auggie, plus two of the volunteer firefighters. The three men were all crouched down in the snow, looking at the ground, while the dog howled. The fox was on Emma's side of the fence, the park side, and he was digging furiously, his black-socked front paws burrowing at full speed.

Moses wagged his tail when he saw Emma, and howled again, and he bowed in excitement, to see that Emma was here, and that she could help. Auggie and the volunteer firefighters looked up. Emma saw that many of the trees behind them were stapled with bright-white missing person flyers. Emma would find out later that was how they'd tracked her dad, following the posters starting behind the coffee shop, different from the others because they looked so freshly printed, and also they had a million-dollar reward on them. Her father had left a trail of crumbs.

"Where is he?" Emma asked.

"In there," Auggie said, pointing to the ground. Her dad was trapped in a hog tunnel, one of those holes dug by the boars when they escaped the park. Emma bent down to where Rasputin was digging.

"Don't touch the fence," Auggie warned. "They didn't turn off the voltage. We're trying to get them to turn off the power, but no one is picking up the phone at park headquarters."

Rasputin was furiously trying to dig his owner out, the only one actually *doing* anything. The fox must have gone through the boar tunnel no problem; he was only seventeen pounds, had gained two pounds since he'd come to live with the Starlings, but still much smaller than a wild boar. But Clive had gotten stuck crawling through. He had underestimated his size, or had overestimated the size of the hole.

"Dad," Emma said. "Hey, Dad, you okay? I'm here."

"He's unconscious," Auggie said. "He was unconscious when we got here."

"We've been trying to pull him out by the feet with no luck," one of the firefighters explained.

"He's getting stuck on something," Auggie said. "But GG, okay, we can do this, this is good, this is good. If you're on the other side, we can push him to you."

"Push him?" Emma asked. She looked up at Mack, saw his broken arm.

"Maybe I can use one arm," he said unhelpfully.

"Emma, you pull," Auggie said, ignoring Mack. Auggie liked Mack, he just wasn't helpful at the moment, and he hadn't been helpful the past week either, with that stupid basketball injury, Auggie had to finish building the *Titanic* set entirely on his own. "Emma," Auggie told his sister, "you grab whatever you can of him and pull, even if you have to pull him by the hair. We have to move fast. He must be breathing in dirt."

Emma got on her hands and knees, pushed Rasputin out of the way, and thrust her arms into the tunnel. She felt a hard shell, like a turtle's back. *What on earth?*

"He's wearing a bike helmet," she said.

"What?" Auggie asked. "His motorcycle helmet?"

"No, I'm pretty sure it's a bicycle helmet. That's what it feels like."

"Grab it," Auggie instructed. "Pull."

Emma grabbed the helmet, got her fingers underneath and she pulled. She worried she was going to separate his head from his spine, if that was possible, but the bike helmet gave her something to grab onto, and there wasn't time for a better plan. They pushed from the other side, and the body moved toward her. She grabbed her father by the collar of his jacket, and got fistfuls of that long hair. She pulled and yanked and pulled. The dog was going nuts, jumping and barking, cheering them on. The fox screeched.

Her father's purple-helmeted head crowned out of the hole, and Emma reached down and was able to get him under the arms. He was definitely unconscious, if not dead. And Emma pulled as hard as she could as she brought him out of the hole, facedown in the dirt. She could feel energy pumping in her hands. Not *magic*-magic, not even healing energy, we realized at Maple Street, but that old amazing trick of adrenaline, when mothers have the superhuman strength to lift cars off babies.

Emma flipped her father over. His hands were blackened, scorched from an electric shock from touching the bottom of the fence. There was dirt in his hair, in his eyelashes, and his face was scraped badly, covered in blood. The fox was yapping at her, Moses howled again, both animals commanding her to *do something*.

"Do what?" Emma asked. "What do I do? What am I supposed to do?"

"CPR," Auggie said. "Emma, check his pulse, and then start CPR if he needs it. Emma, I'm right here."

She was so glad her brother was there, calm in an emergency. Emma had been trained in CPR when she started working at

Guiding Light Hospice, the entire staff had to be, even the ones who weren't allowed to touch the patients. Emma remembered the practice rounds she'd done on the Resuscitation Anne torso doll. She began to pump on her dad's chest cavern. She focused. There was only her father in front of her, and her brother's steady and clear voice.

She pumped.

And pumped.

And pumped.

But when the CPR seemed to be going nowhere, she decided to try it. She paused the chest pumps and put her flat palms against her father's chest where she imagined his heart would be, somewhere behind that bony cage of ribs. His big dumb, stupid heart. Emma's hands burned against her father's chest. She tried hard to believe in the touch, wanted to believe that the Charm could work. She was giving it all she had. Every last drop of energy.

Nothing happened.

No magic trick.

Emma returned to CPR, one last desperate effort of traditionally accepted medical treatment. Auggie continued his coaching, tried to be calm and reassuring, letting Emma know he was still right there, that she shouldn't quit, the EMTs would be there soon. *And then!* Emma felt something change in her father, underneath her hands. More and more members of other search parties had arrived, and so there was a large group of people watching when Clive Starling sputtered to life.

"A miracle," someone whispered, before the cheering began. The hugging began on the other side of the fence, and Auggie told her the EMTs were very close, Mack would be leading them through the woods. Emma checked that her dad really was breathing, and his pulse was back. He was still unconscious, but he was definitely breathing.

"A miracle," we said at Maple Street. Ralph Kelsey (b. 1923–

d. 2014) was happier than we'd ever seen him. We had all been sure Clive Starling was a goner, that we would all meet him at the iron gates of Maple Street Cemetery that coming weekend. *And here—a second chance!* What we wanted most.

"GG," Auggie said from the other side of the fence. "Good job. Really good job."

"We did it," Emma panted. She didn't have much time to dwell on it, but she was so proud of herself. She hadn't panicked, she had kept going, she hadn't quit. Auggie had helped. They had been a team. "I couldn't have done it if it wasn't for you," she said to her brother, and they definitely would have hugged if it hadn't been for the electric fence between them.

The EMTs arrived, tromping through the Corbin forest with their stretcher, and everyone standing on the other side of the fence applauded as they put oxygen on Clive's face, loaded him onto the stretcher, and started to carry him back through the woods to the ambulance. It was during that walk that Emma noticed how solemn the EMTs looked. It was a face she remembered the nurses at the hospice would get sometimes, when a family would misinterpret a positive update for a reversal of some kind: something good had happened, sure, but their relative was still dying, and soon.

Only then did Emma realize the terribleness of what she most likely had done, and that's when all of us at Maple Street realized the possibility of it, too, and it explained why we couldn't hear any of Clive's thoughts: his brain may have been deprived of oxygen for too long, and so that would mean that although he was breathing, his heart restarted, he was most likely brain dead, a living vegetable. Bill Casey (b. 1955–d. 2004), who had been in a coma for three years after a forklift accident, groaned in despair.

54

＊·＊

As the fleshy body of Clive Starling was hurried in an ambulance to Upper Valley Memorial Hospital, Harold Baynes arrived at our cemetery. He opened our iron gate and began the walk up our hill, up the gravel path. He was wearing his neat gray suit, and his face was hangdog, his feet heavy, dragging his soul as if it weighed three thousand pounds. Harold veered off the center path and collapsed on the ground among the stones. There wasn't much for us to say to poor Harold. He had come to us too late for any real advice.

"You saw how close I was," he said, from flat on his back. "You all had to see, didn't you? Clive insisted on climbing through that blasted hole in the ground, while the service entrance was up only a little farther. Surely you all saw that."

"You were lucky," Absalom Kelsey (b. 1745–d. 1837) scolded. "You were really meddlesome. Could have been *Poof, gone,* No More Harold."

"You don't think I was prepared for that?" Harold said, sitting up to face Absalom's grave at the top of our hill. "You think I'm a complete imbecile, Abe? Do you?"

"Hey!" Michelle Blake (b. 1914–d. 1942) said, interrupting the fight, because something was happening across town, a wiggle in the Everton universe, and we all looked and listened. Clive Starling wasn't a vegetable after all. *Look!* His brain had come online.

55

"He's not brain dead," Dr. Higgins announced to the Starlings in the waiting room, hours later, after the tests had been run. Confirming what we at Maple Street already knew.

"He's not brain dead," Emma repeated. Auggie was so excited, he spiked his green Jell-O cup from the hospital cafeteria onto the floor.

"Is he awake? Has he asked to see us?" Ingrid asked.

"Alive, not awake," Dr. Higgins said. "He's in a coma, and he hasn't asked for anything yet. But I would like to let you see him, in case there's a turn for the worse. We believe he was electrocuted by the fence, and that stopped his heart. But that pet fox did him a favor with all the digging. It kept the air circulating into the hole, stopped suffocation. He's breathing on his own, at least."

The Starlings followed Dr. Higgins, squirted hand sanitizer into their palms before they went into the room with curtains around the bed and tubes everywhere, machines beeping. They circled around him, their husband and father, Clive Starling, with a beat-up nose and two black eyes. He looked more wax than flesh.

Emma's hand went to her mouth to catch a sob. "I'm sorry," she said. "I'm so sorry."

"Hey, hey, hey," Auggie said, reaching out to his sister. "Not your fault."

"I was supposed to save him."

"Emma this is absolutely not your fault," Ingrid said. "He never had much time left. I'm the one who should be sorry. In sickness and in—" But Ingrid couldn't finish her sentence, crying now too.

I thought I had until spring, Clive thought from his coma. *When the snow melted.*

We agreed at Maple Street. Clive shouldn't die, not yet. He was an assistant teacher to the fifth graders, and they loved him, and the school year was months from over. He hadn't found out what had happened to Crystal Nash. He hadn't reunited with his wife, or with his band. And the *Titanic* hadn't yet left the dock, even though the ship was all ready to go in the Everton Old Opera House, the last coat of silver paint completely dry. But there's always something you miss out on, at the end.

"Postponed," Auggie would tell his actors, and he would send out a notice to everyone who had already bought tickets: *Due to a family emergency, the show has been temporarily postponed.*

The days passed, and Clive showed no signs of waking up, but he was stable. The Starlings were allowed to camp out in his room, even outside official visiting hours, thanks to some strings Dr. Gary Wheeler had pulled. Gary understood when Ingrid broke up with him, but he also said he would wait for her. She said she wasn't making any promises, and for now she had to be with her husband. Every few hours, she kissed Clive's forehead, wanting him to know she was there.

From his coma, Clive was so glad Ingrid was there by his death-bed, proud to have seen one of his marriages out to the very end. His partner and best friend, his superior in intellect, his equal in good looks. The mother of his children. Maybe his wife could finish her book about Everton's history now that he would soon be dead. He hoped so. She would need to find something to fill all her extra time. The children were fine on their own, grown-ups practically.

"Hey, Sleeping Beauty," Auggie said, walking into his dad's room on the third day of the coma. "Oh man, what are they feeding him? It smells like Snow White and the Seven Farts in here."

The doctors were in fact not feeding Clive anything yet, but if the coma went on much longer, they would need to put in a feeding tube. Emma, his guardian and health proxy, had signed off on it. She'd asked Dr. Higgins to make sure her dad got the most expensive brand of mush, and Dr. Higgins had looked at her strangely, said he was pretty sure all the mush was the same.

"You're a lot like your father, you know," Ingrid said to her son about his fart jokes. "Just like your father to be making a big joke out of a terrible situation."

"Would you prefer I cry all the time, Mom? Do you want me to lie down in the hallway and scream?"

"No," Ingrid said, thinking it over. "They might kick us out then."

Clive's heart swelled to think his son was like him. It showed on the monitor, but of course no one noticed that the beat went slightly irregular. Ingrid went back to her knitting, and Auggie sat down with a book he'd found in his dad's office, a biography of Rasputin the Russian monk, one of the few books in the office not ruined during the destruction by the deer. Dr. Higgins said it's good to read aloud to comatose patients, so Auggie was going to give it a shot.

Auggie's boss had given him the week off at the lumberyard, and Principal Jefferies had put the string of short-term substitutes back in rotation while Emma took the time off to be with her dad. Emma had made sure the kids knew they were welcome to come visit Captain Clive in the hospital, but she told them he would be sleeping and he didn't look great. Michael B. had been first to visit, followed by Ulf and Olivia.

Emma arrived with Bart Nash's old stereo from the house, so they could play her dad some of his old Black Sabbath CDs. Dr. Higgins had said other patients respond to music, if they don't like the reading-aloud thing. Emma had also gone home to medicate Moses, who was struggling with his separation anxiety. Mack had a vet friend who said a little doggie Prozac would improve things, and he had brought the pills over. "Smells like a fart factory in here," Emma said as she crossed the threshold of Room 202.

"You're just as bad as your brother," Ingrid scolded. But secretly, she was impressed with Emma and Auggie, the way they'd acted over the past few days. They'd been acting like functional adults, asking the doctors questions, thanking the nurses, calling their bosses to make arrangements for their jobs, and being generally respectful and kind to each other. She wanted her husband to wake up, to hear what he thought about the kids. How well they were finally turning out. Not such dependent leeches.

"The man can't die," Auggie said from the corner chair, as he read the Rasputin biography. "Stoned to death, stabbed, and survived. He also slept with everyone. He claimed sex with him had medicinal power."

A nurse had come into the room to check Clive's vitals, and she was a little confused; she thought Auggie was telling stories about the man in the bed, his father, still asleep. "He does seem like he's a special person," the nurse agreed. Auggie snorted, but it was Ingrid who really laughed at that, laughed so hard it turned to tears.

"Mom," Emma said. "See if you can calm down."

"I can't," she said, gasping. "I can't."

Emma had to take their mother out for some fresh air while the nurse finished her job. The nurse was unruffled; she'd seen hysterical people before.

"How about this, Dad?" Auggie said, having returned to his

reading after the nurse had gone. Rasputin had saved the life of the son of the Russian tsar by demanding the doctors get away from the boy, throwing all their medicine in the fire. It is now believed that the boy had hemophilia, and so the medicine they were giving him, aspirin, really *was* killing the poor kid.

56

> ⟫·⟪

Leanne Hatfield had not gone to visit Clive Starling in the hospital yet; she was still pissed at him for ruining the musical. She was so depressed that *Titanic the Musical!* had been canceled—*postponed, whatever*—she didn't even want to go to her ten A.M. voice lesson on Saturday, but her grandfather made her get in the car. He said a commitment is a commitment; Hatfields don't lie around the house feeling sorry for themselves.

The Hatfields first stopped at the Wilderness Edge's Express for two apple fritters, David Hatfield trying to cheer his granddaughter up, and then they drove to the front gate of Corbin Park where the gatekeeper looked at the sticker on the windshield before waving them on in. Leanne's grandfather drove the clunker of a station wagon down the long dirt road through the woods toward Hummingbird House, and, as usual, they had to turn off the radio and put on a CD because they stopped getting a reliable radio signal in the park. Even cell phones didn't work in there. There was often talk among the millionaires of getting a cell tower, but it kept getting turned down in park meetings. Once they thought about it, the millionaires always concluded that they liked to be a little unreachable on the weekends. They all had such busy and important jobs; it was nice to shut off for a minute. They could send emails, of course, all the cabins had internet because it was so easy to lay down fiber-optic lines. It wasn't the dark ages. It was just the deep, dark woods.

———

Mavis Spooner had been planning to shoot an email to Leanne Hatfield and her grandfather to inform them that voice lessons would be canceled that day and next week, too, and the week after that, actually, voice lessons canceled until further notice. Mavis didn't want visitors. She was having trouble controlling her anxiety ever since Mack Durkee and Emma Starling had traipsed through her property. Those two young people had walked down her driveway like they'd owned the place, only to be followed by the rest of the search party, and then an ambulance, and two police cars, and ever since then, well, the walls had been closing in on poor Mavis. *What was next? Would Corbin Park's gates be open to the public? What was the point of being so rich if just anyone could walk across your lawn?* Mavis felt violated. She decided to batten down the hatches at Hummingbird House, which meant no more voice lessons for Leanne Hatfield. A shame, too, the girl had real talent.

So, earlier that morning, it was eight-thirty A.M., Mavis Spooner had her email to David Hatfield half-written, she was a slow typer, when Jack the bear had climbed up on the porch again, demanding his breakfast. When Mavis saw Jack on the porch, smudging his nose against the glass, she was angry. She did not need anyone knocking on her door right now, not even a bear. Mavis had gone out to the porch with a broom across her walker to swat at Jack, and, well, the bear didn't like that at all. He went right for Mavis, claws and teeth at her throat. Mavis Spooner didn't put up much of a fight, and Jack went straight into the house afterward, looking around for those bowls of Ol' Roy dog food. The rest of the hard-boiled eggs.

———

When Leanne Hatfield and her grandfather pulled up to the Hummingbird House in their station wagon, it was Jill the bear who came running to meet them. Jill was distraught, and hungry. She had wanted breakfast, too, but she wasn't going to kill anyone over it.

"Don't get out of the car," David Hatfield commanded his granddaughter, but of course Leanne wasn't going to; she was no dummy. They could both see Mavis Spooner's body lying on the porch, and her arm was dangling in an unnatural way. Jack appeared in the doorway of the house, standing up on his hind legs to see who had arrived.

David Hatfield tried to stay calm. He pulled out his cellphone, but there was no signal. It would take almost thirty minutes to get back to the front gate of the park; it was not a quick journey. If Mavis Spooner was still alive up there on her porch, time was of the essence. It looked like she was wearing only a nightgown.

"We should go to the neighbors'," Leanne said.

Her grandfather agreed that was right; they would go to the neighbors' . . . if they could find the neighbors. He put the car in reverse and drove down the road until they came to another dirt driveway, with a sign on a tree that said WELCOME TO FROG HOUSE! in white lettering. As soon as she saw the friendly sign, Leanne thought immediately of the pile of plastic frogs she left piled in the cemetery because frogs were Izzy's favorite animal. Izzy used to complain her dad went to his hunting cabin in Corbin Park on weekends, while she stayed in town with her mom. This had to be his cabin. The Frog House.

"It's Izzy's dad's cabin," Leanne said to her grandfather. "It's a good sign. Izzy will help us." Leanne had never believed in angels, but she felt the spirit of Izzy Eaklin there with her, helping her rescue the old lady next door. There was a black Range Rover in the driveway; the Eaklins were home.

Leanne jumped out of the car and ran ahead, her grandfather was so slow, she would explain to Izzy's dad that the old lady next door was hurt, maybe dead, but they might be able to save her. Leanne did not knock on the door, painted hunter green with a gold frog doorknocker; there was no time to waste. She turned the gold doorknob instead, went right into the house. She saw the moose head above the stone fireplace first, and then the kitchen with gleaming white countertops, a bowl of bananas on the counter, and Leanne was about to call out to Mr. Eaklin for help when she saw a little girl in a purple sweatshirt sitting at the kitchen table, doing something that looked like homework, looking healthy and apple-cheeked and very not dead at all, and a youngish woman with blond hair and brown roots sitting there next to her. There was a chandelier made of antlers above their heads.

"Izzy?"

"Leanne," the girl said. "Hi!"

"Oh my God," the woman said. "Oh my God, can you help me?" she asked, jerking her arm, and Leanne saw the woman was handcuffed to the chair. "There's a key—"

Geraldine Eaklin ran out with a frying pan in her hand, ready to swing it, but she stopped. It was Leanne Hatfield. She couldn't hurt Leanne, that kid had been like one of her own.

"What in the good Christ is going on here?" David Hatfield asked from the front doorway, so much slower than his granddaughter. "Geraldine?"

"Grandpa," Leanne said. "It's Izzy! And they handcuffed Crystal Nash. The missing woman from the posters."

"Please help," Crystal said. "I'm a hostage."

"Shut up," said Geraldine, still holding the frying pan. "Let me think."

Percy Eaklin came out of the first-floor bedroom with his hands up. "I'm sorry. I'm so sorry."

"Grandpa," Leanne said. "We need the cops."

"I think so too," he agreed.

"Definitely," Crystal said.

"David, we can explain," Geraldine said.

"Let me call my lawyer first," Percy said.

Geraldine Eaklin couldn't believe her husband was going down without a fight. They'd made it this far. They'd been to hell and back. "Crystal *cured* Isabella," she said. "She's a miracle worker."

"They kidnapped me," Crystal said. "Percy took me at gunpoint."

"Oh, you were so high you don't know what happened," Geraldine snapped.

"Percy, what did you do?" David looked at his old friend.

"I'm sorry," Percy said. "I was desperate."

"I'm calling the police," Leanne said, reaching for the red phone on the Eaklins' wall. Because even though Izzy was also her favorite person in the world, or maybe her second favorite, after her grandfather, you absolutely cannot kidnap anyone. That was one of the many things Leanne Hatfield knew for sure.

"I'd like to call them myself," Percy said, putting his hand out for the receiver. "I'd like to turn myself in." That was just as well, because the police might not believe it if a little girl called. Kids pranked the 911 number all the time, and the two Everton cops had already heard every wacky story in the book when it came to the mysterious disappearance of Crystal Nash. But if Percy Eaklin called, they would believe what he said, because Percy Eaklin was a respected member of the Everton community, someone who wouldn't say there was a wolf unless there was a wolf, even if he was the one with the sharp teeth, the pointy ears.

"Can you also tell them to send an ambulance?" Leanne asked, remembering what had happened to Mavis Spooner next door.

57

Emma was by the hospital vending machine when she received the strange call from Officer Zinger. Crystal had been found, rescued, after being kidnapped and held hostage by Percy Eaklin and his wife, Geraldine. Emma had no idea how to process that information, but she ran to tell her family. "They found her," she said, in the doorway of her dad's hospital room. "They found Crystal."

"Oh no," Auggie said.

"I'm so sorry," Ingrid said.

"No, they found her *alive*. She was at Percy Eaklin's cabin. He kidnapped her."

"He did what?" Auggie asked.

"Crystal wants us to go see her at the police station. She asked for us."

"Well, let's go," Ingrid said, grabbing her purse and keys.

On the way out of the room, Emma looked back at her father in his bed, half waiting for him to spring up and let out a good old-fashioned Clive Starling whoop. Her dad had been right all along. Something had happened to Crystal. Emma remembered the surveillance photo of Percy Eaklin going into Crystal's trailer, recognizable only because he was wearing a suit. They had been on the right track. They had been so close. But then again, Emma had never really thought Percy was suspicious. She had only felt sorry for him. The unmeasurable loss he had suffered.

That was the other crazy thing Officer Zinger had said on the phone: Isabella Eaklin was still alive. Found in the woods with Crystal Nash.

When the Starlings arrived at the police station, Officer Zinger took them back to the lunchroom, which held a long table and a fridge and a microwave, a poster of Dwayne "The Rock" Johnson on the wall, and the Starlings stood for a moment in the doorway, staring. Crystal had two inches of brunette roots and was wearing her old favorite Upper Valley High sweatshirt from the basketball team, the sleeves rolled up to reveal some of her tattoos. Percy Eaklin had found a way to get Crystal all her old clothes from the trailer, asking Graham Leeches to contribute to the donation drive.

"I always wanted to come back from the dead," Crystal said.

"If anyone could." Emma ran to her friend. Whatever had gone wrong between them didn't matter now. Or maybe it would matter again, at some point, but not in this moment. Ingrid put her face into her hands and started to cry. Auggie put his arm around his mom.

"So, you missed me?" Crystal asked, smiling. She wasn't too thin. The Eaklins had fed her. There were no obvious signs of abuse. But Emma was amazed that someone could smile after what she'd been through. A hostage situation. She'd been wearing an electric ankle monitor as well as handcuffs most of the time. The Eaklins had been careful about not letting her escape. They had been diligent. Percy Eaklin had Crystal's motorcycle crushed into scrap metal, had ditched Crystal's phone. He'd had the money to cover his tracks. No one was allowed in Corbin Park except for the millionaires, and the millionaires left one another alone. The Eaklins' nearest neighbor was Mavis Spooner, and the old lady never left the park. She'd never seen a missing person poster.

"Was it . . ." Emma couldn't bring herself to ask all the questions she had on her mind. There was no telling what Crystal had been through. Officer Zinger hadn't told Emma much.

"There is a lot of bad stuff that did *not* happen to me," Crystal said. "No torture, no rape."

"Okay." Emma was surprised by how blunt Crystal was. But Crystal had always been blunt.

"In a lot of ways, we were like a family."

"Sounds great," Auggie said.

"August." Ingrid swatted at her son. "It's not the time for jokes."

"Jokes are fine," Crystal said. "Jokes are probably good. I mean, while I hate the Eaklins for kidnapping me, I just mean, day-to-day, it was boring and ordinary. Cooking and eating dinner. Working with Isabella on math problems."

"They kidnapped you to be their nanny?" Auggie asked.

"No, no. Isabella was dying, and they thought I could help her. They were at the end of their rope. The doctors had thought she had leukemia, but then it wasn't leukemia, and it seemed like there was nothing they could do to treat whatever it really was."

"A misdiagnosis," Emma said, remembering what Leanne Hatfield had told her.

At Maple Street, we remembered the events of the previous spring and summer well: Isabella Eaklin was in the hospital dying, and the doctors were running out of ideas. Isabella was in so much pain, so Geraldine started looking into alternative therapies. Geraldine had a friend, Sally Hunt, who recommended the teenage healer who worked out of the McDonald's. It sounded crazy, but this girl had cured Sally of some terrible skin condition years before. Sally still kept the worn business card in her wallet. *The Gentle Touch Healing Society*. Geraldine called the number on the card, and it connected her to Crystal Nash, the business manager.

Crystal told the Eaklins that she was so sorry, but there was no way she could save a dying girl, and she wouldn't give them false hope. But Percy knew everyone has a price, and Crystal could name hers. Finally, Crystal agreed to visit the girl in the hospital, thought maybe she could at least help with her pain. And it turned out, Crystal had a way with the kid. Isabella smiled and laughed when Crystal was there, some color returned to her face. She slept peacefully after the visits. She reported to be in less pain. Percy Eaklin said he'd pay Crystal to come to visit every day. Double the money.

But one day Crystal missed a healing session, and another day she showed up strung-out. Percy went to the trailer to confront her. He said he knew what was going on, he had seen the same glassy-eyed look in some of his employees at the gun factory. He could pay for Crystal's rehab, but there wasn't time for weeks of rehab, and he couldn't have an unreliable healer. His daughter had so little time left. He'd left the trailer frustrated, angry.

"You did what?" Geraldine had asked, when Percy explained how he'd panicked, took Crystal by gunpoint from the parking lot after her shift ended that night at the Blueberry Hill Pub. Percy explained to his wife that Crystal was currently detoxing in their hunting cabin in Corbin Park, locked in a room with plenty of food and water, where no one could hear her scream. Geraldine was angry at first, but she came around eventually. She understood. Their daughter was more important than anyone else in the entire world. They would pay Crystal once Isabella no longer needed her, the Eaklins promised, but they needed her to help manage their daughter's pain. They would pay Crystal a lot at the end of this. Isabella was released from the hospital that week, allowed to go home to die.

The surprising thing was, after a week in the cabin with Crystal, Isabella started getting better, something no one could have hoped for. Every day, Isabella seemed to be improving, eating more, getting stronger. Geraldine had read all about cancer patients who take nature baths to shrink their tumors, and countless books about shamans who can cure deadly illnesses, and sometimes they need to draw on the power of the natural world to do it. Crystal Nash must be like that, the Eaklins figured. She needed the power of the natural world to help Isabella.

As their daughter grew healthier, it was Geraldine's idea to fake the funeral, to bury the little coffin at Maple Street. Geraldine had gone a little paranoid, especially with Percy still insisting on going to work in town. Geraldine didn't want people asking him about Isabella, and fewer people would ask if their daughter was thought to be dead. She didn't want him to spark the suspicions of anyone in town. She didn't want to get caught now that they'd found something to keep Isabella alive.

"I understood their choice to keep me there," Crystal said to the Starlings. "Even if I wasn't happy about it. I had performed a miracle."

"You really think you healed her?" Emma asked.

"Seems pretty crazy," Auggie said. "Just my opinion though."

Crystal shrugged. "All I know is that Isabella didn't die. She was dying for a year, and then she wasn't." Emma remembered how certain Crystal used to be about all this stuff, how she'd always been sure that Emma was "the real deal," as advertised on Craigslist. Crystal now believed she was the real deal too. "And I was happy to be clean. It's true what they say; the stuff ruins your life. Maybe the Eaklins can start a program, once they get out of prison," Crystal said. "Frog House Kidnapping and Rehab."

"Whatever works," Auggie agreed.

Emma let out a nervous laugh. Maybe Crystal would be okay.

"Hey, where's Mr. Bird?" Crystal asked, looking out the door waiting for Clive to appear. "I thought he would be first in line for my autograph." The missing person posters Crystal had seen everywhere said PLEASE CALL CLIVE STARLING WITH ALL LEADS.

"We'll go see him later," Emma promised, because Officer Gene had come in to say there were reporters waiting outside. He said Fox News and CNN had sent helicopters from New York City, and he couldn't hide his excitement about that. A kidnapping was a national news story. The big leagues.

58

News travels fast around Everton. By evening, nearly everyone had heard at least one version of the kidnapping story. Nearly everyone had heard Crystal Nash had been found in Corbin Park; nearly everyone had heard the Eaklin girl was still alive.

Except for poor Clive.

In his coma, he didn't know that Crystal Nash had been found, even though it was all anyone was talking about around him. But the longer Clive was under, the more trouble he had stringing together conversations; his brain was getting pretty jumbled. Ridley Willett had started prepping the grave, jackhammering through the frozen ground, since he had to assume Ingrid Starling wouldn't want to leave her husband on ice. Ridley wasn't looking forward to dealing with that woman again.

The TV mounted in Clive's hospital room was even blaring the nightly news, but none of it was getting through to his brain. "Do you think the town of Everton forgot about you?" the interviewer asked on the screen. "Do you blame the police, your friends and family, the general public, for not doing enough to find you sooner?"

"It was dumb luck that I was ever found," Crystal replied. "I don't blame anyone for not having the dumb luck to find me sooner, if that's what you're asking. They put up posters everywhere. They did their best. I don't blame anyone except Mr. and Mrs. Eaklin. I especially do not blame Isabella, who is a wonderful, wonderful kid."

"That's a really well thought out answer."

"Well," Crystal said, giving the interviewer an annoyed look. "I certainly had the time to think."

"My daughter was dying, and then she wasn't," Percy Eaklin explained to the same interviewer, later in the segment. "If your daughter was dying, and she out of nowhere got better, after she'd gone through hell on Earth, and then she was healthy again, no rhyme or reason to it, wouldn't you do everything to make sure nothing changed? Not one thing?"

"If one person was the key to saving the life of your child," Geraldine Eaklin asked, looking right into the camera with her doe eyes, "wouldn't you do it? We only did what most people would have done, in our situation."

"I highly doubt that," Mae Belle Henick (b. 1799–d. 1820) argued with the TV from her grave.

"That woman is certainly something," Donald Brown (b. 1890–d. 1965) agreed.

The rest of us were too relieved by the events of the day to think much about Geraldine's ridiculous statements. We had never known if Crystal Nash would be rescued, if anyone would ever find her. We're dead, but we're not fortune-tellers, not soothsayers. We don't always get it right, so we were overjoyed by this turn of events. We'd seen countless tragedies before, and we hate it when it ends in tragedy.

"Hi, Mr. Bird," Crystal Nash said when she finally made it to Clive's bedside, after the initial media frenzy died down. "I heard how you looked for me." She wiped her tears with her sweatshirt sleeve. It had been an intense twenty-four hours.

"He would be so happy to know you're here," Ingrid said.

"But why?" Crystal asked. "I mean, why didn't he give up? I can see how it looked. I think anyone else would've given up. Except my dad, maybe, but obviously—"

"My dad loves you," Emma said. "We all love you."

"The Bird family," Crystal said, shaking her head and wiping her eyes again.

"My husband . . ." Ingrid started to explain, and sighed. "Well, that man can be a complete and utter trial. But other times, well, sometimes he could surprise me, just how far he'd go for someone he loved. Further than I thought possible, or rational. He would be so happy to see you here in front of him. He would say it was all worth it."

"But he *would* try to take credit for the rescue," Emma said.

Crystal smiled through her tears. "He'd want a piece of that reward."

"That's for sure. And a plaque with his name on it."

It was a damn shame that Clive was too far underneath the coma to hear all this, the nice things they were saying about him. He would be thrilled to hear Crystal Nash had been rescued, even if he hadn't been the one to open the door and be the hero. "The Hatfields, huh?" he would have said. "Those lucky bastards."

And the Hatfields were indeed looking a little lucky. They would be collecting a sizable reward from the estate of Ralph Kelsey (b. 1923–d. 2014). Ralph had added the stipulation to his will back in November, a reward clause in the event anyone found Crystal Nash, after he got the idea one night at dinner. It was not quite a million dollars, but David Hatfield would say it was certainly better than a kick in the pants.

Mavis Spooner deserved much of the credit for Crystal's rescue, too, but she wouldn't be seeing a red cent of the reward. She was interred in Maple Street that coming weekend, another grave for poor Ridley to dig in frigid weather. Mavis Spooner (b. 1928–d. 2015) would arrive at our cemetery holding an imaginary broom in her hand, swatting it at her husband in the next grave, telling Jack over and over again to "get off the porch, go back in the woods, Jack, please go back where good bears belong." But in time Mavis's final earthly moment would fade, and she would return to herself, and she would learn Jack Spooner (b. 1926–d. 2005) had been keeping tabs on her all these years. That her Jack had been watching when she'd thought herself all alone in the world with no one except the bears, the raccoons in the garage, the deer on the lawn, the little girl who came once a week to sing.

59

⇢·⇠

Of course, Crystal Nash wanted to try to heal Clive, now that she fancied herself a big miracle worker, but she said it was important to do it right—one big powerful, well-planned session instead of a lot of shitty mini ones, especially if Emma hadn't been healing successfully lately. Crystal had read so much on *charismata iamaton* over the years, like how the moon can change your energies. Stuff Emma had never bothered to learn because it had come naturally to her, until one day it was gone. Crystal said she wasn't surprised that Emma had lost the Charm. She'd never cultivated it. An unwatered plant will eventually die. "You always resented the attention," Crystal said. "I would have relished it."

"I know," Emma said, and shrugged. Crystal had all the attention she could ever want now. She would see how much she liked it, or didn't.

"And actually, you didn't lose anything," Crystal explained. "You just released it, because it wasn't serving you. The energy belongs to the universe. You were only a vehicle for that energy."

"Okay," Emma said. She had forgotten that Crystal could be a little woo-woo.

"You would know all this if you ever read any of the books I gave you. But whatever. We do need you to reopen your energy pathways if we're going to try to wake up your dad, but that won't be hard. We'll need your mom and Auggie too. We need to harness as much energy as possible."

"Okay," Emma said. "You're the boss." *The worst thing we*

can do is kill him, she thought, before she remembered that was exactly what she was afraid of.

"Great," Auggie said when he heard of the plan. "Let's get as nutso as possible. How much salt do we need?" Emma realized her brother had paid awfully close attention to what she and Crystal were up to back in high school. He had been a little spy in his own house.

"Lots of salt," Crystal agreed. "And lots of candles, green wax, if we can find it, green is best for healing."

Ingrid was also surprisingly up for a big healing session, even with the additional witchy aspects, even with the three bags of green candles from the Dollar Store. Anything to get her husband back, or to kill him for good. No one thought Clive Starling would like being stuck in a coma.

Crystal said the healing would start later that night, at three A.M., which she said is the witching hour, and typically when the hospital was at its quietest. It was smack in the middle of the nurses' night shift, when many of them would try to catch a little snooze.

Hours before the big healing session was due to begin, there was some good news coming out of one corner of Upper Valley Memorial Hospital. Not in Clive Starling's room, no, things were still bleak in Room 202, but upstairs, in pediatric care. After a barrage of tests, plus a consult with a famous doctor from Boston, it was determined that Isabella Eaklin was in perfect health. The doctors' leading theory was that the girl had been suffering from an autoimmune disease, one of those bad and inexplicable ones, where the body keeps attacking and attacking itself, a killing from within. But one day, for whatever reason, Isabella's body had simply decided to stop the assault. To let itself live. The doctors said Isabella's parents had been right to be cautious about changing their daughter's living conditions once she started getting better, in case there had been an environmental trigger.

The famous doctor from Boston also admitted it was possible the healing sessions with Crystal Nash had caused some sort of placebo effect. "If Isabella believed the healing hands would work, that might be very powerful in something like an autoimmune disease," he explained. "Crazier things have certainly happened. Who am I to say this magic woman didn't heal the girl?"

"You're a doctor," someone at the press conference reminded him, but he only shrugged.

At 2:45 A.M., right before the witching hour, Crystal, Emma, Auggie, and Ingrid lit the candles all over Clive Starling's hospital room. Crystal poured a mound of salt in the doorway, and around the window, to keep the good energy in, the bad energy out. Auggie had wanted to bring the fox, sneak him into the hospital in a duffel, because witches have familiars, don't they? Emma told him that that wouldn't be fair to the dog. The dog was beginning to adjust to life without Clive, but he had gotten very, very attached to the fox. Moses and Rasputin could not be separated under any circumstances, or Moses might put his head right in the oven.

At three A.M., Emma and Crystal each put one hand on either side of Clive's head, where his worst ailments were, and held hands with Ingrid and Auggie, forming a circle.

"What now?" Auggie asked.

"Yes," Emma asked. "What now?" This was very different from what she and Crystal had always done at the McDonald's.

"We'll go around and say what we love about him," Crystal explained. "He will see why he needs to wake up, why he shouldn't leave us yet. I can go first. Mine's easy: The man looked for me when no one else did. He treated my disappearance seriously. He never gave up."

"He never did," Emma agreed, and everyone nodded.

"You've been a true friend, Mr. Bird," Crystal said.

Auggie was next in the circle. "Dad was always there for me. I mean, not always. But sometimes. Sometimes, he was there. When it really, really, mattered, he was there."

"I'm so glad you feel that way, Auggie," Ingrid said.

"You're up, Mom. Give him your worst."

Ingrid looked at her husband in the bed. The sleeping face she knew so well, the familiar lines and creases. "Well, what can I say, Clivey? I'm so glad I married you. I'd do it again if I could."

"That's it?" Auggie asked, after a few seconds of quiet, because Auggie didn't understand how much it means for someone to be glad they married the one they married, and not just because of the kids.

"Your father knows the rest," Ingrid assured him.

"Okay, Mom. If you say so."

It was Emma's turn, the last to go. The hospital room glittered in the candlelight, thanks to the get-well cards the fifth graders had made, which had shed some of their sparkles, glitter sticking to surfaces that were supposed to be sterile. "I came home feeling like a loser, and Dad could have made me feel worse, but he didn't. He let me figure it out. He told me not to try so hard as a teacher, because he knew I needed to relax and let my guard down if I was going to get to know the kids. If the fifth graders were ever going to trust me. I probably would have read straight from the textbook for the entire year if it wasn't for Dad."

"Ha," Auggie said. "They would have killed you."

"Torn me limb from limb," Emma agreed.

"Your dad knows it's hard for you to let people in," Ingrid said. "You were always a little uptight."

"Thanks, Mom. Wonder where I got that."

"And now—" Crystal said.

"The human sacrifice!"

"August, shush," Ingrid scolded. "We're not sacrificing any-one."

"*Now,*" Crystal continued. "We concentrate. Focus on that love for him, and let it radiate from your heart and your chest and your head down your veins, down through your arms, out through your fingertips. Put that healing energy into his body. Think of the color green, or pink. Colors of healing and rebirth."

This is stupid, Auggie thought, but he did it anyway. Ingrid and Emma thought something similar, but they also did it anyway. It was the time to do exactly what Crystal Nash said, to close their eyes and focus and radiate green and pink. And if you have never held hands with the people you love most in the world in a dark room surrounded by candlelight and the beeping of various ma-chines keeping your father alive, it is an *experience.* They loved one another so much, at least in that moment. They felt sure they were healing him, that Clive would soon levitate up to the ceiling and float back down awake, good as new.

"What in the world?" the nurse on duty said, flicking on the overhead fluorescent. "Candles? This is a hospital. You can have the funeral when this man is dead. And you know what, you can all come back during regular visiting hours. When the sun is up and the crazy in you is gone." Nurse Shauna was no stranger to the bullshit of hospital visitors. She was not afraid to throw any-one out. Up until this point, she had been Emma's favorite nurse on the hall. Really on top of it. Well, she was on top of this too. She was busting it up. "Candles in the hospital, really," she mut-tered as she shooed Clive Starling's late-night visitors out the front sliding door.

Outside Upper Valley Memorial Hospital, the four of them laughed in the parking lot, remembering the nurse's disapproving face. No, it hadn't worked, but it had been thrilling nonetheless, even—no, *especially*—getting busted by the nurse at the end. It reminded Ingrid Starling of a time in high school, when she and her friends got caught skinny-dipping by the cops in the polluted lake in their town. It was one of Ingrid's most cherished memories, an uninhibited experience that had bonded Ingrid and those two other girls as best friends and fellow mermaids, and it was all the more memorable for the abrupt way it had ended, that crash back to earth, the flashlight in the water, the gruff sound of the cop's voice, telling them all to get the hell out of that water if they didn't all want to grow up to have three-legged babies.

In the car on the drive back to the Corbin Mansion and caretaker's house, Ingrid looked around at the kids she'd ended up with: Emma, Crystal, and then at Auggie, behind the wheel. "Your father would have loved that," she said. "I think it was a beautiful way to honor him."

"I wish it had worked," Auggie said.

"Yeah," Crystal agreed. "That would have been better."

Emma stayed quiet, just looked out the back passenger window as Auggie drove them home. It was too dark to see the trees out on the road, too dark to see the missing person posters, but she knew they were out there. She felt their eyes staring back.

PART VII

The Rats

60

THE CREATURE I LOVED THE MOST

from *The Collected Writings of Ernest Harold Baynes,* © 1925
This Book Is Property of the Everton Historical Society

Mrs. Baynes and her loyal mate.
Photograph by E.H.B.

The last time I saw The Sprite was on New Year's Eve, we toasted him as the grandest little fox on earth, but it was clear that he wasn't enjoying the many guests of the party, and he soon was scratching at the door. I let him out, and he turned once to look back at me in the lamplight, smiled and waved his tail, and then he was gone. He did not return after that, though I've flung open the door many times after a slight noise, my heart always hopeful. I suspect I'll never stop waiting for the funny little chap to come home. In my imagination I see him now on the edge of the wood, with the evening light upon his seemingly weightless fur, his lithe figure in relief against the shadows of the overhanging trees, bright-eyed, alert, and self-possessed.

No memories are more dear to me and to my wife than those which show The Sprite in our home. He would scratch at the door, come into the firelight, smiling and waving his brush tail, happy to see us, yet there was always an air about him which seemed to say: "Awfully glad to see you both here together to-night! I know how deeply you care for each other, despite Mr. Baynes' many flaws. Oh, me? No, I can't stay, I really can't, I've important business on tonight. Got a little supper handy? Out in the kitchen? Oh thanks, this is awfully good. Well, I must be going now."

I suspect a dog got The Sprite, or a bullet, or perhaps it was that simple fall to old age, that reaper who eventually comes to all of our doors. We can do nothing but laugh in death's face when he comes to call, in shock and awe that he finally came to us! It's our turn! We were not overlooked this time, even though we had hoped we might be forgotten. Forgotten, please, just this once!

61

Official visiting hours at Upper Valley Memorial Hospital began at nine A.M., the sun would be up, and the Starlings would be allowed back in the hospital. The nine o'clock hour came, but the Starlings were all still sleeping, zonked out from the events of the night before. Ten A.M. arrived, and then eleven, everyone still sawing logs. At eleven-fifteen Crystal Nash was the first to get up, she'd been sleeping in the guest room, which was her room now, as long as she wanted it to be. Crystal went downstairs and grabbed the keys to Clive's truck; she was supposed to go see Isabella Eaklin at the Hatfields'. David Hatfield had been named emergency guardian by the courts, and Izzy and Leanne were living together like sisters. Crystal was going to stay a big part of Isabella's life. They loved each other.

At eleven-thirty, Ingrid awoke, and so did Auggie. Emma was last to get up, and everyone still had to shower. It would be a while before they got to the hospital. The Starlings had decided Clive's feeding tube should be removed. This was no way for him to go on living, even if he was getting the most expensive brand of mush. Still, it would be excruciating to ask for Dr. Higgins to remove the feeding tube. To give up on their father waking up. No one was in a rush.

It was noon when Clive's eyelids fluttered open. Harold Baynes was sitting there at the edge of his bed, as he often did. We were so pleased to see the old boy still around. We'd lost track of him the past few days, had started to wonder if he had exploded after all.

"Good morning," Harold said. "Crystal Nash was found. She was kidnapped and kept in Corbin Park." Harold said it calmly, as though it wasn't even that out of the ordinary. As if kidnapping victims were found in the park every day. Well, Harold had known where Crystal Nash was for quite some time. He knew that park better than anyone, except for maybe Austin Corbin himself, and Corbin is buried in New York, no use to us here.

Clive Starling sucked in air and tried to make a sound. He tried to say something, but the words were hard to say. He looked for a glass of water next to his bed, maybe he needed a glass of water. No cup of water, but there was a stereo there, playing a song Clive knew well. Clive opened his mouth again, and this time a sound came out, clear as a bell.

When the Starlings arrived at the hospital, Dr. Higgins came running, his stethoscope flapping. "He woke up singing," Dr. Higgins said, meeting them at the sliding entrance doors. "It's something new for me." They could all hear him then, his voice drifting from down the hall.

"That's his favorite song," Auggie said, which Emma knew wasn't true: "War Pigs" was his favorite. Their dad was singing another Black Sabbath classic, a ballad, not what everyone expects from the Prince of Darkness and the vanguard band of heavy metal. It was about losing the best woman you ever had.

"He's okay?" Ingrid asked the doctor.

"Okay is a relative term, and it's really too soon to tell. But it's better than we thought it would be, considering what he'd been through, and how long he's been out. It's something of a—"

"Well, let's go see him," Ingrid interrupted. She had no time for miracles. It was just one of those things. Sometimes people survive the unsurvivable. Beat all the odds.

A delay of death is *a miracle!* That's what we wanted to tell Ingrid Starling. We could spend years talking about it, what we would do with one more earthly day in our fleshy physical bodies. Some of us wanted to run again, to sweat, to feel our legs and our blood pumping with use. Others wanted another go at sex, to really remember to enjoy it this time. World War II nurse Michelle Blake (b. 1914–d. 1942) wanted to see Europe, not in wartime, there had been so much art she'd missed. Ruthanne Jefferies (b. 1938–d. 2009) wanted to eat an entire chocolate cake, since she'd spent her whole life on a diet, only to drown on an empty stomach. The living don't know how good they have it.

"Why can he sing if he can't talk?" Auggie asked.

Dr. Higgins explained that a different area of the brain controls singing and music; it's separate from the language center. "It's actually not uncommon in people who have strokes, that they learn to sing before they speak. Not that Clive had a stroke, but there has been brain trauma, and he'll need quite a bit of rehabilitation before he learns to speak again. But it's somewhat promising that he's awake, that he can sing."

"Promising," Ingrid agreed.

"Totally insane," Emma said. It was the same song over and over; her dad was on some kind of loop. He looked around the room as he sang. Emma wondered if he knew where he was.

My family! Clive thought, but he could only sing. *They're here to see me off. They're here to bury me. Look at how much they love me, they're all here. How I wish I could tell them—*

Crystal Nash waltzed into the room then with a bouquet of lilies, sent over by David Hatfield. "What's going on?" she asked.

When Clive saw Crystal Nash and an armful of white funeral flowers, he knew he was dead, or dreaming, or back in that goddamn coma. But when Clive reached out from the bed to hug Crystal Nash, that angel, she hugged him back! Clive was amazed. She was real, solid flesh, and so was he. He wasn't in heaven, or someplace worse; no, he was here and Crystal was alive! He clutched her to him. The nurses and Dr. Higgins stood by, waiting to make sure this big surprise didn't cause some kind of relapse. Not that anyone has ever gone into a coma from that kind of shock, a shock of happy news, but this also wasn't an everyday situation.

Clive didn't remember much about the day in the woods; he just remembered assuring Harold Baynes that no, he could definitely fit through that hog tunnel, they didn't need to keep looking for the service gate that Harold wanted to find. *Where was Harold*, Clive wondered. *The man should see this*. But he would worry about where Harold had gone later. Crystal was here, in the flesh. Crystal, who loved loud metal music and witchcraft and as a teenager had been a real daredevil, who didn't think twice about riding her mountain bike over the makeshift ski jump behind the high school, and who had grown up to be his bartender and good friend. Clive heard the words "kidnapping" and "hostage" bandied about, and he could only assume he was the one who had saved her from what sounded like a terrible situation. *Why else would he be in this hospital bed? Why else would everyone be looking at him with such wide eyes of astonishment?*

"I'm a hero," Clive said, clear as day, which really sent Dr. Higgins's head into a tailspin. The lights had come on in Clive's language center, a switch suddenly flicked. The brain is a mysterious thing.

A week later, released from the confines of the hospital, Clive Starling wasn't even halfway in the front door of the Corbin caretaker's house, his wheelchair stuck on the doorframe, when the fox and the dog were jumping at him, the fox yipping, the dog licking and licking.

"Hi, little buddy!" Clive said. "Hi, big buddy! Hi, my favorite pals! Yes, yes, we're out of the woods!"

Moses and Rasputin were out of their skin excited to see the silver-haired man, eyes bulging, tails wagging, bodies wiggling. It was like one of those viral videos when a soldier comes home from war and his German shepherd just absolutely loses her shit in disbelief. That's why we like living with animals so much; they exhibit their joy so outwardly, remind us how to be better alive.

62

Opening night of *Titanic the Musical!* finally arrived at the end of March, nearly two months after its original opening date, giving one of its actors time to recuperate from his recent coma. Captain Clive would be onstage in his wheelchair; he was too frail to stand up for that long, but he was ready to act and sing. He was not going to screw this up for his son. He wore his ship's captain outfit to school, and all day the fifth graders couldn't sit still, they were so excited. At recess, they huddled in the far corner of the playground, reciting their lines, going over the big finale number. They were giddy all day, passing notes. Emma didn't mind. She was excited too.

At seven P.M. sharp, people crowded into the theater at the Old Opera House. Emma was helping backstage with the costume changes and organizing the kids, but she kept peeking out from the curtain to see who had arrived. It seemed like the entire town was there: moms, dads, siblings, grandparents, friends, neighbors, the Enraged Old Bags, everyone from Sundown Acres who was mobile . . . Big Hank was there, and all of Clive's old bandmates, including Dennis Hollingdrake. Mack Durkee was front-row center, with his mother, who was feeling a lot better after her final rounds of chemo. Crystal was helping out backstage, too, and Ingrid had been asked *not* to help, to sit in the audience and enjoy the show. More than anything in the entire world, Auggie wanted to impress his mom.

"Look at all these beautiful people," we said to one another about the audience that night. We wished they could know how much we loved them, how hard we were rooting for them.

Before the curtain went up, Emma found her father. He was sitting with Michael B., listening to the boy's plan to become a fish-and-wildlife biologist someday, helping animals like the captain had said he should. Michael B. had already asked the bait shop to stop selling lead tackle; it was poisoning the loons on Sugar Lake.

"What's up, Em?" her dad said, looking up at her.

"I just want you to know how proud I am of you," Emma said, putting her hand on her dad's shoulder. Her father beamed.

"Thank you, Emma," he said. "But wait until you see the show."

Emma had seen about a dozen rehearsals by this point, but she nodded. She would save her praise for after the show.

"Me too, Ms. Starling?" Michael B. asked. "Are you proud of me too?" Michael B. was holding a sign that said BE A MASTER BAITER: DON'T USE LEAD TACKLE! ONLY DOUCHEBAGS KILL LOONS! He was also going to ask the bait shop to redo their billboard.

"I'm extremely proud of you, Michael. Couldn't be prouder."

"Thanks. And nice makeup, Ms. Starling," Michael B. said. For opening night, Emma had done the Ozzy Osbourne heavy eyeliner, made raccoon circles around her eyes so she looked positively deranged. She was going to be backstage all night, she figured; no one would see her, and it matched the all-black uniform that the stage crew had to wear. Really, she knew her dad would get a kick out of it: it was the way she used to do his makeup before his Blacker Sabbath shows.

"You look pretty weird, Ms. Starling," Tobey L. said. "I think I like it."

"Look at everyone out there." Isabella Eaklin had pulled back a corner of the red velvet curtain. Isabella would be playing the role of assistant captain, a role Auggie had tacked on at the last minute. It was Isabella's first starring role in a community theater production, even if she had no lines. She just had to stand next to Clive onstage, and was instructed to kick him in the leg if he started talking to the ghost of Ernest Harold Baynes.

"It's a full house," Leanne said, looking out at the crowd. She did her jazz hands, then hugged her friend. Leanne had hugged Izzy a lot since she'd found her alive. Izzy didn't mind. She'd missed her best friend; it was the worst thing about fake-dying. The girls now wore matching pink outfits most of the time, although that night they were both in costume: Izzy wearing a captain's hat, Leanne dressed as a first-class passenger in red lipstick and pearls. "A full house!" Leanne repeated. "We've never had a full house in the history of community theater!"

It was because of the popularity of the show that Sid Wish almost didn't get a seat. Sid hadn't bought a ticket to the show beforehand, the way nearly everyone else had, so he almost wasn't able to get in. But Principal Jefferies, being polite, asked if one of the ushers would run and go get a folding chair for Mr. Wish, who had once been the director of the community theater, and acquitted of the drug charges, while his wife was probably going to prison for years. Sid Wish sat on a beige aluminum folding chair at the end of one of the aisles, against fire code, most likely, but the volunteer fire chief was in attendance and didn't say anything. It was a big night for the kids in the play, and no one wanted to distract from what would probably be a very nice evening out, if Auggie Starling could pull it off.

The first act went off without a hitch, with some downright beautiful singing from Leanne Hatfield and Clive Starling, and an okay enough solo from Nicole P. There was some nice acting from a few of the sailors and passengers, and tons of brownies and cookies sold at intermission. But in the second act, just as you've gotten to know and love these characters based on real-life *Titanic* passengers, the Unsinkable Molly Brown as well as the more sinkable rest, the iceberg hits, your heart is broken, and death is certain for 1,500 men, women, and children. And in this case, the play was cast with nearly all children, so it promised to be extra-tragic when they sank.

Emma worried that the *Upper Valley News* arts critic, Joanne Fever, was going to rake her brother over the coals for this performance. Joanne Fever was of the opinion that plays, musicals, and novels should lift us up, that art shouldn't depress us. Emma had read that line in Ms. Fever's column more than once. But so far, Emma had noted, not one single community theater actor, not one single fifth grader or fourth grader or third grader, had flubbed their lines. Her brother deserved a rave.

And then, after intermission, Tobey L., who played Night Watchman #1, was about to go onstage to tell Captain Clive Starling sitting in his wheelchair that the ship had hit an iceberg—didn't he feel it?—and the ship was taking on water. The ship was, maybe, possibly, sinking. The boy was supposed to be nervous to talk to the captain, to give him this bad news, but Tobey L. was nervous about going onstage at all. He sucked on his inhaler and wouldn't budge as Leanne Hatfield tried to push him. Emma went over to see what the holdup was, and she held both Tobey L.'s sticky little hands and she said that no one could do a better job at this part than he was about to do. Tobey L. nodded and marched onstage, and Emma felt like a really good teacher, for a moment. One single moment.

Because then Emma saw it: she didn't know if it was Leanne Hatfield's poking and prodding, or if it was her good touch, but the Charm returned for a half second to her hands, the touch she'd been so sure was all gone. Or perhaps it was only some early hormones showing up at the wrong time. But whatever sparked it, Tobey L. went onstage, in front of the entire town, and it was apparent to everyone that the young boy had a boner, perhaps the first boner in his life. With the spotlight on him, and wearing those thin sailor pants, everyone could see it. Emma could certainly see it from the wings of the stage, but she could tell the audience could see it too; there was a collective gasp.

Tobey L., who was quick on his feet, one of Emma's smarter students, knew he had to give everyone something else to talk about. And so, Tobey L. covered the front of his sailor suit the best he could with his little sailor hat, and he looked Captain Clive Starling in the eye and said, "Not an iceberg in sight."

Clive looked at Tobey, confused. This wasn't his cue. He would wait for his cue. Clive was not going to ruin this night for his son.

"Not an iceberg in sight?" Isabella Eaklin asked, piping up as the assistant captain. Unlike Captain Clive, Isabella had gone to theater camp in the third grade, and she knew the Rules of Improv. Rule Number One was: *You must always agree with what your scene partner says, you must not disagree with them, because the show must go on and all that.* If the partner says you are on the moon, then you are on the moon, if he says he is made of steel, then he is made of steel, and if the *Titanic* isn't sinking, then the *Titanic* isn't sinking.

"Not an iceberg in sight," Tobey L. repeated, firmer this time, and looking at Isabella now.

"Okay," Assistant Captain Isabella said. "That's great."

From his wheelchair, Captain Clive moved his trembling hand to his beard. The audience noticed his hand shaking, and wondered if it was stage fright, the fake cold of the Atlantic, or if it was only his degenerative brain disease. Clive was confused, he was pretty sure none of this was in the script, but maybe the script had changed, and he really didn't want to ruin this for his son.

"Where are we going again?" Assistant Captain Isabella asked. "If we aren't going to sink?"

"Orlando, Florida!" Olivia called, running onstage in a fur

coat much too big for her. Olivia was playing one of the first-class passengers, and she thought they could send the *Titanic* to Disney World, the place Olivia wanted to go to most. She had put blue pin after blue pin in central Florida on Ms. Wish's world map of "Where We Have Been and Where We Hope to Go." She didn't know Disney World was a swamp back in 1912, the park not built until the 1970s.

Auggie was gesturing wildly from the other side of the stage, trying to signal to his father or Isabella or Tobey L. to get back on track, to sink the ship and move the musical toward its final numbers. But instead, Isabella Eaklin, improv genius, said: "Why don't you wake up the whole ship, then, and we'll get the day started." Even though the iceberg hit the *Titanic* in the smack-dab middle of the night, 11:40 P.M., it was now a new day. Michael B., who was in charge of the music, put on a Disney song, one all the kids knew, that one from *Frozen*. A pretty messed-up song choice, Emma thought, since so many of the *Titanic*'s dead had perished in the frigid water.

"We're having a party?" Captain Clive finally asked, still shaking. Something really wasn't right. "Harold?" Clive called, but the ghost hadn't come to the performance. He had been alive for the original *Titanic* disaster; he didn't need to see it again. Isabella Eaklin ran over and gave Captain Clive a swift kick in the shins; he wasn't supposed to talk to the ghost onstage. "Ouch!" Clive yelled.

Some of the kids were filling up their plastic martini glasses with more pickle juice, a prop from an earlier scene. Auggie had told Emma he had thought the cloudiness of pickle juice would make the martinis look better than if the stemmed glasses were full of only water. It was only for a one-minute scene earlier in the show, for the richest passengers, and no one was supposed to drink so much of it, only one or two sips, but the New Hampshire Pickle Company had donated a whole barrel, so the pickle juice was limitless. Even the kids who were in steerage had martinis now, and the pickle juice seemed to be getting the kids actually drunk, maybe by some miracle the brine had turned to alcohol while the barrel sat backstage the past two months. The kids were dancing and dancing, and a song from *The Lion King* came on the speakers next. The kids sang louder.

"We've hit the iceberg!" Leanne Hatfield finally said, right into the microphone so you could hear her over the singing. Not all the kids were mic'd, because most of them didn't have speaking parts. Leanne Hatfield was clearly frustrated; her solo was coming up soon, but before she could sing about her drowned husband, the ship had to sink.

"I patched the leak!" shouted Ulf into Tobey L.'s microphone. Ulf was wearing his Viking helmet again, even though Leanne had banned it from the production, and also, Ulf was supposed to be one of the ship's crew, not even onstage for the dancing scene. He was supposed to be down in the steerage of the *Titanic*. He would be one of the ones who drowned. Emma was ready backstage with blue lipstick for his frozen lips. But instead, the show went on and on and on, Leanne announcing that the ship hit iceberg after iceberg, and Ulf patching up leak after leak.

"This is amazing," Crystal said to Emma backstage. "This is real art."

"I don't know if Auggie will think so," Emma said, trying to see to the other side of the stage, where Auggie had been sitting in the director chair. But the chair was empty, because, by that point, Auggie was onstage with the kids too, dancing along to "Hakuna Matata," throwing kicks in the air. "If you can't beat 'em," Crystal said before running onstage to spin Clive around.

Emma was now all alone backstage, and she looked out into the audience. All the dads had stopped filming this theatrical disaster. Sid Wish had found reading material, a magazine. But in the front row, Mack looked gleeful, and Emma's mother was laughing in delight. She was so proud. *Look what her son had done!* He had brought joy back to this musty old opera house, which had seen so many boring shows since its opening in 1872. And Ingrid would know; she kept a catalogue of the productions and reviews in the historical society. In fact, the first known usage of the phrase "a real snooze" was coined thanks to an Everton Opera House play put on in 1897, when every last person in the audience fell asleep.

Emma could see that her students were having the time of their lives, but she also knew the kids were getting too whipped up, and eventually an elbow would accidentally connect with an eye socket. *Too much fooling leads to crying,* her mother had always said whenever Emma and Auggie would wrestle as kids. Emma, the long-term fifth-grade substitute teacher, had to be the one to stop it. It had to be stopped now, while the going was good. She pulled the plug on the music, but the children didn't even notice. The dancing continued.

Emma remembered the foghorn. As stage manager, she was supposed to sound the foghorn when the *Carpathia* ship came to rescue the survivors, but first the *Titanic* had to sink, and the *Titanic* wasn't sinking. Still, she wouldn't be the first that night to go off the script, so she grabbed the foghorn and pulled the trigger, let it rip. The dancing had gone on long enough.

"There's her mojo," Michelle Blake (b. 1914–d. 1942) said from atop her headstone.

"She has a real command over the children," Mary Garvin (b. 1945–d. 2001) agreed.

Emma went onstage in her black T-shirt and black jeans and her dark black eye makeup, which was dripping down her face from the heat of the stage lights and made her look absolutely ghoulish, and some of the Enraged Old Bags in the audience gasped when they saw her, wondered if it was their turn to be haunted. Eunice Vandervoss had a heart palpitation, clutched for her chest. Emma hadn't forgotten about the makeup as she marched onstage; she just didn't care who saw her that way. This was her hometown, let people think whatever they thought about her. In the front row, Mack Durkee felt a stirring in his pants. He loved when Emma got weird. He had made her a necklace of the bear teeth from the rug in the mansion and planned to give the necklace to her after the show. He was going to ask her to be his official girlfriend, long-term. He had even made up a contract, as a joke.

"Attaboy," said Charles Tepper (b. 1932–d. 1998), forever a horny toad.

Onstage, Emma grabbed the microphone from Leanne, and announced that the *Titanic* had landed in New York, at its final destination, safe and sound. And all the kids were hugging, the audience was hugging, and everyone was crying.

"These kids will save the world!" Auggie said, taking Leanne's microphone out of Emma's hands. And the audience was applauding, and everyone started chanting: "Tobey, Tobey, Tobey!" and clomping and stamping and cheering. Jonathan Rat tried to pick up Tobey L., was trying to get other kids to lift Tobey L. up like he was a high school football hero. Ulf and Michael B. were quick to help.

"Jonathan," Emma demanded. "Put him down. Jonathan, stop it. *Rat,* stop it. Rat. Rat. Rat! I said for you to stop it, Rat." Emma didn't say this into the microphone, so no one in the audience heard her, just the kids and her brother and father nearby. But Jonathan Rat Nelson had gotten all the other kids to lift up Tobey, and he was on their shoulders now, Tobey L. way up high in the air.

63

>-•-<

Clive Starling was sitting in his wheelchair, watching it all happen around him, the children cheering. Clive felt so happy, elated, that he had lived to see this. It was a *spectacle*. And that feeling is exactly what we've been talking about—*what we could have done with a little more time!*

Clive watched as one of the children, the one with white-blond hair and strange blue eyes, he could never remember all of their names, that child was trying to lift up Tobey, the poor sailor who'd gotten the boner onstage. And his daughter, his dear Emma, wearing her nightmarish clown makeup, she was yelling something about rats. *Emma has really come into her own this year,* he thought. She wasn't so worried about being impressive or accomplished, wasn't annoying in some of the ways she used to be. He could see that losing the Charm had been good for her, and so had a few months of teaching. She seemed happier. She was desperately trying to control the kids onstage.

"Rat, rat, rat!" Emma was yelling at the kids. "Rat!"

And that was when, all of a sudden, Clive saw that there were rats—big fat rats, extra-large rodents filling up the theater. Big gray ones, brown ones, even a few white ones. Rats everywhere, just like that night he'd seen all the rats in the Blueberry Hill Pub when the health inspector had to be called, but these rats were even bigger. Some of these rats were nearly as big as the children. They seemed to be coming from underneath the stage, from the pit, or from the audience maybe. The rats were coming up on the stage. It was clear to Captain Clive that these rats had come from steerage. The rats wanted to get to higher ground. They didn't want to drown, no one did.

Clive Starling had never minded rats, but these rats might be vicious, and there were so many of them. He'd heard that if you get bitten by a rat or a skunk or even an unidentified dog, you have to get rabies shots. When you get a rabies shot, they put the needle in your belly button, which is much worse than a usual shot. He knew that from what had happened to Ozzy Osbourne, after his infamous episode of biting the head off a live bat on-stage.

"RATS!" Clive yelled. "RATS, RATS, RATS!" Clive yelled, and he was mic'd up, so everyone could hear. "RATS! RUN! RUN, RATS, RUN!" *Run* may have been the operative word, what got everyone moving, butts out of seats and headed toward the exit. Everyone running straight toward the exits in the back of the the-ater, all at once, all of it madness like it must have been the night that the real *Titanic* was sinking. Children, parents, grandpar-ents, all running. Crystal grabbed the handles of Clive's wheel-chair and pushed him down the aisle, while Emma and Auggie herded the children like a gaggle of geese. It was complete chaos as everyone headed for the exit double doors, and it was lucky no one got trampled. Clive Starling might have been slapped with a big fine for yelling the equivalent of *fire* in a crowded theater, ex-cept for what happened next.

An entire panel of stage lights—six spotlights and a beam that held them together—came crashing onto the stage. It was like a small fireworks show, for those who stopped running long enough to look back. The panel had been directly above where Tobey L. had been lifted to the heavens; if it had fallen twenty seconds ear-lier, it would have hit that group of children straight-on. Each spotlight weighed 12.4 pounds, but when dropped from that height, the police said it could have been a real tragedy. A dozen dead children.

But because of Clive, all the children escaped. Not even a scratch on one.

On the street, outside the theater, no one asked Clive Starling about the rats, because everyone in Everton had heard about Clive's hallucinations, had heard about Ernest Harold Baynes and the cats in the Meriden College classroom—a few people had even seen the YouTube video—and most everyone could put two and two together. So instead, the people of Everton took turns hugging Clive, thanking him over and over again for saving the lives of their children. The fifth graders grabbed at his wheelchair, wanted to lift him up in the air too.

"Absolutely not," Ms. Emma Starling said. "Feet on the ground." They could tell their teacher meant it this time, so they listened.

"Who knew you'd be good with kids," Ingrid said.

Crystal put her arm around Emma. "I could have guessed she'd be a good teacher. She always cared too much about grades."

Emma enjoyed the weight of her friend's arm on her shoulder.

"Our Emma was always going to find her way," Ingrid said proudly. "I never worried about her."

"Mom," Emma said, flushing with embarrassment and pride.

"Three cheers for Clive Starling!" Dennis Hollingdrake called out.

Michael B.'s mom was passing around a flask, and Officer Gene went to his cruiser, came back with the bag of medals he'd ordered online for occasions like this one. He'd already given medals out to Leanne and David Hatfield; Officer Gene had given out more medals this year than ever before. It wasn't a real medal, not exactly, but a small black button that read TOWN HERO in yellow lettering. Officer Gene pinned it to Clive's collar on the captain's uniform. The whole town applauded, and Clive stood up from his wheelchair. Someone handed him the flask to make a toast.

"To all my friends here tonight," he said, lifting the silver flask high. "Heaven will be so lonesome without you!"

Later, once the scene in the Old Opera House had been investigated, the best guess about what had caused the lights to fall was all that dancing onstage. All that noise, all those vibrations, must have somehow shaken the screws loose up in the ceiling, and maybe Sid Wish had cut corners with the installation of the lighting system, but no one could say for sure, because Sid Wish was the only one who didn't make it out of the auditorium that night. He had been struck by a single spotlight that had fallen into the audience; the rest of the lights had fallen onto the stage.

Sid didn't run when everyone else did, too concerned with his automobile magazine to even look up when the foghorn had sounded. He'd brought the magazine because he had wanted town art critic Joanne Fever to notice him, and how bored he was. He wanted to be written up, he told us later when he arrived at Maple Street, as "the former director in the audience, visibly unimpressed by the efforts of his replacement." But Sid Wish (b. 1971–d. 2015) wouldn't be mentioned at all in the review, because Joanne Fever had slipped out at intermission. She was sure she had seen enough; she knew what would happen in the next act, and she didn't want to stay and depress herself with the drownings of children dressed as adults. Joanne Fever posted her review on the *Upper Valley News* arts page forty minutes later, with a headline that proclaimed:

TITANIC SINKS, NEW DIRECTOR AUGGIE STARLING SOARS.

———

Back at the Corbin caretaker's house, Emma, Auggie, Crystal, and Mack stayed up to celebrate a successful community theater opening, rehashing every last moment.

"What about the foghorn?" Auggie asked, stroking the fox in his lap. The dog was at his feet. He was wearing one of the costumes, Olivia's big fur coat, so he looked like a real Russian tsar. "Remember when Emma blasted the foghorn?"

"Ending everyone's fun," Mack said, and laughed.

"I was worried someone was going to get hurt. The kids were out of control."

"Well, almost everyone was *supposed* to die," Auggie pointed out. "Sixty-eight percent. That's how many sank in the *Titanic*."

"Aren't you full of fun facts." Crystal threw a piece of popcorn at him.

"We're definitely all lucky to be alive after tonight," Emma said. "After the theatrical work of Auggie Starling."

"Well, *I've* always been lucky," Crystal said.

"Is that so?" Auggie said, and laughed. "Me too."

Emma felt a chill. None of this was that strange, her brother and Crystal and Mack all sitting there around the kitchen table in her parents' house, everyone palling around, and yet all of it was. So strange and so wonderful. She excused herself for a minute, she didn't want to start crying and ruin everything. On her way to the bathroom, she passed her parents' bedroom. She was there at the right time, because her father opened the bedroom door and asked Harold to wait in the hallway, kicked out like a dog who stares during lovemaking. It was nice for us to see Emma laugh so hard, standing outside her parents' bedroom. She ran to tell the others.

"Gross," Auggie said. "Come on, Emma, so gross."

"That's amazing," Mack said.

"I think it's sweet," Crystal agreed. "After all this time."

"They really love each other," Emma said.

"Gross," Auggie said again.

And then our iron gate creaked at Maple Street, and in came Leanne Hatfield and Isabella Eaklin, out after dark, here for a séance, sneaking out after Leanne's grandfather went to bed. Leanne and Izzy plodded bravely through our graveyard, here to pull up the spirit of Rebecca Hatfield (b. 1979–d. 2004), so they could tell Leanne's mom what had happened at the Old Opera House a few hours before. Leanne pulled out her Ouija board from her pink backpack. It was a gift from her favorite teacher. Something Ms. Starling thought the two girls might like.

64

>-•-<

The headstone was installed in midsummer, a few weeks after the burial, and a little lime-green, black-spotted plastic poison dart frog was soon left on top of the stone. Harold Baynes came by to admire the inscription; he doesn't avoid Maple Street the way he used to, now that he knows he has friends here. The engraving reads:

CLIVE J. STARLING
B. JULY 10, 1946–D. JUNE 29, 2015
LOVING FATHER & HUSBAND
HERO TO YOUNG PERSONS
& A FRIEND TO ALL CREATURES

"My kids picked it out," Clive Starling (b. 1946–d. 2015) boasted, which was, of course, something we already knew, but we let him tell us anyway. At Maple Street, we don't mind listening, even when we know how the story ends.

AUTHOR'S NOTE
ON HER RESEARCH

I decided it might be worthwhile to explain how this novel came to be—especially out of respect for the real people of the Upper Valley, New Hampshire.

In December 2016, my husband and I were visiting our friends Chris and Courtney at their recently purchased home in Newport, New Hampshire. We went out shopping for a Christmas tree, and we drove past this enormous yellow mansion. NO TRESPASSING signs were posted at the base of the driveway. *What is that?* I wondered. *Who lives there?* My friends, still new to the area, didn't know.

Dear reader, I googled: "Newport, New Hampshire, enormous yellow mansion," and from there I learned about nineteenth-century robber baron Austin Corbin, who allegedly razed his childhood home, except for the room he was born in, and built his mansion around it. I found out about his hunting park, which he began to build in 1886, buying up land from farmers, which would eventually span 26,000 acres. It was stocked with animals imported from all over the world, among them bison, boar, antelope, elk, beavers, and quail. When the first white-tailed deer arrived by train from Canada, the entire town came to see them—at the time, deer were hunted out of New England—and Corbin Park would help reintroduce deer to the area. I also found—*wowee-zowee!*—the park was still intact today, owned by an anonymous group of hunters. Chris and Courtney had heard something about the park, because the real estate agent had warned them: sometimes wild boars get out and dig up gardens.

"*Someone* should write a book about this," I said, like a big dummy; I'd recently sold my first novel. But I don't write historical fiction—I like my characters to use the internet and tell fart jokes—so I didn't think it was going to be my story to tell. And besides, I was writing another book, one about fifth graders and their substitute teacher.

But my obsession with the park only grew, and once I learned about Ernest Harold Baynes, the real-life Doctor Doolittle who was a naturalist for the park, well, stick a fork in me. I scrapped most of the other novel (but kept the fifth graders). I made up a fictional town—Everton means "Boar Town"—because I didn't want to be bound too closely to the facts, and I made Ernest Harold Baynes a ghost. I started spending more time in Newport, camping out in the attic of the historical society.

Here is one delicious thing I've found about writing novels: if you work on something long enough, the universe starts to send you encouragement. In May 2018, not wanting to keep burdening my friends, I booked a short research stay at Freewill Farm in Newport. By happy coincidence, I learned the woman who owned the farm, Cathryn Baird, also happened to be president of the Newport Historical Society. And when I arrived, her twentysomething daughter was wearing a Black Sabbath T-shirt, which is Clive Starling's favorite band.

In the months following, Cathryn Baird introduced me to Bill Ruger, who was in the final months of his life after a battle with cancer but wanted to meet to talk about my book. Bill owned the gun factory, which I knew, and I learned he also owned the Corbin Mansion. I had already fully assembled the character of Ralph Kelsey, who also owned the mansion and the gun factory, so I was a little surprised by the coincidence, but like I said: *the universe*! Bill Ruger was also one of the few publicly known members of

Corbin Park (formally called the Blue Mountain Forest Association), but we didn't talk about the park much. To be honest, I, like Clive Starling, love the lore the park invites more than what might really be inside. That said, I would *absolutely die* to go in.

(For those really interested in the park: New Hampshire Public Radio had a great segment about it—the episode is called "The Millionaire's Hunt Club"—which outlines how impossible it is to get inside the gates. One local I spoke with called it a black hole in his backyard.)

I also did some key research at the Plainfield Historical Society, which has a treasure trove of Ernest Harold Baynes photos (Baynes actually lived in Meriden, a village of Plainfield, but I moved his house for my purposes). It was there that I learned Baynes had affairs with women at the Cornish Art Colony down the road, a gossipy tidbit I loved.

For Baynes's excerpts used throughout the novel, I repurposed much of his real writing from his various books, cutting up his sentences and collaging them, adding my own writing to provide a bit more of a narrative through line and some of the details about his marriage. Harold Baynes had a documented sense of humor, so I hope he would be amused by my repurposing of his work.

And a last note on my research for this novel, and perhaps my most important note: I am not a writer overly concerned with realism, but I am inspired by true events, and real life is where all my ideas originate. As I began to assemble a story about a small town in Sullivan County, New Hampshire, I found I had to address the opioid crisis. It casts too large a shadow over the real town I was inspired by to ignore it in my fictional one. According to some old *Boston Globe* articles I found, heroin was first brought to Newport by a group of dealers who drove up from Massachusetts and gave out free samples at parties. Once heroin arrived, it stayed. Today, fentanyl has only made the problem worse, and New Hampshire has one of the highest opioid over-dose rates in the country. People under thirty-five are more likely to die from an overdose than a car accident.

I wanted to approach this topic with extra caution, leading with empathy for people struggling with addiction and for their families. I read books and articles, and I watched documentaries. Most important, I consulted several trusted friends willing to share their experiences, insights, and expertise. I am grateful to them for their time and thoughtfulness with me and with the manuscript. Any failings to accurately or sensitively depict the opioid crisis are mine alone.

I hope I've done right by the subject, and I hope I've rendered the characters as complete and complicated people. This book is about rooting for everyone, and about loving a place. And I hope it's clear that I deeply love the place.

ACKNOWLEDGMENTS

Writing this novel sometimes seemed like it would be a never-ending project, and when I worried I'd be walking circles in Corbin Park forever, I would dream about writing the acknowledgments. Now look at us; we're out of the woods! And it is a thrill and a relief to thank these people who helped me find the path out:

Katie Grimm, my marvelous agent and true-blue friend—thanks for your eagle eyes, for pushing me further, for always talking it through, and for generally believing in me. Sara Weiss, my wise and patient editor, thanks for having a vision for the Starlings, for pushing me for more, for giving me space when I needed it, and for supporting me so wonderfully. Thanks also to Elana Seplow-Jolley for giving some really key edits, and for helping me understand it as a fairy tale. I'm also very grateful to everyone at Don Congdon Associates who offered their valued thoughts and kind support along the way: Monique Vieu, Cara Bellucci, Caroline Miranda, Neeru Nagarajan, Zora Driscoll, and Grace Towery. And an enormous thanks to everyone on my team at Ballantine, including Kara Cesare, Kara Welsh, Jennifer Hershey, Kim Hovey, Sydney Collins, Taylor Noel, Melissa Sanford, Rachelle Mandik, Cindy Berman, Dana Blanchette, Greg Mollica, Ella Laytham, and Deborah Foley.

Heaps of gratitude to Chris and Courtney Crowell (plus Parker and Koda too!): this book would not exist without our travels together, and it would have been much harder to write without your generosity. Thank you.

Thanks to these friends, who supported me and this book in some vital way, whether as early readers or late-night texters, gilded-age experts or cartooning teachers: Tessa Fontaine, Marika Plater, Natasha Sokol, Jessica Manly, Caitlin Delohery, Amy Kurzweil, Andrew Martin, Jane Alexander, Clare Beams, James Scott, Robbie Howell, Caleb Johnson, Marya Brennan, Lucas Mann, Kat Solomon, Katie Dieter, Nate McNamara, Victor Wildman, and Ellen Whittet. And a special sentence for Tasha Graff, the crown jewel friend, thank you for reading countless drafts and talking me off just as many cliffs. And another special spot for Erin Craig. You were sunshine itself.

Thank you to the Upper Valley historians who were so generous with their time and expertise: Larry Cote, Cathryn Baird, Jane Stephenson, Christopher Wright, Marylou McGuire, and Ray Reid. I'm sorry a few of the facts got mangled by my imagination. Thanks also to the late Bill Ruger for taking the time to talk to me and for welcoming me to the grounds of the real Corbin Mansion.

I am so grateful to MacDowell, where I wrote the most important draft of this book, and where I had some extremely valuable conversations about the project. Thanks also to the ghost of Thornton Wilder for showing up when he did.

Beyond the help of Thornton W., this book owes a debt to many other authors, and I'd like to especially acknowledge the works of John Irving and Barbara Kingsolver.

Thank you to my parents, Liane and Paul Hartnett, for their abundant love and support, and to my brothers, Jake and Michael, and to Nomin and Sway too. A bonus thank-you to Jake for his help with Russian curse words, even though I had to cut them all. Thanks also to my extended family—Hartnetts, Callahans, Linsleys—who are all always so supportive, and a very special thank-you to my uncle Bob Hartnett, who made it out of that La-Z-Boy chair alive.

This book is dedicated to my husband, Drew. I could have never made it out of the woods without you. Thank you for everything you did to help me get here, for our destressing runs and our brainstorming talks, for taking the morning childcare shift, for reading whatever I asked you to read, for watching whatever movie I thought might help. I could never have hoped for a better partner, and I treasure our life together. Thank you to Leora, my little heart, the creature I love the most, and a thank-you to Willie, too, of course. Heaven knows I would never forget to thank the dog.

To any readers of this book who are writers too: if you're still in the woods of your own novel—keep going. Exit this way.

About the Author

ANNIE HARTNETT is the author of *Rabbit Cake*. She has received fellowships from the MacDowell Colony, Sewanee Writers' Conference, and the Associates of the Boston Public Library. She studied philosophy at Hamilton College, has an MA from Middlebury College, and an MFA from the University of Alabama. When she began writing this book, she was living in the groundskeeper's house in a cemetery. She now lives in Providence, Rhode Island, in an ordinary house with her husband, daughter, and darling border collie, Mr. Willie Nelson.